The Voice
of Elizabethan
Stage Directions

LIBRARY

TEL. 01244 375444 EXT. 3301

This book is to be returned on or before the last date stamped below. Overdue charges will be incurred by the late return of books.

UNIVERSITY COLLEGE CHESTER

A College of the
University of Liverpool

The Voice
of Elizabethan
Stage Directions

The Evolution
of a Theatrical Code

Linda McJannet

DELAWARE

Newark: University of Delaware Press
London: Associated University Presses

Associated University Presses
440 Forsgate Drive
Cranbury, NJ 08512

Associated University Presses
16 Barter Street
London WC1A 2AH, England

Associated University Presses
P.O. Box 338, Port Credit
Mississauga, Ontario
Canada L5G 4L8

The paper used in this publication meets the requirements
of the American National Standard for Permanence of Paper
for Printed Library Materials Z39.48-1984.

Library of Congress Cataloging-in-Publication Data

McJannet, Linda.
    The voice of Elizabethan stage directions : the evolution of a
theatrical code / Linda McJannet.
        p.   cm.
    Includes bibliographical references and index.
    ISBN 0-87413-660-1   (alk. paper)
    1. English drama—Early modern and Elizabethan, 1500–1600—
Criticism, Textual. 2. Stage directions—History—16th century.
3. Theater—England—Production and direction—History—16th
century. I. Title.
PR658.S59M38   1999
822'.309—dc21   97-51314
                                                                        CIP

PRINTED IN THE UNITED STATES OF AMERICA

Contents

Preface

In talking with friends and ordinary readers about Shakespeare, I am always amazed at how many recognize or can quote, along with lines from famous speeches, a stage direction from *The Winter's Tale: "Exit, pursued by a bear."* The appeal of this particular direction is doubtless multiple: it seems touchingly quaint; it suggests either that Shakespeare was prone to fantasizing about *coups de théâtre* or (alternatively) that trained animals might have been available on the Elizabethan stage; it sums up in a humorous image the inevitable harassments and precariousness of life; and so on. But in addition to the appeal of their content, stage directions fascinate and delight us as a language unto themselves, a code specific to the world of the theater and the collective exercise of imagination on which it depends for its effects. Like *"Exit pursued by a bear," "Enter the king"* is recognizable to any literate speaker of English as a stage direction. But where does it come from, this unique formula with its inverted grammar and uninflected verb?

This book began as a study of the cues for movement, props, costumes, and stage business implicit in the dialogue of Elizabethan plays. In pursuing this topic, I planned a brief preliminary chapter on stage directions per se to "get them out of the way." However, the more I tried to describe Elizabethan stage directions, the more I realized how little was actually known about their origin, their unique verbal and visual form, and their importance as an element of dramatic discourse—not just for what they tell us, but for the efficiency and suggestiveness with which they address their various audiences. To remedy my own ignorance and to satisfy my curiosity, I eventually abandoned my original topic and roamed as far back in the history of English drama as seemed necessary to answer the questions that presented themselves.

For example, when does the now-familiar scheme of functionally discrete directions (for entries, exits, speech prefixes, and midscene action) first appear? When are stage directions presented as marginalia and when are they integral to the text of a play? When they are in the margins, does this necessarily mean they are "marginalized" or subordinate in importance? When do English plays begin to indicate a change of speaker by beginning the speech on a new line with an indented left-hand speech prefix? Classical plays simply insert the new speaker's initial in the middle of the line, if necessary, and preserve the dialogue in an unbroken block. What advantages and disadvantages do these different conventions have for an actor or a lay reader? Or, for a final example, given that the classical plays familiar to the playwrights of the day do not themselves provide any models to imitate, why do Elizabethan stage directions boast so much Latinate diction and syntax? Why has their Latinity survived so long? What purposes does it serve? The chapters that follow try to answer these and other questions about the form and voice of English stage directions from the early 1500s till the closing of the theaters.

Beyond answering such questions, the fruits of this effort bear on a number of larger issues. One of these is the communal and collaborative nature of drama. As the professional London theaters became well established, it is clear that the form and voice of stage directions increasingly followed a set of conventions, both verbal and visual, shared by authors, the keepers of the theatrical promptbook, scribes, and even printing-house personnel. The evolution of stage directions, particularly in their visual deployment on the page, also illuminates the slow transition from a manuscript culture to a print culture and the effect of a wider readership on the form of plays. The accommodation of stage directions to the printed page reveals both the continuation and the modification of established manuscript traditions for representing drama; it does not, however, support the view that printed editions systematically transformed theatrical playscripts into literary texts specially designed for lay readers.

In addition, the study of stage directions reminds us of the multiplicity of Elizabethan drama. Some years ago, Alfred Harbage argued that there were "rival traditions" in the Elizabethan theater,[1] one popular and morally optimistic and one elitist and morally disillusioned, and that they were epitomized by the Globe and its repertoire, on the one hand, and the Blackfriars, on the other. This particular dichotomy has been challenged in recent years, but it is important to remember that the world of Elizabethan drama was not homogeneous or monolithic. The professional men's companies, the boy players, and the amateurs of the universities and the Middle Temple constituted a complex of different communities involved in generating and presenting plays. What sometimes seems a randomness in the form of stage directions is, I hope to show, really the confluence of rival conventions, one growing out of the native religious drama and one based on an emerging neoclassical tradition. Adherence to one or the other convention generally coincided with adherence to popular versus neoclassical canons of literary excellence and dramatic decorum. Due in part to posterity's preference for Shakespeare over his more classically minded rivals, such as Jonson, the popular tradition prevailed in both areas.

Finally, and perhaps most important, the different conventions for conveying staging information in classical plays, medieval religious drama, and the plays written for the professional London theaters embody different concepts of dramatic discourse and of the possible relations between dialogue and action on the stage. Stage directions are virtually nonexistent in classical drama. The explicit directions that have been identified in extant Greek dramatic texts number only fourteen.[2] Renaissance editions of Roman dramatists such as Plautus and Seneca also lack explicit directions for action or gesture. In Greek and Roman drama, all action that does occur on stage is implied in the dialogue itself. Further, as is well known, classical decorum required that violent action, such as Jocasta's suicide or Oedipus's putting out his own eyes, happen offstage and be reported in a *narratio*, a descriptive speech by a messenger or other character. In effect, in classical tragedy the characters are "speakers" rather than "actors," a distinction often preserved in the Latin texts, where they are sometimes listed as *Interloquitores*. Although we may speculate about traditional movements and gestures employed by the choruses and individual actors in classical drama, the virtual absence of stage directions independent of the dialogue means that the dramatists did not envision—or at any rate that the scribes did not transmit in any extant texts—action that could communicate *without* words.

Medieval religious drama takes the opposite approach. The events of sacred history, such as the murder of Cain or the passion of Christ, are not merely retold and reflected upon; they are literally en-acted on the stage, often with robust realism. Unlike classical plays in which dialogue dominates the page to the exclusion of all else, in medieval plays action and spectacle often seem primary. Some early religious plays present the dialogue within a highly articulated set of instructions for production—a so-called production narrative. Elaborate sets may be described, the necessary preparations for special effects spelled out, and advice given for rehearsing the actors. Not all medieval religious plays do this, but those that do, as Gary Chancellor has observed, resemble a "production notebook" from a modern theater.[3] The result is a performance-oriented text that emphasizes action as much as the spoken word.

Shakespeare and his fellow dramatists obviously drew upon and developed aspects of both the classical and medieval religious drama, but with respect to onstage action, they placed themselves squarely in the native, medieval tradition. Thus, as David Bevington stressed in choosing the quotation that serves as the title of his book,[4] in the plays of Shakespeare and his contemporaries "Action is eloquence." As a result, in Elizabethan plays stage directions are an integral part of the playscript, verbally and visually. While they often confirm actions already implicit in the dialogue, they also make possible such poignant and electrifying moments as that in which the exiled Coriolanus, after seeming to have rejected his mother's pleas for mercy towards Rome, "*holds her by the hand silent.*" The gesture that communicates his capitulation is encoded only in the stage direction. Neither classical nor medieval drama permits precisely this kind of effect. At the same time, the voice of Elizabethan stage directions, unlike that of the medieval production narrative, is not dominant or restrictive; it is one of many voices in a polyvocal script. While it calls attention to required action or other visual effects, its extreme economy of words and its frequent silence create ample opportunities for the actors to supplement or elaborate upon what is required. How the form and voice of Elizabethan directions became conducive to these effects is the concern of the following chapters.

Many people were of invaluable help to me in the researching and writing of this book. I am grateful to Maureen Goldman, then department chair, and to Bentley College for a sabbatical in 1989–90, during which I began my research. I am also indebted to Sherman Hayes and Lindsey Carpenter of the Solomon Baker Library at Bentley College and Mary Wright and all the staff at the Huntington Library, San Marino, California, where I spent eleven months in a setting as ideal for the spirit as it is for scholarship. Several colleagues, notably Marie A. Plasse of Merrimack College and Arthur Kinney of the University of Massachusetts, Amherst, read the entire manuscript and offered valuable criticism and suggestions. G. Blakemore Evans of Harvard University also generously read several chapters and, as always, referred me to important resources and saved me from errors and overstatements. Those that remain are entirely my own. The British Library, the Folger Shakespeare Library, the Bibliotèque municipale de

Tours, and the Huntington Library kindly gave permission to reproduce photographs of manuscripts and early editions in their collections. For unfailing encouragement, affection, and personal support I owe Michael O'Shea more than I can express, but he is used to reading in the margins and between the lines.

The Voice
of Elizabethan
Stage Directions

Introduction

In a session at a conference on Elizabethan theater, an accomplished actor from the Stratford (Ontario) Shakespeare Festival explained her approach to a role. Her rule, she said, was "clarity first": she would start with the words, consulting the *Oxford English Dictionary* for "all the words [she] didn't understand, and then all the words [she] thought [she] understood," and she would check the Variorum and different editions on matters of punctuation. Only after such painstaking work with the text would she attempt to "get into the character," asking questions of herself, listening to the ideas of the director and her fellow actors, and gauging the reactions of audiences. After the talk, I asked her if she approached the stage directions with the same reverence as she did the dialogue. The question seemed to take her by surprise. "What stage directions?" she responded. "You mean *Enter, Exit?*"

Assuming that she and I were using the term "stage directions" in the same sense,[1] her response points up a paradox. Since the rapprochement between the literary and stage-oriented study of Elizabethan drama in the 1970s, many literary scholars attend closely to the theatrical aspects of dramatic texts, particularly to stage directions. Even inconsistencies in the directions (for example, in character designation) are now scrutinized for clues to "authorial intention" or interpretive nuance.[2] However, as her comment testifies, modern actors do not always approach Elizabethan stage directions with the same reverence that some scholars now do. This may be less true at theaters devoted to the production of Shakespeare's plays, but even in these specialized communities, Elizabethan stage directions are more or less invisible and taken for granted.

Actors are not the only ones who find stage directions to be a minor—even nonexistent—element of an Elizabethan playscript. Theater semioticians often observe that, whereas modern plays tend to be heavily annotated with directions, in traditional or "classic" drama, such as Shakespeare and

Racine, "didascalia are virtually absent from the text" and "all performance information provided must be concentrated in the dialogue."[3] That is, explicit italicized directions regarding stage business, such as one finds in Ibsen, Shaw, or Tennessee Williams, are relatively rare, and the basic requirements of movement, props, costumes, or vocal delivery are implied in phrases (such as "on my knees" and "by this sword"), commands ("Let him go, Gertrude"; "Take your fingers from my throat"), questions ("Why do you bite your lip?"), and descriptive statements ("He takes her by the palm; ay, well said, whisper"). Theater historian David Bradley refers repeatedly to the "reticence" of Elizabethan texts with respect to performance instructions and the "extreme meagerness of their stage directions."[4] Patricia A. Suchy likewise finds pre-nineteenth-century directions to be relatively rare and unproblematic compared to those of later eras. She notes that only with the introduction of realistic, representational settings did cues for performance disappear from the dialogue and move "into the margins of the read playscript," where they acquired "new functions."[5] Contemporary playwrights also view Shakespeare's plays as lightly annotated compared to their own. Janusz Głowacki, author of *Fortinbras Gets Drunk,* casually observed in an interview, "[O]f course, Shakespeare doesn't have any stage directions."[6] Horton Foote hyperbolically sums up a common perception among modern playwrights: "Shakespeare doesn't have a single stage direction in the whole of his works. Exits and entrances, and alarms and flourishes, that's about it."[7]

It is quite true that, compared to Ibsen, Shaw, Ionesco or Beckett, Elizabethan and Jacobean plays are lightly annotated; most performance information is inscribed in the dialogue rather than in italicized directions. It is also true that some kinds of stage directions common in the nineteenth and twentieth centuries are rare or unknown in Elizabethan times. Of the eight categories of directions distinguished by Michael Issacharoff, for example, only two or three are regularly found in Elizabethan drama.[8] Issacharoff's categories include: "extratextual" directions (like the prefaces of Shaw or Corneille, describing the mise-en-scène), "autonomous" directions (privileged, often humorous additions, aimed at a sophisticated reader), "technical" directions (detailed modern cues for lighting, sound, and camera movements), and "normal" directions (for stage action, etc., subordinate to the dialogue). Of these only "normal" directions for stage action (*"They fight"*) and rudimentary "technical" directions (*"Sound trumpet"*) are regular features of Elizabethan playscripts. Issacharoff further distinguishes among directions that identify who is speaking ("attributive"), to whom ("directional"), how ("melodic" directions regarding the emotional state of speaker or addressee), and where ("locative" directions regarding decor and setting, time of day, etc.). In Elizabethan plays, speakers are identified via speech prefixes, but addressees are often left ambiguous (though some asides are marked). The location of the action is usually conveyed in the dialogue ("So this is the Forest of Arden"), though it may be suggested in an entry direction via details of costume *("dressed as foresters")* or other brief phrase *("as from dinner," "at work")*. "Melodic" directions concerning how a line is spoken are almost unknown in Elizabethan plays; in my sample of fifty-odd plays, I have encountered only a handful.

Nonetheless, stage directions are by no means absent from Elizabethan plays. As many editors, performance-oriented critics, and theater historians have repeatedly demonstrated, Elizabethan directions frequently contain vital information regarding subtle and powerful stage effects. What needs to be accounted for is why Elizabethan stage directions *seem* invisible. How do they manage to impart much information (or suggestion) without seeming intrusive or burdensome to the performers' sense of creative autonomy? Part of the reason lies in the predominance of cues "hidden" in the dialogue. But, equally important, Elizabethan directions adhere to a set of conventions that foster both unobtrusiveness and authority. Although some of these conventional elements are familiar to all students of Elizabethan drama, they have not to my knowledge been thoroughly described, nor has the unique voice with which they address their interpreters been appreciated. Describing their form and voice, and their evolution from the drama of the Middle Ages, is thus one of the main tasks that this book undertakes. It is further the argument of this book that the form and voice of Elizabethan stage directions result in their economy and "invisibility," and that these qualities, in turn, are the source of their relative authority with generations of performers.

Authority as well as unobtrusiveness is a key issue for stage directions. At least from the point of view of the modern theater professional, stage directions are often sites of contention. They attempt to impose a vision (sketchy or full) of how the script might be staged. Whereas the scholar values directions as evidence of the original staging or the "virtual performance" inscribed in the text,[9] performers often see them as mere relics of past performances and obstacles to the exercise of their creative freedom. Ironically, as Patricia Suchy notes, although a stage direction seems "to emanate more directly from an author than dialogue, it is most often understood [by theater personnel] to be an option, not a given."[10] Playwrights who were actors, theater managers, or directors (such as Shakespeare, Molière, Beckett, and Anouilh) could personally supervise the actual staging of their plays. But other authors must exert their influence from afar, relying on their knowledge of the companies and theaters for which they write, their personal authority, and the persuasiveness of the form and content of the stage directions themselves.

Though often used as a metaphor in contemporary literary and cultural studies, the phrase "sites of contention" can in this case also be taken quite literally. At least in our own day, more than one playwright has resorted to legal means in an effort to control how his or her play is produced. In 1984, Samuel Beckett's agents contested a production of *Endgame* at the American Repertory Theater, Cambridge, Massachusetts, because director Joanne Akalitis set the play in a post-nuclear-holocaust subway tunnel.[11] Such a setting suggests an obvious (if partial) explanation for the extreme behavior of the characters, whereas the skewed domesticity and gray impassivity of the set described by Beckett offers no such help: *"Bare interior. Grey light. Left and right, high up, two small windows, curtains drawn."* Similarly protective of his authorial intentions, Edward Albee has contracts written so that textual cuts must be approved by him, and performers are forbidden to be cast against gender in productions of *Who's Afraid of Virginia Woolf?*[12] We have no records of such conflicts over staging in Elizabethan times, but some surviving documents attest to companies' efforts to control who had access to the texts. When Shakespeare's company was still the Chamberlain's Men, its sponsor wrote to the stationers, presumably at the company's request, to protest the unauthorized publication of allegedly corrupt versions of its plays.[13] Playwright Richard Brome's contract with the Salisbury Court Theater explicitly prohibits his publishing any plays written for the company without its permission.[14]

Short of legal means, modern playwrights resort to the firmest possible language to indicate their wishes. For example, in the opening direction of *'night, Mother* (1983), Marsha Norman speaks emphatically to forestall directorial decisions that would, she feels, subvert her intentions: *"Under no circumstances should the set and its dressing make a judgment about the intelligence or taste of Jessie and Mama. . . . Heavy accents, which would further distance the audience . . . , are also wrong."* Marvin Carlson agrees that in contemporary plays, stage directions are increasingly "the major site" in the "struggle for interpretive control of the production."[15] But ironically, as Suchy observes, "in the contemporary theater, the use and parameters of stage directions have become so diverse that they have lost conventional force."[16] In other words, although contemporary stage directions are now given greater space and independence with respect to the dialogue, they are no more likely (and may be less likely) to be observed than their humble predecessors, *Enter* and *Exit*.

To date, the content rather than the form of Elizabethan stage directions has been of interest to literary scholars. Theater historians, such as

Walter Hodges, Bernard Beckerman, G. E. Bentley, T. J. King, and more recently, Andrew Gurr, S. P. Cerasano, and John Astington,[17] have valued them as indirect testimony to the architecture and spectacle of the Elizabethan theaters (*"Enter the king above," "Enter with a devil . . . with fireworks"*). William B. Long's study of manuscript directions has challenged the assumptions of earlier textual critics regarding systematic editing in the playhouse.[18] Alan Dessen has examined their theatrical logic in an effort to recover the grounds on which spectators and players agreed to meet.[19] The form and "voice" of Elizabethan stage directions, on the other hand, have been more or less taken for granted.

The Voice of Stage Directions

The voice of stage directions has been described as "a real voice, that of the author" addressing "other real people," actors and directors.[20] They have been seen as instances of "natural discourse," as opposed to the "fictive discourse" of the characters.[21] Setting aside, for the moment, the question of whether the author of an Elizabethan play is the "author" of all of its directions, the notion that the voice of traditional stage directions is "natural" or "real" is not entirely satisfactory. Whoever speaks through them, stage directions constitute a distinct code, a set of verbal and visual conventions that vary from period to period, and sometimes, as we shall see, among genres and venues of a single period.

Surveying the conventions of directions in various periods, one finds a range of "authorial" or "directorial" voices analogous to that which Wayne Booth found among narrative voices in his *Rhetoric of Fiction* (1961). Alongside the "self-effacing" narrator of some Hemingway stories, one might set the practice of ancient Greek drama, which is silent on all matters of staging.[22] Alongside the "self-dramatizing" narrators of Fielding and Cervantes, one might set the novelistic prefaces and directions of Shaw and the ironic, playful directions of Ionesco (*"A long moment of English silence. The English clock strikes 17 English strokes"*).[23] The conventions of diction, syntax, typography, and page design determine what kind of voice speaks through this element of the dramatic text; and, just as a command of the language of any craft is necessary for authority on the job, mastery of the relevant conventions is one way that the voice of stage directions acquires authority.

In Elizabethan times, stage directions, particularly those in plays for the professional London theaters, were defined by a fairly narrow range of typographical, syntactical, and rhetorical conventions, which it will be the purpose of subsequent chapters to analyze and explore. As with the structure of natural languages, the conventions governing stage directions within the London theatrical community "can be abstracted from usage and stated explicitly . . . only with difficulty and never completely."[24] Though one can, I shall argue, speak of clear norms in the stage directions of the popular Elizabethan drama, norms are not the same as absolute rules; there are always idiosyncratic usages, throwbacks to earlier forms, and other deviations.

Although Elizabethan stage directions are notorious for their lack of "regularity" (when compared to modern promptbooks and editions), what *is* regular about them often goes unnoticed owing to its familiarity, its apparent naturalness or inevitability. This is so because many aspects of the form that eventually developed in Elizabethan directions became standard for plays in English. But, as I shall try to show, what now seems to us natural and unremarkable was the result of a long process of experimentation and change in the habits of the writers, readers, and performers of dramatic texts.

ELIZABETHAN STAGE DIRECTIONS AND THEIR WRITERS

It has generally been assumed that the stage directions in an Elizabethan dramatic text may be the product of more than one hand. The presence of many hands in playhouse manuscripts suggests that scribes, bookholders, or other theatrical personnel sometimes left their mark on the directions in the texts they interpreted. The communal transmission of directions is particularly evident in *Sir Thomas More* and *Thomas of Woodstock*. Stage directions in *More* appear in the hands of the various authors and a "playhouse reviser"; the *Woodstock* manuscript contains annotations in eight different hands in addition to that of the scribe responsible for the bulk of the play.[25] Certain scribes—Ralph Crane is a notable example—sometimes embellished directions and sometimes shortened them.[26] Those responsible for a play's being printed may have further edited the directions in some way; the compositor struggling with a shortage of space on a page might influence what appeared in the printed version.

Recently, William B. Long has challenged the assumption that authorial stage directions were routinely and significantly altered in the playhouse. He argues that the supposed process of *systematic* annotation of an "authorial" manuscript in the playhouse is not well grounded in the evidence of the documents that survive. Theatrical manuscripts full of contradictions and loose ends seem to have been adequate to the needs of performance. His study of extant playbooks leads him to conclude that theatrical alter-

ations occur so infrequently "that, if a stage direction exists in a contemporary text—manuscript or printed—it is most likely authorial."[27] At the same
time, he acknowledges, Elizabethan playbooks "tend to become reposito-
ries. They accumulate inscriptions of various kinds" during their lifetime
in the playhouse, though not all of these are, in his view (or mine), properly
described as "stage directions."[28]

Approaching the problem from a different perspective, Antony
Hammond, an editor of the forthcoming Cambridge edition of Webster's
plays, concludes that much information about onstage action included in
authorial manuscripts tends (at least in the case of Webster) to be omitted
in promptbooks. Thus, in his experience, far from adding to or altering
existing directions for action (which he terms "directions of the third kind"),
some playhouse scribes seem to have omitted them.[29]

For the purposes of the present book, however, the important point is
that whoever was responsible for the stage directions in plays written for
the professional London theaters, the various hands generated and observed,
to a great extent, a common code. As David Bradley found in his study of
how an Elizabethan playscript was prepared for performance, the "Plotter"
or annotator of the script usually employed "the standard formulas of stage
directions found in all the texts."[30] Bookholders or printers might abbrevi-
ate or elaborate the *content* of a direction, but with a few exceptions they
observed a set of shared conventions when it came to the *form* in which
directions of various kinds were typically cast.

ELIZABETHAN DIRECTIONS AND THEIR AUDIENCES

The audience of a playscript and thus of its stage directions is diverse,
encompassing both prospective performers, past or future spectators, and
other readers. This diversity is suggested in the manuscripts of some medieval plays. In the Digby *Mary Magdalen*, players, readers, and spectators
are all addressed, albeit through separate channels. The stage directions
give blocking and costuming instructions to the players: *"And all the seven
Dedly Sinnes shal be conveyid into the house of Simont Leprous; they shall
be arayid like seven dylf [devils]"* (563, S.D.). The epilogue blesses the
spectators and begs their indulgence of "the sentens [narrative] / That we
have playid in yowr syth [sight]" (2133–38), while the scribe adds his own
valedictory in a postscript to the readers:

> Iff onything amisse be,
> Blame [lack of] conning, and nat me.

> I desire the redars to be my frynd,
> Iff ther be ony amisse, that to amend.
>
> (2141–44)

Christ's Burial, an Easter play dated c. 1520 from the e Museo 160 manuscript, also addresses readers as well as performers. A notation at the bottom of fol. 140ᵛ (the second page of the text) makes suggestions for performing the play in two parts, one on Good Friday, one on Easter morning. The note also alludes to lines that might be cut in performance, though damage to the manuscript obscures the reference to the particular lines marked for omission. The prologue, however, is explicitly directed to readers:

> A soule that list to sing of loue
>   of Crist that com tille us so lawe
> Rede this treyte, it may him moue,
>   And may hym teche lightly with-awe. . . .
>
> (Pro. 1–4)[31]

An interlude offered for acting might also address itself to readers as well as performers. On its title page, *The Marriage of Wit and Wisdom* manuscript (c. 1579) presents itself as convenient for six players and as "mixed full of pleasant mirth as well for The beholders as the Readers or hearers." Similarly, *The Life and Repentance of Mary Magdalen* advertises on its title page that it is "by the learned clarke Lewis Wager," that "foure may easely play this Enterlude," and that is "very delectable for those which shal heare or reade the same."[32]

Elizabethan directions, however, are assumed to have been addressed in the first instance to actors and other playhouse personnel, and this historical circumstance is sometimes taken as establishing a gulf between the original audience of stage directions ("players") and later audiences ("readers"). This inference, however, creates a false dichotomy. Although stage directions (closet drama excepted) are always initially directed to theater people, this means that they are the play's first (and often most dedicated) readers.[33] In our own day, theatrical production requires many kinds of reading (a director's quick read through, an initial rehearsal "reading," an actor's solitary reading of his part to con or "map" his role, to name just a few),[34] and some of these forms of reading must have also occurred in the Elizabethan theater.

Elizabethan stage directions, however, had to be conducive to reading in one further—and paradoxical—sense. In Elizabethan times, actors might have heard the play read to them prior to reading it (or the "sides" with their individual parts) themselves.[35] Thus their first encounter with the text might have been aural rather than visual. According to G. E. Bentley, "a normal part of the dramatist's preparation of his play for the acting troupe was the reading of his manuscript to them for their approval."[36] These presentations were apparently convivial affairs, often conducted at taverns, not in the cold, empty theater. In March 1598/99, Henslowe advanced players five shillings to cover the cost of a reading "at the Sun in New Fish Street," and in 1602 he laid out two shillings "when they read the play of Jeffa for wine at the tavern."[37] Potential performers were also sometimes given some or all of a new play to read,[38] but an oral presentation to some or all of the company seems to have been common. Thus playwright Robert Daborne writes to Henslowe in 1613: "On Tuesday night if you will appoint I will meet you and Mr. Alleyn and read some, for I am unwilling to read to the general company till all be finished."[39] Thus it appears the company often approved the purchase of a play on the basis of such a private "reading." Actor Robert Shaw writes to Henslowe in the summer of 1600, "We have heard their play and like it. Their price is £8, which I pray pay now to Mr. Wilson, according to our promise."[40]

This custom of reading the play aloud to its potential performers had several practical advantages. It allowed the playwright to give it what we might call a lively "concert" reading (here the actor-playwrights may have had an edge), and it might have alleviated difficulties if the author's papers were indeed "foul" and hard to read owing to corrections, interlineations, and so forth. (Daborne apologizes to Henslowe for a fragment being "not so fair written as I could wish.")[41] More important for our purposes, the custom of this initial reading would also have reinforced certain elements of the form of Elizabethan stage directions. Presumably, if a dramatic text was to be intelligible when read aloud, the author would have to read some, if not all, of the directions aloud as well. It would obviously be helpful if their diction and syntax differed from that of the dialogue. Further, a distinctive visual appearance (their position in the margin as glosses, or their being set out in a different script) could aid the playwright or other reader in distinguishing them vocally. As Ivan Illich has pointed out, in performing the liturgy medieval clerics had developed a variety of vocal styles or "accents" to accompany a variety of biblical texts. As a result, "the literally mono-tonous *cantus lectionis* for the glosses" was clearly distinguishable from "the *tonus prophetiae, epistolae,* [or] *evangelicae.*" According to Illich, the different tones were so familiar that "anyone, without understanding a word, would know that the Old Testament, St. Paul, or the Gospel, respectively, was being read," and these tonal differences survive in the traditional forms of Christian liturgy to this day.[42] It seems likely that the marginal position and Italian script of Elizabethan stage directions would have similarly helped the playwright's oral interpretation of the different parts of his script for his player audiences.

The various sorts of reading involved in accepting, memorizing, and rehearsing a play may differ from the sort of reading done by a nontheatrical reader, and both differ from the reading habits of a professional scholar.[43] Nonetheless, as readers (or hearers) of the play, all these have some things in common. For example, all need to be able to distinguish directions from dialogue, to follow the sequence of speakers, to perceive scene breaks, and to grasp the relation between a given direction and the corresponding lines. In this sense, performers and all others who approach the play at least initially through the text as written or read aloud are the audience for stage directions, as opposed to spectators who witness the performers' responses to the directions, not the directions themselves.[44]

The supposed gulf between theatrical and lay readers is also assumed because the Elizabethan playwright has been portrayed as writing with no thought of print.[45] However, many plays were published (some with, some without the playwright's permission), often in multiple editions. There was clearly an appetite for dramatic texts on the part of the Elizabethan and Jacobean reading public. Caroline playwright Richard Brome's contract with the Salisbury Court companies prohibits him from allowing the plays written for them to be printed "without the license from the said company or the major part of them."[46] Presumably this restriction was intended to protect the company's financial interest in a profitable play, but it also implies that the company might decide to authorize a printed edition. Although Brome is a late example, it would seem that the printing and reading of playtexts was in the minds of the theatrical community, at least as a commercially sensitive issue.

The prefaces and dedications written by the playwrights themselves in printed editions that were apparently authorized seem to assume a well-defined reading public for plays. Heywood, in the 1600 quarto of *The Foure Prentices of London with the Conquest of Jerusalem* perhaps playfully dedicates the play "To the honest and high-spirited Prentices, the Readers." Middleton's preface to the 1611 quarto of *The Roaring Girl* is addressed "To the Comicke, Play-readers" as if that were an established group. In the Preface itself, Middleton implies that his "booke" has a dual life, one on the stage and one in readers' private rooms: it is, he asserts, like its heroine "fit for many of your companies . . . and may bee allowed both Gallery roome at the play-house and chamber-roome at your lodging" (A3). As Frederick Kiefer has pointed out, before Jonson's folio elevated plays and masques to the status of "workes," "it was common for authors to *affect* the pose of an amateur, whose writings somehow found their way into print."[47] But the key word is "affect"; the modest and ingratiating rhetoric of authors' prefaces should not be read too literally or naively. In his preface to a quarto edition of *The English Traveller* in 1633, Thomas Heywood offers three reasons why his own plays have not been collected and published in folio. One reason is, he claims, that "it was never any great ambition in [him], to bee in this kind Voluminously read"; but the other reasons have to do with the acting companies having "negligently lost" the plays and the "Actors, who thinke it against their peculiar profit to have them come into print," retaining their control of the playtexts.[48] The undertone of animosity in his statement of the latter reasons rather undercuts the self-effacing modesty of the first.

Once a play was printed, the rhetoric of title pages and prefaces suggests that the Elizabethans deemed playscripts from the theater as adequate and appropriate for the lay reader. The prefaces to the published versions of plays for the London theaters are explicitly addressed "to the reader" (or the "learned" or "knowing" or "the great variety of readers"), but at the same time their title pages often invoke the authority (or perhaps the notoriety) of performance. Some printers (like that of *1 Tamburlaine*) claim to have edited the play for readers,[49] and others, like that of the Beaumont and Fletcher folio, claim to present in the printed edition a more authoritative and complete text than any actually staged.[50] But many more claim fidelity to the stage version as a selling point. (In the thirty-five printed plays examined in chapter 3, for example, twenty-eight allude on their title pages to their having been acted, and only seven do not.) The formulae are familiar: *"As it was acted by His Majestie's Servants," "As it was sundry times performed in the City of London to great applause."* Others assume, like the printer of *Alphonsus, Emperor of Germany*, the goodwill of any reader who has "seen this Piece presented with all the Elegance of Life and Action on the *Black-Friers* Stage." In the First Folio of Shakespeare, Heminge and Condell claim to present texts more perfect than those previously printed, basing their claim on the authority of Shakespeare's "papers" as delivered to the playhouse. They imply the primacy of the theatrical versions based on these "papers" when they preempt would-be critics, asserting that the plays "have had their triall alreadie [on the stage] and stood out all Appeales" (A3).

As we shall see in chapters 1 and 2, printed texts did alter somewhat the visual design of a playscript and thus the position of some directions (notably speech prefixes) in relation to the dialogue. The mere fact of printing, however, did not result in wholesale rewriting of the stage directions. Most of those who presented dramatic texts to the reading public (Jonson's folio of 1616 is the great exception) did not find it necessary to alter the stage directions. While modern readers may have difficulty interpreting Elizabethan directions, and while some late private transcripts seem to have tried to "flesh out" playhouse directions for the benefit of readers unfamiliar with the staged play, the stage directions adequate to the needs of the Elizabethan and Jacobean playhouse were generally seen as intelligible to ordinary readers of the time.

EARLY TAXONOMIES: "LITERARY" VS. "THEATRICAL" DIRECTIONS

Early attempts to distinguish elements of the form of Elizabethan stage directions grew out of the effort to determine the provenance of the texts in which they resided. Textual scholars, such as W. W. Greg, A. W. Pollard, R. B. McKerrow, and J. Dover Wilson, distinguished between "literary" and "theatrical" directions in their effort to determine whether authorial "foul papers" or a theatrical "prompter's copy" lay behind a printed text of a Shakespeare play.[51] While they recognized that both types might appear in a given manuscript, in distinguishing between different kinds of directions they provided the first taxonomy of Elizabethan stage directions according to their content, diction, point of view, and (to a degree) their syntax.

For example, they noted that some directions (likely, they thought, to be authorial) were "permissive" or indefinite ("Three or four officers, soldiers as many as may be"), whereas others (presumably those of the playhouse) were precise about the actual numbers. They also distinguished between descriptive directions, such as "Mycetas comes out alone with his crown in his hand," and imperative directions, such as "Sound trumpet," "Make as if ye would fight." (The former they viewed as more likely to be authorial, and the latter theatrical.) They also pointed out directions that included contextual information not readily translatable (they thought) into concrete details of staging: "Enter the Mayor and citizens marching as at Mile-end" or "Enter the king and lords to banish the Duchess." (These directions were also considered to be signs of an author's hand.)[52] Greg and later Richard Hosley noted the difference between "fictive" and "theatrical" diction in Elizabethan stage directions. "Slipping into his narrative," an author, they thought, might write in fictive terms ("on the walls," "before the gates," "into the city," "at the window") rather than the technical stage terms ("above," "aloft," or "within").[53]

Directions originating in the playhouse, in addition to lacking these authorial touches, were thought to be more consistently informative about blocking ("at one door," "at another"), props ("a bed thrust out"), warnings *("One ready with pen and ink"),* and special effects (flourishes, fire-works, drum and colors, etc.).[54] The presence of *Ready* directions for actors (especially by name), "early" entries (entries that precede the entering character's first speech by several lines), and notations for props not needed or not revealed until later in the scene were also assumed to characterize a playhouse manuscript and (perhaps) to have originated with playhouse personnel rather than the author in the throes of composition.[55]

Although not all who followed them paid heed, Greg and R. B. McKerrow warned that both kinds of directions could be found in authorial and theatrical manuscripts, and thus could not guarantee the nature of the copytext in which they resided.[56] Indeed, they concluded that mixed forms were likely to be the norm. As McKerrow put it:

> What could be more natural than that a skilled dramatist closely connected with the theater and writing, not with any thought of print, but with his eye solely on a stage production, should give stage directions in the form of directions to the actors (as they might appear in a prompt-book) rather than as descriptions of action viewed from the front of the theater. Probably he would use either type of direction as it happened to occur to him, just as we find them mixed in the manuscript of *The Two Noble Ladies,* which is held to be in the hand of its author.[57]

Other examples of "mixed" directions are not hard to find, early and late in the period, particularly with respect to fictive vs. technical theatrical diction. In the manuscript of *Edmond Ironside* (c. 1590), which bears many signs of playhouse use, technical and fictive terms coexist:

> *He beates them about the* stage.
>
> (TLN 560–61; emphasis added)
>
> *The Herrold departeth from the kinge to the* walls
> *sounding his trumpit.*
>
> (TLN 872–73; emphasis added)
>
> *assayle the* walls.
>
> (TLN 914; emphasis added)
>
> *They fight againe Edm[ond] drives Canute*
> *back about the* stage.
>
> (TLN 1996–97; emphasis added)

Instances of mixed diction also occur in *Hengist, King of Kent* by Middleton, a relatively late play. The manuscript, which appears to be a private transcript, c. 1616–20, of a partially annotated promptbook, calls for characters to enter *"on the walls"* (V.ii.0, S.D.). At the same point in the quarto, published in 1661 after the theaters had been closed for almost twenty years, the theatrical term appears, and the characters enter *"above."*[58] Thus it seems that a manuscript with some connection to the theater might contain literary or fictive terms, and the printed edition, presumably aimed at readers unfamiliar with the performed play, might include theatrical directions.[59]

In addition to its unreliability as a indication of textual provenance, the "literary" vs. "theatrical" distinction is less than satisfactory in other ways. Many directions thought (perhaps correctly) to be authorial in origin are clearly "theatrical" in many other respects. For example, permissive directions, such as *"soldiers as many as may be,"* traditionally taken to be authorial, are clearly addressed to those responsible for staging the play, not to a lay reader. They show an insider's awareness of limitations regarding casting, while making the desire for maximum spectacle clear. The very recognition of the players' responsibility for the details of the action (the actual number of soldiers) is in keeping with the collaborative nature of the theatrical enterprise. Indeed, in plays for the London theaters, nearly all directions considered "authorial" and thus "literary" by the traditional criteria outlined above efficiently accomplish theatrical ends—as the mixed practice of existing playhouse manuscript demonstrates. For truly "literary" annotations to a playtext, one might cite the marginalia Jonson sometimes provides in his 1616 folio. In act 3 of *Sejanus*, for example, he clarifies family relationships (*"His daughter was betrothed to Claudius, his sonne"*) and glosses unfamiliar words (*"A forme of speaking they h[a]d," "A wreath of laurell"*).[60]

While the early attempt to distinguish between "literary" (authorial) and "theatrical" directions provides a beginning taxonomy of Elizabethan directions, the terms themselves do not describe the most significant variations in the voice and viewpoint of Elizabethan stage directions.

I propose, then, to examine Elizabethan stage directions from the point of view of their voice and address, their conventions as an effective verbal and graphic code. My concern will be to describe their characteristic visual deployment, their grammar, and their rhetorical stance. A particular rhetorical stance may or may not coincide with the "real" relationship that obtains between speaker and audience; indeed, my assumption is that in most rhetorical situations, one's stance is influenced partly by convention, partly by "real" conditions (power, money, status, personal feelings), and partly by an effort to influence or determine the relationship that emerges from the sum of those conditions. Consequently, while I shall try to keep in mind what we know about the "real" relationships of writers of stage directions and their audiences, my goal is chiefly to describe the conventional voice of Elizabethan directions, at least as it strikes my twentieth-century ears.

My sample for this survey is a group of about fifty plays written for the professional men's companies during the late sixteenth and the first half of the seventeenth century. To highlight the conventions of these plays and their theatrical community, I contrast them with plays from other venues and their antecedents in religious, academic, and popular drama. I focus on plays for the professional men's companies and the London stage because, as we shall see, the form of directions varies somewhat from venue to venue. University plays, court masques, and many plays written for the boys' companies often imitate the apparatus of classical drama. It was plays for the adult companies at the Theatre, the Globe, the Rose, the Fortune, and later the Blackfriars and the Cockpit that established the form of stage directions largely maintained by later generations of English playwrights.

For the sake of brevity, the term "Elizabethan" in the title of this book refers to the conventions observed in plays of the Elizabethan, Jacobean, and (sometimes) Caroline periods; this liberty can be justified, since most of the conventions were initiated, though perhaps not fully established, during the latter part of Elizabeth's reign. In selecting the plays, I drew initially upon Irving Ribner's list in *The English History Play in the Age of Shakespeare* (Princeton: Princeton University Press, 1957), which spans the genre from Skelton's *Magnificence* (1519) to Ford's *Perkin Warbeck* (c. 1633). This provided a manageable sample with a broad chronological range, which I have extended by comparing Elizabethan plays with a large number of their medieval forebears.

Reliance on one genre, historical plays, may introduce bias into the evidence, so prudence would seem to suggest that my conclusions cannot be extended to other genres without risk. Indeed, one of my findings is that a few playwrights used different conventions regarding dramatic apparatus for plays of different genres. However, the history play is in itself a mixed genre, containing plays in tragic, comic, and pastoral modes, and it could be said to offer a reasonable cross-section of the dramatic materials popular in the London theaters. Many plays now classified as comedies and tragedies were based upon historical sources, and thus leaven the sample. For example, *John a Kent and John a Cumber*, *The Shoemakers' Holiday*, *Macbeth*, and *King Lear* all appear on Ribner's list. Nonetheless, particularly in chapters 3 and 6, where I attempt to tally certain practices, I broadened the sample with plays representing other genres, such as romance and city comedy. Further, although it will be clear that Shakespeare's plays of all genres follow the practices described below, I cite a wide spectrum of authors and plays, quartos "good" and "bad," to demonstrate that with a few exceptions these practices characterized not just a few writers, but the entire community of the public theaters in London.

The discussion that follows is divided into two parts. Part 1 deals with the material text and the visual aspects of the Elizabethan code for stage directions. The first chapter discusses the transformation of the univocal "production narrative" that characterized early medieval drama and the genesis of the now-familiar scheme of functionally discrete directions (entrances, exits, speech prefixes, etc.) and the corresponding page design of a dramatic text. Though visual means were used both early and late to distinguish the stage directions from the dialogue, different visual schemes affected how the voice of the directions addressed its interpreters. Chapter 2 focuses on the evolution of the left-hand speech prefix and its role in reintegrating dialogue and directions into a polyvocal but readable text. Chapter 3 analyzes the visual deployment of midscene directions, and the tension between the marginal design of playhouse manuscripts and the greater integration and linearity of printed editions.

Part 2 looks closely at the grammar and rhetoric of the stage directions themselves. Chapter 4 introduces some general differences between the directions for the London theaters and their medieval predecessors. It traces the shift from Latin to English, and it analyzes the influence of this shift on verb mood and the decline of "self-consciousness" in English stage directions. Chapter 5 focuses on the authoritative Latinate diction and syntax of Elizabethan entries and exits, and chapter 6 on the more laconic form of midscene directions for action and special effects.

Medieval stage directions, though sampled fairly extensively here, are cited to highlight by contrast the particular conventions of the later period. In speaking of the "evolution" of Elizabethan directions from their medieval roots, I mean to suggest neither hierarchy nor teleology, but only to show that it was the directions of medieval religious drama that later generations adapted to suit their own theatrical conditions and communities. Medieval texts vary widely in their annotation. Some, like the Wakefield *Noah*, have almost no directions. (The *Noah* as we have it has only one, directing Noah to meet his wife, and little apparatus altogether save speech prefixes.) As in their Elizabethan successors, much action in medieval plays is inscribed only in the dialogue, without any confirmation or clarification in stage directions. I make no claim to have described the full range and variety of medieval directions, though this strikes me as a fascinating and worthwhile project. I have only attempted to sketch the outlines of medieval practice in some plays that do have directions, and to compare their visual, grammatical, and rhetorical features with those of their Elizabethan counterparts. Though I have not been able to resist speculating about the effect of the form of medieval directions on their interpreters, my goal in doing so has been to sharpen our familiarity-blunted senses with respect to Elizabethan directions.

After this study was essentially complete, I had the pleasure of reading T. H. Howard-Hill's article, "The Evolution of the Form of Plays in English during the Renaissance,"[61] which is concerned with many of the issues discussed in this book. Since Howard-Hill bases his analysis of the medieval roots of Elizabethan practices on a survey of "all manuscripts of plays composed [in English] before 1500,"[62] I am gratified that my conclusions, based on a sampling (albeit a large one) of medieval plays, are consistent with his, though arrived at independently. In general, Howard-Hill's findings and those I present in this book are complementary. We both find in the "native" medieval drama the main source of the visual and grammatical conventions of Elizabethan playscripts and consider the influence (often superficial) of the rival "classical" method for presenting a dramatic text. However, our work differs in scope, focus, and purpose.[63] My focus is more narrowly on stage directions per se, whereas he is equally interested in the apparatus of the text (arguments, dramatis personae, act and scene divisions, etc.), the last of which he sees as "the fundamental distinction" between the "native" and "classical" methods of presenting a dramatic text.[64] Our purposes also differ. Howard-Hill is interested in establishing the general outlines of the two methods chiefly because "the transmission of Renaissance plays, and especially the functions of their scribes, can hardly be understood without reference to the mixed traditions that eventually determined the form of modern play texts."[65] This book, on the other hand, is concerned not so much with the process of transmission as with the rhetorical implications of the various forms that stage directions have historically taken. Whereas he is interested in the influence of the existing conventions upon scribal hands, I am concerned with how the different conventions create distinctive voices or reveal distinctive conceptions of the nature of drama and of dramatic discourse. In the notes to the chapters that follow, I will try to indicate where Howard-Hill's insights have refined my own and where we differ.

Finally, a note on the typographic representation of early texts cited in this study. The practice of setting stage directions in Italian script or an italic typeface was not universal in the texts I will be discussing, especially the earlier ones. Nonetheless, if the stage directions quoted in the following chapters were distinguished from the dialogue by *some* visual means, I have placed them in italics to signify the same. As a result, all but the very earliest examples will appear in italics, even though something other than an italic script or typeface may have identified them to a contemporary

reader's eye. I have not preserved proper names and other words that appear in roman type in directions that are otherwise italicized. In general,
when quoting from early printed plays, I have preserved the original spelling except for u/v, i/j, archaic characters, such as thorn or long ess, and
abbreviations involving tildes. I have sometimes silently modernized punctuation. In quoting manuscript sources, if I have consulted a transcription
that modernizes capitalization, spelling, and punctuation, the edition will
be cited in a note. As far as possible, when illustrating a particular convention, I have listed the examples in roughly chronological order. Chapters 1,
2, and 3, which discuss the visual layout of early texts, necessarily rely on
facsimiles or the quarto and folio texts themselves, which are cited by siglia
(for original texts or unlineated photographic facsimiles) or Through Line
Numbers (TLN), the system of the Norton Facsimile of the 1623 Folio of
Shakespeare's plays and of the Malone Society reprints and some other
print facsimiles. Where the verbal rather than the visual form of the stage
directions is discussed, more readily accessible modern editions will be
cited using the old system of upper- and lowercase roman and Arabic numerals for act, scene, and line numbers, respectively; some plays are ap-
propriately cited by line number, or by scene and line number only, so
using Arabic numerals exclusively could be confusing. A list of the plays
cited and the editions consulted can be found at the end of this book.

Part One

The Material Text:
Page Design, Typography, and Mimesis

1

Distinguishing Directions
from the Dialogue

Unlike the amateur actor Flute, who speaks "all [his] part at once, cues and all,"[1] an actor memorizing his part needs to be able to distinguish his own lines from the cue lines and stage directions that were also written on his "side" or portion of the script. For similar reasons, a bookholder, actor, or other reader needs to be able to distinguish stage directions from the dialogue of a play. The stage directions and the characters speak from what the discipline of discourse analysis would call different "author positions," and the text would be incoherent if it confused the voices of the characters and the voice that conveys staging information, entries, and exits. In the medieval and Renaissance periods, those responsible for playscripts developed various conventions to help their interpreters distinguish the different voices. In early vernacular drama, the distinction between dialogue and stage directions is partly linguistic: the directions appear in Latin, the dialogue in the vernacular. The different voices are assigned different tongues. This convention constitutes a nominally visual distinction, as well, since Latin and vernacular languages such as Anglo-Norman or Middle English "look different" on the page to those who can read them and even to those who cannot.

Once both directions and dialogue began to appear in English, a specialized syntax and diction, including some Latin terms and Latinate syntax, helped to differentiate stage directions from dialogue. Such verbal codes were particularly important in entries and exits, as we shall see in chapter 5. However, in the transmission of medieval and Renaissance playscripts, many of the conventions that evolved were visual, matters of calligraphy (or typography) and page design. The next three chapters explore the design of the material text and its contribution to the voice of English stage directions.

35

In addition to distinguishing between directions and dialogue, Elizabethan playscripts also differentiate directions by function. With certain exceptions (such as the complex directions for dumb shows or ceremonial entries discussed in chapter 5), directions in plays for the London theaters can generally be classified as speech prefixes, entries, exits, or midscene directions for action and special effects.[2] In some cases, most notably speech prefixes and entries that initiate a scene, the directions occupy a distinctive position on the page. For example, entries that begin a scene are usually written across the entire page (in manuscripts) or centered within the text column (in printed editions). Speech prefixes usually appear in or near the left margin of the text column. In both these cases, the position of the direction on the page signals its function and clarifies its relation to the dialogue. Ultimately, in printed plays, page design served both to distinguish directions by function and to reintegrate directions and dialogue into a readable text.

As Robert S. Knapp has observed, drama as text and drama as "presence" or theatrical event coexist in a complex tension: "[T]extuality enables presence, yet also threatens it; so when plays become fully readable, they lose presence, as do actors who altogether become creatures of the script."[3] As noted in the introduction, this paradox is particularly true of stage directions. On the one hand, they provide necessary or helpful information about staging. On the other, they may seem to preempt the theatrical imagination of their interpreters or to intrude a nondramatic voice into the dramatic text. I hope to show that during the Elizabethan period, the visual design of playscripts became more readable without sacrificing—and indeed while emphasizing—"presence." By "readable" I mean something perhaps more basic than what Knapp means in the passage quoted above, but making the material text more readable was an important step in the creation of a drama that has survived both as theater and as literature.

To some eyes, while printed Elizabethan plays exhibit a semblance of a visual design that modern editions have refined and codified, Elizabethan manuscripts, especially playhouse manuscripts, reveal a disconcerting freedom and absence of regularity. According to Marion Trousdale, for example, the visual design of extant playhouse manuscripts is so complex as to be haphazard; it reveals no "scheme" at all. She argues that in the fifteen manuscripts discussed by W. W. Greg in *Dramatic Documents from the Elizabethan Playhouses* (1931)

> neither the positioning nor the nature of the stage directions is consistent
> with any established procedure, with the possible exception of the exits,

which most often appear on the right. But "most often" is the operative phrase. Exits for *Edmond Ironside* occur on the right, but they are also combined with entrances in the center. In *Sir John van Olden Barnavelt,* ... two exits are centered while other exits are marked on the right.[4]

Trousdale and other commentators, such as William B. Long,[5] are right to stress the differences between the sometimes casually and confusingly annotated scripts that survive from Elizabethan playhouses and the greater neatness and regularity of later promptbooks, and of printed texts both Elizabethan and modern. However, in focusing on what is not regular, it is easy to overlook what is. Moreover, in seeking regularities, one can hope only to describe norms, not absolute "rules"; in the use of any communal code, exceptions and eccentric usages can always be found.

The significant regularities of Elizabethan and Jacobean dramatic texts, both manuscript and printed, and the implications of their design for the tenor of dramatic discourse emerge more clearly when we compare them with their predecessors. This chapter will focus on general schemes for distinguishing directions from dialogue and the placement of initial entry directions. The following chapter will discuss speech attributions and mimesis in the design of dramatic texts. Visual conventions peculiar to midscene directions touched on here will be discussed in greater detail in chapter 3. As noted in the introduction, when discussing plays of the late sixteenth century, I will focus on plays associated with the professional London theaters and the men's companies, rather than on academic plays, like *Gammer Gurton's Needle,* and other boys' plays, which adhere to a slightly different set of conventions.

EARLY DRAMATIC MANUSCRIPTS

The earliest surviving dramatic manuscripts make no effort to distinguish staging directions from dialogue: both appear in Latin without any alteration in the size or mode of script. In the tenth century *Visitatio Sepulchri* or *Quem Queritis*, to call it by its familiar opening words, the Latin text and directions move across the page without any effort at visual differentiation. The small-script notations in Old English that are visible between the lines are glosses to aid the reader in translating, not staging, the text. Folio 21[v] of this play is reproduced in fig. 1.[6] An English translation of the first four lines of this folio, preserving the visual presentation of the original, would look like this (the first words conclude the opening stage direction):

[. . . let him begin in a sweet and moderate voice] to sing: Whom do you
seek. When this has been sung to the end let the three answer with one
voice: Jesus of Nazareth. He to them: He is not here, he has risen as he
had foretold; go announce that he has risen from the dead. This command
having been voiced, let the three turn to the choir saying Alleluia, the
Lord has risen. . . .

In addition to the uniform presentation of dialogue and staging directions, the rubrics themselves are undifferentiated; that is, sequence, movement, gesture, and speech attribution may be handled altogether in a single
complex direction. The one elliptical phrase ("He to them") and the subjunctive verbs ("Let the three turn") signal *verbally* that this is a dramatic
version of the *Sepulchre* episode, but, unlike the playscripts to which we
have become accustomed, nothing distinguishes it *visually* from a
nondramatic text, such as a biblical narrative or a philosophical treatise.

To an eye used to Elizabethan or modern conventions for dramatic
texts, this "mass of [chirographic] protoplasm" (to adapt Walter J. Ong's
phrase)[7] seems difficult to sort out as a script for performance. An individual actor's speeches are not easy to identify, nor is it easy to tell where
a stage direction ends and spoken dialogue begins. Of course, this may not
have been the case for its intended audience, English Benedictine monks
accustomed to the beautiful but dense columns of text in manuscripts of
the day. Ong sees the unbroken columns that characterize medieval manuscripts as a sign of a strong oral residue in medieval culture. According to
Ong, such texts, though written, were conceived of as existing in time, as
the unbroken utterance of a single "speaker." Thus it is not surprising that
the earliest manuscripts do not clearly differentiate the voices of a dramatic
text; text and dialogue are conceived of as a unified set of instructions for
the play. In addition, Ong argues that most medieval manuscripts were
"producer-" rather than "consumer-oriented," that is, they were meant to
be deciphered by other professionals (teachers, priests, and scribes), not
the lay public.[8] If we may stretch the term, medieval playscripts are also
"producer-oriented" in the theatrical sense: they are addressed to the person(s)
in charge of a future production, not an individual player or a lay reader.

Nonetheless, the desirability of visually distinguishing dialogue from
staging directions for the benefit of readers and performers made itself felt
early in the transmission of medieval dramatic texts. As noted above, maintaining the directions in Latin for decades (even centuries) after the dialogue had shifted to the vernacular created a linguistic distinction, and at
least a slight visual distinction as well. But additional visual means were
soon developed.

In the *Mystère d'Adam* manuscript, usually dated 1225–50 though the play is believed to be fifty to one hundred years older, the directions are in Latin, the dialogue in Anglo-Norman.[9] In the first part of the manuscript, the scribe makes no further effort to distinguish dialogue from staging information by a contrasting size or style of script or other visual means; using every possible bit of writing area, the text unfolds uniformly.[10] Later in the manuscript, however, the scribe begins to leave white space between the end of a stage direction and the beginning of the next line of verse (see fig. 2), and a few pages further on he takes care to begin each direction and each speech on a new line. As a result, the poetic qualities of the text (the verse line, often shared by more than one speaker) are subordinated to its theatrical features (the change of speakers). This tension between the poetic and theatrical aspects of a play will be a recurrent theme in our discussion of the visual design of the playtext. For our present purposes, the important result of the *Adam* scribe's innovations is that the directions and the dialogue are further distinguished by being granted their own space, their own lines of the text.

Fourteenth- and fifteenth-century manuscripts developed additional conventions for the differentiation of stage directions and dialogue. Innovations cannot be dated precisely, since one cannot be sure whether an extant manuscript, if late, preserves an earlier tradition in the presentation of a dramatic text or updates it. Nonetheless, the plays preserved in the Macro manuscripts, the York and the Towneley (Wakefield) cycles, and the noncycle plays in Digby 133 and e Museo 160 may be said to offer a reasonable sample of scribal and perhaps authorial practices from the late 1300s to the early 1500s. They exhibit a variety of visual schemes to distinguish directions from dialogue, but they have four common features: the use of space to the right of the text column, including the right margin, for directions; the use of ruled lines (or "rules") between speeches and around directions; some variation in size or style of script; and, on occasion, the use of red ink for speech attributions and staging information.

For example, *The Castle of Perseverance* in the Macro manuscript, usually dated 1397–1440, differentiates stage directions visually as well as linguistically. The directions appear in Latin in or near the right margin as a gloss (see *"Tunc verberabit eum,"* near the top of fig. 3)[11] and occasionally within the text. In the latter arrangement, they are set off by rules, and both direction and rules stretch from the left margin across the page (see the bottom of fig. 3). Although they are in the same style of script as the dialogue, the directions appear to be slightly reduced in size, thus further distinguishing them visually.

Mankind (c. 1464), another Macro play, also places directions in the margin and uses rules to highlight them. The play, which appears to be intended for a professional troupe,[12] has only about a dozen directions excluding speech attributions, some in Latin and some in English.[13] All the directions appear in the right-hand margin, set off from the dialogue by white space.[14] However, since the tail rhymes of each stanza and the speakers' names are also set to the right of the main text column, the scribe often separates the directions with a right-angled, or "hooked," rule.[15] While the speakers' names appear to be in slightly bolder script,[16] the directions are not clearly so distinguished. (Overall, this manuscript is relatively congested and difficult to read.)

Occasionally a scribe, perhaps weary of crowding speech attributions and directions into the margins, alters his scheme midway through the manuscript. This is the case in *Christ's Burial* (c. 1520, e Museo 160). After the first fourteen pages, the scribe puts the directions "neatly spaced in the middle of the pages."[17] In *The Killing of the Children* (c. 1490–1500, Digby 133), the stage directions, which are in English, appear within the text column between rules, often preceded by a dash or other mark to distinguish them from the dialogue.[18] This results in a more spacious and legible presentation, and the addition of the dash ensures ready recognition of the directions as such.

In addition to using marginal space, rules, and varied scripts, scribes occasionally made use of red ink to highlight staging information. In doing so, the scribes followed the tradition of placing the directions for the conduct of the liturgy in red ink, from which they acquired the name "rubrics" (*ruber* meaning "red"). For example, on folios 160[v] and 161 of *The Castle of Perseverance* two stage directions and six speech attributions appear in red ink.[19] The speech attributions on four other pages are also "touched with red."[20] The use of red ink in this manuscript is not sustained; it is employed on only six pages out of a total of seventy-six. The red-ink direction at line 574, inserted as was the custom after the dialogue had been written, is crowded in between a tail rhyme and the next speaker's name. Red ink is very helpful in this particular instance, but other similarly crowded right-margin directions and speech attributions are not distinguished by colored ink.

In other manuscripts, scribes used red ink to highlight both theatrical and nontheatrical aspects of the text. The red paragraph tokens employed in the left margins of the so-called *Ludus Coventriae* mark the beginning of each stanza, not a change of speaker, which sometimes coincides with the stanza break, but often does not. In the Northampton *Abraham and Isaac*, the use of colored inks is more functional; speeches are separated by a red line. But in this manuscript, too, other touches of red (to highlight the

first letter of each verse and the rhyme brackets) are purely ornamental.[21]
In the Brome *Abraham and Isaac*, the first word of each speech is under-
lined in red throughout the play (which serves to highlight the change of
speakers), but "a large number of words within speeches" are also under-
lined in red, "many of them for no obvious reason."[22]

In the Towneley (Wakefield) cycle, stage directions, in Latin and English,[23] appear either to the right of the text in the margin, or within the text
column, set off by rules above and below or on all sides. For example, fol.
51[v] containing lines from the *Magi* shows two directions within the text
column and one in the margin at the very bottom.[24] Two plays in the cycle
have directions entirely in red, and in fifteen plays the marginal directions
are marked by a hooked underline in red or set off by the red rule that
generally divides the speeches. (Twelve of the plays have no directions
other than speech attributions.) In the first seven plays, the first letter of
each speaker's name is also touched with red.

According to A. C. Cawley and Martin Stevens, the rubrication in the
Towneley cycle is "almost entirely functional," with the aim of making the
manuscript "easier to use, whether for reading or staging."[25] The most prominent visual features of these texts, however, are the large-script words *Incipit*
(begins) and *Explicit* (ends), at the beginning and end, respectively, of each
play. These phrases highlight the textual boundaries of each play rather
than specific performance information.[26] Of course, emphasizing where
one pageant ends and another begins is an aid to performance, too, especially when different groups of players are responsible for different plays.
But, in the design of this manuscript, though both textual and performative
aspects of the plays are stressed, the emphasis is on the textual.

In a few plays, however, the use of red ink to highlight stage directions
is more sustained and systematic. This is the case in the York cycle, the
Ludus Coventriae, the Digby *Mary Magdalen*, and *Christ's Burial* (e Museo
160). In these plays, though nontheatrical elements of the text may also
appear in red, speech attributions, speech rules, and/or directions in red ink
are the norm rather than the exception. For example, in the Digby *Wisdom*,
the scribe uses brown ink for the text and speech attributions and red for
the stage directions.[27] *Christ's Burial* also has directions and speech attributions in red throughout.[28] The result is a text both beautiful and functional, easy to read and interpret. Similarly, in the *Play of the Sacrament*, in
an uncanny anticipation of the modern felt-tipped pen, someone has highlighted both speech attributions and directions with yellow crayon.[29]

All but the very earliest dramatic manuscripts thus make some attempt
to distinguish directions from dialogue, the most common methods being
the use of the space to the right of the text, including the right margin, and

the use of rules and contrasting ink. In highlighting staging information, however, medieval manuscripts are not always consistent. Moreover, non-theatrical elements of the text (stanza breaks, biblical and Latin quotations, and rhyme schemes) may also be emphasized, and effort is sometimes expended to ornament the text for purely aesthetic reasons.

ELIZABETHAN MANUSCRIPTS

The design of Elizabethan dramatic manuscripts resembles that of medieval texts in many ways. *Thomas of Woodstock* may serve as a representative example of a manuscript associated with the London theaters (see fig. 4).[30] Like their predecessors, Elizabethan manuscripts often vary the size of the script or its boldness to differentiate stage directions and speech attributions from dialogue. They also use rules to separate one speech from another and to highlight directions. In the manuscript of *Thomas of Woodstock*, the rules between speeches are short, but the rules on either side of the major entry directions run the full width of the text column. Some playhouse manuscripts also use rules "above, under, or all round"[31] to highlight the marginal directions.

In addition, in the extant playhouse manuscripts, dialogue and directions generally inhabit different spaces. The dialogue dominates the central text column; with the exception of initial entries (to be discussed below), the directions are placed in the margins, both on the right, as in earlier manuscripts, and on the left. As we shall see in chapter 4, the shift from self-conscious to self-effacing directions had the effect of verbally integrating the disparate elements of dramatic discourse: it permitted the interpretation of both dialogue and stage directions from a single point of view. Visually, however, most directions in manuscript plays remained, like their medieval counterparts, glosses on the text rather than integral parts of it.

Whereas some medieval manuscripts use contrasting ink, Elizabethan dramatic manuscripts generally use a contrasting hand to differentiate stage directions from dialogue: the dialogue is normally in an English secretary hand and the directions in an Italian.[32] The degree of contrast varies, of course, with the care and/or skill of the author or scribe. Muriel St. Clare Byrne, editor of the manuscript of *John a Kent and John a Cumber*, notes that its author, Anthony Munday, provides directions "in what may by courtesy be termed . . . Italian script," but that the Italian hand is rather inconsistent and amateurish.[33] The important point for our purposes, however, is that the distinction is at least attempted.

The design of Elizabethan dramatic manuscripts differs from that of

their predecessors in two important ways: the placement of speech attributions (which will be discussed in the next chapter) and the prominence of
initial entries.

In Elizabethan manuscripts, midscene entries and other directions may
appear as marginal glosses, but entries that initiate a new scene are regularly given special treatment. They are usually written across the entire
page, extending beyond the text column both to the left and the right, and
set off by rules. Thus, they both interrupt the text column vertically and
extend its margins horizontally. Alternatively, initial entries in Elizabethan
manuscripts may be centered *within* the text column, breaking its boundaries with white space to the left and right of the direction.[34] (The centered
position became the norm in printed texts and may have exerted an influence on later manuscripts.) Though the across-the-page initial entry is more
common, initial entries are centered within the text column in *Edmond
Ironside* (e.g., TLN 1039, S.D.), a playhouse manuscript, and in the late
Hengist, King of Kent (c. 1616–20), which seems to be a private transcript.[35]
Thus the variation does not divide altogether neatly between playhouse
and nonplayhouse manuscripts.

Whether written across the entire page or centered within the text column, initial entries break up what was the dominant feature of most medieval dramatic manuscripts, namely, the uniform central column of the text.
Moreover, the visual break corresponds to a "break" in the flow of the
performance, the momentarily cleared stage and the entry of characters to
begin a new scene. Thus, whereas medieval directions are limited to the
boundaries of the text column or confined to the space to its right, Elizabethan initial entries break and divide the text column to emphasize the cleared
stage and the beginning of a new scene; the design thus stresses the theatrical aspects of text.

Strictly speaking, initial entries have no exact counterpart in medieval
drama. In medieval plays, the characters enter and exit or move about the
playing space, but the action usually proceeds continuously. Space also
tends to be continuous, especially if several "mansions" or playing stations
are visible simultaneously, as in *The Castle of Perseverance*. The closest
analogue to the Elizabethan initial entry is thus the opening moment of the
play, when the characters enter the playing space. But at this point medieval manuscripts tend to emphasize textual, rather than theatrical, features,
providing a title or *Incipit* rather than an entry direction per se. For example, the two Wakefield shepherds' plays begin *"Incipit pagina pastorem"*
[The shepherds' play begins] and *"Incipit alia eorum"* [Their other {play}
begins]. The first speaker's name then simply appears in the right margin.
The text is silent on the character's physical entry into the playing space.

Compared to their medieval predecessors, the design of Elizabethan dramatic manuscripts might be said to emphasize the theatrical rather than the textual aspects of the plays. But it would also be accurate to say that while both performance and text were continuous in medieval drama, the discontinuous structure of popular Elizabethan drama is likewise reflected in the design of the material text. The treatment of initial entries, like the left-hand speech prefix to be discussed later, illustrates how playscripts of either period translate their particular versions of dramatic decorum onto the page.

Early Printed Plays

Although the conventions for visually distinguishing directions from dialogue are fairly well established in dramatic manuscripts by the mid 1500s, plays in English printed before the theaters were built exhibit various typographical arrangements—one is tempted to say experiments.

In *Wealth and Health* (S.R., 1557, Q [undated]), Gothic type or black letter is used for both the dialogue and the directions, but various design features contribute to the distinction between the two. Speech prefixes are placed in the margins, left and right, and a dark "paragraph" symbol identifies entry directions, which are centered on their own line: see "¶ Here commeth remedy in and to him saith" in the middle of the recto page in fig. 5. Occasionally, however, the same symbol is used to signal a new stanza, so the visual token is not limited to emphasizing staging information. When the paragraph symbol is omitted and the direction is not given its own line of text, confusion can result. The far-right exit direction, "thei sing / & go out" (about a quarter of the way down the recto page of fig. 5) at first glance seems part of the dialogue. No white space or paragraph symbol precedes it, although a half-parenthesis is placed before "& go out." Thus, while this printed text anticipates the later practice of centering entries and placing midscene exits to the right, it also illustrates the confusion that may result if directions are not clearly distinguished from the dialogue by the use of white space, a different typeface, or some other means.

Like *Wealth and Health*, *King Darius* (Q 1565) presents both dialogue and directions in Gothic type and marks speech attributions and directions by a paragraph symbol to distinguish them from the dialogue (see fig. 6). In addition, however, directions for entries and actions (but not speech attributions) are set in a smaller type, which further sets them apart from the dialogue. The second quarto of this play (1577) fails to do either of these things and is accordingly more difficult to read or interpret. In one instance, staging information is placed in the left margin, indicating gestures to accompany Iniquitie's dialogue: "He ca/steth [a brass pan] at Constan/cye," a candlestick "At Char/ytye," and a taper "At [E]qui/tye" (E3ᵛ–E4). As we shall see in chapter 3, use of the left margin to isolate directions from the dialogue is common in many Elizabethan playhouse manuscripts but rare in printed texts.[36]

A slightly different scheme can be found in the 1567 quarto of *Horestes*. In this text, both dialogue and directions are set in Gothic type of the same size, but page layout compensates for the lack of contrasting type. Speech prefixes are centered on a separate line, and directions for midscene action are clearly distinguished from the dialogue; they appear in the outer margins of facing pages (see fig. 7).[37] As a result, the often lengthy directions for stage business run down the margins in a separate column of text. Such marginal directions are the visual equivalent of the self-conscious directions we will examine in chapter four. Though efficient and highly discreet in their fashion, they step aside from the text to comment on it from the margins. They thus require their interpreters to tune in, as it were, quite separate channels, one self-consciously referring to the other.

In the quarto of *Cambises* (S.R. 1569/70), one finds an early use of contrasting typefaces to distinguish directions from dialogue,[38] the convention that came to be the norm in printed London plays. The dialogue is in Gothic, speech prefixes and all directions are in roman. This simple but effective convention for distinguishing directions from dialogue has its basis in Elizabethan dramatic manuscripts, as we have seen, in which the dialogue was usually in an English secretary hand, and the directions in an Italian.

The choice of contrasting typefaces for stage directions in printed editions has its own interesting history. When black-letter or Gothic typeface was the norm for English works, the stage directions appeared in roman, as in *Cambises*. This was in keeping with the historical associations of certain typefaces: English was associated with Gothic type, and Latin (in which stage directions had long appeared, even in plays otherwise in the vernacular) was associated with roman.[39] Later, when the more legible roman type became the norm for books in English, stage directions shifted into italic typeface, perhaps also for its association with the home of the Latin language.[40]

It has been suggested that after 1475, the overall design of English dramatic manuscripts and printed plays might have been influenced by the printed editions of classical drama, which first appeared in England about this time: Plautus (1472), Seneca (1474), and Terence (1470).[41] It is certainly true that playwrights, like other educated Elizabethans, would have been exposed to the design and apparatus of printed classical plays at school and university, and it is also true that amateur academic playwrights throughout the period often imitate aspects of what came to be the method of presenting a classical play (massed entries, act and scene divisions, Latin stage directions, and the like).

But the design of the earliest editions of classical authors seems to be influenced more by long-standing scribal practices than by neoclassical ideas about dramatic form that later became current among the literati. In the 1472 edition of Plautus, for example, there are no act or scene divisions, no stage directions, and no "entries" as such (the names of the characters are merely listed at the beginning of unmarked scenes), and lines of verse are not broken when the speaker changes. The only feature that might have influenced the native tradition is the position of an abbreviated speech prefix in the left (rather than right) margin. In fact, rather than classical editions altering the design of English playscripts, the influence seems to have gone the other way. As T. H. Howard-Hill has observed, by the end of the sixteenth century, English school texts of classical playwrights are "manifestly influenced by native practice," and the printed form of English plays also "owes more to their native origin than to imported fashion."[42] Not only was "the native tradition rooted in the increasingly professional 'theatre,'"[43] but the increasingly professional theater was rooted in the native tradition.

To sum up, in both manuscripts and early printed plays, the distinction between the voice of stage directions and the voices of the dialogue is visually underscored. Directions are differentiated from the dialogue and, to some extent, from one another according to function. The degree to which the directions are marginal or included within the main text column varies considerably, but both manuscript plays and early printed editions continue to place many directions in the margins, as glosses on the dialogue. This design maintains a separate channel for the voice of stage directions.

According to Ong, unlike printed texts, manuscripts "with their glosses or marginal comments (which often got worked into the text in subsequent copies) were in dialogue with the world outside their borders."[44] This is certainly true in the playhouse manuscripts that have survived; they are a palimpsest of the players' negotiations with the script, and some playhouse additions have willy-nilly become part of the received texts. At the same time, the manuscript tradition remains in other ways more conservative; it defers to the inviolability of the central text column, i.e., the dialogue, and marginalizes staging information as if it were a separable, rather than an integral, part of the script. Or to put it another way, the manuscript tradition, with its marginal stage directions, still tends to view drama as speech to which action is ancillary, rather than as the marriage of speech and action in a single, expressive whole.

Reintegrating the voice of stage directions into the dramatic text, while still visually and verbally distinguishing it from the voices of the dialogue, was accomplished in the printed editions of the 1590s and early 1600s. This development in the code for stage directions depended partly on the technology of printing itself, and partly on the handling of speech attributions, to which we must now turn.

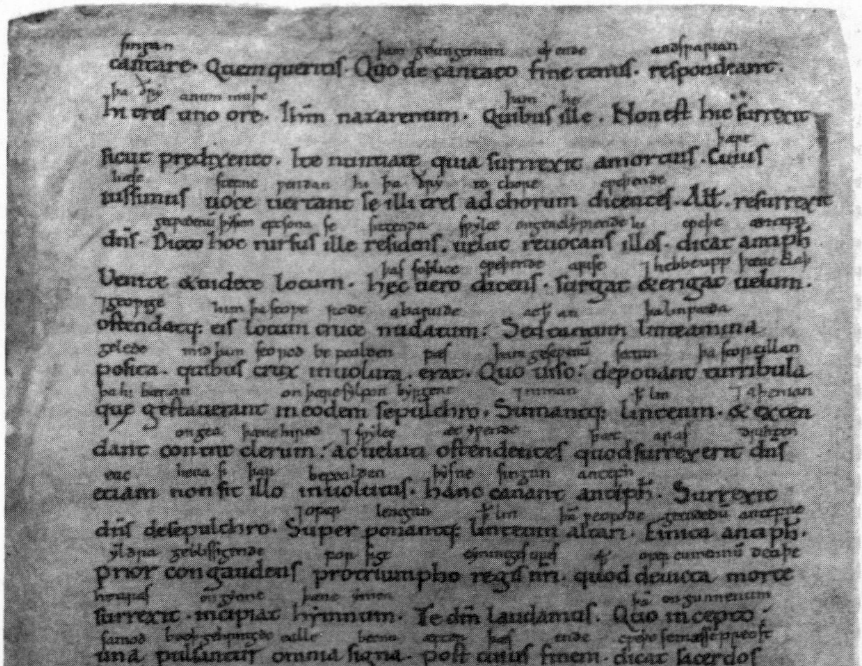

Fig. 1. ***Visitatio Sepulchri* or *Quem Quaeritis,* Cotton ms. Tiberius A. III, fol. 21v. By permission of the British Library and the Harvard College Library.**

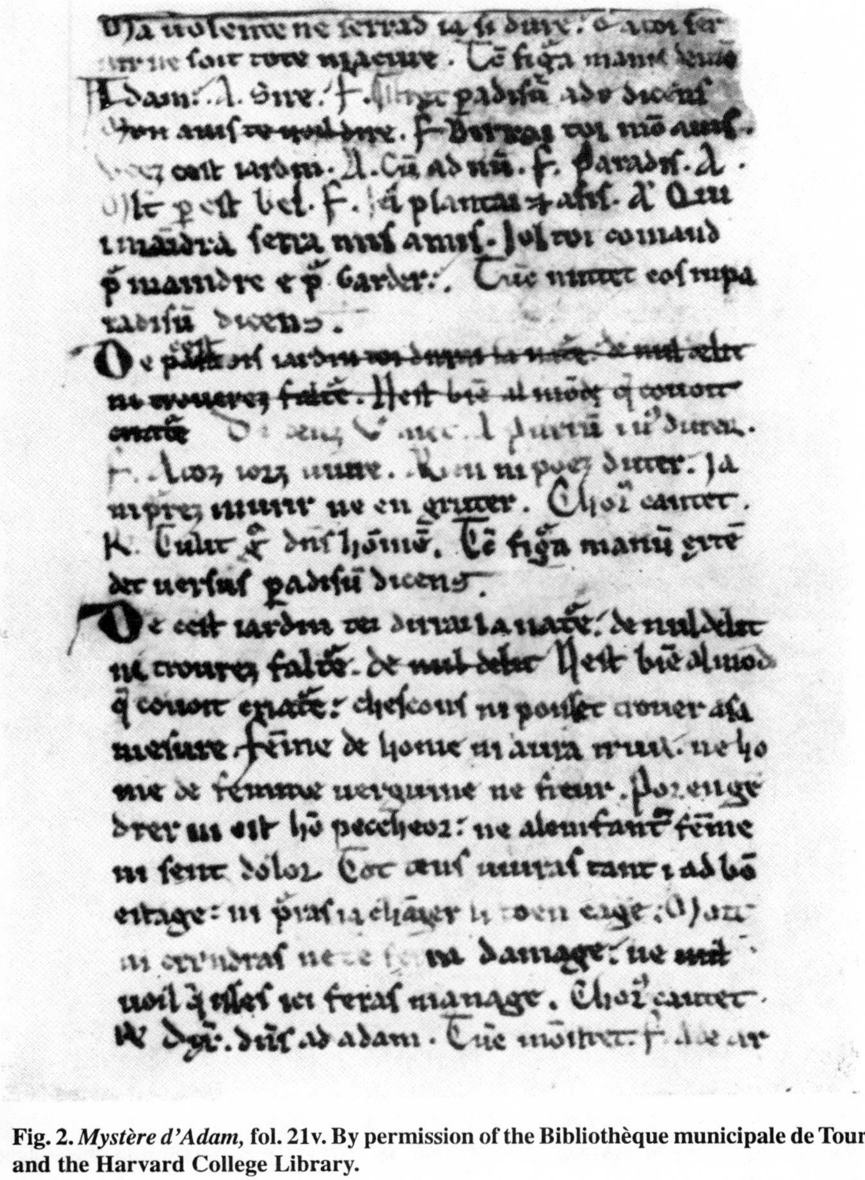

Fig. 2. *Mystère d'Adam,* fol. 21v. By permission of the Bibliothèque municipale de Tours and the Harvard College Library.

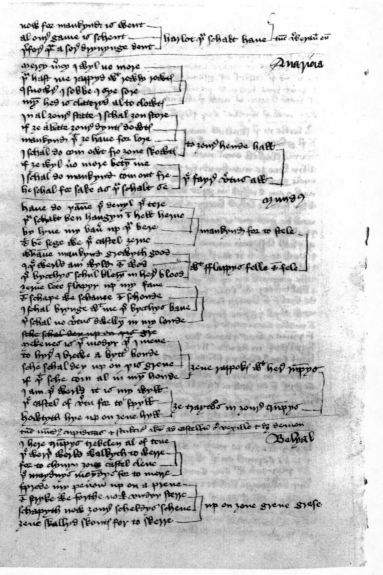

Fig. 3. *The Castle of Perseverance*, V.a.354, fol. 171v. By permission of the Folger Shakespeare Library.

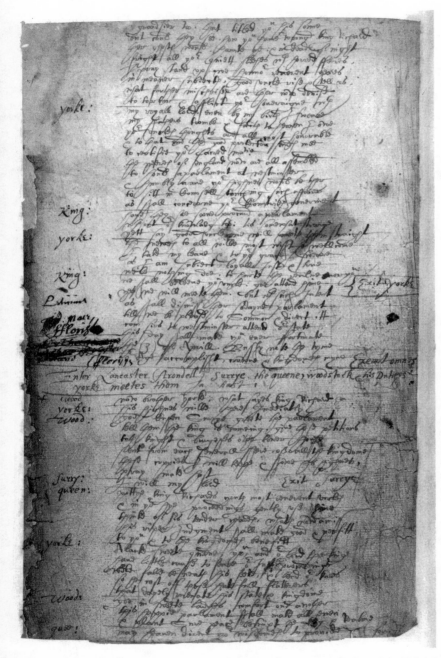

Fig. 4. *Thomas of Woodstock,* Egerton ms. 1994, fol. 167v. By permission of the British Library.

Health. To haue you both to scrape I am content
Now I say you liberte will, neither to consent
Wyll and wit, god hath vs sent
We may be glade of them

Liberti. Of we wolde refuse wyll and wyt
we were to blame for thyr profyt
Therfore by my wel thyr that not dye
Dey be welcome to me,

Wyll. God I thanke you masters all thre
ye shall finde vs prest but true but cannot by
My tonge somtimes, I suppou mercy
Dir wyll be true I occud say,

Wealth. Syrs go your way home vnto one place
And he ch pshye vs after grace
And thei when we cure be stall set you in case

Health. To haue a pstyng eluer,
Thu loke ye do not traitp and leus
for we wyll put you in grete trust
All our housoulde guide ye must
Behaue you selfe well

Wyll. Masters feare not tes I haue wit though
To be yple my selfe, and le begyn upon you
I haue begyled many one I may say to you
I pray you kepe that in counsell

Liberty. Be ware of that, to hat both be seyr
Begyle vs all, yet I charge ye nay
De shall not begule vs yet I way
I wyl be ware be tyme

Wyl. Syr be not angry I you pray
The foole woreth, now ye doth say
Demeneth that he wyl be profitable also ay
And saue you many thinges.

what

What be meaneth I can not tell
But his saying is not well
Depart hence syrs by my counsell
And care vs at our lodging

Now and it please ye, wyll ye there any synging
Thervn I tell you I am somthyng cunnyng
ye shall heare and ye lust.

Syr I pray you sing and geten
Now lo I begin this a little blowth th. the singe
Syrs now go out they of you I am glad (go out
As of any (remaineres that euer I had
for these can do very good aboued
We must nedes haue such men
What were we yet to lacked thus
And without this, but this be true yit
Therfore wyll and wit I went pray cht.
I promise you I loue them

Syr your maieste thu is partly welcome
Like your place here about as it is reason.
I pray you pardon as I wot not to not what ye be
ye seme a man of honour, and of great autority
Syrs to know wherfore ye come we are desyrous
I am he that ought for to be wel knowen
Of nowte the detail, and of suerte
Great payne and businesse as for mine owne
for you I haue taken because I lone your batteli
To sustaine you is all my besyr and facutly
yet hard it is to doo, the people be so variable
And many be so wilfull, they will not be refo/mable
Syr, I pray you pardon vs of our ignoraunce now
If well ye know vs better than we be yon

C.ii.

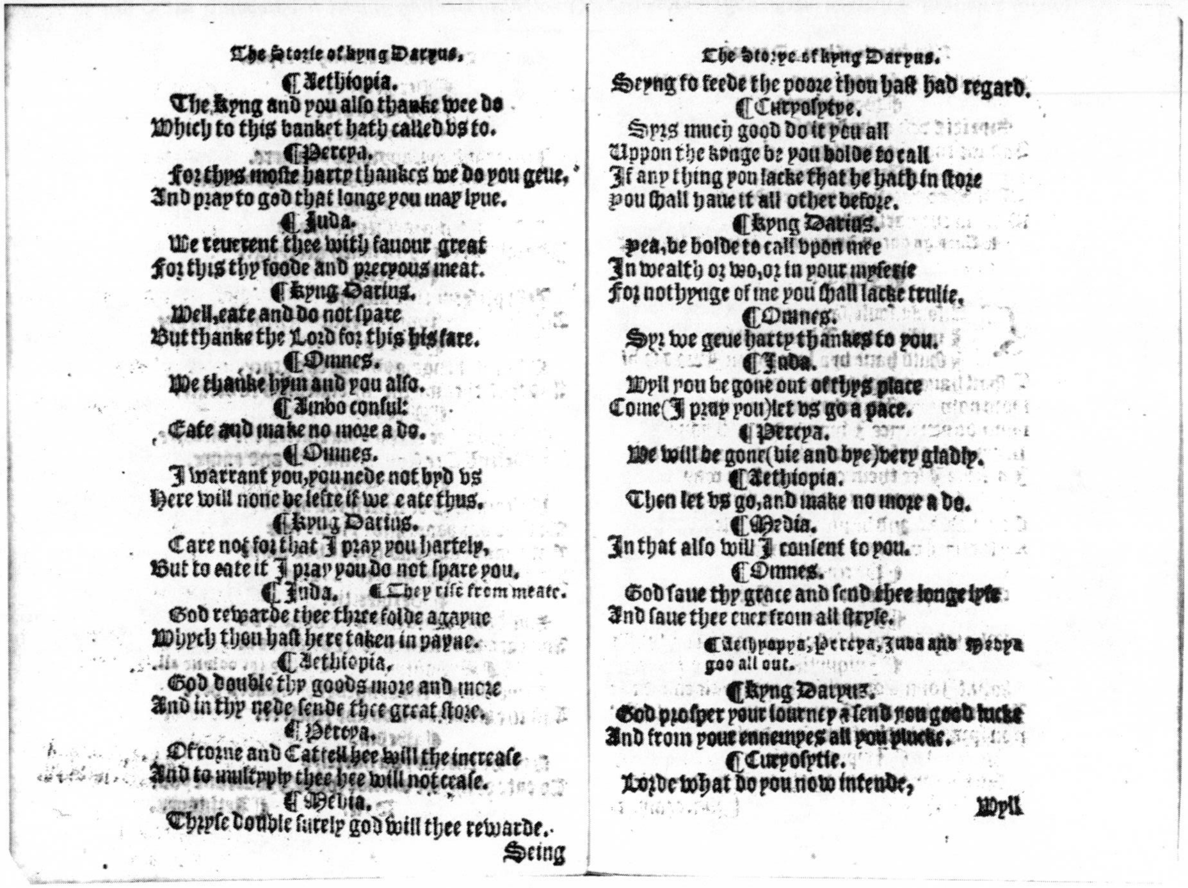
The Storie of kyng Daryus.

¶ Aethiopia.
The kyng and you also thanke wee do
Which to this banket hath called vs to.
¶ Percya.
For thys moste harty thankes we do you geue,
And pray to god that longe you may lyue.
¶ Juda.
We reuerent thee with fauour great
For this thy foode and precyous meat.
¶ Kyng Darius.
Well, eate and do not spare
But thanke the Lord for this his fare.
¶ Omnes.
We thanke hym and you also.
¶ Ambo consul:
Eate and make no more a do.
¶ Omnes.
I warrant you, you nede not byd vs
Here will none be lefte if we eate thus.
¶ Kyng Darius.
Care not for that I pray you hartely,
But to eate it I pray you do not spare you.
¶ Juda. ¶ They rise from meate.
God rewarde thee three folde agayne
Whych thou hast here taken in payne.
¶ Aethiopia.
God double thy goods more and more
And in thy nede sende thee great store.
¶ Percya.
Of corne and Cattell hee will the increase
And to multyply thee hee will not cease.
¶ Media.
Thryse double surely god will thee rewarde.
Seing

The Storye of kyng Daryus.

Seyng to feede the poore thou hast had regard.
¶ Curyositye.
Syrs much good do it you all
Uppon the kynge be you bolde to call
If any thing you lacke that he hath in store
You shall haue it all other before.
¶ Kyng Darius.
Yea, be bolde to call vpon mee
In wealth or wo, or in your mysery
For nothynge of me you shall lacke truly.
¶ Omnes.
Syr we geue harty thankes to you.
¶ Juda.
Wyll you be gone out of thys place
Come (I pray you) let vs go a pace.
¶ Percya.
We will be gone (bie and bye) very gladly.
¶ Aethiopia.
Then let vs go, and make no more a do.
¶ Media.
In that also will I consent to you.
¶ Omnes.
God saue thy grace and send thee longe lyfe
And saue thee euer from all stryfe.
¶ Aethyopya, Percya, Juda and Medya goo all out.
¶ Kyng Daryus.
God prosper your iourney a send you good lucke
And from your enemyes all you plucke.
¶ Curyositie.
Lorde what do you now intende,
Wyll

Fig. 6. *King Darius,* 1565, D3v–D4r. By permission of the Huntington Library, San Marino, California.

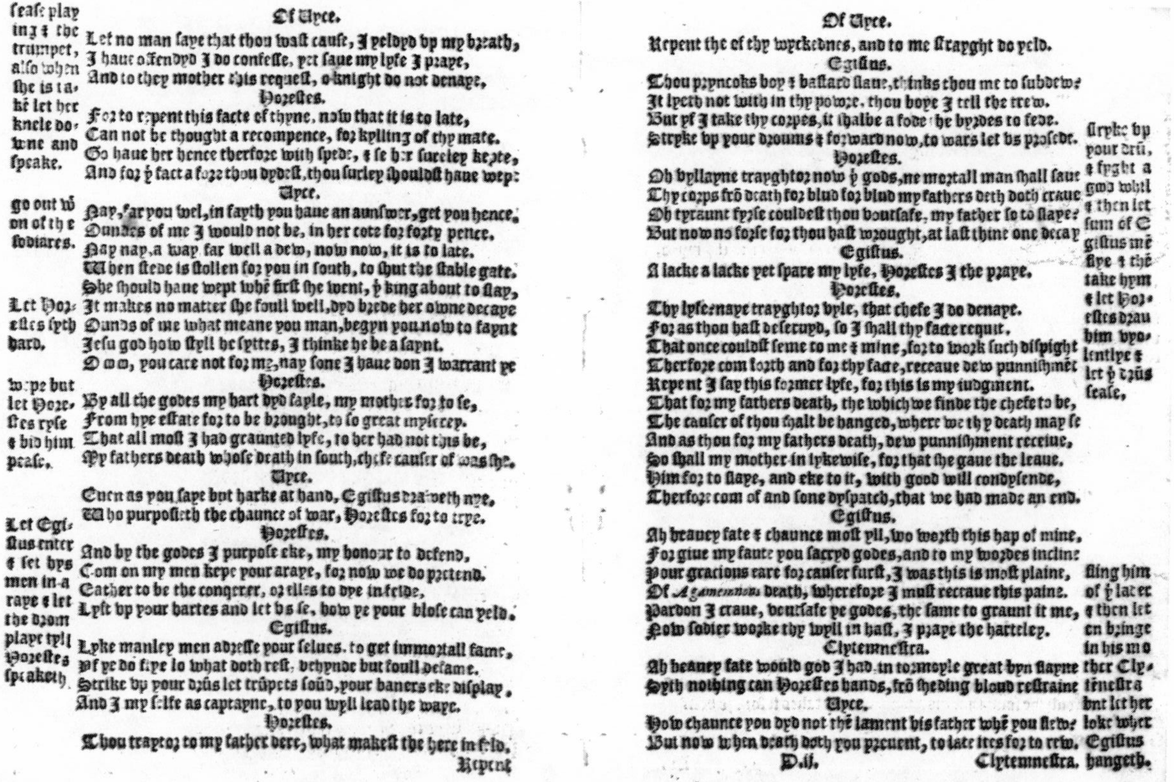

Fig. 7. John Pickeryng, *Horestes*, 1567, D1v–D2r. By permission of the British Library.

To feeke out forrow that dwels euery where,
Defolate defolate will I hence and die:
The laft leaue of thee takes my weeping eie.   *Exeunt.*

Enter Lord Marfhall and the Duke Aumerle.

Mar. My Lord Aumerle is Harry Herford arnde?
Aum. Yea at all points, and longs to enter in.
Mar. The Duke of Norfolke fprightfully and bold,
Staies but the fummons of the appellants trumpet.
Aum Why then the Champions are prepard and ftay
For nothing but his maiefties approach.
   The trumpets found and the King enters with his nobles; when
      they are fet, enter the Duke of Norfolke in armes defendant.
   King Marfhall demaunde of yonder Champion,
The caufe of his arriuall here in armes,
Aske him his name, and orderly proceede
To fweare him in the iuftice of his caufe.
   Mar. In Gods name and the Kings fay who thou art,
And why thou comeft thus knightly clad in armes,
Againft what man thou comft and what thy quareil,
Speake truly on thy knighthoode, and thy oth,
As fo defend the heauen and thy valour.
   Mow My name is Thomas Mowbray Duke of Norfolke,
Who hither come ingaged by my oath,
(Which God defende a Knight fhould violate)
Both to defend my loyalty and truth,
To God, my King, and my fucceeding iffue,
Againft the Duke of Herford that appeales me,
And by the grace of God, and this mine arme,
To proue him in defending of my felfe,
A traitour to my God, my King, and me,
And as I truely fight, defend me heauen.

      The trumpets found. Enter Duke of Hereford
            appellant in armour.
   King Marfhall aske yonder Knight in armes,
                    B 2   Both

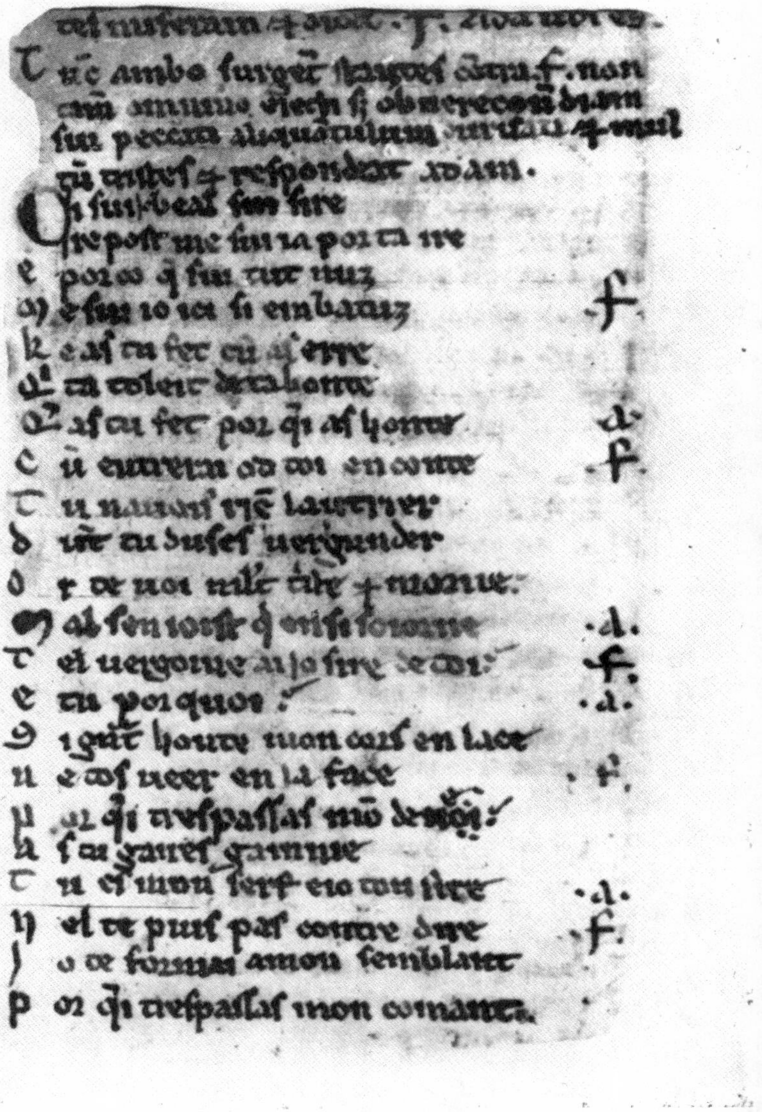

Fig. 9. *Mystère d'Adam,* fol. 27r. By permission of the Bibliothèque municipale de Tours and the Harvard College Library.

2

Speech Attributions

In printed Elizabethan plays, the norm with respect to speech attribution can be described as follows: speeches are introduced by a prefix or heading in which the speaker's name or title appears, usually in a brief or abbreviated form, in a contrasting, usually italic, typeface, indented slightly from the left margin of the text column (see fig. 8). Each change of speaker consequently breaks the text column, albeit slightly, and even a single verse line will be broken if shared by two speakers, the second half-line being indented only to the extent required by the new speech prefix. This is the norm, not an absolute "rule," of course, but deviations from the norm are relatively rare in plays associated with the professional London theaters. This now familiar textual design may seem so commonsensical as to be unworthy of comment, but its importance to the writing (or printing) and reading of dramatic texts emerges if we compare it with its predecessors in the manuscript tradition and with early experiments in printed drama.

Early Manuscripts

As noted in the previous chapter, many speech attributions in early medieval drama are not visually differentiated at all. They are part of a detailed production narrative that combines exits (of some characters), entrances (of others), blocking, details of costume or business, and speech cues, all in one rubric. In the *Mystère d'Adam*, for example, one finds:

Tunc Figura vocet Adam propius, et attentius ei dicat:
[Then let the Figure {of God} call Adam nearer and say to him more intently:]

(48, S.D.)

57

Tunc Figura manu demonstret paradisum Ade, dicens: Adam!
[Then let the Figure {of God} point out Paradise to Adam with his hand,
saying: *Adam!*]

(80, S.D-81)

Tunc aspiciet Evam uxorem suam, et dicet:
[Then he will look at Eve his wife, and say:]

(357, S.D.)

According to nineteenth-century scholar Marius Sepet, these undifferentiated rubrics formed an "enveloping monologue" from which the dialogue "struggled to free itself."[1] Perhaps one need not view the matter as a
struggle, but it is certainly true that the embedded speech cues remain close
to the conventions of narrative, with its distinctive "he said, she said." More
particularly, the attributive tags (*dicens, dicet, dixit,* and their English equivalents) seem an echo of biblical narrative in which verbs of speaking and
saying hold a prominent place. (As Walter Ong has noted, God nearly always speaks to his people; he only rarely writes to them.) *Dixit* and *dicens*
are ubiquitous in the Latin Vulgate; and the Geneva Bible is replete with
such formulae as "And God spake unto Noah, saying . . ." (Gen. 8:15) and
"Samuel answered, and said . . . (1 Sam.9:19). The rubrics of medieval
drama similarly emphasize "the word" no less than "the Word," and the
theatrical emphasis is an analogue of the theological. That is, narrative
speech cues emphasize the act of speaking, and this emphasis metaphori-
cally reflects the central importance of the Divine Word and its reception in
the content of that drama.

Narrative speech cues persist even after marginal, freestanding speech
attributions become common for speeches not otherwise preceded by a
stage direction. For example:

Tunc ibunt Voluptas et Stultitia, Malus Angelus et Humanum Genus ad
Mundum, et dicet:
[Then Lust-and-Liking and Folly, the Bad Angel and Human Kind will
go to the World {at his scaffold}, and he {Lust-and-Liking} will say:]
                            (*The Castle of Perseverance*, 574, S.D.)

Tunc exibunt demones clamando; et dicit primus:
[Then the demons will go out exclaiming, and the first demon {reenter-
ing} says:]
                            (Wakefield *Creation*, 131, S.D.)

Tunc capit Cherubin Adam per manum, et dicit eis Dominus:

[Then the Cherubin takes Adam by the hand, and God says to them:]
(Wakefield *Creation*, 197, S.D.)

Here shall the knigtes gete spicys and wine: and here shall enter a dylle
[devil] in [h]orebill aray, thus seying:
(*Mary Magdalen* [Digby] 962, S.D.)

Here the Jewys goon and lay the [h]ost on the tabill, say[i]ng:
(*The Play of the Sacrament* [Croxton], 392, S.D.)

In some cases the central stage direction retained a speech cue even when a speech attribution followed. For example, near the bottom of fig. 3, the direction that precedes the speech attributed to Belial in the right-hand margin reads (in translation):

Then the World, Covetousness, and Folly will go to the castle with the banner, and the Devil will say,
(1898, S.D.)

Similarly, in the Digby *Killing of the Children*, both directions and right-margin speech attributions at the end of a ruled line introduce speeches, as in the following example:

Here shall Symeon bere Jhesu in his armys, goyng a procession rounde
aboute the tempille, and al this wyle the virgynis synge Nunc dimittis and
whan that is don, Symeon seyth:
——————————————————————————— *Symeon*
O Jhesu, chef cause of oure welfare. . . .
(484, S.D.-485)[2]

The narrative speech cue, *dicens* or an English equivalent, survives as late as the mid 1500s, especially in humanist and academic drama. In *Wit and Science*, written c. 1530–48 for the boys of St. Paul's by their master, John Redford, one finds:

. . . And when the galiard is doone, Wit saith as folowith and so fal[l]ith
downe in Idlenes' lap:
(330, S.D.)

And similarly, in Bale's *King Johan* (c. 1530–60), in both the scribal and autograph portions of the manuscript, directions for entries or stage business often end with a speech attribution:

Here enter Pandwlfus, the cardynall, and sayth:

(1197, S.D.)

In genua procumbens Deum adorat, dicens:
[He adores God falling on his knees, saying:]

(1956, S.D.)[3]

In such instances, the characters are still creatures of the rubrics, from which their words directly spring. On some occasions, the stage directions even anticipate or include the character's line:

Here sett down, and Nobelyte shall say benedicyte. [Nob.] Benedicite.
                                    (*King Johan*, 1148, S.D.-1149)

Here answerrit[h] all the pepul at ons[e], "Ya, my lord ya."
                                    (*Mary Magdalen* [Digby], 44, S.D.)[4]

Although narrative speech cues persist in medieval dramatic texts, free-standing speech attributions occur quite early. In the *Adam*, when no stage direction immediately precedes a speech, the scribe uses the character's initial followed by a period to indicate the change of speaker: "a." for Adam, and "f." for the Figure [of God]. The effect is that of a speech prefix embedded in the text (see fig. 2). Like the "℞" symbol that identifies responses sung by the choir and the orthographic abbreviations common in medieval texts, the use of initials to signal changes of speaker helps save space. But it also introduces a visually distinctive, abbreviated speech prefix rather than a full-sentence or narrative speech cue, such as those in the "*Quem Queritis*" and elsewhere in the *Adam* itself.

In addition, in the last quarter of the *Adam* text (fols. 27–28, and fols. 32ᵛ to 40), changes of speaker not prefaced by an attributive stage direction are indicated by the character's name or initial near the *right* margin, rather than embedded in the text (see fig. 9). The embedded initial is "delayed" by white space to the end of the line, from which highly visible position it introduces the speaker of the following line. This early scribe thus points toward the differentiation of the speech prefix as a freestanding direction and the development of the visual scheme in which directions are distinguished not only from the dialogue but from each other, according to their function.

Although the right-hand speech attributions in the *Adam* resemble a marginal gloss, strictly speaking they are not marginal. They reside within the main text column and can be read in linear sequence with the dialogue. The scribe has simply used white space to isolate the initial at the end of the text line. It was a small matter, however, to move the speech attribution from the end of the line into the right margin and thus open up a new and independent channel for the voice of the stage directions, in the tradition of marginal commentary well established in medieval manuscripts of all sorts.[5]

This is the practice in many late medieval dramatic manuscripts. In *The Castle of Perseverance* the speakers' names appear prominently in the right margins, in a somewhat larger and bolder script. A ruled line runs from the character's name above the first line of the speech, thus effectively separating the speech from the previous one (see fig. 3). Unlike the *Adam* scribe's solution, this practice is genuinely marginal. Although lineation is not precise (as it is in a printed text), the speech attributions appear to be on the same level as the new speaker's first line, not at the end of the previous speech. Thus they are not strictly in sequence, as one reads left-to-right. They address our peripheral vision from a marginal space to the right of the dialogue column.

A similar scheme is observed in *Mankind* and the Wakefield plays. The speakers' names appear in or near the right margin at the end of a ruled line extending from the left margin that separates the speeches. Even though these speech attributions are not set in clearly contrasting size or style of script, their position in the margin, usually surrounded by white space at the end of a (sometimes bold) rule, makes them highly visible. The plays in the Digby manuscript also routinely put speech attributions on the right, some with ruled lines, some without. In *The Killing of the Children* in the Digby manuscript, the attributions seem to straddle the line between speeches, and thus they might be read, like those in the much earlier *Adam*, as technically "in sequence" rather than as marginal. But their position well to the right of the dialogue column makes them more gloss than prefix, and they are clearly separated from the stage directions placed within the central text column.

The emergence of the visually distinct, freestanding speech attribution is significant in the evolution of English dramatic discourse. Wherever a freestanding speech attribution is located (left, right or center), it signals the autonomy and integrity of the character. He or she has a vocal and therefore "existential" independence, appearing in the dramatic text without introduction or qualification by any other discernible voice. Though the characters may be brought on stage by an authoritative entry direction, they speak autonomously, unmediated by anything more than the usually abbreviated appearance of their names. When a play is performed or read, the characters seem to speak spontaneously and of their own volition, and this immediacy and vitality is visually encoded in the efficient convention of the speech prefix. It is one sign, if you will, of the victory of the dialogue over the production narrative that dominates early medieval texts. It is a sign of the separation of medieval drama from its narrative sources.

Although the early Tudor manuscript tradition regarding speech attributions thus respects the independence of dramatic characters, the textual design is geared to the oral culture of a cry of players, rather than to the linear logic of reading. The right-margin position of the speech prefix creates a separate, rather than an integrated, channel for staging information. The interpreter experiences a stereophonic alternation of voices rather than the modulation of a polyvocal text. Only towards the end of the fifteenth century does a genuine, left-margin "speech prefix" appear. The earliest I have encountered is in the late-fifteenth-century manuscript of the Brome *Abraham and Isaac*. Two other instances occur in the latest manuscripts in the Digby collection. *The Play of the Sacrament*, a manuscript "undoubtedly of the sixteenth century,"[6] has left-margin speech prefixes, as does a scene for Belyall and Mercury inserted c. 1550 into *The Conversion of St. Paul*.[7]

ELIZABETHAN DRAMATIC MANUSCRIPTS

The Belial scene shows the pattern that came to be the norm in manuscripts connected with the professional London theaters. As can be seen in the manuscript of *Thomas of Woodstock* (see fig. 4), the speech prefix moves to the primary left-hand position (primary, because readers enter the text from left to right).[8] It can thus be assimilated in the normal sequence of reading, but it is still very visibly in the margin, still more gloss than part of the text. Even if characters share a single line of verse, the speaker's name is placed in the left margin, and the speech begins on a new line. The theatrical fact (the change of speakers) takes precedence over the literary or verbal fact (a single poetic line).

As noted by W. W. Greg,[9] *John of Bordeaux* has been viewed as a partial exception to this convention among surviving playhouse manuscripts. It contains an unusual number of "doubled" speech prefixes, that is, a second or third prefix embedded within a single pentameter line. William Long's more recent examination of the manuscript, however, shows that even in this anomalous text, doubled or embedded speech prefixes are distinctly in the minority: 84 percent of the time, the speech prefix is found on the left, beginning a new line.[10]

Elizabethan manuscripts thus found a compromise between a position convenient for readers and a visual prominence that might be helpful to a bookholder in the theater. The text column is reserved for dialogue exclusively—except when it is broken by the entries, centered or written across the entire page, that begin each scene. Here, as we have seen, the stream of dialogue is visually interrupted in accordance with the fundamental element of Elizabethan dramatic structure: the clear stage and the entrance of a new set of characters to begin a new scene. But the mere change of speaker does not itself break the text column, unless the characters share a single line of verse.

Overall, Elizabethan playhouse manuscripts, like their medieval predecessors, show the "vestigial orality" that Ong attributes to manuscript culture generally.[11] Although they discard the verbal emphasis on speaking or saying encoded in the old narrative speech tags (*dicens, dicet,* and their English equivalents), visually, they preserve the dominance of the spoken word (the dialogue). The text column is chiefly reserved for the dialogue and nearly all staging information is relegated to the margins. The text column may be marked by ruled lines between speeches, but, with the important exception noted above, its borders remain inviolate. Speech prefixes and midscene stage directions still speak to us stereophonically from the margins, and the dialogue occupies the central position. Certain practices in the physical production of playhouse manuscripts reinforce the centrality of the dialogue. The scribes seem generally to have written all the dialogue first, in one continuous effort, and then to have come back and added the stage directions, *including* the speech prefixes.[12] The Word (as Derrida would have it) was the still the thing.[13]

EARLY PRINTED PLAYS

As if recapitulating the manuscript tradition, plays printed before most of the London theaters were built exhibit various typographical arrangements with respect to speech attributions.

In *Wealth and Health* (S.R., 1557), the speech attributions are placed wholly in the margins. Unlike early manuscripts, however, these attributions appear in the *outer* margins of *facing pages:* in the left margin on the verso pages, in the right margin on the recto (see fig. 5). (The same arrangement was used in *Everyman,* c. 1510.)[14] This scheme is consistent with the manuscript convention of the speech attribution as a marginal gloss, rather than as a discreet but integral part of the text. (It also has the advantage of preventing the speakers' names from being obscured by the binding when the printed book is opened.)

In the 1565 quarto of *King Darius,* however, the speakers' names are centered on separate lines within the text column, not in the margin. To distinguish them further from the dialogue, they are preceded by the paragraph symbol ¶ (see fig. 6). When a direction for an entrance, exit, or other business is inserted in the blank space following a speech attribution, it is also preceded by a paragraph symbol that separates it from the speech heading (see "¶ They rise from meate" in the lower third of the verso page in fig. 6). To a modern reader's eyes, this practice results in a much lighter and more inviting text than the relatively dense look of *Wealth and Health*. It also makes every speech attribution literally a "prefix"; in the normal course of reading, one meets it before one encounters the speech itself. In *Wealth and Health* this was only true on the verso pages; on the recto pages, the speech attribution appeared at the end of the first line of a speech. It also has the result that the characters' speeches are separated by vertical white space. Thus the central text column is broken not only for entries but also for the alternation of speakers.

In *Horestes* (Q 1567) speech prefixes are also centered on a separate line, once again providing vertical white space between speakers. In this text, however, the dialogue is visually broken only when the speakers change and not for entries or exits. As noted above, even extended directions are run in the margins, rather than integrated into the text (see fig. 7). In this instance, the speech heading is both differentiated from other directions and integrated into the normal progress of reading, but all staging information is relegated to the margins, as in the manuscript tradition.

Although freestanding speech attributions are the norm in these early printed interludes, narrative speech cues are still quite common and sometimes confusing, as in the first example below (I have not preserved the lineation of these marginal directions):

> *Enter a woman lyke a beger rouning [roaming] before they* [sic] *sodier,*
> *but let the sodier spek first but let the woman crye first pitifulley.*
> > (*Horestes*, Q 1567, TLN 740–53 [C3ᵛ])

> *Let Egistus enter and set hys men in a raye, and let the drom playe tyll*
> *Horestes speaketh. . . .*
> > (*Horestes*, TLN 903–7 [D1ᵛ])

> *Pause a while till he be gon out and then speak tretably.*
> > (*Horestes*, TLN 1121–27 [D4ᵛ])

> *Here they go out and then entereth Constancy, saying as it*
> *were a sublocutio.*
> > (*King Darius*, Q 1565, H3)

In printed plays associated with the London theaters, however, we find an important set of changes. Speech prefixes or headings consist of the speaker's name or title in a brief or abbreviated form, in a contrasting typeface (usually italic), indented slightly from the left margin of the text column (see fig. 8). In the early editions surveyed for this book, I have encountered only one in which the practice of slightly indenting the left-hand prefix is not consistently observed, namely the 1599 quarto of *George a Green*, printed by Simon Stafford for Cuthbert Burby. Other products of Stafford's shop, such as *Old Fortunatus* (Q 1600), observe the normal convention. The 1605 quarto of Rowley's *When You See Me You Know Me* is also partly anomalous. In gatherings A–C of this quarto, speech prefixes are usually flush to the margin, and on C3^v and C4, one or two are embedded within the line. But this edition seems the exception that proves the rule: beginning with gathering D to the end of gathering L, prefixes are regularly indented, one per line.

Occasionally one finds a narrative speech cue *instead* of a speech prefix in a play for the London theaters. They are more common in earlier plays, such as those of Peele, who often wrote for the boys' companies where the older convention of undifferentiated directions survived, but they occasionally crop up in plays by other hands. For example:

> *The Lluellen spieth Elinor and Mortimer and saith thus*
> *(Edward I*, Q 1593, TLN 1013–14)

> *A dead march, and passe round the stage, and Guildford speaks*
> *(Sir Thomas Wyatt*, Q 1607, A4)

Certain other anomalous forms in Peele also show the vestigial influence of the older, undifferentiated rubrics. Thirteen prefixes in this play are combined with an entry or other brief direction. Thus one finds, centered, with no speech prefix following, *"Bishop speaks to her in bed"* (TLN 2153) and *"Enter Soldiers"* (TLN 2370). And, in the usual left-hand position as a speech prefix one finds: *"Enter Katherina"* (TLN 2310), *"Potter strikes"* (TLN 1509), and *"Frier kneeles"* (TLN 1518). Similarly one finds in Marlowe's *Edward II* a centered direction that reads *"Edward kneels, and saith"* (TLN 1517), and in the Folio text of *2 Henry IV*, *"All kneel"* appears as a speech prefix (TLN 44).

But these are exceptions, even in Peele. In *Edward I* there are about seven hundred and twenty left-hand speech prefixes and only ten centered directions with narrative speech tags. In some cases, a compositor seems simply to have transferred to the printed page a left-margin note in his copytext. This at least seems a reasonable explanation for a few anomalous instances in *Sir Thomas Wyatt* (Q 1605):

> *Lady to one.* Sirra is this the English gentleman
> *Of the attendants.* Which brought the horses.

Generally speaking, in plays for the professional London theaters the narrative speech tag disappears, and the left-hand speech prefix alone attributes the dialogue.

In printed editions, as in the playhouse manuscripts, only one speech prefix and therefore one speaker appears per line. Even if two characters share a single pentameter verse or are engaged in brief prose exchanges, the text will place the second speaker's words on a new line preceded by speech prefix. On occasion, two half-lines or brief speeches are combined in the same line of printed text, but this is clearly the exception, not the rule. The 1598 quarto of *1 Henry IV*, for example, contains about 750 speech prefixes, and only sixteen are embedded midline; in the 1613 quarto, only fourteen are embedded. In both editions, these doubled or embedded speeches occur chiefly where lack of space seems to require them.

Lack of space would not arise as a problem in a quarto edition, of course, unless the printer had decided to expedite the printing by casting off copy rather than setting each page of a gathering consecutively. Since errors in casting off copy might affect the layout of a page and thus the position of its stage directions, this printing-house practice needs to be considered here.

If the eight pages of a normal quarto gathering are set consecutively, all but the last page has to be in type before either side of that sheet can be printed. For example, in gathering A, the outer forme contains type for pages one, four, five, and eight (or A1, A2^v, A3, and A4^v), while the inner contains pages two, three, six, and seven (or A1^v, A2, A3^v, and A4). Thus the inner forme can be printed as soon as the seventh page, A4, is complete, but not sooner. By casting off, or estimating, the manuscript copy for each page of a gathering, the compositors could set either the inner or outer forme, and these four pages could be printed and dried while the type for the other forme (the other side of the sheet) was being set. As soon as the printing of the first forme was complete, the type could be returned to the type case and reused. Casting off copy thus made most efficient use of the available fonts by reducing the number of formes that had to be standing in type at any one time. In addition, since typesetting is more time-consuming than printing, being able to begin printing after only four pages were set in type was a further boon to efficiency, especially in a small printing house.

Determining the manner of composition of each of the plays consulted is beyond the scope of this study. However, William H. Bond[15] has described the hallmarks of cast-off copy in the printing of a quarto, and his description permits an estimation of its influence on the issue of embedded speech prefixes. First, Bond's analysis shows that if cast-off copy were employed, overset (crowded) or underset pages would tend to occur in one or the other forme, whichever was set last. If the compositor began with the outer forme of gathering A, siglia A1, A2^v, A3, and A4^v would be set first, and the surplus text or slack space resulting from errors in estimating the copy would necessarily appear on the pages of the inner forme, that is, on A1^v, A2, A3^v, or A4. If the inner forme were set first, the expectation would be the reverse. So, one sign of cast-off copy in a quarto is that anomalies appear in the pages of either the inner or outer forme, but not in both. Second, Bond reasons that errors in casting off copy are more likely to occur in prose than in verse passages. Copy primarily in verse could be counted out line by line, and unusually long lines could be "turned over and tucked in." The number of printed pages needed for prose passages, however, would be would be harder to estimate. Thus, in estimating the effect of the exigencies of the printing process on the placement of speech prefixes (or other stage directions), one could check whether they appear in the pages of one or both formes of a gathering, and whether they tend to appear in verse or in prose passages. Using these two criteria, a spot check of some quartos with anomalous speech prefixes suggests that, at least in these cases, a shortage of space on the page *was* a factor.

For example, the extended prefixes in *Edward I* (*"Friar strikes,"* *"Mortimer kneeles,"* *"Enter Katherina"*) may be the result of an attempt to save space by combining two stage directions (which would normally appear on their own lines of text) with an indented speech prefix. These unusual prefixes occur in only one forme of gatherings E, F, and G, though they are equally likely to appear in verse as in prose. In gathering I, however, the inner forme has two anomalous speech prefixes and the outer has one. In the case of *1 Henry IV* (Q 1598), the embedded speech prefixes seem more clearly to be the result of casting off copy. Gatherings G and K have two instances each, both in the outer forme. Gatherings D and E have five and two instances of embedded speech prefixes, respectively; although in these gatherings at least one instance occurs in each forme, all occur in pages primarily in prose. Gatherings B and H have only one instance each, so no judgment is possible.

In a later play, Wilkins's *The Miseries of Enforced Marriage*, the evidence seems even more compelling that cast-off copy, rather than a weakening of the convention, led to anomalous speech prefixes. In this 1607 quarto, all but two gatherings contain one or more instances of a second speech prefix embedded within the line. Gatherings A, B, H, and K have only one example each, but all four are in the outer forme; the sole example in gathering E is found in the inner forme. Gatherings C, D, F, and G have between two and six examples each (for a total of fifteen instances), all in the inner forme, and nine of the fifteen occur in prose pages. Cumulatively the number and placement of the anomalies in these editions suggest that they are likely to have been the result of casting off copy, rather than of ignorance or caprice. And in any case, their small number as a proportion of the total number of speech prefixes does not really challenge the overwhelming evidence that, in plays associated with the professional theaters, the dominant convention was one speech prefix per line of text, even if this meant dividing a line of verse.[16]

In the Caroline period, however, embedding two or even three speakers within a single line of text in a verse speech occurs fairly often. In the 1634 quarto of *Perkin Warbeck* is this example:

> *Kath.* Where my obedience is (my lord) a dutie,
> Love owes true service. *Warb.* Shall I? — *K.Ia.* Cousin, yes.
>
> (E1^v)[17]

Embedded speech prefixes were the norm in Renaissance editions of classical authors, such as Seneca and Plautus.[18] Not surprisingly, they are common in university plays, and Jonson employs them in his 1616 folio. Embedded speech prefixes may arise partly as a means of saving space and thus reducing printing costs, but it is hard to see why this motive would not have been as compelling for printers earlier in the period as well as later.

From both an actor's and a reader's point of view, however, embedded speech prefixes, by failing to highlight the change of speakers, are harder to interpret. Since proper names are often italicized even in a dialogue speech set in roman, italic speech prefixes occurring in midline could easily be mistaken for dialogue—direct address, or an allusion to another character. Embedded speech prefixes are also less faithful to the dramatic nature of the text than left-hand prefixes: the preservation of the pentameter line takes precedence over theatrical matters (the change of speakers). Finally, at least to this reader, embedded speech prefixes seem more disruptive even from the point of view of the pentameter line. They burden it with words extraneous to both rhythm and meaning (though this is less true when mere initials are used). Perhaps for these very reasons, the neoclassical, "literary" convention of embedded speech prefixes did not make a lasting mark on the design of dramatic texts. Like their Elizabethan forebears, later plays in English preserve the tradition of a new line of text for each speaker and of speech headings either centered or near the left margin.

Mimesis and the Printed Text

The conventions governing speech attribution in Elizabethan printed editions suggest how page design may enhance readability and still emphasize the play as theatrical event. The Elizabethan speech prefix is fully integrated into the linear process of reading, rather than functioning as a marginal gloss. It occupies the primary left-hand position, where the reader's eye enters the text. Set in italics and indented, it identifies the speaker with maximum efficiency and yet is easily differentiated from the dialogue. All these features increase the readability of the text as a text.

At the same time, the freestanding speech prefix and the rarity of narrative speech tags in Elizabethan printed texts emphasize the "presence" of the characters. They speak autonomously, without lengthy introduction via a stage direction. In addition, the previously inviolate column of the dialogue is discreetly broken by the indented speech prefix each time the speaker changes, even if two speakers share a line of verse. The indentation parallels the change in voices, a feature of the auditory experience of the play. The text column is not, however, interrupted by vertical white space for a new speaker, as happens with the centered speech attributions in early printed texts like *King Darius* or *Horestes*. Major (vertical) breaks in the text column are reserved for discontinuities in what the audience would see, such as major entrances, complex stage business (such as a fight sequence), or (sometimes) an exit that results in a cleared stage and the end of the scene. Finally, the left-hand speech prefix and the usually right-of-center exit direction represent the entry of the character into the readers' ken and his or her subsequent departure from our imaginative field of vision.

The mature Elizabethan page design thus has a mimetic dimension; keyed to the way we read a page (top to bottom, left to right), it suggests aspects of an audience's aural and visual experience in the theater. This mimetic design may not be conscious, any more than is the tendency of texts "to assimilate utterance to the human body" by the use of terms such as "headings," "chapters" (from *caput*, "head"), and "footnotes."[19] Nonetheless, though highly schematic, the mimetic features of Elizabethan page design are unmistakable.

Lest this last assertion seem fanciful, let me close by noting other mimetic uses of typography and page design in printed plays. As the medium of print increased control over space and variations in typeface, the playful exercise of that control was not uncommon. Examples include the mimetic setting of textual props, such as proclamations and letters, and the expressive use of different typefaces.

As we have seen, choice of typeface can be expressive as well as utilitarian. Italics commonly highlight quotations or dialogue in Latin (such as the conjuring in *Doctor Faustus*). They are also used for dialogue in Romance languages (such as Henry's wooing of Katherine in broken French in *Henry V*). In *Alphonsus, Emperor of Germany* (Q 1654), in a witty variation, Gothic typeface is used to represent the German spoken by the unfortunate heroine, Hedwick. In the folio edition of *The Alchemist*, Jonson also uses Gothic type for German expressions and names, such as "Ulen Spiegel," one of Face's aliases. Although the practice may seem humorous only to modern eyes, one twentieth-century editor preserves this typography as "too good a visual joke to miss."[20] Jonson may also be tweaking Face's gullible victims, since the Gothic typeface was sometimes felt to appeal to lower-class readers. Howard-Hill asserts that a printer would probably simply follow his copytext in setting elements of the play in different typefaces.[21] If so, this suggests that play manuscripts likewise used different scripts mimetically, as visual cues to highlight dialect, texts within the text, or varied modes of delivery.

Italic typeface is also used to differentiate from normal dialogue the text of letters and proclamations read aloud; it suggests the need for a different way of speaking such texts-within-the-text. In I.iii of *1 Henry VI*, for example, the officer's "lowd" public reading of the mayor's proclamation is suggested both by italics and a dialogue cue:

> *Maior.* Come Officer, as lowd as e're thou canst, cry:
> *All manner of men, assembled here in Armes this day, against Gods peace and the Kings, wee charge and command you, in his Highnesse Name, to repayre to your severall dwelling places, and not to weare, handle, or use any Sword, Weapon, or Dagger hence-forward, upon paine of death.*
> (F 1623, TLN 444–49)[22]

The italics signify a "text to be read" rather than spontaneous dialogue; and for this and other official proclamations, some formal, declamatory way of speaking also seems to be encouraged.

Related to the use of italics for texts-within-the-text is the use of italics (or quotation marks) to set off lines of dialogue that claim the distinction of being *sententiae*, whether quoted from Seneca or other classical worthies, or composed by the playwright himself. For examples, see Chapman's *Bussy d'Amboys* and Middleton's *Perkin Warbeck*. Perhaps this was again a cue to the actor to give the lines added solemnity and weight. In this case, however, the typographical flourish emphasizes a literary as well as a theatrical element.

A playtext may also imitate in its layout the form of documents read aloud. Letters are sometimes presented mimetically on the page. In Marlowe's *Edward II* (Q 1594), a letter regarding the Queen's activities in France is read; the closing phrase, *"Your honors in all service, Lewne [Levune]"* is indented as it would have been in an actual letter (TLN 1820). Similarly, in *When You See Me, You Know Me*, two letters contain indented closing phrases in imitation of a letter format:

> *Heaven send thee life to inherite thy election,*
> *To God I commend thee, who still I pray preserve thee.*
> Thy loving sister, *Elizabeth.*
>
> (TLN 2417–19)

Other examples of the mimetic layout of letters occur in *Edmond Ironside* (TLN 1274), *Love's Labour's Lost* (Q 1598, both letters from Don Armado), *2 Henry IV* (Q 1600, TLN 827–30), *Hamlet* (Q 1604 and F 1623, Hamlet's letters to Ophelia and to the King), *The Roaring Girl* (Q 1611, F2^v and F3), *Every Man Out of His Humor* (Q 1600, TLN 2327–41), and *King John and Matilda* (Q 1655, H1 and H3).

The 1604/5 quarto of *Hamlet* sets Hamlet's commentary on the play-within-the-play literally "aside," speech prefixes and all, in the right-hand margin. Thus we read his commentary literally as marginalia parallel to the players' speeches:

____[Play-within-the-play]___	
_____	*Ham.* That's
_____	wormwood.
	(H2)

_____	*Ham.* If she should
_____	breake it now.
	(H2^v)

Even white space within a direction might have a mimetic function. A stage direction in one late play seems to use white space to suggest the stage space separating entries at opposite doors:

> *Enter Cranwell ushering the Duchess of Suffolk, a gentlewoman bearing*
> *up her train, Bertie, and Gentlemen.*   *at the other door, beggars.*
>   (*The Duchess of Suffolk*, Q 1631, A3)

Perhaps the best-known and most amusing example of mimetic design is the setting of the tavern bill that Peto filches from Falstaff's pocket and reads aloud in *1 Henry IV*. It is represented in the Folio text (and in most modern editions) as follows:

Peto. Item, a capon.	iis.iid.
Item, Sawce.	iiid.
Item, Sacke, two Gallons.	vs.viiid.
Item, Anchoves and Sacke after Supper.	iis.vid.
Item, Bread.	ob.
	(F 1623, TLN 1503-7)[23]

The normal "look" of the dialogue is replaced by a layout that visually imitates the genre of the text-within-the-text and cues its appropriate vocal interpretation.

CONCLUSION

As with other aspects of the English code for stage directions, visual conventions evolved slowly and in revealing ways. Overall, the visual codes that ultimately evolved integrated theatrical apparatus into the text of the play as unobtrusively as possible without creating a confusion of voices and discourse. Although the conventions observed by Elizabethan manuscripts and printed plays are not identical, there is a good deal of overlap: both found ways to display and distinguish the multiple voices of a dramatic text through different hands or typefaces and judicious breaking of the main text column. The differences that did arise between manuscripts and printed editions correspond to the generic differences between manuscript and print illuminated by Walter Ong and Martin Elsky. In brief, printed editions relied more heavily on a spatial order. In response to the needs of a larger and more varied audience, they devised a text that was both polyvocal and inviting to read.

Scribal practices in the transmission of a play manuscript may help explain why brevity was, from a practical point of view, a virtue in Elizabethan stage directions. It has been argued that the dialogue was written first and speech attributions and stage directions had to be fitted into whatever space had been left for them. Not all scholars accept this argument, but even if it is true, it is not the only reason why directions might tend to be brief. Rhetorically, brevity is also a virtue; it conveys confidence and authority, and it enhances speed of comprehension. It ensures that the directions are efficient and visible, yet unobtrusive, whether they are placed in the margins or in the center of the text column. Further, the link between page design and conciseness was a two-way street: page design encouraged brevity, but reliance on visual conventions such as the freestanding speech prefix rather than the discursive narrative speech cue helped make concise, functionally differentiated, easily integrated directions possible.

Finally, the design of printed plays, in particular, had mimetic qualities: it preserved or extended dramatic decorum onto the page by suggesting special vocal effects (such as reading aloud, dialects, or foreign languages), textual props (such as letters and proclamations), a cleared stage, and the movement of characters in and out of our field of vision. The early quartos allowed a reader to enjoy a play in private, to give it and its characters (as Middleton said) "chamber-roome in his lodging." But in doing so, these texts for readers, I would argue, bridge to a remarkable degree the divide between the stage and the study. The design of an early quarto, like that of the play manuscript itself, retains distinctive marks of the theatrical qualities of the text it displays. Fundamental to this design was the prominent place given to entries after a cleared stage and the seemingly simple device of the left-hand speech prefix, which efficiently encoded the change of speakers and preserved the autonomy and "presence" of the characters even on the printed page.

3

Midscene Directions

This chapter will focus on the visual deployment of midscene directions, excluding speech prefixes: that is, directions for entries, exits, action, sound, and special effects that occur within a scene, between one initial entry and the next. Even more than speech prefixes and initial entries, midscene directions reflect the various ways in which the transmitters of stage directions negotiated the transition from manuscript to the printed page and grappled with representing the many voices of a dramatic text.

As we have seen, the prominent initial entry and left-margin speech prefix of Elizabethan dramatic manuscripts were readily adapted in the design of printed plays. Whereas in manuscripts entries were written across the whole width of the page and speech prefixes were placed in the left-hand margin, in printed texts they were each placed within the central text column, indented and set off by white space. Initial entries thus preserved their prominence and speech prefixes their left-hand position, but both were integrated into an ever more unified text. The handling of midscene directions shows a similar compromise: nearly all midscene directions in printed texts are technically integrated into the text column, but they increasingly imitate the manuscript tradition of marginalia, a tradition that seems at odds with the linear logic of print. For the greater part of the period before the closing of the theaters, the impulse to integrate midscene directions and the impulse to place them in the margins seem to have existed more or less in equilibrium. Texts frequently employ both conventions, though some may prefer one, and some the other. As a result, midscene directions vary considerably with respect to their place on the page and the visual means used to highlight and distinguish them from the dialogue.

In addition, in the case of midscene directions, what counts as an instance is less clear-cut than in the case of speech prefixes and initial entries. The midscene landscape is complicated by the presence in manuscripts and in some printed texts of notations generally understood to be playhouse additions to the script.[1] As is well recognized, many of these notations simply reproduce or highlight directions elsewhere on the page. For example, in *John a Kent*, both entries and sound cues that appear centered or in the right margin in the predominant scribal hand are sometimes emphasized in the left margin by another (presumably playhouse) hand:

Musique. Chime

> A daint<y fit>
> of musique
>
> (TLN 1138–41)

Musique

> Musique
> whi<. . .
>
> (TLN 776–77)

Enter Shrimpe

> Enter Shrimp skipping.
>
> (TLN 1009–12)[2]

Other playhouse notations preview or list properties implied in the dialogue of an upcoming passage or scene. In the manuscript of *Sir John Van Olden Barnavelt*, the main scribe (Ralph Crane) writes:

> ———*A Bar brought in.*
>
> (TLN 2160)

Another hand, presumably the bookkeeper's, adds just above it on either side of the entry:

———

Barre   *Table*

———

Above another entry, added on both sides and apparently at different times,[3] one finds:

————————   ————————

Hornes   *Hornes*

————————   ————————

> (TLN 1726)

Other bookkeepers' notations include so-called ready directions for specific characters or actors, usually one or two of the actors taking minor parts.

Since the aim of this study is to describe the code for stage directions associated with plays for the professional theaters, a bookkeeper's or "playhouse reviser's" approach to annotating stage directions is relevant. At the same time, as William B. Long has suggested, many of these theatrical inscriptions, while evidence of (rather casual) playhouse practice with respect to annotating a manuscript, are not properly termed "stage directions."[4] In deciding which should and should not be considered, I have proceeded as outlined below.

First, in discussing manuscript plays, I include in my tallies all playhouse inscriptions regarding movement (entries or exits), stage business, sound, and props, even those that are redundant, oddly timed (early or late), or subsequently deleted. Notations concerning specific actors are counted only if they use a standard formula for a direction (e.g., *"Ent. H. Gibs"*). This decision inflates slightly the total number of directions in a given text, but my interest is in where directions of different kinds tend to appear, not their frequency. Further, as we shall see in chapter 6, many directions for sound and special effects eventually adopt the abbreviated grammatical form of bookkeeper's notes. Thus, it seems appropriate here to consider the page position of both authorial/scribal directions for action or special effects and bookkeepers' notations in response to them.

Second, I have recorded the characteristic position of bookkeepers' marginal notations concerning casting (i.e., the name or initial of an actor taking a minor role) and "ready" directions, but I have not included them in tallies of entries or other stage directions per se. Third and last, I have ignored playhouse alterations of speech prefixes, the addition of act and scene divisions, and indications of textual cuts. Though I have tried to be consistent, there are enough anomalies that my attempts below to quantify practice should be understood as necessarily judgment-based and approximate. Nonetheless, certain norms are very clear, both in manuscripts and printed plays.

MIDSCENE DIRECTIONS IN ELIZABETHAN MANUSCRIPTS

My sample of manuscript practices is based on print facsimiles of nine manuscript plays associated with the professional theaters, four from before 1600 and five from 1616 to 1637. The plays are:

John a Kent and John a Cumber (c. 1589), in Munday's hand
Edmond Ironside (c. 1590)
Thomas of Woodstock (c. 1592)
Sir Thomas More, Hand S [Munday] only, c. 1592[5]
Sir John Van Olden Barnavelt (c.1619), a Ralph Crane transcript, apparently made for performance[6]
Hengist, King of Kent (c. 1616-20), a transcript apparently based on a promptbook but intended for a private client[7]
Two Noble Ladies (c. 1622-23), an authorial manuscript[8]
Bonduca (c. 1627-37), a transcript of "fowle papers of the authors," i.e., Beaumont and Fletcher[9]
Believe as You List, (c. 1631), a manuscript in Massinger's hand with many bookkeepers' notations; apparently a promptbook for the King's Men[10]

I have also examined the photographic facsimiles of pages of other manuscript plays in Greg's *Dramatic Documents from the Elizabethan Playhouses* and consulted print facsimiles of two manuscript plays not represented in Greg, *John of Bordeaux* and *Tom a Lincoln.*[11]

Integrated vs. Marginal Design

As noted in chapter 1, in medieval dramatic manuscripts stage directions do not occasion a noticeable break in the text. They are either marginal, or, like the dialogue, they conform to the normal borders of the central text column, particularly the left margin. During Elizabeth's reign, initial entries, those that follow a cleared stage and initiate a new scene, begin to interrupt the text column, extending beyond it left and right, or centered within it, framed by white space on the left and right. Other stage directions, however, tend to appear in the margins or in the space to the right of a line.

In the manuscripts before 1600 in my sample, entries that occur in midscene as well as initial entries may also be placed across the page or centered. In *John a Kent*, for example, midscene directions in general are found mostly in the margins, but midscene entries are more likely to be centered (twenty-five instances) than marginal (three instances). In addition, one long direction for midscene action and three descriptive exits are also centered:

> *The chime plays, and Gosselin with the Countesse goes turning out. . . .*
> *The chime again, and they turn out in like manner. . . .*
> *The chime again, and so they.*
>
> (TLN 1158–64)

Edmond Ironside shows the greatest tendency to place midscene directions within the central text column.[12] Fourteen midscene entries are found
within the text column, while only eight are marginal. In addition, almost
half the brief directions for action and special effects (twenty-one of fifty-
one instances) are also centered, as are four of the thirty-one exits (three of
which appear combined with entries). For example:

> *Vskataulfe whispereth in Canutes eare.*
>
> (TLN 96)
>
> Exeunt Swetho with the poore Daines.
>
> (TLN 137)[13]
>
> *The Drumme soundes a far off.*
>
> (TLN 1771)

In other manuscripts of the 1590s, however, marginal midscene directions are the rule. In portions of *Sir Thomas More* ascribed to playwright
Anthony Munday (Hand S), twelve entries are centered, but seventeen entries and the rest of the one hundred and seven midscene directions are
found in the margins. In *Woodstock*, nearly all directions that break the
central column are initial entries. Of the entries that occur midscene, three-
quarters are marginal (forty-one on the left, four on the right), and only one
quarter (fourteen) are written across the page, like an initial entry. (One
additional entry is indented on its own line of text.)

Further, in the *Woodstock* manuscript, only one direction that is *not* an
entry resides on its own line of text, namely *"Manett Trisillian"* at TLN
1240, and even this apparent exception might be explained away. First, as
a *"manet"* direction, it is first cousin to an entry direction, and thus may
have some residual claim to a centered position on a separate line. Second,
it occurs at the very bottom of fol. 171a and shares the last line with a
marginal exit direction that begins to the right of line 1239 (a dialogue line)
and extends down the margin:

> . . . com Anne to our great hall
> wher Richard keepes his gorgious ffeastivall—-*Exeunt*< . . .
>   *Manett Trisillian*   *with*< . . .
>
> (TLN 1239–40)

Thus, the scribe may have impulsively taken advantage of the empty space
at the bottom of the page rather than adding a third or fourth line to the
existing marginal direction.

The centered midscene directions are often elaborate processional entries or extended action sequences, so their visual prominence is not surprising. They underscore significant aspects of the spectacle. For example:

> The boy trips around about Oswen and Amery sing<
> chyme, and they one after the other lay them<
> using very sluggish gestures, the Ladyes amazed<
> about them.
>
> > (*John a Kent*, TLN 1145–49)

> They play and the boy singes, whereat the Bridgroomes come foorth
> in their nightgownes and kerchers on their heades, to them Oswen<
> Amery making themselves ready.
>
> > (*John a Kent*, TLN 581–83)

> *Enter Thomas of Woodstock in Freese: The Mace<*
> *The Lord Mayre & Exton, & others with lightes afore them<*
> > (*Woodstock*, TLN 115–16)

> Alarum Enter Canutus flyinge Edmond followinge
> they fight The Two kinges parley sounde a Retreate
> and parte.
>
> > (*Ironside*, TLN 976–78)

> *The* Trumpittes sound and the Armies do Compasse
> the Twoe kinges in the middest, they fight.
> > (*Ironside*, TLN 1977–78)[14]

In these instances it is easy to see the theatrical logic of placing such directions across or within the central text column, even though they do not initiate a scene. They signal major action or spectacle and thus emphasize what the audience would see.

Textually, too, centering such lengthy directions makes sense. Like the left-hand speech prefix, centered directions help one to read the text as a polyvocal but integrated whole. Compare, for example, the manuscripts of Thomas Legge's *Richardus Tertius* (1579), a university play, in which extensive directions for action are run in the left margin opposite the dialogue (I cite the manuscript in the Huntington Library):[15]

Some armed, with	_____
privy coates	_____
with gowns	[Latin Dialogue] _____

thrown over.   _____
Some unarmed.   _____

                                        (P. 87 [III.ii.11ff.])

Let the Protec   _____
tor give a blow   _____
on yᵉ Counsel-table   [Latin Dialogue] _____
and let one of yᵐ   _____
of the yᵉ gard break   _____
in thereat with   _____
his halbt and   _____
strike yᵉ L. Stan   _____
ley on yᵉ head.

                                        (P. 105 [V.vi.73ff.])

The parallel text in the left margin requires one to pass over this portion of
the page twice, once to read the dialogue and once to digest the marginal
directions for action. By contrast, the practice of centering extensive
midscene directions integrates longer directions syntactically and visually;
they can be read in sequence rather than as parallel texts, one central and
one marginal; the directions point "ahead, instead of away."[16]

On the other hand, in the playhouse manuscripts we have been examining, brief entries for individuals or pairs of characters, some elaborated
with details and some not, may also be centered. For example:

Enter Shrimp skipping.

                                        (*John a Kent*, TLN 1012)

Enter Edricus solus:

                                        (*Ironside*, TLN 277)

Enter Swetho the Two Pledges
and Stich with an Axe:

                                        (*Ironside*, TLN 643–44)

Enter a messenger runninge

                                        (*Ironside*, TLN 735)[17]

Brief midscene entries may also be centered in some later manuscripts,
such as *The Two Noble Ladies*. In a way, centering even such brief entries
results in a page design that is "theatrical" in an even more radical sense
than the scenic structure signaled by the prominent initial entry. After all,
to think in terms of "scenes" does require one to step back from the moment-by-moment flow of the action. Thus, in some manuscripts, the mere

arrival of a new character on the stage seems sufficient to interrupt the text column. While the change of speakers is indicated by a left-margin speech attribution, even a routine entry can occasionally claim the emphasis of white space and its own line of text.

Having given this important minority of midscene directions their due, however, it must be emphasized that in the nine manuscripts I have examined, the vast majority of brief midscene directions are placed in the margins. Moreover, the practice increases over time. In manuscripts after 1615, both those used in the playhouse and those intended for private use, a marginal position for midscene directions is the norm. These later manuscripts are more generous with vertical white space than their predecessors, but unlike the earlier manuscripts, they rarely break the central text column, even for entries. The *Hengist* scribe centers only one of forty-two midscene entries, and all other midscene directions are marginal. Similarly, *Barnavelt* centers only one of forty-eight entries and places all other directions in the margins. *The Two Noble Ladies* centers fourteen entries and five other midscene directions, but this represents less than half of the number of midscene entries (thirty-four in all) and a small fraction of the one hundred and sixty-four other directions that reside in the margins. The scribe of *Bonduca*, presumably following the authors' foul papers, centers only eight of the forty-five midscene entries and places all other directions in the left margin. Neither Massinger nor the bookkeeper (or "stage adapter") centers any midscene directions in the manuscript of *Believe as You List*; both place all of them in the margins.

Taking all midscene directions into account (entries, exits, and directions for action and special effects), the overall tally for nine manuscript plays is as shown in table 3.1.

Table 3.1

	Total midscene directions	Across page or Centered	Marginal
John a Kent	115	25.0%	75.0%
Ironside	104	37.5%	62.5%
Woodstock	172	8.7%	91.3%
Sir Thomas More	107	11.0%	89.0%
Barnavelt	102	1.0%	99.0%
Hengist	111	4.5%	95.5%
Two Noble Ladies	183	10.0%	90.0%
Bonduca	106	7.5%	92.5%
Believe as You List	120	0.0%	100.0%

Thus while major (and some minor) entries and extended action sequences
may be integrated into the text column in earlier playscripts, midscene directions generally tend to appear as marginal glosses. Placing most midscene
directions in the margins reinforces the design of playscripts discussed in
the previous chapters. The directions for midscene business and movement
are clearly visible to the left and right of the dialogue, and the text column
is broken chiefly for initial entries. The needs of a bookholder are met, the
scenic structure of the play is visually stressed, and word and action are
represented in parallel textual columns as distinct but simultaneous voices.

In addition to placing midscene directions largely in the margins, playhouse manuscripts employ other visual devices to isolate them from the
dialogue and call attention to them on the page. As noted in chapter 1,
directions are usually written in a contrasting Italian hand, and sometimes
in a larger or bolder script. In addition, midscene directions are often highlighted by the use of dashes, slashes, brackets, parentheses or half-parentheses, and rules. In playhouse manuscripts, these devices are presumably
for the benefit of "the glancing bookholder"[18] preparing or managing a
performance with his fellows. They call attention to staging information
and make it stand out on the page (although a modern observer might sometimes wonder how to digest at a glance what often becomes a welter of
competing notations!). These visual elements also occur in transcripts for
private clients, where they may be unthinking carryovers from the playhouse copy, or they may be deemed useful for a lay reader, who also needs
to distinguish directions from the dialogue to make sense of the text.

The particular visual embellishments vary. The *John a Kent* manuscript, in the hand of author Anthony Munday, employs slashes or occasionally half-brackets before its right-margin directions (which he does not
italicize):

> / he pulles
> / his beard
>
> (TLN 299–30)
>
> / he offers
> to depart
>
> (TLN 254–55)
>
> / winde his horn
>
> (TLN 469)

Slashes are also used in Munday's portions of the *Sir Thomas More* manuscript:

/ offering to depar<t

(TLN †1824)

/ with great reverenc<e

(TLN †1237)

Even more common in manuscripts early and late is the use of rules, "hooked rules" (rules plus slashes), or brackets on two or on all four sides:

Trumpetts sound

(*Woodstock*, TLN 627)

wind Hornes
w^{th}in

(*Woodstock*, TLN 584–85)

hee beates
them about
the stage

(*Ironside*, TLN 562–63)

In the *Barnavelt* manuscript, Crane sometimes precedes an indented or marginal direction with a dash:

———*A Bar brought in*

(TLN 2160)

———*Enter Modes-*
bargen. . . .

(TLN 1727)

———*Enter 2.Captaines*

(TLN 146)

In *Two Noble Ladies*, many midscene directions, both centered and marginal, appear in boxed rules. In *Bonduca*, exits and sound effects are often preceded by dashes or brackets or set between rules:

                              ⎰*sitt downe.*

                                                    (TLN 1683)

                        ————⏋fightes:

                                                    (TLN 1678)

In *Believe as You List,* Massinger encloses nearly all his midscene directions in boxes, while the bookkeeper places his redactions of them and
other notes between heavy rules.

Most of these devices call attention to the directions and isolate them
from the dialogue, reinforcing their status as marginalia. Dashes and brackets, however, also seem to indicate where the direction intersects with the
dialogue, and thus they simultaneously separate and reintegrate these two
aspects of dramatic discourse. As long as directions run in the margins,
however, their point of contact with the dialogue will always be approximate, not exact, and they will leave a good deal to the discretion of the
players. In the passage from *Woodstock* below, for example, the dialogue
as well as the stage direction cues Woodstock to yield the emblem of of-
fice, but the precise timing remains open. The actor could explore various
expressive possibilities of when to give over the mace, such as angrily
anticipating his own words or delaying (as if reluctant) until all three lines
have been spoken:

> *Wood:*   but be it as it will: low here king Richard   ———————
>   I thus yield up my sad protectorshipp   *gives the*
>   a heavey burthen hast thou tayne from mee   *Mace up*
>   ———————

                                                    (TLN 900–902)

To sum up, in dramatic manuscripts of plays associated with the professional theaters, most midscene directions are marginal and thus syntactically and spatially discontinuous with the central text. They run parallel
to it, as a gloss in either margin, set off by rules or boxes, as in the following examples from *Thomas of Woodstock:*

                        ———————

> *Greene*: Farewell Tressillian still be neere the courte
>   anon king Richard shall confirme thy state
>   We must attend his grace to westminster

to the hye nuptialls of ffaire Ann a Beame

that must be now his wife, & Englands queene   *Exeunt Greene*
                                                    & Baggott

Triss: So let them pass   *Manett Tressill*

(TLN 275–81)

Surry: It is his custome to be prodigall
          to any but to those doe best deserve

wind Hornes	*Ar*: be cause he knewe you would be stowe them well
w^{th}in	he gave it such as for ther privat gayne
	neglect boeth honnor and ther countryes good

lanc: how now what noyse is this

(TLN 582–87)

Occasionally exit or other directions are written to the right of a line of dialogue, and thus can be read in sequence with it and with the one that follows:

Amilcar: . . . . . . In what wee may
          wee are your freindes. breake up the court. │ exeunt Carthaginians

(*Believe as You List,* TLN 1175–76)

But the rules on three sides of the direction suggest that such directions are
to be viewed as marginal and supplementary, rather than as integrated into
a linear text.

Although the underlying logic of the manuscript tradition implies a
strict division of space between dialogue and brief midscene directions,
play manuscripts did not consistently adopt an obvious way to observe this
distinction in practice. As T. H. Howard-Hill has noted in describing Ralph
Crane's transcripts and surviving playhouse manuscripts, the columns created by the folds in the manuscript page were not consistently used to separate the dialogue from marginal directions.[19] Nonetheless, though scribes
and authors may not have taken full advantage of the folds of the page to

indicate the marginality of midscene directions, such directions nonetheless clearly function as marginalia. They are set off by rules or other visual means; they often run down an independent column of two or three lines' duration; and they are only roughly positioned with respect to the point at which they take effect in relation to the dialogue. It is clear from the general practice that midscene directions in dramatic manuscripts follow a marginal *logic* even if its execution is somewhat relaxed with respect to the folds on the page.

At the same time, the marginal directions are relatively brief. Compared to the lengthy marginalia in some academic drama, such as those in *Horestes* or *Richardus Tertius* cited above, they can usually be taken in at a glance. Thus they steer a middle course, creating a design that can be read at one pass (if not strictly linearly), rather than a design that requires the eye to move down lengthy, fully distinct, parallel columns of text.

Differentiating Midscene Directions, Left, Right, and Center

In manuscripts of plays associated with the professional theaters, directions may be found in both margins, but sometimes right and left margins are devoted to particular kinds of directions. No doubt the choice of margin was sometimes dictated by the white space available on either side of a particular stretch of dialogue, but space alone does not seem to have been decisive. In the *Woodstock* manuscript, some left-margin sound cues and midscene entries in the hand of the main scribe (not the bookkeeper) have clearly crowded the speech prefixes that presumably have a prior claim on the space. This is the case at the top of fol. 166[a] (the directions parallel TLN 584–85 and 589–90). Similarly, the boxed direction *"Enter the / queene"* to the left of TLN 1365–66 is squeezed between two speech prefixes and crowds a prefix for Greene to the right of its normal position, reducing it to a mere initial *g* instead of the usual *Gre*. Or again, the boxed direction *"Enter Cheney / wth blankes"* (TLN 1343–45) appears in the left margin, but there is equal or greater space for it on the right. Most important, however, since marginal directions are free to run vertically in their own column for more than one line, the horizontal space available on each side of the dialogue becomes less of a limiting factor: the directions can simply be fit into whatever vertical space is available.

As a result, in some manuscripts, the choice of margin sometimes seems determined by the kind of direction (or in the case of bookkeeper's annotations, to the hand that was writing them)[20] rather than the space available in one margin or the other. Logically enough, entries and sound cues that precede a character's lines are often placed on the left, "before" them in space as well as time, while action that may accompany or follow spoken lines often appears on the right, parallel or in sequence spatially as well as temporally. In the *Woodstock* manuscript, for example, the majority of both midscene entries and directions for sound (76 and 68 percent, respectively) appear in the left margin, many in the hand of the chief scribe, as in the examples below:

/ *Trumpets sound* /

(TLN 627)

$\left\{ \begin{array}{c} \textit{wind Hornes} \\ w^{th}\textit{in} \end{array} \right.$

(TLN 584–85)

sound

(between TLN 823 and 824)

a flourish

(TLN 914)

$\left\{ \begin{array}{l} \textit{Enter a spruce} \\ \textit{courtier a horsebacke} \end{array} \right.$

(TLN 1424–25)

$\left\{ \begin{array}{c} \textit{Enter one A} \\ \textit{whisling} \end{array} \right\}$

(TLN 1706–7)

$\left\{ \begin{array}{c} \textit{(Musicke) Then} \\ \textit{Enter Cheney} \end{array} \right\}$

(TLN 2149–50)

Along with four midscene entries, all eleven midscene directions for action in this play appear on the right:

---

gives the
Mace up

(TLN 901–2)

seale them

(TLN 1629)

They Daunce

(TLN 2149)

he drawes the curtaynes

(TLN 2432)

stickes hime

(TLN 2608)

Edmond Ironside has one left-margin midscene direction, a freestanding call for an *Alarum* at TLN 956, while all directions for action that are not centered appear on the right. In most manuscripts in my sample this spatiotemporal logic is discernible but not absolute. In *John a Kent*, most entries and directions for midscene action appear on the right, though a few of each appear on the left. *Sir Thomas More* also places most entries and action cues on the right, with a few of each on the left.

In later manuscripts, too, though one margin may be preferred, both seem available. In the *Hengist* manuscript, most of the midscene directions (other than those for routine entries and exits) are for sound cues: eight appear on the left, while fifteen appear on the right. *The Two Noble Ladies* shows a slightly more consistent distribution. Twenty-four of the twenty-nine left-margin directions are for sound, while most other directions (eighty in all, including many *asides*) appear on the right. *Bonduca*, however, contains no left-margin directions; except for the eight centered entries, all other directions—action (sixteen), special effects (eight), entries (thirty-seven), and exits (thirty-seven)—appear on the right. In the latest manuscript, *Believe as You List*, Massinger puts only two midscene directions (one entry and one flourish) in the left margin and the rest (sixty-one) on the right, while in annotating the manuscript after him, the bookkeeper prefers the left margin for most of his reiterations (forty-five), placing only twelve on the right. In so doing, he follows what Greg took to be the norm for bookkeepers generally, using the space in the left margin to highlight the existing directions on the right and to add his own "ready" instructions, notes concerning properties, and so on (an additional nineteen annotations).

There is one kind of direction, however, that almost invariably appears on the right. In manuscripts both early and late, nearly all explicit exit directions are on the right.[21] In *John a Kent*, 92 percent of the exit directions are on the right. In *Edmond Ironside*, the figure is 87 percent, and in *Sir Thomas More* and *Woodstock*, 100 percent. In later manuscripts, the trend is undiminished: *Hengist* places 98 percent of exits on the right; *The Two Noble Ladies*, 95 percent; and *Bonduca*, 100 percent. Even the exceptions tend to prove the rule. The three exits in *John a Kent* that are centered include descriptive bits of business that carry "antick" characters offstage (quoted above). The sole exception in *Hengist* is a centered direction at the end of the play proper, and just before the final chorus:

fflourish Exeunt:

In using both margins for stage directions and other kinds of annotations, play manuscripts resemble nondramatic manuscripts of the day. At the same time, in concentrating some kinds of staging information on the right and others on the left, they further rationalize, or logically organize, the design of dramatic texts. Like the left-margin speech prefix, brief sound cues on the left could easily be absorbed in the normal left-to-right process of reading. Moreover, many sound effects did in fact precede the actual entrance of a set of characters, and thus the sound cue logically precedes the entry direction in the space of the text. In addition, the consistently right-hand exit direction suggests that the mimetic aspects in the design of dramatic texts did not originate entirely in printed texts. Entries in manuscript plays might appear left, centered, or in the right margin; exits, though occasionally centered in the plays reviewed here, *never* appear on the left. The convention of the right-of-center or right-margin exit direction ensures that a character exits our mental field of vision as our eye "exits" a line of text.

As one might expect, a more linear page design emerges in printed plays from the professional theaters; but as we shall see, some printed editions also preserve to a degree the simultaneous or "stereophonic" voice of brief midscene directions, even while organizing the text, in other respects, to facilitate linear reading.

Printed Plays

My analysis of the visual conventions governing printed plays relies chiefly on twenty-nine plays published in quarto between 1593 and 1661. This is a modest sample of the extant plays of the period, but a small sample thoroughly digested seemed preferable to a large one that might prove unmanageable. I focus on quarto editions, since these were most common form in which plays were published, but the innovative and influential conventions of folio texts—a fascinating subject in itself—will be mentioned from time to time. The plays were chosen with an eye to variety with respect to author, genre, printer or publisher, and date of publication. All are plays associated with the men's companies, although the sometimes contrasting conventions employed in plays written for the boys' companies will be noted. Since my goal is to describe the practice of the professional theatrical community, I made no attempt to exclude texts once or still classified as "bad quartos." The plays by short title, date of publication, author, printer, and stationer are shown in table 3.2.[22]

Table 3.2

Through 1599:

Edward I (1593), Peele	Abell Jeffes for William Barley
1 Contention (1594), Shakespeare	Thomas Creede for Thomas Millington
Edward II (1594), Marlowe	Richard Bradock for William Jones
Friar Bacon (1594), Greene	Adam Islip for Edward White
Love's Labour's Lost (1598), Shakespeare	William Shite for Cuthbert Burby
Famous Victories (1598), Anon.	Thomas Creede
Mucedorus (1598), Anon.	Unknown for William Jones
Blind Beggar of Alexandria (1598), Chapman [?]	Unknown for William Jones
George a Greene (1599), Greene [?]	Simon Stafford for Cuthbert Burby

1600-1642:

1 Contention(1600), Shakespeare	Valentine Simmes for Thomas Millington
Old Fortunatus (1600), Dekker	Simon Stafford for William Aspley
Every Man Out of His Humour (1600), Jonson	Richard Braddock for William Holmes
Sir John Oldcastle (1600), Munday et al.	Valentine Simmes for Thomas Pavier
2 Henry IV (1600), Shakespeare	Valentine Simmes for A. Wise and Wm. Aspley

Hamlet (1604-5), Shakespeare	James Roberts for Nicholas Ling
King Leir (1605), Anon.	Simon Stafford for John Wright
Captain Thomas Stukeley (1605), Anon.	Unknown for Thomas Pavier
If You Know Not Me (1605), Heywood	Thomas Purfoot for Nathaniel Butter
When You See Me (1605), Rowley	Humphrey Lownes for Nathaniel Butter
Miseries of Enforced Marriage (1607), Wilkins & Heywood	William Jaggard for George Vincent[23]
Sir Thomas Wyatt (1607), Dekker and Webster	Edward Allde for Thomas Archer
King Lear (1608), Shakespeare	Nicholas Okes for Nathaniel Butter
The Roaring Girl (1611), Dekker and Middleton	Nicholas Okes for Thomas Archer
The Valiant Welshman (1615), Anon. ("R.A.")	George Purslowe for Robert Lownes
A King and No King (1619), Beaumont and Fletcher	John Beadle for Thomas Walkley
The Duchess of Suffolk (1631), Thomas Drue	Augustine Matthews for Jasper Emery
Perkin Warbeck (1634), Ford	Thomas Purfoot for Hugh Beeston

Interregnum/Restoration editions:

King John and Matilda (1655), Robert Davenport	Unknown for Andrew Pennycuicke

Hengist, King of Kent, or The
    Mayor of Quinborough
    (1661), Middleton
	Unknown for Henry Herringman

Examples are cited from other plays, but these twenty-nine were the basis of my attempt to tally various practices.

In judging historical trends, I examined the plays by date of publication, since printing-house practices might have changed over time and influenced the "look" of a given text. However, in some instances (such as *The Famous Victories*, c. 1588, Q 1598) a play published some years after its probable date of composition resembled more closely quartos of the earlier period, and overall the trend in printed plays resembles that in the manuscripts discussed above. Thus the changes over time may simply result from the compositors following the layout of their manuscript copytexts as far as possible.

Integrated vs. Marginal Design

In adapting the manuscript tradition to the exigencies and advantages of print, compositors faced certain challenges. As we saw in chapters 1 and 2, the solution for speech prefixes and initial entries was not difficult. Speech prefixes had already migrated to the left margin in playhouse manuscripts, and it was a small adjustment to indent them slightly on the left-hand side of the text column. Similarly, the manuscript practice of emphasizing initial entries found its counterpart in the printing practice of centering initial entries so that the white space on each side, and sometimes above and below, broke the text column, calling attention to the cleared stage and subsequent entry of a new set of characters.

The manuscript tradition of placing midscene directions in the margins would seem to pose a greater problem. Unlike a folio-sized manuscript page, which affords ample space for marginalia to the right and left of a central column, the page of a quarto or other small-format volume seems most suited to a single column of text. As Walter J. Ong has shown, however, printing houses were capable of producing elaborate page designs for Ramian textbooks of rhetoric and other treatises influenced by Ramus's "method," in which information was organized schematically in columns or branched trees.[24] While such abstract designs are not suited to dramatic texts, marginal directions were not uncommon in printed versions of humanist plays. As we saw in chapter 2, speech prefixes reside in the outer margins of facing pages in *Wealth and Health* (S.R. 1557), and extensive directions for action, as well as descriptive entries and exits, similarly run down the outer margins in *Horestes* (Q 1567) (see figures 4 and 6). In a departure from its normal practice, the 1565 quarto of *King Darius* has three left-margin directions on E4. Marginal directions also appear in some printed academic plays, such as *Aristippus*, a university play published in London in 1630.

A page design employing truly marginal directions has some advantages. It makes full use of the space on the page, which helps control costs: in the sixteenth and seventeenth centuries, paper was the single largest expense in producing a printed book. Further, if the printed page closely follows the design of the manuscript, the compositor need not spend time inventing his own. On the other hand, setting two or three columns of text on each page rather than one must have been more labor-intensive. Aesthetically, too, the marginal design of a play like *Horestes* seems crowded and hard to read, but of course this may have been less true to Elizabethan eyes that were used to marginalia.

Strictly speaking, the manuscript convention of marginal midscene directions did not become the norm in printed texts. The use of the left margin, in particular, is very rare in printed plays associated with the professional theaters. In the twenty-nine quartos discussed in this chapter, I have encountered only two texts with truly marginal directions, that is, directions placed wholly outside the normal text column: two entries appear in the left margin in the 1608 quarto of *King Lear*. Marston's *The Malcontent* (Q 1604) contains twenty instances of genuine marginalia, both left and right of the normal text page.[25] Even in the large-format, folio collections of Jonson, Shakespeare, and Beaumont and Fletcher, only Jonson's undertakes to create a spacious, single-column page with true marginalia that do not encroach upon the space reserved for the dialogue.[26] The Beaumont and Fletcher and the Shakespeare folios adopt a double-column format that does not readily accommodate marginalia.

In the quartos examined here, the printing houses devised three ways to accommodate midscene directions: to center them within the text column on their own line of text, like initial entries; to indent them well to the right of center on their own line of text; or to *approximate* a marginal position by placing them flush right in the space at the end of a line or lines of dialogue. All three printing-house solutions (centered, indented, or flush right) integrate midscene directions more fully into the linear flow of the text than was the case in playhouse manuscripts. However, if a single direction is set flush right, especially to the right of *more* than one line of dialogue, something very much like a marginal gloss is preserved, even though it resides within the normal text column. Let us consider each solution in turn.

The central position for midscene directions is preferred in the early plays of my sample. *Edward I* (Q 1593) centers almost all midscene entries and directions for action, as well as some exits. Scene 5, for example, contains the following (mostly violent) midscene directions, all centered:

Meredith stabs him into the armes and shoulders.

(TLN 969)

He shows him hote Pinsers.

(TLN 973)

He cuts his nose.

(TLN 981)

Mortimor goes for Elinor, and conducts her in.

(TLN 1006)

> *Then Lluellen spieth Elinor and Mortimor,*
> *and saieth thus.*
>
> (TLN 1013–14)

Excluding exits for the moment, only ten of fifty-seven midscene directions in this play are indented well to the right on their own line or positioned at the end of a line of dialogue. Four of these are entries, and six are directions for sound or stage business, such as *"They kneele downe"* (TLN 1723), *"Here they sing"* (TLN 1907), *"Sound Trumpets"* (TLN 2156), and *"Here shee dies"* (TLN 2345).

Centered midscene directions, both brief and extensive, are also preferred in some other relatively early printed texts. In *Friar Bacon and Friar Bungay* (Q 1594), the conjuring scene (scene 11 in modern editions) contains the following centered directions:

> *Here Bungay conjures, and the tree appears with the Dragon*
> *shooting fire.*
>
> (84, S.D.)

> *Here the Head speaks, and a lightning flasheth forth, and a hand*
> *appears that breaketh down the head with a hammer.*
>
> (90, S.D.)

> *Hercules appears in his lion's skin.*
>
> (93, S.D.)

> *He begins to break the branches.*
>
> (98, S.D.)

The Famous Victories (Q 1598) may betray its early date of composition (c. 1588) by centering fifty of its seventy-eight midscene directions.[27] As we have seen, early playhouse manuscripts provide a precedent for centering some midscene directions, particularly extended ones that govern major entries or spectacles (such as the conjuring scene above). Thus the printers of these earlier plays are likely to have been following their copy.

Extensive, centered directions have a visual kinship with the design of medieval plays, in which the production narrative alternated with the dialogue in the central text column. However, unlike their medieval predecessors, and like their playhouse originals, centered directions in printed plays break the text column with horizontal (and sometimes vertical) white space: they are set with white space on each side, rather than flush to the left margin, and they are sometimes preceded and followed by a blank line.

Thus, these midscene directions (especially if long) have much the same gravity and prominence as initial entries, which they visually resemble.

The second solution for representing midscene directions is to indent them to the right of center on their own line of text. Take, for example, *1 Contention* (Q 1594, the "bad quarto" of *2 Henry VI*):

> *Sound Trumpets.*
>
> (A2^v)
>
> *Duke Humphrey lets it fall.*
>
> (A2^v)
>
> *The Cardinall dies.*
>
> (F1^v)[28]

To my eye, this placement gives the directions less prominence than if they were centered, but it still breaks the text column with the white space created by the indented position. Further, like the first solution, it integrates the direction visually and syntactically into the text. This solution also has its precedents in earlier manuscript plays, particularly *Ironside* and *John a Kent*, where directions for midscene entries and battle sequences were often indented quite far to the right, rather than centered. So once again, the printers may have simply followed their copy.

The third solution is to place midscene directions flush right (more or less) in the space at the end of a line of dialogue. Verse lines often do not fill the whole text column. Long stretches of prose dialogue, especially if justified, are likely to fill the text column completely for a time, but they may end with a short line followed by ample space for a brief direction. Thus directions can and do appear flush right at the end of verse passages or following a short line of prose, as in the following example from *1 Contention*:

> *Armou.* Hold Peter, I confesse, treason, treason.   (he dies.
> *Peter.* O God I give thee praise.   He kneeles downe.
>
> (D2)[29]

When placed in this way, midscene directions encroach upon the main text column (as could often happen in dramatic manuscripts), but they do not interrupt it with vertical white space. Consequently, especially if slashes, dashes, or half-parentheses are used to separate the direction from the dialogue (as in the first case above), brief flush-right directions may seem simultaneously part of the linear text and "marginal," as they were in manuscripts.

Some printed plays imitate the manuscript tradition even more closely. In these texts, midscene directions occasionally run in a column down the right-hand side of the dialogue, often set off by parentheses or other visual devices. Thus, with or without parentheses or the like, the directions *cannot* be read in strict linear sequence with the dialogue; they speak like marginalia from a separate, parallel column of text. *Sir John Oldcastle* (Q 1600) has several parallel, multiline, "marginal" directions for action and four such entries:

Both at
once al this

(TLN 84–85)

pointing
to the
beggars

(TLN 363–65)

L. Warden and
Oldcastle whisper.

(TLN 1906–7)

gives them
a purse

(TLN 2697–98)

Thomas Lord Cromwell (Q 1602) also employs several marginal directions:

Here within they
must beate with
their hammers.

(A1ᵛ)

One stands at one end
and one at tother.

(C2ᵛ)

The mu-
sicke playes
as they go in.

(D3ᵛ)

An unusually large number (sixteen) are also found in *If You Know Not Me* (Q 1605):

> *Exit*
> *Dodds*
>
> (TLN 94–95)

> *(They sit,*
> *(shee kneeles.*
>
> (TLN 362–63)

> *(They fight,*
> *(he hurts the*
> *(Spaniard.*
>
> (TLN 931–33)

As in the case of anomalous or embedded speech prefixes (more than one per line), it is possible that flush right or "marginal" midscene directions are a printer's response to a shortage of space on a page as a result of errors in casting off copy. However, an examination of the three texts in my sample in which "marginal" directions are most common suggests that casting off copy was probably not a factor. *Old Fortunatus*, *Sir John Oldcastle*, and *If You Know Not Me* were printed by three different printers (Valentine Simmes, Simon Stafford, and Thomas Purfoot). In my sample, these three plays have the highest numbers of multiline, "marginal" midscene directions (eleven, fifteen, and sixteen, respectively); overall, they place 76, 60, and 47 percent, respectively, of their midscene directions to the right of one or more lines of dialogue rather than centered or indented on a separate line. According to William Bond's analysis of cast-off copy in quartos, if the flush right and "marginal" directions were a response to errors in estimating copy we would expect to find them in one or the other forme of a gathering, but not in both; and we would expect to find them concentrated in prose passages rather than in verse and prose randomly.[30]

The evidence against cast-off copy being a factor in *Old Fortunatus* is reasonably clear: in two gatherings (B and C) such directions appear only in one forme, the outer; but in the remaining complete gatherings (D–K), they appear equally in both formes. Further, flush right or "marginal" directions appear randomly in verse and prose portions of the text, not primarily in prose passages. The evidence of the other two editions is even stronger: in both *Oldcastle* and *If You Know Not Me*, without exception, such directions appear in both formes of every gathering and with roughly equal frequency in prose and verse passages. Further, since the three plays were printed by three different printers, it is unlikely that an individual compositor's or printer's preference accounts for them. Thus erroneous estimates made in casting off copy do not seem to account for the presence of flush right and "marginal" directions in these plays. It seems that in these instances the printers were simply approximating the marginal directions in their copy.

Table 3.3 summarizes the practice of the printed plays in my sample regarding midscene directions that interrupt the text column (centered or indented on their own line) vs. those that do not (flush right or "marginal"):

Table 3.3

Printed plays	Centered or indented		Flush right or or "marginal"	
through 1599	556	(80%)	139	(20%)
1600–42	812	(44%)	1028	(56%)
1655, 1661	5	(2%)	222	(98%)

With two exceptions, the nine quartos published through 1599 break the text column for midscene directions between 72 and 99 percent of the time; and all do so more than half the time. With six exceptions, the eighteen quartos printed from 1600 to the closing of the theaters also do so at least 40 percent of the time, with the average distribution varying from 40/60 to 60/40. The two plays published during the Commonwealth or immediately thereafter rarely allow midscene directions to break the text column at all.

The exceptional cases are interesting. *Love's Labour's Lost*, printed by William White, and *The Blind Beggar of Alexandria*, printer unknown, are the only quartos in the group through 1599 that center significantly less than 70 percent of their midscene directions (53 percent and 58 percent, respectively). Since the printer of the latter is unknown, we cannot speculate about the influence of a particular printing house, but part of the reason for the apparent departure from the norm seems to lie in the nature of the plays themselves. Compared to the early history plays in the sample, which tend to stress action and spectacle, these two plays are lightly annotated for action: the quarto of *Love's Labour's Lost* has only ten midscene directions for stage action, and *The Blind Beggar* only five. Thus the entries (which tend to be centered or indented) and exits (which in these two plays tend to be flush right) more or less balance each other.[31]

Some exceptions among the plays published between 1600 and 1642 suggest that particular printers may have had an effect on the tendency to center or indent midscene directions. *The Roaring Girl* and *King Lear*, both printed by Nicholas Okes, center or indent only 34 and 28 percent, respectively, of their midscene directions. And two quartos printed by Simon Stafford, *Old Fortunatus* and *King Leir*, are at or below the low side of the normal range, 40 and 36 percent, respectively. On the other hand, in *Sir John Oldcastle*, printed by Valentine Simmes for Thomas Millington, only 24 percent of the midscene directions break the text column; but two other editions printed by Simmes in the same year (1600) are at or above the norm: *2 Henry IV* breaks the text column for 44 percent of the midscene directions, and the 1600 quarto of *1 Contention* permits 73 percent of the midscene directions to interrupt the central column. The high percentage in the latter play probably reflects the fact that it is essentially a reprint of the earlier quarto of this play, printed by Thomas Creede also for Millington, which centers or indents 84 percent of its midscene directions. Overall, the evidence of these exceptions suggests that the habits of a particular printing house might affect the design of a printed play but that such influence does not seem to have been consistent or decisive. On the whole, printers seem to follow their copytexts using a common set of conventions.

While midscene directions that interrupt the text column are less numerous after 1600, on average nearly half of them continue to do so. The preference for directions that do not break the column increases in the two plays written in the 1620s and 1630s, respectively, and published after the theaters had been closed for a decade or more.[32] In the quartos of 1655 and 1661, nearly all midscene directions are flush right or "marginal." Since all the later plays in my sample of manuscripts prefer marginal midscene directions to those that break the text column, the design of the copytext rather than printing-house economics (the desire to save paper and thus control costs) seems the determining factor. In the 1661 quarto of *Hengist*, only one midscene direction breaks the text column, but this is consistent with the surviving manuscripts of the play: in Bald's print facsimile of one of them, only five midscene directions are permitted to do so.

Nonetheless, an important difference remains between printed plays and the manuscript tradition. While the marginal midscene directions in playhouse manuscripts were often brief and could be digested at a glance, the dominant design (always excepting initial entries) preserved separate channels for dialogue and directions. While the two late quartos closely imitate the manuscript tradition, most of their midscene directions can still be read in linear sequence with the dialogue: about 30 percent of them run parallel to the dialogue in a separate column, while more than 60 percent are flush right at the end of a single line of dialogue. Thus, even though these late quartos rarely break the dialogue column to insert a stage direction on its own line of text, the majority of the midscene directions can be read in sequence with the dialogue, as in printed editions generally.

Differentiating Directions: Centered, Indented, or Flush Right

In early printed plays, directions for action and special effects are variously positioned. *1 Contention* (Q 1594), in addition to the indented and flush-right directions cited above, has centered directions as well:

He sinkes downe again.

(C1)

Bullenbrooke makes a circle.

(B4ᵛ)

She kisseth him.

(F1ᵛ)

King Leir (c. 1594, Q 1605) presents a similarly mixed practice. Centered are:

Then they draw lots.

(TLN 550)

She opens the letters.

(TLN 1169)

Give him two purses.

(TLN 1327)

Indented on a separate line are:

Flings him a purse.

(TLN 1017)

She opens them.

(TLN 994)

In *Sir John Oldcastle* (Q 1600), twelve midscene directions for action are centered, one is indented, twenty-one are flush right, and seven (including four entries) are "marginal."

Common sense suggests that longer directions might be centered, shorter ones indented, and the shortest squeezed into the space at the end of a verse line. But this logic does not seem to hold consistently in the examples above. Most relatively long directions are centered, but so are some very brief ones. In addition to the examples above, one could cite these centered directions in *Captain Thomas Stukeley* (c. 1596, Q 1605):

Putting out his hand.

(TLN 395)

Turning to the King of Portingall.

(TLN 2347)

Panting for breath.

(TLN 2799)

Thus, as in dramatic manuscripts, the rationale for centering, indenting, or placing midscene directions flush right is not based only on the length of the direction.

Like dramatic manuscripts, printed plays show some tendency to place different kinds of midscene directions in particular positions. Up to the closing of the theaters, midscene entries are most likely to be centered, as shown in table 3.4.

Table 3.4. Entries

	Centered	Indented	Flush	"Marginal"
through 1599	218	15	15	0
1600–1642	516	39	132	22
1655, 1661	0	0	34	33

For the twenty-seven plays published before 1642, the percentage of centered midscene entries is high: 89 percent for the editions through 1599, 73 percent for those to 1642. The two late editions reverse prior practice, placing all midscene entries in the margins. Thus, like the earlier manuscript plays, most of these plays give midscene entries considerable prominence, corresponding to a change in on-stage personnel and the tension occasioned by the arrival of a new character.

Directions for action and special effects (table 3.5) show a slightly different pattern. After 1599 there is an increasing tendency to relegate midscene directions other than entries to a flush right or "marginal" position.

LINDA McJANNET

Table 3.5. Action and Special Effects

	Centered	Indented	Flush	"Marginal"
through 1599	140	25	19	1
1600–1642	162	33	225	55
1655, 1661	3	1	38	29

Before 1600, 76 percent of such directions are allowed to interrupt the central column; after 1600 only 34 percent do so. Once again, the very late editions are still more consistent: only 5 percent of such directions interrupt the text column. In interpreting these figures, it is well to remember that some major "action sequences" (such as dumb shows, fights, and battle scenes) are likely to take the form of elaborated entry directions, and might thus be centered. The flush right and "marginal" directions are likely to be brief cues for action or gesture aimed at a single character. Thus their discreet page position and, if you will, their sotto voce tone seem appropriate to their function.

As was the case in dramatic manuscripts, the placement of exits is the most consistent over the entire span of my sample. An indented right-hand position was preferred from the first, and as time passed a flush right or "marginal" right position became the overwhelming norm (table 3.6).

Table 3.6. Exits

	Centered	Indented	Flush	"Marginal"
through 1599	35	123	107	1
1600–1642	23	39	557	38
1655, 1661	0	1	82	6

Like playhouse manuscripts, printed editions quickly establish a mimetic design in which exits are keyed to the left-to-right rhythm of reading, and the preference increases without alteration over the entire period of our sample.

All in all, the design of printed plays meets the needs of readers while preserving many aspects of the manuscripts on which they were based: in both manuscripts and printed plays, midscene entries are likely to break the text column, while directions for action and most exits speak discreetly from the right "margin" without interrupting the visual flow of the dialogue. The chief difference is that in printed plays, some directions that were probably marginal in manuscript are integrated into the main text column, indented on their own line of text.

Coordinating Directions and Dialogue

Centered or indented, midscene directions in printed texts may interrupt the text column, but they do not usually disrupt an individual *line* of dialogue. Unlike some modern plays (Beckett's come to mind) in which parenthetical directions are freely interspersed in the dialogue, Elizabethan midscene directions rarely if ever appear midline. In all the texts surveyed for this study, I encountered only two midline directions for action in a play for the professional theaters: the parenthetical phrase *"gives his purse"* that occurs in the middle of a prose speech in Heywood's *1 Edward IV* (F2), and the direction *"Strikes him"* in the middle of a prose speech in *The Miseries of Enforced Marriage* (TLN 568, C1ᵛ). In the latter case, casting off copy may explain this anomaly. As we saw in chapter 2, the presence of two speech prefixes in a single line in this edition follows the pattern one would expect if the printer was using cast-off copy to expedite the printing process: that is, the embedded speech prefixes occur on only one forme of a gathering. The page on which this midline direction occurs, C1ᵛ, makes up part of the inner forme, which also contains all three instances of doubled speech prefixes in this gathering. The fact that both midline exceptions occur in prose speeches strengthens the likelihood that casting off copy may have been a factor in their placement on the page. Thus, although there is a trend in printed editions to present a more integrated, unitary text, as a rule the dialogue and directions still maintain distinct voices and a degree of spatial separation.

Occasionally, an entry or direction for action appears as an extension of the speech prefix. Some examples in *Edward I* have already been cited:

> *Enter Katharina.* At hand Madam.
>
> (TLN 2310)

> *Potter strikes.* He must needs go that the divel drives. . . .
> *Frier strikes.* I with maister proud Potter the Divel have my soule:
> (TLN 1509–12)[33]

As noted in chapter 2, these extended speech prefixes might be seen as vestiges of the undifferentiated directions of the medieval drama, in which cues for action and speech appear together without distinction. Extended speech prefixes are most common for directions indicating to whom to address a speech, such as *to the Priest* or *aside*. In *Sir John Oldcastle*, extended speech prefixes appear in four out of five occasions where asides occur in prose passages; in the verse passages, however, *aside* appears in the margin.

"Asides" aside, however, directions and dialogue generally run parallel or alternate, rather than cohabiting within the line. Even extended speech prefixes simply stretch the space already allotted to a normal stage direction. They do not *interrupt* a line of dialogue. As a result, midscene directions are only moderately precise with respect to their point of operation. Most playscripts for the professional theaters seem content to let the player (or the reader) determine exactly when a given direction takes effect.

The desire to place directions more precisely with respect to the moment of their operation is more common in academic drama. Presumably, since in this venue both playwright and actors were amateurs, they felt a greater need for specificity regarding the details of performance. In *The Rival Friends*, a university play published in 1632, one finds directions of all sorts in midline. Typical is the following (the speech prefix is embedded within the line of dialogue):

> . . . *Ant.* let me see *[He looks upon his watch]* 'tis just eight now.
>
> (D3)

Midline exits also can be found: *"[Ex. Lou. & Bedlam]"* occurs midline on L4ᵛ. This play sometimes uses asterisks in the dialogue to signal precisely where a marginal direction applies:

> Dost thou not blush to speak't,* thou shame of woman?
> But here he comes . . .   *Enter*
>   *Nean[der]*
>
> (C2ᵛ)

> A thiefe
> I and the worst of thieves————*villaine thou liest.   *aside*
>
> (C3)

Marston, who sometimes follows the academic, neoclassical convention for dramatic discourse, also occasionally uses asterisks to coordinate dialogue and stage directions. In I.ii of *The Malcontent* (Q 1604), for example, Malevole's offstage rantings are cued by an asterisk after the speech prefix and a marginal direction rather than by the more familiar *within:*

*Mal.** Yaugh, God a man, what dost thou there? . . .   **Out of his*
chamber.
(B1)

Jonson, the professional playwright most drawn to neoclassical conventions, also experiments with tighter directorial control and more explicit description of stage business in the folio versions of some plays. One device he adopts is inch-long dashes or "breaches" inserted into a dialogue passage to which a marginal direction is then keyed. In the induction to the folio version of *Cynthia's Revels*, for example, one finds:

At the breaches   *3 [3rd Child-player].* First the title of this
in this speech   play is *Cynthia's Revels*, as any man can witness.
following, the o-   . . . ————————————Pray let me alone. . . . But I
ther two inter-   should have told you————(Looke, these emets
rupt him, still.   put me out here) that with this Amorphus, there
                         comes along a citizen's heire. . . .
                                            (F 1616, p. 182 [Ind. 37–68])

3. I wonder that any man is so mad to come to   *At the breaches*
see these rascally Tits play here————They   *he takes his ta-*
so act like so manie wrens, or pismires————   *bacco [sic].*
not the fifth part of a good face amongst them
all————and their music is abominable————
able to stretch a man's eares worse then tenne—
————pillories. . . .
                                            (F 1616, p. 183 [Ind. 120–25])

These directions prescribe or retroactively describe clever stage business; the timing of the last tobacco puff is particularly astute: "worse then tenne——[puff]—pillories." But Jonson's directions are quite different from those in the quartos we have been examining. They are textually self-conscious,[34] referring not only to the dialogue *("in this speech following")* but also typographical features of the text *("the breaches")*. Moreover, in their desire to dictate so precisely the timing of word and gesture, they depart from the more laissez-faire attitude of the other London playwrights, who usually indicated individual bits of business less precisely or not at all. In general, directions from the boys' plays or "literary" folio editions are more prescriptive and detailed, while those in quartos of plays associated with the men's companies are more laconic and give the actors more power and more discretion.

E. A. G. Honigmann, calling for greater standardization of modern editorial practices, has suggested that all directions that become operative midway through a line ought to be so placed.[35] Going further, Gary Taylor and Stanley Wells, in the modern spelling Oxford edition of Shakespeare,[36] place many of their own editorial directions midline, some in broken brackets and some merely in parentheses:

> They please me well. *(To Suffolk)* Lord Marquis, kneel down.
> *Suffolk kneels*
> We here create thee. . . .
> *Suffolk rises*
>   (*1 Contention [2 Henry VI]*, I.i.60–61)

> And this *(pointing to the chair of state)*, the regal seat, possess it, York.
>   (*The True Tragedy [3 Henry VI]*, I.i.26)

> *Rutland ⌈reviving ⌉:* So looks the pent-up lion o'er the wretch . . . .
>   (*The True Tragedy [3 Henry VI]*, I.iii.13)

Like Marston's asterisks and Jonson's breaches, these editorial practices "improve" the approximate placement of Elizabethan stage directions and seek to integrate staging information more fully into the text. However helpful to the modern student, those that interrupt the line risk destroying the rhythm of the verse in the reader's ear. They also significantly alter the visual design of Elizabethan editions and the implied responsibilities of their readers. At least to my eye and ear, while Elizabethan editions present a readable text, they also preserve a decorous separation of the voices of the dialogue and the voice of the stage directions. Directions and dialogue inhabit subtly distinguished spaces, and, while they can be read more or less linearly, they are syntactically self-contained. Further, their interpreters are expected to read with attention to the performance cues in the dialogue and to coordinate dialogue and directions on their own.

In a modernized edition such as the Oxford, however, the voice of stage directions is merged so completely with the dialogue that it loses its distinctness and its formal, decorous tone. More important, in the interpolated directions above, the voice of the stage directions is ever at our elbow as we read, pointing out what should be obvious to any practiced reader of drama. It burdens the actor with fairly rote directions and preempts the general reader's attempt to approach the text in an "actorly" fashion, probing it for tone and possible stage business. It makes the reader passive rather than active.

Conclusion

The evolution of the visual aspects of dramatic discourse bears on the question of marginality and centrality on the printed page. As it happens, what is "marginal" or "central" in the theoretical or figurative sense is not altogether decided by literal marginality or centrality on the page. Sometimes the marginal is privileged and primary. That is, marginal commentary (as in some medieval texts or in scholarly editions of our own day) may be the most important part of a text. As Evelyn Tribble has demonstrated in her study of margins and marginality, the authority and status of these aspects of a text are not "historical constants." In the printing of the vernacular Bibles, for example, "margins . . . were not places of the other but of authority itself, while the margins of humanist texts teem with social and literary guarantors."[37] In her analysis, during the early modern period "the marginality of the margins . . . is shifting, as major and minor, center and margin, are yet to be firmly established."[38] Whereas the post-eighteenth-century convention of the footnote reflects "a firm subordination" of note (or subtext) to text, she argues, "[s]uch subordination is by no means characteristic" of early modern texts.[39] Tribble's caveats would seem to apply to dramatic texts as well. A speech attribution in red ink in the right margin of a medieval playscript can hardly be viewed as "marginalized" or unimportant.

In the dramatic texts that have concerned us here, however, the distinction between the center and the margin, as a metaphor for greater or lesser importance, seems ultimately less relevant than the issue of how *all* the spaces on the page might be used to represent the multiple voices of drama. True, the early medieval production narrative gains some of its authority by inhabiting the central column in a more or less seamless unity with the dialogue. But the practical inconvenience of this visual presentation soon led to the various conventions of page design and calligraphy or typography discussed in these three chapters. The solution of the manuscript tradition was to maintain the marginal space as a separate channel unique to the voice of stage directions; speech attributions and many other directions resided wholly in the margins, and initial entries were written from margin to margin, extending the boundaries of the line and dividing the central text column into scenes. With the advent of print, a different solution was found, namely to place most stage directions within the text column, differentiating them by italics and white space to create an integrated, polyvocal text. While this design restored many directions to the "central" position, the overall effect was to integrate them more discreetly, to make them less disruptive visually and cognitively. Such a text served the needs of readers by deploying significant elements as a reader would meet them, top to bottom, left to right, in the normal course of reading. However, to call the text thus created "unitary," with the pejorative connotation the term now tends to carry, seems to me to miss the independence of voices and the degree of theatrical presence preserved by this textual design.[40]

Since any playtext is by its nature polyvocal, the voices of the characters and that of the stage directions vie for attention and authority. Since that competition is an important part of drama as a genre, the preservation of visually distinct, even quasi-marginal, stage directions in a playtext seems especially advantageous. Overall, through the use of italics, white space, and an effectively (if not literally) marginal position for some stage directions, Elizabethan printed plays succeeded in creating a text that invites reading yet still preserves the polyvocal nature of drama. As if in recognition of that fact, modern scholarly editions increasingly seek, and rightly so, to preserve the integrity of the apparatus and visual design of their copytexts as well as the integrity of the dialogue.

Part Two

The Grammar and Rhetoric of
Elizabethan Stage Directions

4

Self-Conscious and Self-Effacing Directions

When the voice of the stage directions speaks, what position does it take relative to the fictive world of the play? In the last chapter, we saw that the spatial relationship of stage directions and dialogue varied in medieval and Renaissance dramatic texts. The unified production narrative of early medieval drama, in which directions and dialogue were presented in an unbroken, seamless column of text, gave way to a scheme in which some directions spoke in a parallel voice, as marginal glosses on the text, while others (chiefly entries) interrupted the text column to mark the beginning of a scene. Ultimately, the design of printed plays for the professional theaters reintegrated dialogue and stage directions into a coherent, polyvocal text, which invited reading without sacrificing "presence" and dramatic decorum.

Just as the visual design of a playscript may position the directions inside or outside the text column, the directions may position themselves, grammatically and rhetorically, inside or outside the fictive world of the play. On the one hand, stage directions and other dramatic apparatus may be self-effacing; they may blend into the fictive world without calling attention to themselves, to the backstage world of the theater, or to the play as a written text. On the other hand, directions and other apparatus may be self-conscious about the theatrical or the textual aspects of the play, or both. Their stance or point of view is one of the most fundamental features of theatrical discourse.

Whether textually or theatrically aware, self-conscious directions address their interpreters from a position outside the world of the play. They address themselves directly to their interpreters as readers of "words," "lines," or other textual elements, or as producers of a play concerned with theatrical illusion and the time and space of performance. Self-effacing directions, on the other hand, though still clearly distinct from the dialogue, do not address their interpreters directly; they operate within the theatrical illusion and the fictive world of the play.

The practice of any theatrical community is rarely purely one or the other, but, in general, stage directions in English plays move from self-consciousness in medieval period to relative self-effacement in the late sixteenth and early seventeenth centuries, particularly in plays for the professional London theaters. Consequently, most of the syntactic features discussed in this chapter help us understand the voice of Elizabethan stage directions by contrast and indirection. That is, the vestiges of self-conscious syntax in directions for plays associated with the London theaters illuminate their usually self-effacing norm. Understanding the exceptions when they do appear is useful, but more important is appreciating how much the voice of Elizabethan directions depends on silence, ellipsis, and indicative verbs, rather than on the more explicit and self-conscious rhetoric of its antecedents.

Self-consciousness in directions may be signaled through diction, syntax, or both. As noted by earlier scholars, theatrically self-conscious diction includes the use of technical theatrical terms for stage machinery or architecture and "permissive" phrases ("others as many as may be"). Self-consciousness is also implied in references to theatrical illusion per se (in phrases such as "seeming" or "as though") and deictic or ostensive references to the sequence of the action ("Then," "Here," "In this fight," "wherein"). Less commonly, stage directions or other apparatus may also be textually self-conscious, referring to the play as a series of speeches, verses, lines, or words.

In addition to containing self-conscious diction, directions may be syntactically self-conscious. Self-conscious syntax includes verbs in the subjunctive or imperative mood that imply direct or indirect address of the actors and thus contribute to the awareness of the theatrical world. In addition to verb mood, direct address via second person pronouns ("Go thy ways out") creates self-conscious directions, as do other grammatical constructions that depart from the moment-by-moment decorum of the world of the play. Let us begin by looking at changes in the mood of the verb.

VERB MOOD: SUBJUNCTIVE, IMPERATIVE, INDICATIVE

One of the chief signs of self-consciousness in stage directions is the use of verbs in the imperative or subjunctive moods. Such verb forms were the

norm in medieval Latin directions, the most common being the subjunctive with imperative force. For example:

> *Tunc vadat figura ad ecclesiam, et Adam et Eva spacientur. . . . Interea*
> *demones discurrant per plateas . . . et veniant vicissim juxta paradisum.*
> *. . . Tunc veniat Diabolus ad Adam, et dicet ei:*
> [Then let the Figure {of God} go to the church and let Adam and Eve walk
> about. . . . Meantime let devils run to and fro . . . and let them come, one after
> the other, close to paradise. . . . Then let the Devil come to Adam and say:]
> *(Le Mystère d'Adam*, 112, S.D.)[1]

> *Exiant simul. Cantent:*
> [Let them go out together. Let them sing:]
> *(Mankind,* 161, S.D.)

> *Exiat*
> [Let him go out]
> *(Mankind,* 564, S.D.)

> *Dicant omnes*
> [Let them all say]
> *(Mankind,* 724, S.D.)

In addition to this "jussive" (imperative) subjunctive, one also finds the
future indicative, which also carries imperative force (the "shall/will" distinction, mostly lost to modern American English, but still available to other
English speakers). For example:

> *Tunc Figura manum extendet versus paradisum*
> [Then the Figure {of God} will stretch forth his hand toward Paradise]
> *(Adam,* 88, S.D.)

> *Tunc exibunt demones clamando*
> [Then the devils will go out clamoring]
> (Wakefield *Creation*, 131, S.D.)

> *Tunc ascendet Humanum Ge[n]us ad Mundum*
> [Then Mankind will go up to {the station of} the World]
> *(The Castle of Perseverance,* 614, S.D.)

Following their Latin models, early English stage directions are typically couched in the subjunctive or its English equivalents, the future indicative with "shall" and auxiliary verbs such as "must":

> *Here shal Satan go hom to his stage, and Mary shal entyr into the place alone. . . . .*
>
> *(Mary Magdalen* [Digby], 563, S.D.)

> *Here shall the clerk goon to ser Aristory, saluting him. . . .*
> *(Play of the Sacrament* [Croxton], 248, S.D.)

> *Here the ovyn must rive asunder. . . .*
> *(Play of the Sacrament,* 712, S.D.)

> *Let Worldly Man look suddenly about him.*
> *(Enough is as Good as a Feast,* c.1564, 1186, S.D.)[2]

These subjunctives address the players indirectly, through a third-person command. Rhetorically, they address nobody in particular; they seem aimed at a disinterested third party, perhaps the equivalent of the producer or stage manager, or the group as a whole. For their contemporary readers, the tone of the vernacular subjunctives may have been formal and polite rather than godlike and imperious. (I am thinking of an analogy with the Romance languages, in which the subjunctive *veuillez ouvrer la porte* becomes a polite form of request, in contrast to the brusque imperative *ouvrez la porte.*) But the tone is objective and impersonal, a dramatic analogue of "To whom it may concern." It may also be heard as rather grand and magisterial if echoes of biblical subjunctives, such as the *Fiat lux* of Genesis, are operative.[3]

Gradually, however, subjunctive verbs give way to the more familiar forms. The process can be seen in the late Tudor moralities. The directions in *Cambises*, for example, use subjunctive, imperative, and indicative verbs freely. In addition to the subjunctive

> *Here let him swinge them about.*
>
> (187, S.D.)

> *Here let him quake and stir.*
>
> (1165, S.D.)

one finds imperatives

> *Step aside and fetch him.*
>
> (417, S.D.)

> *Smite him in the neck with a sword to signify his death.*
>
> (460, S.D.[4])

and indicatives

> *He falleth down; she falleth upon him and beats him, and taketh away his weapons.*
>
> (273, S.D.)

Similarly, *Enough is as Good as a Feast* contains not only subjunctives (like the one cited above) but also: *"Go towards him"* (741, S.D.), *"be going out"* (577, S.D.), and *"fall down"* (1402, S.D.).

The imperative verbs alter the voice and address of directions. Now the players appear to be addressed directly in their professional capacities. This is especially true if, as is sometimes the case, the imperative is reinforced with second-person pronouns. For example, one occasionally encounters such directions as:

> *Up with* thy *staff, and be ready to smite* . . .
>
> (*Horestes*, TLN 175–78; emphasis added)

> *Make as if* yee *would fight.*
>
> (*Edward I*, TLN 467; emphasis added)

> *Sit down and knock* your *head.*
>
> (*Friar Bacon and Friar Bungay*, xi.56, S.D.; emphasis added)

The point of view in some early plays is not rigorously maintained, however, as the sometimes confusing pronoun shifts in *Horestes* illustrate:

> *Go a fore her and let her fal[l] downe upon* thee *and al[l] to beate* him.
>
> (TLN 755–61; emphasis added)

But sometimes, as in the following example from *Horestes*, the address of the company seems deliberately precise and direct (second-person plural), while references to a particular player revert to third-person subjunctive:

> *Go and make* your *lively battel, and let it be longe eare* you *can win the Citie and when* you *have won it, let Horestes bringe out his mother by the arme.* . . .
>
> (TLN 861–85; emphasis added)

For a time, the choice of imperative or indicative seems to have been an author's choice: John Bale in *Kynge Johan*, for example, prefers the imperative or subjunctive thirty out of thirty-eight times, whereas in the popular *King Darius* (Q 1565) the preference is reversed, twenty-nine indicatives to one imperative.[5] By the time of the London theaters, however, the indicative is clearly preferred (thirty-eight to eight in *The Spanish Tragedy*, forty-four to eleven in *Edward I*, twenty-six to three in *The Famous Victories*, twenty-three to four in the manuscript play *John a Kent and John a Cumber*).

Eventually indicative verbs (or, as we shall see, in the case of entries, a unique hybrid of the indicative and imperative) became the norm. Indeed, some forms that appear to be imperative, such as *"Draw"* or *"Sit,"* may be elliptical forms of plural indicative directions (*"[They] draw," "[They] sit"*).[6] Perhaps as the players and playwrights/script annotators were more likely to be acquaintances and colleagues, their relationships were sufficiently well established that simple indicatives served. As William B. Long has put it, the evidence of extant playhouse manuscripts attests that playwrights and players "generally understood and respected each other's professional capabilities."[7] In any event, as the theaters flourished, the stage directions assumed a voice that could indicate stage business economically, without elaborate politeness, and performers and writers alike became accustomed to a code that depended upon simplicity and economy rather than formality and syntactic completeness.

Like the left-margin speech prefix, third-person present indicative directions contribute to a more readerly text without abandoning dramatic decorum. To be sure, the third-person indicative is also the usual form of mediated narrative. *"He dies"* may thus seem less in tune with the mimetic decorum of drama than *"Die"* or *"Let him die."* But the present tense distinguishes such directions from ordinary narrative, in which the past tense is the norm ("There once was a king who had three daughters . . ."). The present indicative thus observes the decorum of drama: everything is happening in the present, here, now, as we watch or read.

In addition to blending with the present of the action, third-person present indicative directions allow the actor or other interpreter to maintain a consistent "third-person" relation with the text. Unlike imperatives, which address the actor-as-actor, third-person directions address the actor obliquely, through his character: *"He dies."* Thus, a lay reader coming to the text for pleasure need not cognitively adjust for an imperative or jussive subjunctive addressed to others. Compared to either subjunctives or imperative directions, third-person indicative directions are less self-conscious and thus less obtrusive.

On the face of it, for a stage direction to speak *about* the character rather than *to* the actor may also seem a narrative or literary technique. In fact, however, third-person indicative directions reflect theatrical practice.

They merge the actor into his character, as the audience is encouraged to do—or, for that matter, as theatrical companies, in Shakespeare's time and our own, do in rehearsing or discussing a production. As others have noted, playscripts used in Elizabethan theaters sometimes identify minor characters by inscribing the name of the player or apprentice in the margins ("Mr. Gibson," "Kit"), but the major characters are invariably identified by their fictive names alone. This is still largely true. Lists for props and diagrams for processional entries at the Royal Shakespeare Theatre and Oregon Shakespeare Festival follow the same practice today: major characters are identified by their characters' initials (KH for King Henry) and only minor figures, often doubled, are labeled with the actors' initials.[8]

Verb mood in English directions thus moves in a curious spiral. The Latin and English subjunctives address the players or their supervisors impersonally through a third-person command; the briefly reigning imperative verbs address the players directly in their capacities as actors; and the ultimately adopted third-person indicative verbs address the players obliquely through the characters their playing was bringing to life.

TEMPORAL AND SPATIAL MARKERS

Even apart from verb forms, medieval stage directions are highly self-conscious. Many directions attend explicitly to the temporal sequence of the performance. For example, the *Mystère d'Adam* begins with the rubric *"Tunc incipit lectio"* (Then the lesson/reading begins). The temporal sequence of actions and speeches is highlighted throughout the text with a verbal marker, most often *Tunc* (Then):

Tunc Figura manu demonstret paradisum Ade, dicens: Adam!
[Then the Figure {of God} will point out Paradise will his hand, saying: *Adam!*]
(80, S.D.)

Tunc mittet eo in paradisum, dicens: Dedanz vus met.
[Then he will send them into Paradise, saying: *I place you within.*]
(84, S.D.-85)

In other Anglo-Norman plays from this period one finds additional temporal markers, such as *Interim* (meanwhile), *Postea* (thereupon), and *Item* (again) used with a speech prefix, as in *"Item Rachel,"* for a character's subsequent speeches.[9]

Such temporal markers locate the directions outside the world of the play, fitting them into a production narrative contained in the rubrics and mediated by "then, then." As we have seen, in later periods the visual sequence of speeches and stage directions on the page was sufficient to represent the temporal sequence of the performance, but in early texts the spatial sequence on the page was verbally reinforced by an explicit narrative framework.

Rhetorically, just as the subjunctive verbs seemed addressed to someone other than the player in the here and now of the play, the audience for temporally marked directions is someone "outside" the play, managing the sequence of the performance or contemplating it in advance. In one Anglo-Norman text, *La Seinte Resurrection*, the directions not only begin with *"then,"* but they are also versified and cast in the past tense. They provide a complete and coherent narrative framework, perhaps meant to be read aloud between the passages of dialogue.[10] In this unusual instance, the directions may address spectators at the time of performance as well as performers prior to it. But in either case, the verbal marker "Then" self-consciously mediates the text to its various interpreters; the stage directions collectively create a narrative that contains (or at least runs parallel to) the unmediated and developing present of the fictive world.

The temporal or sequential emphasis in medieval directions testifies once again to the "auditory" mentality, the "oral residue," that Walter J. Ong attributes to the culture of the Middle Ages. As noted in chapter 1, the visual design of medieval manuscripts preserved the sense of the word as spoken, not as an object fixed in space, on the page.[11] Texts were identified not by title pages or even titles so much as by their *incipit*, their first words (as in the case of the Lord's Prayer being known as the "Our Father").[12] According to Ong, early dramatic manuscripts, in particular, were a unique blend of chirographic (writing-based) and oral cultures, since they were "composed in writing and then memorized verbatim to be presented orally."[13]

Given Ong's analysis of the link between oral cultures and temporality, it is easy to see why medieval stage directions and dramatic apparatus emphasize temporal sequence. Before plays came to be called "plays" *(ludi),* the notion of order or sequence is often preserved in their Latin titles, as in the *Ordo Repraesentationis Adae* (literally "the order of the representation of Adam").

Finally, the emphasis on the order of events, which is largely preserved in dramatic texts for the next two centuries, is understandable given the processional context of much medieval religious drama. The players were often literally in motion on pageant wagons succeeding each other in a single outdoor playing space. The processional mode lingers in the rubrics of the later Corpus Christi plays, which are sometimes entitled *Processus* (Bevington translates as "story") and concluded with an indication of which story "follows" *(sequitur)*.[14] The nomenclature also suggests that the writers and interpreters of such directions thought of the play primarily as a narrative unfolding in time through speeches and gestures orchestrated by the stage directions.

The subsequent evolution of the temporal marker *Tunc* (then) testifies to the changing relationship between the writers of directions and their interpreters, and to the growth of a spatial (rather than temporal) mentality in manuscript plays. *Tunc* is still common in some English Corpus Christi plays, such as the Wakefield *Creation:*

> *Tunc cepit Cherubim Adam per manum*
> [Then the Cherubim takes Adam by the hand]
>
> (197, S.D.)

and in morality plays, such as *The Castle of Perseverance:*

> *Tunc ascendet Humanum Ge<n>us ad Mundum*
> [Then Mankind will go up to the World]
>
> (614, S.D.)

By the fifteenth century, however, especially in vernacular directions, a "spatial" marker (*Hic*, here) is often provided instead. In a French saint's play, c. 1450, one finds *Cy (Ici)* introducing both dialogue and stage business:

> *Cy [S. Pierre] parle a S. Estiene*
> [Here St. Peter speaks to St. Stephen]
>
> *Cy se revestent*
> [Here they put their clothes back on][15]

Similarly, in the Wakefield *Creation:*

> *Hic Deus recedit a suo solio*
> [Here God withdraws to his throne]
>
> (76, S.D.)

and in the Digby *Mary Magdalen:*

> *Here entyr Syrus the fader of Mary*
>
> (48, S.D.)

The preference for "Here" over "Then" seems to reflect the shift in perception that Ong notes, namely the growth of "spatial" thinking as writing and especially print, with its regularizing tendencies, fixed the word in space rather than time. In addition, and more important for the purposes of this book, the change from temporal to spatial marker suggests an altered conception of the text and a change in the point of view. Whereas "Then" locates readers or interpreters outside the text, "Here" locates them inside it. And whereas the "Then" formula seems to address itself to someone contemplating a production, looking ahead, with the whole of the narrative in mind, the "Here" formula invokes a spatiotemporal present. Like the indicative verb forms evolving at the same time, the spatial marker addresses those involved in the production moment by moment, within the here and now of actual (as opposed to potential) performance.

Despite these subtle changes, the "Then" or "Here" formulae remain both theatrically and textually self-conscious; they refer equally to a point in the text and a moment in the action as it unfolds. Both actor and stage manager are addressed self-consciously although efficiently in their professional capacities.

To a great extent, the rhetorical point of view of such directions is conventional, not reflective of the actual circumstances of address. Presumably, except when orally prompted during performance (the exception and not the rule), the player receives and interprets his portion of the text prior to performance to con it.[16] The bookholder also reads the directions prior to performance to plan or rehearse stage business, blocking, and special effects, though he also presumably uses them to monitor the performance proper.

At the same time, the discursive formality of late medieval and early Tudor directions ("here" plus the English subjunctive) seems well suited to their real rhetorical situations, namely the address at a distance of dedicated amateurs or professional traveling troupes. Mystery plays performed year after year on ritual or festive occasions were handed down, presumably from one group, even one generation, of players to another. In the interludes offered for acting, the identity and particular circumstances of future players was likewise unknown. Consequently, the authors and publishers sought to be of all possible assistance. They included doubling patterns and assured prospective performers that the piece was "most convenient" for performance, or that "seven may easily play this Interlude."[17] The tone of the directions is of a piece with the title-page rhetoric and doubling lists: it is at once authoritative and ingratiating, and brevity is sacrificed for syntactic completeness and specificity.

Temporal and spatial markers do occur in early plays for the London theaters. They can be found, for example, in the anonymous *Famous Victories of Henry the Fifth* (c. 1588, Q 1598). In the somewhat later *Arden of Feversham* (Q 1592), many entries begin *"Here,"* and, what is more unusual, almost all ten of its mid-scene directions for action begin with *"Then"*:

> *Then Arden draws forth Mosbie's sword.*
>
> (i.307, S.D.)[18]

> *Then she throws the broth on the ground.*
>
> (i.365, S.D.)

"Then" occurs once in Marlowe's *Edward II* (Q 1594):

> *Then Gurney stabs Lightborn.*
>
> (xxii.115, S.D.)[19]

Marked directions also occur occasionally in Heywood's *1 Edward IV* (1594-99, Q 1600):

> *Here the rest offer to follow him.*
>
> (C2ᵛ)

> *Here enter the Queen and Duchess with their riding rods.*
>
> (C3)

Heywood's directions are often idiosyncratic, including one unusual *"There"* marker:

> *There he draws his sword and knights them.*
>
> (D4)[20]

Peele's *Edward I* (Q 1593) contains several temporally marked directions, including three *"Then"* formulae and other temporally explicit directions:

> *Here let the Potter's wife go to the Queen.*
>
> (TLN 2543)

> *Here she dies.*
>
> (TLN 2345)

After the christening and marriage done, the heralds having attended,
they pass over. . . .

(TLN 2133–34)

Then all passe in their order to the king's pavilion.

(TLN 2141–42)

After the show, and the King and Queen with all the lords and ladies in
place, Longshanks speaketh.

(TLN 2182–83)

After the sight of John Baliol is done, enter Mortimer pursuing of the
rebels.

(TLN 2299–2300)

Then make the proclamation upon the walls.

(TLN 2304)

Even so, these instances are exceptions to Peele's normal usage. In a total
of approximately ninety directions for entries and stage business in *Ed-*
ward I, such temporal markers occur only eleven times.

Similarly, an initial *"Here"* can be found in some plays by Shakespeare
in directions for stage business, although it does not occur in entries and
exits, as was common in medieval drama:

Here alarum; they are beaten back. . . .

(*2 Henry VI*, I.ii.21, S.D.)

Here they fight, and Joan de Pucelle overcomes.

(*2 Henry VI*, I.ii.103, S.D.)[21]

Here they both call him.

(*1 Henry IV*, I.iv.80, S.D.)

Here they embrace.

(*1 Henry IV*, III.iii.30, S.D.)[22]

But these Shakespearean examples are also exceptions, and the unmarked,
self-effacing directions familiar in most Elizabethan texts are the rule. In
the directions in all the extant texts of Shakespeare, quarto and folio, *"Here"*
occurs only thirty-eight times, and three of the earliest plays (*1, 2,* and *3*
Henry VI) account for fifteen of them.[23] In several instances where the quarto

text has *"Here,"* the comparable Folio direction eliminates the old-fashioned marker. In *Richard III*, I.ii, for example, the quartos have:

> *Here she lets fall the sword.*
>
> (Q1–6)[24]

The folio reads:

> *She falls the sword.*
>
> (F1, TLN 376)

Similarly in *1 Henry IV*, the quarto has:

> *Here they embrace.*
>
> (Q 1598, V.ii.100, S.D.)

The Folio substitutes:

> *They embrace.*
>
> (F1, TLN 2889)

In unmarked directions, those without either *"Here"* or *"Then,"* reliance on page design replaces the verbal marker.[25] It is understood that the direction comes into play vis-à-vis the dialogue in accordance with its placement on the page. It has the advantages of efficiency and a balance between visibility and unobtrusiveness. The absence of the temporal or spatial marker also means that the voice of the direction is less self-conscious and obtrusive. While the status of a direction will still be clear if normal typography and page layout are observed, the disappearance of the temporal/spatial marker is one of the changes that resulted in the generally self-effacing directions of plays for the professional theaters.

Temporally marked directions do survive in plays for the London theaters within processional entries and midscene directions for extended stage business, such as battle sequences or dumb shows. The grammar and rhetoric of such paragraph-length directions will be discussed more thoroughly in chapter 5, but it should be observed at this point that the appearance of an initial *"Here"* is rare in such directions. The temporal markers (*"then," "next," "before"*) tend to be internal, not the first word of the direction. In such extended, complex directions it is not surprising that explicit sequencing should appear, but this is different from the convention of an initial temporal marker for every direction, which, as argued above, regularly locates the voice of the directions outside the text and/or performance, referring to either or both self-consciously.

Theatrically Self-Conscious Directions

While self-conscious verbal markers in early medieval drama create awareness of the temporal sequence of speeches and events, medieval directions are often self-conscious in a more specifically theatrical way. These directions provide detailed instructions on what effects are required and how to achieve them. They stress specific theatrical illusions, not the mere fact of sequence. They differ in syntax from what I would call "theatrically informative" directions valued by theater historians, and they heighten the degree of self-consciousness occasioned by technical diction, such as "stage," "within," or "above."

For example, in the Anglo-Norman *Adam*, several stage directions are explicit about how to achieve the desired theatrical illusions. The murder of Abel is to be enacted as follows:

> *Then Abel will kneel to the east. And he will have a pot concealed in his garments, which Cain will strike violently, as though killing Abel. Abel will lie prostrate as though dead.*
>
> (722, S.D.; Bevington's translation)

Such a direction is theatrically self-conscious in that it is addressed to performers with the goal of securing vigorous and realistic stage effects. The concealed pot will protect the actor playing Abel and relieve the actor playing Cain of the necessity of pulling his punches. The voice of the directions is also theatrically self-conscious in another respect: the players are to perform certain actions *"as though . . . ,"* a phrase which clearly acknowledges theatrical illusion. Although in the performance the actor playing Cain must *"strike as though killing"* Abel, in the world of the play, Cain really kills his brother. The wonderfully graphic directions for violence in *Cambises* are similarly self-conscious and explicit about the means of illusion. A postexecution indignity is cleverly simulated:

> *Flay him with a false skin.*
>
> (464, S.D.)

and a bloody murder is accompanied by

A little bladder of vinegar pricked.

(729, S.D.)

The consciousness of theatrical illusion also comes through whenever directions directly refer to prior preparations regarding stage furniture. For example, in the *Adam* the altars of Cain and Abel are

> *two great stones that have been readied for the purpose. One stone will have been set at a distance from the other so that, when the Figure [of God] appears, the stone of Abel will be on his right hand, the stone of Cain on his left.*
>
> (666, S.D.; Bevington's translation)

The present perfect, future, and future perfect tenses clearly remove such a direction from the here and now of the action. In a complex sequence of tenses, the direction retroactively instructs the players about the desired placement of stage furniture before the play begins.

Comparative (as opposed to simple) references to costume are also theatrically self-conscious. In the procession of the prophets that concludes the *Adam*, one direction reads:

> *Let Solomon come forward, with the same adornments as those in which David advanced, except that he should seem younger. . . .*
>
> (790, S.D., Bevington's translation)

By comparing the costumes of characters at different moments in the action ("*the* same *adornments. . . in which David* advanced"), the direction maintains an atemporal, outside perspective, from which the details of all aspects of the production are simultaneously available for discussion. Like the phrase "*as though,*" the verb "*seem*" locates the direction outside the reality of the dramatic world. In the play, Solomon *is* younger; from the point of view of the makeup and costume master, he must be made to *seem* so.

The acknowledgment of illusion sounds strange to ears used to the voice of Elizabethan directions. "*As though dead*" looks at Abel's demise as acting and directs him how to achieve the desired effect. In an Elizabethan play, the voice of the direction typically remains inside the illusion; the conventional form is "*He dies*" or "*Dies.*" And if a direction does use the phrase, e.g., when Falstaff "*falls down as if he were dead*" (*1 Henry IV*, V.iv.76, S.D.), the character is pretending, as well as the actor.

Sometimes the information supplied in a direction suggests a descriptive rather than strictly theatrical point of view. That is, the emphasis is on intangible matters such as atmosphere or the motivation of a character, rather than on the concrete means of illusion:

> *Then they will both go to a place apart and, as it were [quasi] secret, where Cain, like a madman, will rush upon Abel, wishing to kill him.*
>   (*Adam*, 678, S.D., Bevington's translation)

The parenthetical insertion, *"as it were [quasi] secret,"* expands descriptively on the more concrete phrase *"a place apart."* The provision of information about motives (*"wishing to kill him"*) and the descriptive simile (*"like a madman"*) would all be at home in an epic or other mediated narrative. Except for the future tense (an alternative form of the imperative), the voice of this direction is more narrative than theatrically self-conscious. But it is easy to see that the purpose of this narrative information is ultimately to guide the players in performance by describing the manner of required actions and motives that the players presumably are to convey as best they can through gesture, facial expression, and so on. And, like more strictly theatrical directions, the syntax of such directions mediates the dramatic world to its interpreters.

Typically, the directions in the production narrative of the *Adam* and other early medieval plays are descriptively and theatrically self-conscious all at once:

> *Then let Adam eat part of the apple. When he has eaten, he will recognize his sin at once, and will bend over so that he cannot be seen by the people. And he will strip off his festive garments and will put on poor clothes sewn together with fig leaves, and, manifesting great sorrow he will begin his lamentation.*
>   (314, S.D., Bevington's translation)

In sum, by means of their syntax, such as temporal markers, verb mood, verb tense, and subordinate, especially adjectival, clauses (*"the same adornments* in which *David advanced," "a pot . . . ,* which *Cain will strike violently"*), these early directions view the action from outside the here and now of the dramatic world. Freed from the moment-by-moment action of the plot, the voice of the directions mediates the dramatic world. It moves freely back and forth over the events of the play and the preparations for its production, supplying information in a confidential channel to performers and other readers.

As in the case of the temporal marker, self-consciously theatrical directions seem addressed to the medieval equivalent of the producer, or stage manager, even more than to the individual actor. This inference is borne out most clearly by the extraordinary prefatory directions in the *Adam* and some later medieval texts, like the *Castle of Perseverance*. In the *Adam*, a preface regarding the scenic requirements of the play and the coaching of the actors anticipates Hamlet's instructions to the players at Elsinore:

> *And let this Adam be well coached when he must give answers; lest in answering he should be either too hasty or too slow. Nor him alone, but let all persons be coached thus, so that they may speak in an orderly manner and make gestures appropriate to the things of which they speak; and, in their verses, let them neither add nor subtract a syllable but pronounce them all steadily and speak those things that are to be spoke in their due order. Whoever will mention the name of Paradise, let him look in its direction and point it out with his hand.*
>
> (0, S.D., Bevington's translation)

The well-known prefatory apparatus of *The Castle of Perseverance* is similarly detailed about preproduction matters. The tone of this later play seems a little more relaxed, however. The manuscript includes a diagram of the desired staging, with such annotations as:

> This is the watyr a-bowte the place, if any dych may be mad, ther it shal be pleyed, or ellys that it be strongly barryd al a-bowt.[26]

Though equally theatrically self-consciousness, this voice is more flexible voice than that of the earlier *Adam;* it is willing to offer alternatives and imagine the contingencies of different production companies and spaces. Nonetheless, the putative audience for such directions is Peter Quince, bookkeeper, prompter, and stage manager extraordinaire, or the company as a whole, not an individual player like Bottom. Rather than coaching the individual actors moment by moment, such directions address the producer or the players as a group.

In some later medieval plays, stage directions are less frequent as well as less detailed and self-conscious. The text of *Everyman* (c. 1495), for example, is virtually devoid of directions other than speech prefixes, and *Mankind* (c. 1465) is also lightly annotated. Perhaps as the tradition of playing developed, some writers implicitly relied more heavily on traditional business, and on the experience of the veteran amateurs of the Corpus Christi cycles and the professional players of the traveling troupes. Nonetheless, though the sheer bulk of the production narrative waned, the directions in most Tudor interludes remained theatrically self-conscious.

For example, Skelton's *Magnificence* (c. 1520) is full of directions that frankly acknowledge theatrical illusion (in English translation):[27]

And let him make as if he doffs his cap ironically.

(748, S.D.)

Here let him make as if he were reading the letter silently. . . .

(324, S.D.)

The subjunctive verbs and *"as if"* phrasing clearly evoke the theatrical perspective. Theatrical self-consciousness comes through also in the following:

Here let Folly enter, shaking a bauble and making a commotion, beating on tables and suchlike.

(1040, S.D.)

The permissive tag *"suchlike"* self-consciously delegates the rest of the business to the players, but in its comparative reference *("beating on tables and suchlike")* it creates a further element of self-consciousness, similar to that created by *"accordingly"* and *"in similar manner"* in the directions in the *Adam*, quoted above. A particular form of theatrical self-consciousness occurs in John Bale's *King Johan* and other early interludes. The scribal portion of the *King Johan* manuscript contains (sometimes erroneous) doubling instructions:[28]

Here kyng Johan and Sivile order go owt and Sivile order drese hym for Sedewsyon.

(556, S.D.)

Here Nobelyte go owt and dresse for the cardynall.

(1533, S.D.)

As we have seen, directions in plays for the professional London theaters moved away from the theatrically self-conscious "directorial" voice of medieval stage directions towards a more self-effacing voice that addressed the players indirectly, laconically, and unobtrusively. However, when they do occur, theatrically self-conscious references to stage business in Elizabethan directions take interesting forms and reveal interesting priorities.

The formula, *"as at work,"* or *"as from dinner,"* or *"as in his study,"* or *"as at Mile End"* (or some other locale) is fairly common in Elizabethan plays:

Enter Falconbridge with his troops marching, as being at Mile-end.
                                                    (*1 Edward IV*, C4)

*Enter Cambridge, Scroop, and Gray, as in a chamber, and set down at a
table consulting about their treason. . . .*
                                    (*Sir John Oldcastle*, TLN 2086ff.)

This formula would seem to be an outgrowth of the *"as if"* directions in
medieval drama. Such directions are best understood, as Alan Dessen has
argued, not as calls for elaborate scenic effects but as calls for certain evoca-
tive props (such as stools and needlework, napkins, a book, or pike staves).[29]
"As being at Mile-end" might suggest marching in a routine, training mode,
as opposed to weary troops on a forced march or a tense and aggressive
prebattle muster. Similarly, although there is no way to convey nonverbally
the location of the nobles' imminent deaths (Pomfret), the tableau of the
prisoners surrounded by halberdiers might indeed be a sign of "nobles being conveyed to their deaths," in contrast, say, to the unceremonious cart-
ing of common offenders to hanging in *Edward I*. In any case, in contrast
to their unself-conscious equivalents *"at work,"* and *"in prison,"* such directions speak, if only vestigially, in terms of theatrical illusion, rather than
dramatic reality.

In his most recent discussion of such directions, Dessen speculates
that directions beginning with *as* implicitly contain the mentality of the
earlier *"as if"* directions, and that they attest to the fundamentally presentational mode of Elizabethan drama. As he puts it, they "call our attention
to a revealing gap between theatrical effects linked to imaginative play and
game . . . and theatrical effects geared to verisimilitude."[30] I agree with
Dessen's analysis, in the main, but the difference between the fully self-
conscious *"as if"* and the more descriptive *"as at"* is important for the
evolving voice of English stage directions. While the presentational mode
of "play and game" is available to the Elizabethan dramatist, so is a much
greater degree of verisimilitude. While this greater realism is not usually
expressed scenically in realistic stage furnishings such as trees or tents
(which Dessen discusses), the drama does encourage a far greater historical and psychological realism than its medieval forebears. The evolution
of the grammar of stage directions, as I have been arguing, seems itself to
capture and convey this particular blend of dramatic decorum. Thus I would
emphasize, not downplay, the difference between the theatrically self-conscious diction of the medieval stage *("as if")* and the more descriptive
Elizabethan phrases *("as at," "as in,"* or *"as from").*

In addition to phrases with *"as,"* self-consciousness in Elizabethan directions can take other forms. In an otherwise unremarkable direction for the masque in *Perkin Warbeck,* some details of costume are indicated by a kind of "cultural shorthand":

> *Enter at one door four Scotch antics, accordingly habited; enter at another four wild Irish in trouses, long-haired, and accordingly habited. . . .*
> (II.iii.111, S.D.)

"Accordingly" steps for a moment outside the here and now of the play, indicating in shorthand to the players the desired, presumably traditional, ethnic costume. Just in case, in the second clause, *"trouses"* ("fitted trousers with stockings attached worn by Irishmen and Scottish highlanders" is Anderson's gloss), are specified, but other costume details are again delegated to the players *("habited accordingly")*. Like the phrase *"as being at Mile-End,"* such a direction alludes implicitly to the real-life knowledge of the players. In this respect, though arguably examples of self-conscious directions, they contrast with the medieval examples above: rather than instructing the players in detail, they rely on the assumed shared experience (theatrical and otherwise) of their interpreters to fill in the blanks.

A series of three directions in *The Spanish Tragedy* suggest that theatrically self-conscious directions were sometimes motivated by simple economy. The first gives us the Elizabethan norm: third-person indicative, present tense:

> *He takes the scutcheon and gives it to the King. . . .*
> (I.iv.25, S.D.)

But explicit references to this earlier direction in two subsequent ones creates a momentarily self-consciousness voice. Although the past tense of the first repetition is softened into the present participle of the second, the comparative references speak from a vantage point outside the dramatic present:

> *He doth as he did before.*
> (I.iv.35, S.D.)

> *Doing as before.*
> (I.iv.47, S.D.)

In this case, economy of reference takes precedence over consistency of point of view. Similar directions can be found in the 1619 quarto of

Heywood's *1 Edward IV* (c. 1594–99). Here a need for clarity about a character's intermittent disguise results in a backward-looking reference:

> *Enters again muffled in his cloak.*
>
> (H3ᵛ)

> *King enters in his former disguise.*
>
> (I3)

A similar instance occurs in Munday's *John a Kent* manuscript:

> *Enter at one door John a Kent, hermit-like, as before. . . .*
>
> (TLN 406)

An unusual deictic reference to a group of characters can be found in the same manuscript:

> *Enter Pembrook, Morton, Oswen, Amery, and to them this crew, marching, one drest like a Moor. . . .*
>
> (TLN 367f.)

In this case, in addition to the self-conscious reference to the characters, the term *"crew"* seems to abandon the usually dispassionate, objective voice of Elizabethan directions; the professional playwright permits himself a moment of superiority vis-à-vis the preposterously dressed tradesmen and their amateur pageant.

In Munday et al.'s *Sir John Oldcastle,* two battle sequences also begin deictically (emphasis added):

> In this fight, *the Bailiff is knocked down. . . .*
>
> (TLN 23)

> In this fight, *the Lord Herbert is wounded. . . .*
>
> (TLN 55)

In *Friar Bacon and Friar Bungay* (Q 1594), Greene also cues some stage business deictically:

> *All this while Lacy whispers Margaret in the ear.*
>
> (xi.40, S.D.)

> *With this a great noise. The Head speaks.*
>
> (xi.60, S.D.)

However fleetingly, the demonstrative pronoun introduces a self-conscious reference to the action per se.

Slightly different are clauses beginning *"wherein"* or *"whereat,"* alternative mediating constructions found elsewhere:

> *Here is a very fierce assault on all sides, wherein the Prentices do great service.*
>
> (*1 Edward IV*, Cᵛ)

> *Shore and his soldiers issue forth and repulse him, after excursions, wherein the rebels are disperst. . . .*
>
> (*1 Edward IV*, D3)

> *They play, and the boy sings, whereat the Bridgrooms come forth in their nightgowns and kerchers on their heads.*
>
> (*John a Kent*, TLN 581–82)

> *Alarum: Excursions, wherein Talbot's son is hemm'd about, and Talbot rescues him.*
>
> (*1 Henry VI*, IV.vi.0, S.D.)

> *Alarums to the fight, wherein both the Staffords are slain.*
>
> (*2 Henry VI*, IV.iii.0, S.D.)

The *"wherein"* clause does not self-consciously refer to the dramatic text or action as such, but it does introduce a mediating syntactic element. A strictly unmediated, moment-by-moment version of the last direction can be found by comparing its counterpart in the "bad" quarto of this play, which eschews any subordinate constructions (or subject-verb agreement):

> *Alarums to the battle, and sir Humphrey Stafford and his brother is slaine. . . .*
>
> (*1 Contention* (Q 1600), F4ᵛ)

In other instances, an occasional *"who"* may be introduced to clarify a complex direction. Heywood uses such constructions in his characteristically descriptive directions:

> *Enter the Queen, and the Marquis of Dorset leading Jane Shore, who falls down on her knees before the Queen fearful and weeping.*
>
> (*2 Edward IV*, P4ᵛ)

Two examples can also be found in the Shakespeare Folio:

King takes his seat, whispers Lovell, who goes to the Cardinall.
(Henry VIII, III.ii.35, S.D.)

Enter Douglas, he fights with Falstaff, who falls down as if he were dead. . . .
(1 Henry IV, V.iv.76, S.D.)

At the same point in the quarto of *1 Henry IV*, however, no clause mediates the dramatic information; pronouns are left in strict moment-by-moment sequence, even though ambiguity results:

Enter Douglas, he fighteth with Falstaff, he falls down as if he were dead. . . .

In general, throughout the Elizabethan period self-effacing directions were the norm. When one finds a self-conscious theatrical direction in the medieval form, such as

Here within they must beat with their hammers.
(Thomas Lord Cromwell, A2ᵛ)

it is an exception to the more common (though less informative and explicit) *"Noise within."* Even more unusual is the theatrically self-conscious specificity of the following direction from *Alphonsus, Emperor of Germany:*

They must have axes made for the nonce to fight withall, and while one strikes, the other holds his back without defense.
(Q 1654, E1ᵛ)

Such a direction is reminiscent of those in the *Adam* and other early religious dramas. Far from relying on the experience and resources of the players, it does not assume a supply of prop axes will be on hand; they must be *"made for the nonce."* The title page of the quarto of 1654 refers to the play's having been performed at the Blackfriars Theatre "by his late Majesties Servents," but the direction has more in common with those for amateur players at the universities than it does with plays for the professional theater.

Overall, while theatrically self-conscious directions can be found in playtexts to 1600 and beyond, the trend is away from self-conscious directions towards self-effacing ones that remain within the dramatic illusion. This in turn signals a comparable shift in the implied audience. Instead of directly addressing the stage manager or actor in his professional capacities,

Elizabethan directions evolve into the tactful and indirect address of actor-as-character (or actor-as-reader). This rhetorical distinction complements, I think, one William Long has drawn between the content of directions written by amateur and professional playwrights in the Elizabethan period: the amateurs are more likely to specify *how* something should be done, whereas the professionals in their "advisory directions" describe *what* they want and leave implementation to the players or later consultation.[31]

TEXTUALLY SELF-CONSCIOUS DIRECTIONS

In the directions of early religious drama, theatrical and textual self-consciousness are not always distinguishable. Both are often subsumed in the emphasis on temporal sequence and on the spoken (or sung) word. At the beginning of the *Adam*, for example, we read:

> *Qua finita chorus cantet:* ℞ *Formavit igitur dominus.*
> [When this is finished let the choir sing: {the response} *Formavit igitur dominus.*]
>
> *Quo finito dicat Figura* Adam! *Qui respondeat* Sire!
> [When this is finished let the Figure {of God} say: *Adam!* Who must answer: *Sire!*]
>
> (0, S.D)

These rubrics are self-conscious in that the demonstrative pronoun *("this")* refers deictically to particular elements of the sequence. The demonstrative pronoun is not common in the *Adam;* it seems reserved for references to the singing of the responsorial verses that occur at key points of the play proper. Nonetheless, it points up a feature of the earliest directions. The reference of *"this"* is ambiguous: it may refer to the scriptural passage per se or to the *act* of its being sung or spoken. Thus, *"this"* might be construed as either theatrically or textually self-conscious. Given that no "action" in the usual sense has occurred, the textual (or perhaps more precisely, the verbal) element seems uppermost. But the important point would seem to be that the two are not clearly distinguishable. The script is a seamless blend of speaking and doing, and the stage directions cue both self-consciously. Recalling the prefatory instructions for directing the actors, one might speculate that at this point action (especially gestures) were so stylized and so fused to the words that to refer to one was to refer to the other.

In later Tudor religious plays and interludes, however, stage directions refer more clearly to the play as a spoken text or to textual elements within the play. Sometimes the self-conscious, deictic reference is still general, as in the Brome *Abraham and Isaac* (c. 1470–80):

> *Here Abraham leyd a cloth on Ysaaces face,* thus *seyyng,* . . .
> (289, S.D.; emphasis added)

> *Here Abraham mad hys offryng, knelyng and seyyng* thus, . . .
> (382, S.D.; emphasis added)[32]

In the Digby *Mary Magdalen*, however, the reference is specific:

> *With* this word *vij [seven] dyllys xall de-woyde [go out] frome the woman . . .*
> (691, S.D.; emphasis added)[33]

In Skelton's *Magnificence*, at least one direction seems textually self-conscious:

> *Despairingly let [Poverty] say* these words. . . .
> (2038, S.D.; emphasis added)[34]

A comparable direction immediately following is cast in terms of action (though the action is that of emotional speaking):

> *Here Magnificence dolorously maketh his moan.*
> (2048, S.D.)

Some directions in *Wit and Science*, written c. 1530–48 for the boys of St. Paul's by their master, John Redford, are more clearly textually self-conscious in coordinating the speakers, or in this case the singers:

> *Here Wit, Instruccion, Studye, and Diligence sing "Wellcum, my nowne":
> and S[c]ience . . . come in at "As" and answer ev're second verse.*
> (985, S.D.)

Song verses are self-consciously alluded to in Bale's *King Johan*, too. Two characters enter *"singing one after another,"* and their Latin songs are cued deictically:

> *Us[urped] P[ower] (syng* this*): Super flumina.* . . .
> *Pr[ivate] W[ealth] (syng* this*): Quomodo cantibimus.* . . .
> (764–65; emphasis added)

In a later manuscript play, *The Marriage Between Wit and Wisdom* (c. 1579), perhaps by Francis Merbury, instructions about the logistics of the songs and special musical effects are also often self-conscious, both theatrically and textually:

> *Here shall Wantoness sing* this song *to the tune of "Attend thee, Go play thee."* . . .
>
> (Fol. 10ᵛ; emphasis added)

The directions in this interlude also refer deictically to the text itself:

> *Enter Good Nurture speaking* this.
>
> (Fol. 11; emphasis added)

> *Here he [Idleness] espieth Search coming in and goeth up and down saying* . . . as in the first five lines.
>
> (Fol. 21; emphasis added)

Directions in university plays are also likely to be "metatextual," as in these examples from the induction to Peter Hausted's *The Rival Friends* (Q 1632):

> *At* the first word that Venus sung, *the curtain was drawn and they discovered.*
>
> (B1ᵛ; emphasis added)

> *At Phoebus his going in, the Chorus sing* the last two lines.
>
> (B2; emphasis added)

The directions from Merbury and Hausted that refer to *"lines"* most clearly imagine the text as visually presented on the page, rather than as words or speeches to be spoken in a temporal sequence.

Though not uncommon in humanist and academic plays such as those cited above, self-conscious textual references are relatively rare in plays for the London theaters. A few references to the spoken text occur in plays by Heywood and Munday, two playwrights often idiosyncratic and discursive in their directions. In Heywood's *2 Edward IV*, some directions refer explicitly to portions of the text or a character's speech precisely to indicate the stage effects he desires:

> {*All this aside.*
>
> (M3ᵛ)

This while the hangman prepares. Shore at this speech *mounts up the ladder.*

(R1ᵛ; emphasis added)

One direction also alludes directly to the improvised dialogue delegated to the performer:

Jockie is led to whipping over the stage, speaking some words, but of no importance. . . .

(L5)[35]

Sir John Oldcastle by Munday and others also has a self-conscious textual reference coordinating simultaneous speeches:

} *Both at once all this.*

(Bracketing TLN 83–87)

A self-conscious reference to a textual *prop* occurs in a long direction for the funeral procession in *King John and Matilda* by Robert Davenport (1628–34, Q 1655) written for Queen Henrietta's Men at the Cockpit and later also performed there by Beeston's Boys:

Enter the King and Lords, the Lady Abbess, ushering Matilda's hearse, born by Virgins, this motto *fastend unto it: . . . To Piety and Chastity. . . .*

(V.iii.0; emphasis added)[36]

However, the few textually self-conscious directions in plays for the professional theaters tend to emphasize the word as spoken rather than as written.

Our examination of point of view in stage directions from the professional theaters highlights the emergence of an efficient, unobtrusive, self-effacing dramatic code that paralleled (and in part empowered) the emergence of a mixed presentational *and* representational drama from the more purely presentational drama of the medieval period. Drama is never a pure genre. It always blends presentational and representational, mediated and unmediated, verisimilar and symbolic elements. Elizabethan plays employ metadramatic address, narration, and description, as well as dramatic representation, both in their apparatus (directions for dumb shows and battle sequences) and in their dialogue (appeals to the audience, reports of offstage action, exposition of prior events, etc.). Unlike some medieval drama, however, the persistence of presentational aspects in Elizabethan drama did not entail a thoroughgoing self-consciousness of illusion in the voice of the stage directions. Rather, Elizabethan playwrights developed an oblique, self-effacing, yet authoritative code that communicated staging information to theater professionals and lay readers without burdening or distracting them with an awareness of the mechanics of stage illusion.

5

Entries and Exits

All actors know the importance of entrances, but anyone who has experimented with productions on models of the Elizabethan scaffold comes to recognize their meaning in a particularly acute way. It is not an exaggeration to say that the action of an Elizabethan play *consists* of entrances. They are the means by which the story is told; the controllers of the illusion of time and place; the sign-posts for the understanding of the plot.

—David Bradley, *From Text to Performance*
in the Elizabethan Theatre

In the anecdote that began this study, actor Nancy Palk responded to my question about her approach to Shakespeare's stage directions by asking, "What stage directions? You mean *Enter, Exit*?" Her question served at that point to highlight the invisibility of many Elizabethan directions, but it also testifies to the relatively greater visibility of Elizabethan entries and exits.

Entry and exit directions are more visible and memorable partly because they are so fundamental. As the quote from David Bradley above suggests, the cleared stage followed by an entrance defines the boundaries of each scene, and thus highlights the essential element of the play's dramatic structure. Together with the two doors through which the actors come and go, entries and exits create (to quote Bradley again) "the systole and diastole of the great heart-beat of the Elizabethan stage."[1] Students of Shakespeare and later English drama probably consider entries and exits an inevitable element of dramatic apparatus, although strictly speaking they are not. As noted previously, classical plays do not employ them. However, to those used to them, entries and exits plus speech prefixes may seem the necessary and sufficient apparatus for a play.

Entries and exits are also, of course, by far the most common directions in Elizabethan plays. Even a cursory familiarity with the drama of the time yields this impression, and Marvin Spevack's concordance to Shakespeare

139

emphatically confirms it.[2] In his collation of the directions in all the extant
texts of Shakespeare's plays, quarto and folio, *"Enter"* and its abbreviations and variant forms occurs no fewer than 5,779 times, and *"Exit"* and
"Exeunt" and their abbreviations, 3,686 times. Their nearest competitors
are not very near: *"Manet,"* *"Man.,"* and *"Manent"* account for only 130
instances; *"Alarum(s)"* and *"Excursion(s)"* in all their variations and com-
binations account for only 260. Thus the sheer frequency of entrances and
exits partly explains their greater visibility.

Even beyond their numbers, however, entry and exit directions as they
evolved in plays for the London theaters are more visible and memorable
because of their authoritative form. Entries, especially entries that initiate a
scene, are the most highly developed and codified of all Elizabethan stage
directions. As we have seen, the importance of initial entries was recognized in the design of the page. In manuscripts and printed editions alike,
they broke the text column: they extended across the whole page or were
centered and set off by white space. Their verbal form was also distinctive
and is still recognizable today. *"Enter the king"* signals a stage direction to
virtually any literate speaker of English.

The medieval Latin heritage of Elizabethan stage directions was particularly influential on entries and exits. The transition from Latin to English was touched upon briefly in chapter 3, which traced the shift in verb
mood from Latin subjunctives to their English equivalents and finally to
simple English indicatives. This chapter will revisit the Latin roots of English stage directions to trace the development of the diction and syntax of
Elizabethan entries and exits. In both vocabulary and grammar, the *Enter/
Exit* code relies prominently on Latinate features. It is worth stressing—
since the opposite inference is so tempting—that these Latinate features
belong wholly to the "native" English tradition, not to the imitation of classical texts. As Howard-Hill points out, "Enter" and "Exit" "do not occur in
the classical editions" of the Renaissance.[3]

In many medieval plays one cannot speak precisely of "entry" directions since the characters are directed to move about the open playing space,
rather than to "enter" and "exit." In citing the antecedents of Elizabethan
entries and exits, therefore, I will draw chiefly on Tudor interludes and
early plays for the London theaters.

LATIN AND LATINATE DICTION

As we have seen, in the earliest medieval plays, both dialogue and directions were in Latin. With the rise of the vernacular languages, the two chan-

nels of dramatic communication were differentiated: the dialogue moved into the vernacular, presumably for the better understanding of the unlearned general audience, while the stage directions remained for a time in Latin, a language familiar to the clerical guardians and producers of the playscripts.

During the Middle Ages, Latin was a special language used for liturgical, scholastic, and administrative functions. According to Robin F. Jones, since it was "the written vehicle for the transmission of truth and authority" medieval Latin stage directions in both form and content powerfully asserted their "control over the vernacular dialogue," and presumably over the speakers of that dialogue, as well. Their "preferred mood," the jussive subjunctive, she observes, is the same as, and no less authoritative "at least for the grammarian" than, the *Fiat lux* of the Creation.[4] Moreover, as we have seen, in some early manuscripts stage directions (Latin and English) were written in red ink. This visual emphasis may have furthered their authority: in many editions of the Bible, the words of God appeared and still appear in red ink. Whether Latin stage directions preserved something akin to divine authority for Tudor and Stuart interpreters is debatable, but they did powerfully influence the diction and syntax of English entry directions. The impersonal Latinate form of both simple and elaborated entries is an important source of their verbal economy and authority.

Although stage directions in the popular drama generally abandoned Latin for English, a small but important group of Latin terms survived into Elizabethan times and still survive today. This "grammar hallowed by tradition," as Richard Southern calls it,[5] includes *"Exit," "exeunt," "manet," "manent," "solus,"* and *"omnes"* and bears particularly on directions to enter, exit, or remain *(manet/manent)* upon the stage:

Exeunt Duke, Qu[een], man[ent] Bush[y]. Green.
                              (*Richard II*, Q 1597, E1)

Exeunt Marquesse, and Jane and theirs.
                              (*2 Edward IV*, Q 1600, P3)

Enter Bagot a Broker, solus.
                              (*Thomas Lord Cromwell*, Q 1602, A3ᵛ)

Exeunt omnes.
                              (*1 Henry IV*, F 1623, TLN 2217)

Entries and exits thus stand out among Elizabethan directions in part for their diction, the persistence of Latin terms.

In addition to the common phrases listed above, some playwrights, especially those with university training, occasionally used other Latin terms in entry and exit directions. *"Exeunt ambo"* [both exit], can be found in Peele's *Edward I* and Marlowe's *Edward II*, among other plays. Marlowe sometimes elaborates entries or exits with Latin phrases, such as *cum caeteris"* [with others], or *"cum servis"* [with attendants]. In *Edward II*, there are five instances of entries or exits elaborated with Latin terms other than the familiar ones, but such Latin elaborations were the exception, not the rule, in plays for the professional London theaters.

Once again, the particular venue—plays for the professional London theaters—is important here. Entry and exit directions (and indeed all directions) entirely in Latin are the rule in many early humanist dramas, such as those of John Bale. See, for example, the portions of the manuscript of *King Johan* in Bale's own hand. Latin directions are the norm in many university plays throughout the period. In plays like *Misogonus*, the academic playwrights show off their classical learning. Directions entirely in Latin are also fairly common in plays for the boys' companies. Chapman's *Bussy d'Ambois* (Q 1607), for example, has eleven directions entirely in Latin except for the characters' names. These include entries and exits *("Exit cum Guise," "Intrat Umbra Friar")* as well as midscene directions for blocking and stage movement *("Surgit spiritus cum suis," "Descendit Friar," "Procumbit")*. But, for the most part, in plays for the professional theaters the survival of Latin was limited to the few familiar terms listed above.

As stage directions wholly in Latin gave way to English ones, *intrare* was variously rendered as *"enter," "enter in,"* or *"come in":*

Here entyr Syrus, the fader of Mary.
(*Mary Magdalen* [Digby], 48, S.D.)

Here entereth in Vertuous Living.
(*Like Will to Like* [Q1568], TLN 724)

Here cummyth Saule rydyng in with hys servantes.
(*The Conversion of St. Paul* [Digby], 168, S.D.)

Here Sedycyon cummyth in.
(*King Johan*, 626, S.D.)

Then comyth in the Holy Ghost comforting Man. . . .
(*The Creation of Eve* [Norwich, 1565], 122, S.D.)

They go out and Inquitie commeth in synging.

(*King Darius*, Q 1565, D4ᵛ)

Sometimes "*intrat*" itself was preserved in an otherwise English direction. Several of these forms might appear in the same play, as the following examples from *Like Will to Like* (Q 1568) demonstrate:

Tom Tosspot commeth in with a fether in his hat.

(TLN 267)

Here entereth in Vertuous Living.

(TLN 724)

Intrat God's Promise and Honour with him.

(TLN 896–98)

The Devil entereth.

(TLN 1290)

Exire was also variously translated. It appeared most often as "*go out*" or "*go away*" (or sometimes as "*run out*" or "*run away*"):

Here Titivillus goeth out with the spade.

(*Mankind*, 551, S.D.)

Here goeth the Jewys away. . . .

(*The Play of the Sacrament*, 335, S.D.)

And so they go out of the place.

(*Magnificence*, 823, S.D.)

Thei sing & go out.

(*Wealth and Health*, TLN 519–20)

Aethyopya, Percya, Juda, and Medya goo all out.

(*King Darius*, D4)

Go out with on[e] of the sodiares

(*Horestes*, TLN 885–88)

They sing this song as they go out from the place.

(*Like Will to Like*, TLN 804)

Run out.

(*Enough Is as Good as a Feast*, 1056,S.D.)

On occasion it was left as *Exit*:

Exit Lucifer.

(*Like Will to Like*, TLN 258)

Exeunt they all.

(*Like Will to Like*, TLN 966)

Fairly soon, however, the two-word translations (*"come in," "enter in," "Go out"*) yielded to the more efficient *"Enter"* and *"Exit"/"Exeunt."* Strictly speaking, only exit directions actually retain the Latin verb; but the preference for *"Enter"* over *"come in"* provided a Latin-derived and conveniently alliterative English complement for *"Exit."*

The preference for *"Enter"* and *"Exit"* was, of course, not instant or absolute. Relatively early plays for the London theaters, such as Kyd's *Spanish Tragedy*, contain exits and entries such as the following:

She in going lets fall her glove, which Horatio, coming out takes up.

(I.iii.99, S.D.)

In *1 Tamburlaine*, the following noncanonical entries occur:

To the battle, and Mycetas comes out alone. . . .

(II.iv.0,S.D.)

Sound trumpets to the battle, and he runs in.

(II.iv.41, S.D.)[6]

These examples are also unusual in that they reverse the usual prepositions: Horatio enters by coming *"out"* and Mycetas exits by running *"in."* Thus the directions view things from the audience's point of view rather than the players'.

Noncanonical, descriptive exits also appear occasionally:

They hale Edmund away, and carry him to be beheaded.

(*Edward II*, xxi, 107, S.D.)

Mistress Blague departs. . . .

(*1 Edward IV*, I3)

one goes.

                     (*Captain Thomas Stukeley*, TLN 1404)

Runs in [i.e., offstage]
           (*The Death of Robert Earl of Huntingdon*, TLN 2626)

But, as with entries, the Latinate theatrical formula increasingly became the norm in plays for the professional London theaters.

The process may be glimpsed in the revisions of the *Sir Thomas More* manuscript. In scene viii, Hand S (playwright Anthony Munday, ten years the senior of his apparent collaborators) writes *"they lead him out,"* and in the revised scene Hand C (a playhouse bookholder, possibly Shakespeare himself)[7] writes *"exeunt"* (Add. IV, 1.91). Or again, where Hand S in the original scene has *"Faukner is brought,"* Hand C in revising substitutes *"Enter Faukner and Officers"* (Add. IV, 1.24). In comparing such revisions of stage directions, one also becomes aware of how the theatrical code, though abbreviated, conveyed a considerable number of details regarding staging. *"Enter with Officers"* is implicitly the equivalent of *"brought in"* or *"prisoner"* or *"guarded"* and thus contains within it cues for blocking (officers on either side, for example) and perhaps props and costume (a prisoner manacled or stripped of former finery and weapons).

An apparently redundant pair of exit directions in *The Comedy of Errors* (F 1623) also exhibits the increasing preference for the Latinate form. The first, in ordinary English, reads *"Runne all out"* (TLN 1445). The second, a half-line of dialogue later, is cast in the theatrical form: *"Exeunt omnes, as fast as may be, frighted"* (TLN 1448). It seems a reasonable speculation that the first direction dates from an early version of the play, c. 1594, and the second reflects a later revision or addition.

The important practical advantage of the Latinate *Enter/ Exit* code is that entry and exit directions begin with an unvarying theatrical command, rather than a character's name or another word, which might also be mistaken for dialogue. In the medieval formula for directions, the temporal or spatial marker (*"Then let him . . ."* or *"Here they shall . . ."*) fulfilled a similar function. It signaled a direction of some sort, but it was not specific as to what kind. The Elizabethan code is more informative. The *Enter/Exit* formula indicates not only a stage direction but its specific function as well. Like the freestanding speech prefix, it is immediately recognizable as a particular kind of direction. As we have seen, in most cases some visual distinction, such as script, typeface, or page position, also distinguished an entry direction from the dialogue, so the verbal and visual codes reinforce one another. For an actor, bookholder, or lay reader, the status and the essential import of these basic directions are immediately clear.

THE SYNTAX OF ENTRIES AND EXITS

Typical entry and exit directions also exhibit the influence of Latin in their inverted, impersonal syntax. Both entries and exits typically place the verb first and the characters' names afterward, inverting normal English word order. In the case of some exits, the names are omitted, and the verb alone suffices. In addition, entries are distinctive in their lack of subject-verb agreement and the ambiguous mood of the verb. Whether one character enters or more, the verb is unvarying: *"Enter Bardolph"* or *"Enter Sheriff and the Carrier."* In early texts, such as *The Famous Victories*, one may find equally indifferently *"Enters Jockey"* (A2) and *"Enters two Receivers"* (A2ᵛ). In the standard entry form, the mood of the verb is elusive; it hovers between the English equivalent of the old Latin subjunctive ("Let Bardolph enter") and an uninflected, inverted version of the present indicative ("Bardolph enters"). Sometimes an inflected verb does appear in entries. However, as we saw above in examining the revisions of directions in *Sir Thomas More*, the tendency was to replace "natural" or descriptive entries and exits with the theatrical formula. For example, the 1597 quarto of *Richard II* contains the following descriptive directions:

> *The trumpets sound, and the King enters with his nobles. . . .*
>
> (I.iii.6, S.D.)

> *His man enters with his boots.*
>
> (V.ii.84, S.D.)

> *The murderers rush in.*
>
> (V.v.105, S.D.)

The comparable passages in the Folio read:

> *Flourish*
> *Enter King, Gaunt, Bushy, Bagot, Greene, and others:*
> *Then Mowbray in Armor, and Herald.*
>
> (TLN 299–302)

> *Enter servant with boots.*
>
> (TLN 2457)

Enter Exton and Servants.

(TLN 2775)

The verb mood and thus the tone of Elizabethan entries is unique. On balance, at least to a reader of this century, an Elizabethan entry maintains an imperative quality, but its authority arises from matter-of-fact impersonality rather than the biblical grandeur of the English third-person subjunctive ("Let him . . .") or the more personal, confrontational tone of the second-person imperative. If its tone is godlike, it resembles the impersonal force of destiny in classical drama, not the voice of Jehovah.

Exit and *Manet* directions, on the other hand, are often inflected. Although the singular *exit* is sometimes supplied for more than one characters' departure, the plural forms *Exeunt* and *Manent* are also common. Exits and *manet*s are thus less codified than entries with respect to their grammar, which attests to the greater importance of entry directions in Elizabethan scripts. As many editors have noted, in both promptbooks and early printed editions exit directions are omitted altogether far more often than entries. Dialogue cues for a character's departure seem often to have been sufficient.[8]

Nonetheless, taken together, entries, exits, and instructions to remain on stage have a special prominence among Elizabethan directions, and this prominence is in large part due to their Latinate features. Impersonality (lack of verb agreement), brevity (no auxiliary verbs or temporal markers), Latin or Latinate diction, and inverted syntax generate the authority of such directions. Magisterial in tone, they resemble a magic formula, complete with a sprinkling of Latin terms, that conjures a character to appear, remain, or vanish from the stage.

THE SYNTAX OF ELABORATED ENTRIES

The brief formulae *Enter x*, *Exit x*, or simply *Exit/Exeunt* govern most entries and exits in Elizabethan plays, but some entries, especially those that initiate a new scene, contain much more than the basic entry instruction and the characters' names. They may specify props, costumes, blocking (who enters with whom), stage level (*"above"*), or manner of movement (*"running"*). Some even convey information about the character's frame of mind, intentions, or previous whereabouts. These "elaborated entries" contain much of the information we have about subtle and spectacular visual effects on the Elizabethan stage, but their form is as interesting and important as their content.

The basic direction *Enter x,* or *Enter x, y, and z* can be elaborated with any number of descriptive words and phrases, but the syntactical norm for elaboration, within the initial period, is remarkably clear and consistent. It admits adjectives, adverbs, and appositives; it also admits prepositional or participial phrases, including ablative absolutes; but it avoids dependent clauses and inflected verbs.

An elaborated entry for one or two characters might employ one or more of these constructions. Simplest are descriptive participles, appositives, and prepositional phrases (including those indicating use of stage doors or entries "above"):

Enter King Edward, mourning.

(*Edward II*, iv. 304, S.D.)

Enter John of Gaunt, sick, with the Duke of York, etc.

(*Richard II*, II.i.0, S.D.)

Enter the Shrieve with Faulkner, a ruffian,[9] *and officers.*

(*Sir Thomas More*, viii.24, S.D.)

Enter soldiers with the Earl of Kent prisoner.

(*Edward II*, xxi. 80, S.D.)

Enter on the walls the Mayor of York and his brethren.

(*3 Henry VI*, IV.vii.16, S.D.)

Enter the two Kings with their powers at several doors.

(*King John*, II.i.333, S.D.)

Enter at one end John Lincoln with [the two Bettses] together, at the other end enters Frances de [Barde, and Doll] a lustie woman, he haling her by the arm.

(*Sir Thomas More*, i.0, S.D. [Dyce's reading])

Enter a woman with a shoulder of mutton on a spit and a devil.

(*Friar Bacon and Friar Bungay*, ii.130, S.D.)

Enter at one door, Burgundy, chafing, with him Sellinger, disguised like a soldier; at another, the constable of France, with him Howard, in the like disguise.

(*2 Edward IV*, O1)

Enter Puntarvolo, Carlo: two serving men following, one leading the Dogge.
(*Every Man Out of His Humour*, TLN 1867–68)

Enter Bellafronte with a Lute, pen, inke, and paper being placede before her.
                                        (*The Honest Whore*, III.3.0, S.D.)

*Enter Symon and all his brethren, a mace and sword before him, meeting
Vortiger, Castiza, Roxena, Horsus, two Ladies.*
                                        (*Hengist, King of Kent*, IV.i.0, S.D.)[10]

The apparent premium placed on syntactic conformity (or perhaps simply
the force of habit) also helps to account for such curious directions as:

Enter the King, Salisbury and Warwick to the Cardinal in bed.
                                        (*2 Henry VI*, III.iii.0, S.D.)

Enter Cromwell, standing amazed.
                                        (*Henry VIII*, III.ii.372, S.D.)

In Elizabethan directions, it would seem, grammatical and rhetorical codes
sometimes superseded normal logic, or, as Alan Dessen puts it, the distinctive grammar and rhetoric of Elizabethan directions generate their own
"theatrical logic."

Although entries can become highly elaborated, the syntactic principles
of simplicity, economy, and objectivity remain in force. Additional information is added in the concise and impersonal form of participles and ablative absolutes (*"the Ancient borne in a chair"* in the first example below),[11]
rather than subordinate clauses with inflected verbs. Enclitics (a, an, the)
and some connectives are often omitted, stripped away, even as visible
details of staging are multiplied:[12]

> *The trumpets sound, and enter the train, viz. his maimed soldiers with
> headpieces and garlands on them, every man with his red cross on his
> coat: the Ancient borne in a chair, his garland and his plumes on his
> headpiece, his ensign in his hand. Enter after them Mortimer bareheaded,
> and others as many as may be. Then Longshanks and his wife Elinor,
> Edmund Couchback, and Joan and Signior Monfort the Earl of Leicester's
> prisoner, with sailors and soldiers, and Charles de Monfort his brother.*
>   (*Edward I*, i.45, S.D.)

> *Enter the Emperor with a pointless sword; next, the King of Castile, car-
> rying a sword with a point; Lacy, carrying the globe; Ed[ward]; War[ren],
> carrying a rod of gold with a dove on it; Ermsby with a crown and a
> scepter; the Queen with the Fair Maid of Fressingfield on her left hand;
> Henry; Bacon; with other Lords attending.*
>   (*Friar Bacon and Friar Bungay*, xvi.0, S.D.)

Enter at one Doore the Armorer and his Neighbors, drinking to him so much that hee is drunke; and he enters[13] with a Drumme before him, and his Staffe, with a Sand-bagge fastened to it: and at the other Doore his Man, with a Drumme and Sand-bagge and Prentices drinking to him.
                                        (*2 Henry VI*, TLN 1115–19)

Enter Stukeley with bagges of money. After him thronging Arthur Crosse the Mercer, John Sparing the Vint[ner], William Sharp, Thomas Thump, George Haz[ard] tennis keeper, Henry Cracke the Fencer, Jeffery Blurt Baliffe of Finsbury; with written notes in their hands.
                                        (*Captain Thomas Stukeley*, TLN 583–87)

Enter hastily at several doors: Duke of Lancaster, Duke of York, the Earls of Arundel and Surrey, with napkins on their arms and knives in their hands, and Sir Thomas Cheyney, with others bearing torches, and some with cloaks and rapiers.
                                        (*Sir Thomas More*, i. 0, S.D.)

Enter Cambridge, Scroop, and Gray, as in a chamber, and set down at a table consulting about their treason: King and Harry and Suffolk listening at the door.
                                        (*Sir John Oldcastle*, TLN 2086–88)

Enter the Heralds first, then the Trumpets next the guard, then Mace-bearer and swords, then the Cardinal, then Brandon, then the King, after him the Queen, Lady Mary, and Ladies attending.
                                        (*When You See Me, You Know Me*, TLN 2914–17)

Enter Trapdore like a poore Souldier with a patch o're on eie, and Teare-Cat with him all tatters.
                                        (*The Roaring Girl*, K2ᵛ)

Enter Cranwell ushering the Duchess of Suffolk, a gentlewoman bearing up her train, Bertie, and Gentlemen.   at the other door, beggars.
                                        (*The Duchess of Suffolk*, A3)

The first and longest of the above examples, from Peele's *Edward I*, is also the earliest. It has an unusual feature—the word *"viz."* preceding the detailing of Edward's train—and a "permissive" tag, *"as many as may be."* But it exhibits the basic entry code: inverted word order, economy, impersonal syntax (the uninflected *"Enter,"* five ablative absolutes in the initial period), and a plethora of phrases but no subordinate clauses.

Elaborated exits are less common than elaborated entries, and elaborated directions to remain (*manet*) are even more rare.[14] Most are laconic: *Exit* or *Exeunt, Manet X* or *Manent X, Y.* But elaborated exits can be found in plays for the London theaters. Some follow the same syntactic rules as entries, relying on efficient, impersonal participles and phrases:

> *a ducking curtesy—exit into the C[astell].*
> > (*John a Kent and John a Cumber*, TLN 791)

> *Exeunt roaring.*
> > (*Friar Bacon and Friar Bungay*, xv.84, S.D.)

> *Exeunt with curtesies.*
> > (*James IV*, TLN 106)

> *Exit running.*
> > (*Captain Thomas Stukeley*, TLN 2791)

> *Exit pursued by a Beare.*
> > (*Winter's Tale*, TLN 1500)

> *Exeunt severally Weeping.*
> > (*Duchess of Suffolk*, C2)

> *Exit crying help.*
> > (*Duchess of Suffolk*, F3)

> *Exit weeping.*
> > (*Duchess of Suffolk*, H2)

Other directions elaborate upon a canonical exit with a finite verb or an independent clause:

> *The Frier having song [sung] his farewell to his Pikestaff a [he] takes his leave of Cambria, and Exit the Frier.*
> > (*Edward I*, TLN 2395-96)

> *Exit into the Castell and makes fast the dore.*
> > (*John a Kent*, TLN 847–48)[15]

> *Exeunt, and as they are going out, Doncaster puls Warman [aside].*
> > (*Death of Robert, Earl of Huntingdon*, TLN 128–29)

> *Exit the King, frowning upon the Cardinall, the Nobles throng after him smiling and whispering.*
> > (*Henry VIII*, TLN 2080–81)

The first example in this group, also from the relatively early *Edward I,* seems a transitional instance. The phrase *"a takes his leave"* may have been the original descriptive exit direction, to which a more canonical *"Exit"* was later added. A similar duplication occurs in Munday's *John a Kent* manuscript. In a series of descriptive, choreographed exits, two of the three are followed by a normal exit direction:

> *The chyme playes and Gosselin with the Countesse goes turning out.*
> (TLN 1158)

> *The chyme agayn, and they turne out in like manner.*
>   *exeunt*
> (TLN 1161)
> *The chyme agayn, and so they.*
>   *exeunt*
> (TLN 1164)[16]

In general, however, exits are less likely than entries to be elaborated, and when elaborated, their form is less consistent or predictable than that of elaborated entries. Once again, the primary importance of the entry direction seems confirmed in its greater degree of codification.

The characteristic constructions—prepositional phrases, participles, and ablative absolutes—account for the muscular Latinate style and tone of elaborated entry and exit directions. They imitate their Latin models rather than resorting to subordinate clauses, the preferred English idiom. Like early Protestant translations of the Bible, they claim authority and objectivity by staying grammatically close to their Latin roots.[17] At the same time, rhetorically, the participles and absolute constructions seem more "open" and less intrusive than the comparable subordinate clauses might be. Their telegraphic spareness seems to leave room for interpreters to fill in the blanks, both semantically and theatrically. Compared to the novelistic directions of Shaw or Ibsen, say, they maintain a less personal and therefore a less intrusive voice.

This is true even though the provision of a certain kind of narrative or descriptive information in Elizabethan elaborated entries is fairly common. Entries not infrequently contain "inside" information about a character's intentions or contextual information such as where a character has just been or is going. But in contrast to Shaw or Ibsen's directions, they do so without violating their impersonal, compact grammatical form. Examples from plays of widely differing dates include:

Enter the Novice and his company to give the Queen music at her tent.
(*Edward I*, TLN 1887–88)

Enter a Devil to seek Miles.
(*Friar Bacon and Friar Bungay*, xv. 0, S.D.)

Enter the King and State, with Guard to banish the Duchess
(*2 Henry VI*, II.iii.0, S.D.)

Enter Sir Richard Ratcliffe with Halberds, carrying the nobles to death at Pomfret
(*Richard III*, III.iii.0, S.D.)

Enter Falconbridge with his troops marching, as being at Mile-end.
(*1 Edward IV*, C4)

Enter Buckingham from his arraignment, Tipstaves before him, the axe with the edge towards him, Halberds on each side. . . .
(*Henry VIII*, II.i.53, S.D.)

Enter two soldiers with a hamper, the boy in it.
(*King John and Matilda*, C3ᵛ)

Such information is often taken as evidence of authorial origin and of literary rather than theatrical intention. But as other scholars have pointed out, such directions are quite common in playhouse manuscripts as well as in printed editions.[18] Even if they violate our narrow sense of the "stageable," they are theatrical in that they observe the conventional syntax and are thus unobtrusive, objective, and authoritative. Or, to put it another way, it would seem that the formal conventions of Elizabethan directions were more significant than the distinctions we retroactively and perhaps anachronistically draw regarding their content.

Very occasionally, in both early and late editions, narrative information is conveyed in a subordinate clause, the preferred English idiom, rather than in the compressed phrases and participles of the Latinate norm:

Enter Gaveston, reading on a letter that was brought him from the King.
(*Edward II*, i.0, S.D.)

Enter king Phillip: leaning on Stukeley's shoulder, Alva, Davita, Valdes that was the messenger. . . .
(*Captain Thomas Stukeley*, TLN 2044–47)

Enter Cranwell staggering, and falls near the bush where the [lost] child
is.

(*The Duchess of Suffolk*, F2ᵛ)

Occasionally, too, one finds an entry in the middle of a scene that is coordinated via a subordinate clause with some other action occurring on the stage:

While the music plays, enters on the walles Llwellen, Chester with his
Countess, Morton with Sydanen.

(*John a Kent*, TLN 918–19)

As he is going up the stayres, enters the Earles of Surrye
and Shre[wsburie].

(*Sir Thomas More* xvii, †1920)

As they are marching, Enter Curteis and Old Stukeley.

(*Captain Thomas Stukeley*, TLN 808–9)

As they are lifting their weapons, enter the Maior of Hereford, and His
officers and Townes-men with clubbes.

(*Sir John Oldcastle*, TLN 30–32)

As he kisses her, Enter Vortiger and Gentleman.

(*Hengist, King of Kent*, B4ᵛ)

The entry direction per se in each of these is unexceptional, but the introductory adverbial clause seeks to be specific about the timing of the entry, a matter which is usually indicated visually (not verbally) by where the entry occurs on the page. The relationship of these "timed entries" to midscene action sequences (to be discussed in chapter 6) is suggested in the examples above, and in another direction from *Sir John Oldcastle*, where the entering character is immediately involved in the onstage action:

Here as they are ready to strike, enter Butter and drawes his weapon and
steps betwixt them.

(TLN 1590–95)

In plays for the professional London theaters, however, the use of subordinate clauses in entries is relatively rare.

While the voice of Elizabethan entries builds its authority partly on the objectivity of its condensed and codified syntax, once in a while a different tone can be heard. Both instances I have encountered concern the reworking of a morality topos, namely the appearance of a "soldier" (usually the Vice) in ridiculous and deformed armor. Here is the first entry direction for Ambidexter in *Cambises:*

> *Enter the Vice, with an old capcase on his head, an old pail about his hips*
> *for harness, a scummer and a potlid by his side, and a rake on his shoulder.*
>
> (125, S.D.)

This antiheroic emblem occurs several times in the later history plays (including perhaps Falstaff's cannon fodder in *2 Henry IV*), but in two instances it is accompanied by a unusually vehement, judgmental direction:

> *Enter Murley and his men, prepared in some filthy order for warre.*
>
> (*Sir John Oldcastle*, TLN 1194)

> *Enter Richard and Buckingham in rotten armor, marvellous ill-favored.*
>
> (*Richard III*, III.v.0, S.D.)

One can speculate why it should be so, but both the ragtag rebel tradesmen and the cunning poverty of the would-be king elicit a voice that is momentarily ironic and emotionally colored. In contrast to the prescriptive directions in *Cambises*, however, the playwrights delegate to the actors what details of costume are needed. Though magisterial in tone, the directions are permissive in content; they aim to inspire, not dictate, the players' interpretations.

ENTRIES-PLUS-ACTION-SEQUENCES: MASQUES AND DUMB SHOWS

Directions for masques, dumb shows, and other entries-plus-action usually begin canonically, but the syntax of elaborated entries may not be sustained after the opening period. Since a sequence of actions beyond the "entry" is required, several finite verbs in dependent and independent clauses often follow the initial, uninflected entry direction:[19]

> *Enter the Prince marching, and Falstaff meets him playing upon his trun-*
> *cheon like a fife.*
>
> (*1 Henry IV*, III.iii. 87, S.D.)

> *Enter three Antiques, who dance round, and take Slipper with them.*
>
> (*James IV*, TLN 1724–25)

> *Hoboyes. Enter King and others as Maskers, habited like Shepheards,*
> *usher'd by the Lord Chamberlaine. They passe directly before the*
> *Cardinall, and gracefully salute him.*
>
>   (*Henry VIII*, F 1623, TLN 753–56)

> A *noyse within crying roome for the Queene, usher'd by the Duke of*
> *Norfolke. Enter the Queene, Norfolke and Suffolke; she kneels. King riseth*
> *from his State, takes her up, kisses and placeth her by him.*
>
>   (*Henry VIII*, F 1623, TLN 319–23)

Such entries are often preceded by a sound cue and followed by full sentence directions for additional actions or blocking. In addition, when followed by an action sequence, a canonical entry may be followed by a noncanonical exit:

> *Enter Adam, and Antiques, and carrie away the Clowne, he makes pots,*
> *and sports, and scornes.*
>
>   (*Death of Robert, Earl of Huntingdon*, TLN 2398–99)

As a result, something reminiscent of the medieval production narrative temporarily returns to the dramatic text.

The momentary return of the production narrative is most striking in the case of directions for dumb shows, dream visions, and the like, in which the sequence of actions with no dialogue is likely to be extensive. Many dumb shows and visions are allegorical and/or convey a deliberately old-fashioned or amateur quality (like the dumb shows that precede the plays within the play in *Hamlet* or *A Midsummer Night's Dream*); thus their being cued by directions reminiscent of those in medieval drama seems appropriate:[20]

> *Musicke playing within.*
> *Enter After Oberon, King of Fairies, an Antique, who dance [sic] about a*
> *Tombe, plac'st conveniently on the stage, out of the which, suddenly starts*
> *up as they daunce, Bohan, a Scot, attyred like a ridstall man, from whom*
> *the Antique flyes.*   *Oberon manet.*
>
>   (*James IV*, Ind., 1–5)

> *The trumpets sounds [sic]. Dumb show follows.*
> *Enter a King and a Queen, the Queen embracing him and he her. He*
> *takes her up and declines his head upon her neck. He lies him down upon*
> *a bank of flowers. She, seeing him asleep, leaves him. Anon come in an-*
> *other man, takes off his crown, kisses it, pours poison in the sleeper's*

ears, and leaves him. The Queen returns, finds the King dead, makes passionate action. The pois'ner with some three or four come in again, seem to condole with her. The dead body is carried away. The pois'ner woos the Queen with gifts; she seems harsh awhile but in the end accepts love.

(*Hamlet*, III.ii.135, S.D.)

After the initial entry direction, the diction for subsequent entries and exits often departs from the usual formulae. *"Enter"* and *"exit"* still appear, but alternate forms, such as *"leaves him," "comes in," "returns,"* and *"departs"* also appear. The syntax also relaxes, permitting full sentence descriptions of various actions:

Drawe the curten, the king sits sleeping, his sword by his side. Enter Austria, before whom commeth Ambition: and bringing him before the chaire, king John, in sleepe, makes signes to avoid, and holdeth his crowne fast with both his hands.

(*Death of Robert, Earl of Huntingdon*, TLN 925–29)

Nonetheless, despite their freer, more descriptive form, such directions still maintain the moment-by-moment decorum of the drama. They are cast in the present tense and employ compact and efficient syntax.

The directions for the four dumb shows in *If You Know Not Me, You Know Nobody* (Q 1605) are particularly good examples of this spare, moment-by-moment decorum:

A Dumb show.

Enter Six with torches.
Tame and Shandoyse, bare headed, Phillip and Mary after them; then Winchester, Beningfield, and Attendants: at the other dore, Sussex and Howard; Sussex delivers a peticion to the King, the King receives it, shewes it to the Queen, she shewes it to Winchester and Beningfield. They storme, the King whispers to Sussex and raises him and Howard, gives them a piticion, they take their leaves and depart, the King whispers a little to the Queen.

Exeunt.[21]

The first two periods observe the usual syntax of an elaborated entry, *"Enter x, y, z"* plus adjectival and participial phrases.[22] Thereafter independent clauses in strict temporal sequence indicate the actions to be mimed; no mediating conjunctions order the sequence or subordinate one action to another; they are simply given in the order that they occur.

Not all dumb-show directions in plays for the London theaters are so spare as those in *If You Know Not Me*, but their relatively unmediated voice emerges more clearly when they are compared to their predecessors in other venues. In *Gorboduc*, for example, the directions for the entr'acte dumb shows are in fact descriptions cast in the past tense and with glosses on their allegorical significance:

> *The Order and Signification of the Dumb Show Before the Third Act*
>
> *First the music of flutes began to play, during which came in upon the stage a company of mourners, all clad in black, betokening death and sorrow to ensue upon the ill-advised misgovernment and dissension of brethren, as befell upon the murder of Ferrex by his younger brother. After the mourners had passed thrice about the stage, they departed, and then the music ceased.*

In Thomas Hughes's *The Misfortunes of Arthur* (Q 1587), like *Gorboduc* a neoclassical, historical tragedy performed for the queen by gentlemen of the Inns of Court,[23] all five dumb shows are also described in the past tense and interpreted:

> *The Argument and manner of the fourth dumbe shewe.*
>
> *During the Musicke appointed after the third act, there came a Lady Courtly attyred with a counterfaite Childe in her armes, who walked softly on the Stage. From another place there came a King Crowned, who likewise walked on an other part of the Stage. From a third place there came foure Souldiers all armed, who spying this Lady and King, upon sodaine pursued the Lady from whom they violently tooke her Childe and flung it against the walles; She in mournefull sort wringing her hands passed her way. Then in like manner they sette on the King, tearing his Crowne from his head, and casting it in peeces under feete drave him by force away; And so passed themselves over the Stage. By this was meant the fruit of Warre, which spareth neither man woman nor childe, with the ende of Mordreds usurped Crowne.*
>
> (E1ᵛ)

The differences are not surprising. Both *Gorboduc* and *Arthur* were occasional pieces, one-time-only productions for which the printed text provided a record, not a script for reenactment. In plays for the professional London theaters, however, even the dumb-show directions preserve dramatic decorum. Though they may organize and smooth out the sequence of actions, they remain within the here and now of the fictive world.

MANUSCRIPTS VS. PRINTED EDITIONS

The basic form of Elizabethan entries does not differ greatly in manuscript and printed versions of a text, even when many years separate the two. This assertion may seem to contradict previous editors' efforts to stress the difference between the stage directions in manuscripts and printed texts, especially late quartos presumably aimed at lay readers. But most differences rightly noted by editors have to do with content, abbreviations, and incidental syntax, rather than the basic grammatical form of an entry or exit. A brief look an extreme case will suggest the formal continuity that underlies the differences often noted by others.

In his print facsimile edition of Middleton's *Hengist, King of Kent, or the Mayor of Quinburough*, R. C. Bald[24] devotes several pages to variants in the stage directions of the extant manuscripts, which date from 1619–20, and those in the quarto of 1661. He notes that the quarto reduces the number of directions for music and noises *"within"* and that it adds new directions or new material to existing directions to clarify stage action. For example:

	MS	Q 1661
II.i.0	*Enter Vortiger* *a Gentleman meeting him.*	*Enter Vortiger (crowned)*
III.ii. 20–22	*Enter Vort: & and Hersus.*	*Enter Vortiger and* *Horsus disguised.*

The rationale of these revisions seems to be that the quarto was aimed at readers for whom the staged version of the play would have been unavailable following the closing of the theaters in 1642. The changes in content are not all in one direction, however. Sometimes the manuscript direction is more expansive and descriptive, and the quarto is more laconic, using theatrical shorthand:

	MS	Q 1661
Prologue, 0	*Enter Raynulph a Munck the* *Presenter.*	*Enter Raynulph.*
II.iii.8–12	*Enter Heng: Horsus with* *with Drums & Colours,* *Soldiers leading prisoners.*	*Enter Hengist and Horsus* *prisoners.*
V.i.0	*Enter Symon: Clark Glover fell-* *monger etc: graz[ier] Musique*	*Enter Symon and his* *Brethren, Amindab* *his Clerk.*

Overall, however, as far as form is concerned, a comparison of the entries and exits in the manuscripts and the quarto reveals the predominance of canonical diction and syntax in all versions of the play. In the printed text, punctuation is altered, abbreviations are expanded, and details of staging are sometimes added or clarified, but the essential grammatical form is usually unchanged:[25]

	MS	Q 1661
I.i.0,	*Shout Enter Vortiger*	*Shouts within; Then enter Vortiger.*
I.i.28	*Musick Enter Certaine Muncks, Germanicus; Constantius being one as at a procession*	*Enter Constantius as a Monck, attended by other Moncks) Vortiger stays him*
III.ii.0	*Enter Castiza A Booke: Two Ladyes:*	*Enter Castiza (with a Book) and two Ladies.*
III.iii. 259	*Exeunt*	*Exit cum suis*

IV.i.0: (MS)	*Enter Vortiger Castiza two Ladyes Roxena Devon: Staff[ord] at one Doore Symon and his Brethren at the other.*
(Q)	*Enter Symon and all his Brethren, a Mace and Sword before him, meeting Vortiger, Castiza, Hengist, Roxena, Horsus, two Ladies.*

In one instance where the manuscripts omit the word "*Enter,*" the quarto restores it:

V.ii.210–11	*Devon Staff[ord]: leading Hengist prisoner.*	*Enter Hengist, Devon. Staf[ford] & Soldiers.*

On only two occasions do the quarto directions depart from the theatrical norm:

III.ii.111	*Ext vort: Castiza*	*Vortiger snatches her away.*
V.i.156	*Enter Oliver.*	*Oliver is brought in.*

But these two exceptions hardly provide evidence of a thorough revision to eliminate theatrical diction and syntax. In most instances, the theatrical form we have been examining predominates in both the manuscripts and the quarto.

As we have already seen, although the compilers of the Shakespeare Folio of 1623 clearly considered the reader's eye in designing this handsome volume, they made little or no effort to translate theatrical directions for the benefit of "the great variety of readers." Indeed, in instances already examined, the Folio texts are more consistent in their use of the theatrical formulae than the earlier quartos. The editors of the Oxford Shakespeare argue that the Folio texts are in general "more theatrical" (that is, closer to a promptbook) than their "good" quarto counterparts, although the differences between the two are sometimes "relatively minor."[26] If they are correct, it would seem that in spite of the example of the Jonson folio of 1616,[27] Heminge, Condell, and the Jaggards saw no need to tamper with the theatrical form of the stage directions.

Like the entry directions, directions for the dumb shows in the printed version of *Hengist, King of Kent* show editing to smooth out complex manuscript instructions for the benefit of the reader, but both versions are also relatively unmediated, especially given their great length. If anything, the quarto directions often seem less descriptive, owing to their smoother, more efficient syntax.

For example, the manuscript version of the second dumb show is as follows (though not italicized beyond the first line, the entire direction is set off from the dialogue by double rules extending across the page):

Hoboys Dumb show. Enter 2 Villaines, to them Vortiger seemeing to solissitt them, gives them gold, then sweares them—Exit *Vortiger Enter* to them *Constantius* in private meditation, they rudely Come to him, strike down his Booke and Draw their swordes vppon him, he fiarely spredds his armes, and yields to thire furys at wch they seeme to be over Come wth pittye, But lookeing on ye gold kill him as hee turns his Back, and hurry away his bodye. Enter *Vortiger, Devon: Stafford* in private conference: to them Enter ye murders presenting ye head to *Vortiger*, he seems to express much sorrow, and before ye astonished Lordes, makes officers lay hold on em; who offering to Com towardes *Vortiger* are Commanded to be hurryed away as to execution: then ye Lordes, all seemeing respect, Crowne *Vortiger*, then bring in Castiza, who seems to be brought in vnwillingly by Devon & Stafford who Crowne her and then give her to *Vortiger*, she going forth with him, wth a kind of Constraind Consent; then enter *Aurelius & Uther* ye two *Brothers* who much astonished seeme to fly for there safety.

The temporal sequence remains largely unmediated by conjunctions and other connectives, but as in highly elaborated entries and dumb shows generally, some temporal connectives do occur. There are two "then's" and one "at which." There are four adjectival clauses describing characters' actions or reactions ("wno seems to be brought in unwillingly," "who much astonished seeme to fly for their safety"). The several occurrences of "seem" and "seeming" step outside the world of the play to refer to theatrical illusion per se. Vortiger's sorrow is in fact pretense, and refers to the character's, not the actor's, "seeming." Castiza's unwillingness and the brothers' fear for their safety are genuine, on the other hand, so these two references to "seeming" appear to be theatrically self-conscious. The evidence of other dumb-show directions suggests that "seeming" was the preferred term to describe the miming required of the actors. Perhaps the acting style in a dumb show was more stylized or "old-fashioned," and the diction of the stage direction thus echoes that of the old-fashioned medieval production narrative.

The quarto version of this dumb-show direction does differ from the manuscript, but not because it is more descriptive and expansive. Rather, in addition to modifying somewhat the content of the direction, the quarto provides a more condensed version of the stage business. The passage is streamlined grammatically and concentrates on action (rather than reaction, as in the case of the "astonished Lords" and the "astonished" brothers of the manuscript). As a result, owing to its greater brevity, it preserves a sense of theatrical decorum as great or even greater than its counterpart in the manuscript:

> *Dumb show. Enter two Villains, to them Vortiger, who seems to solicit them with gold, then swears them, and Exit. Enter Constantius, meditating, they rudely strike down his book, draw their swords, he kneels and spreads his arms, they kill him, hurry him off. Enter Vortiger, Devonshire and Stafford in conference, to them the villains presenting the head, he seems sorrowful, and in a rage stabs them both. Then they crown Vortiger and fetch in Castiza, who comes unwillingly, he hales her, and they crown her. Aurelius and Uther, brothers of Constantius, seeing him crowned, draw and fly.*

The printed version has half as many words (97 vs. 189), only two subordinate clauses, and two instances of *"seems"* (versus six in the manuscript). Both directions generally observe the basic syntax of an elaborated entry, but the quarto has fewer finite verbs indicating actions and fewer descriptive phrases containing inside information about motives and emotions.

This is the opposite of what one might expect in a late quarto aimed at readers unfamiliar with the staged play. The explanation would seem to be that the theatrical convention of presenting extended action on stage in an unmediated, unself-conscious way survived the closing of the theaters and became a standard element of dramatic discourse in English. While such lengthy directions admit syntactic constructions that organize the information rationally, rather than providing the barest "mimetic" sequence of events (such as that found in the dumb-show directions in *When You See Me*), nonetheless they respect the moment-by-moment unfolding of the action and eschew confidential address of the players or readers.

TWO TRADITIONS: TO ENTER OR NOT TO ENTER

Before leaving the topic of Elizabethan entries, we must not fail to account for their very existence, for the presence of entry directions in an Elizabethan dramatic text was not inevitable. From the seamless production narrative of medieval drama, Elizabethan playwrights developed the entry as a separate functional category. This convention came to be the norm for playwrights associated with the London theaters, but their practice contrasts sharply with the neoclassical conventions observed by many academic dramatists, and the differences between the two conventions are significant.

The rival tradition for the presentation of a dramatic text can be seen most clearly in Renaissance translations of Greek and Latin drama. In the English edition of Seneca's *Hercules Furens* (in *Tragoediae Maiore*, London, 1589), for example, stage directions other than those implicit in the dialogue are absent from the text; the Latin phrases at the beginning of a scene and in the margins are not stage directions but indications of the meter of the verse (*"Trimetri Iambici"* [Iambic trimeters], *"Euisdem rationis"* [in the same manner]) or editorial comments (*"Hic nos primis distinximus ex veteri manuscripti . . ."*). The page design of these editions also differs from that of plays for the professional theaters. They observe the older manuscript tradition, preserving the text column except for act and scene divisions. All speech prefixes are embedded within the dialogue to preserve the integrity of the metrical line.

Renaissance editions of classical plays also had their own convention for initiating a scene. Each scene simply begins with a list of the characters who will take part in it; no details are provided about posture, dress, or hand props. Further, all the characters in the scene are named at the beginning, regardless of when they enter. This convention is usually known as a "massed entry," and the name is accurate insofar as the characters' names are "massed" at the beginning of the scene, even though the dialogue may indicate that one or more characters are not onstage until later.

In one respect, however, the term is misleading and glosses over an important difference between classical and popular dramatic apparatus. Strictly speaking, the list of characters is not an "entry" direction at all. The word *"enter"* does not appear at the beginning of the scene, and, as noted above, the text takes no notice of the theatrical facts of entrances and exits once the scene is underway. Rather than "entry directions" as such, a classical text provides a list of speakers for each scene. As in early manuscript plays, the text column for each scene is not broken to indicate changes of speaker. All speech prefixes are embedded to preserve the metrical integrity of the line. The dialogue within each scene is not interrupted by white space or stage directions. Overall, these plays are presented as texts to be spoken or read, not "acted." This alternate tradition was, as one might expect, influential on university plays.[28] For example, *Misogonus* (c. 1577) and Peter Hausted's *Rival Friends* (Q 1632) have massed entries, embedded speech prefixes, lists of "interloquitores,"[29] and directions entirely in Latin.

It is clear that playwrights for the London theaters were also familiar with this alternate tradition. Webster uses massed entries consistently in *The Duchess of Malfi*. In *1 Tamburlaine*, Marlowe observes some elements of the classical convention. The directions that begin each scene do not contain the word *"Enter";* the names of the characters are simply listed. One modern editor ascribes this omission to "neglect,"[30] but more likely Marlowe was imitating (to a degree) the classical convention. About half the initial entries in Chapman's *Bussy d'Ambois*, initially performed by Paul's Boys and later by the Queen's Revels Children, also omit the entry command.[31]

Strictly speaking, however, neither Marlowe nor Chapman employs the convention of "massed entries": characters who enter midscene are not included in the initial list, as they are in classical drama; they are given normal entries: for example, *"Enter Pero with a letter"* (*Bussy d'Ambois* IV.ii.138, S.D.). Further, the initial entries in these plays follow normal Elizabethan practice in providing staging details (*"Tamburlaine all in black and very melancholy,"* V.ii.0, S.D.), which were not typical of the neoclassical system. Still, *Tamburlaine* and *Bussy d'Ambois* illustrate that alternate entry forms were not unknown in plays for the public stages, especially in those by some university-educated playwrights. Nonetheless, as we have seen, most London playwrights eschewed the classical convention and followed the entry code discussed above.

Perhaps the most interesting use of the neoclassical convention in plays written for the men's companies is Ben Jonson's. Jonson's quartos follow different conventions, apparently depending on genre as well as venue. His "Humour" plays first appeared with normal, sequential entries.[32] His classical tragedies, not surprisingly, employed versions of the classical convention, as did his classically constructed comedies, *Volpone* and *The Alchemist*.[33] In the folio of 1616, however, Jonson regularized the stage directions of all his plays to conform more or less to the classical model. Massed entries were used to reduce the "distractions" of sequential entries, and theatrical terminology (*Enter, exit,* and other Latin phrases) was systematically removed. This is not surprising, given Jonson's view of himself as a proud (if isolated) follower of classical standards and practices of playwriting. However, as Peter Wright as shown, even in this self-conscious attempt to produce a classically "clean" reading text in the folio of 1616, Jonson was not willing to jeopardize or sacrifice the theatrical richness of his plays. Although Jonson used massed entries and rigorously deleted sequential entries, "what was 'banished' as an 'entry' often 're-entered' to provide the same information [disguised] as [a direction for] property, costume, or business."[34]

It would seem, then, that the adoption of the familiar theatrical formula by most playwrights associated with the professional London theaters was the result of choice, not chance or isolation. The native and popular form highlighted the essential action verbs (*Enter* and *Exit*) and indicated the timing of characters' entries and exits with respect to the dialogue (as opposed to massing all the "entries" at the beginning). Just as plays associated with the professional theaters developed a mimetic, "theatrical" page design, they also developed a form for entries and exits that emphasized the visible movement of the characters on and off the stage. The dramatists gravitated to the scheme that emphasized the theatrical aspects of the script— the vivid details of action, sound, gesture, costume, and properties that defined a new scene after a cleared stage and the sequence of entries and exits as the scene developed.

CONCLUSION

On the whole, the initial entry direction with its codified, impersonal syntax has the most authoritative voice of all Elizabethan directions. Unlike midscene directions, to be discussed in the next chapter, initial entry directions stay close to their Latin origins: they preserve Latin diction and syntax, and (in the case of entries) they rely on a verb form reminiscent of the third-person subjunctive in directions for medieval religious plays. Their grammar and rhetoric thus distinguish them from the voices of the dialogue and create a powerful, impersonal voice whose instructions are hard to overlook, resist, or ignore. This authoritative voice signals the start of a new scene to a lay reader, and it seems well calculated to capture the attention of players and other theater professionals.

It may seem that all this authority is expended on directions the least likely to be contested, namely those that get the necessary characters onstage to begin a specific scene. After all, if the dialogue requires x, y, z to be present, what players would not allow them to enter? It would seem to be a case of piling up symbolic authority, flexing verbal muscle, precisely on those occasions that are safe from controversy, like having a military parade in the heart of the generals' power base. Perhaps the hope is that the authority granted on one occasion will spill over into other contested areas, where authority must be exercised with greater tact. On the other hand, we know that characters are sometimes cut from scenes, indeed from entire plays. Moreover, the specific details of elaborated entries need greater support than the appearance of the characters themselves; few productions actually follow entry directions to the letter. Therefore the authoritative diction and syntax may be more justified than at first appears.

In stressing the issue of authority, I do not imagine that an actor/playwright such as Shakespeare anticipated a pitched battle with his colleagues over entries and other matters of staging. But not all playwrights worked so closely with the players who acted their plays. Hamlet, patron and playwright for the nonce, goes out of his way to give the players some pretty authoritative advice, and Peter Quince's struggle to convince his players to follow the script is a scene of enduring comic appeal. The mechanicals are amateurs, and rather dimwitted to boot, and this explains a good deal of Peter Quince's struggle, but the players in *Hamlet* are respected professionals, and the bookish prince still seeks to influence their behavior onstage. The two scenes reflect to varying degrees the fruitful give-and-take of theatrical collaboration. With the inevitable stresses of that collaboration in mind, the compact, Latinate form and diction of the typical initial entry ensures that, as each scene begins, the stage directions muster the players (and orient the reader) with a firm and efficient hand.

The evidence of printed plays written for venues other than the professional London theaters suggests that the code I describe here was a specific *theatrical* code, determined by the conventions of a particular theatrical community, not the mere fact of publication. In cases where manuscripts of plays are extant, though their directions differ in some respects from those in printed editions, they employ largely the same code, as illustrated in the examples from the *Woodstock*, *Sir Thomas More*, and *Hengist, King of Kent* manuscripts. The evolution of the elaborated entry is, to my mind, a microcosm of the twin roots of English Renaissance drama: the eloquence of classical drama and the vivid action and spectacle of the native tradition. Entries employ the authority of a Latinate verbal code in the service of the concrete, visual theater inherited from medieval drama. The Elizabethan entry form persists to this day, alongside more discursive, narrative directions. In the contemporary play, *Titanic*, Christopher Durang honors (even while satirizing) this grammar hallowed by tradition in creating directions that are outrageous in content but traditional in form, such as the following: *"Enter the Captain in his underwear with a slice of bread stuck on the dildo on his forehead"* (scene 5).

In retrospect, Nancy Palk's response in my introductory anecdote—"What stage directions? You mean *Enter, Exit?*"—is not so surprising after all.

6

Action, Gesture
and Special Effects

And so our scene must to the battle fly;
Where—O for pity!—we shall much disgrace,
With four or five most vile and ragged foils
(Right ill-dispos'd in brawl ridiculous)
The name of Agincourt. Yet sit and see,
Minding true things by what their mockeries be.
                              —*Henry V*, chorus, IV.49–53

1 Cheater: We have a play wherein we use a horse.
Symon: Fellowes, you use no horse play in my house. . . .
Give me a play without a beast, I charge you.
                              —*Hengist, King of Kent,* V.i.98–102

It snows, and raines, and thunders.
                              —*Duchess of Suffolk*, F2ᵛ

As the passages above remind us, Elizabethan and Jacobean plays were often lively affairs, with considerable stage action, spectacle, sound, and other special effects. In 1596, the residents of the Blackfriars district successfully petitioned the Privy Council to prevent Richard Burbage and the Chamberlain's Men from using their already converted buildings as a theater. Among other things, the neighbors objected that "the same playhouse is so neere the Church that the noyse of the drummes and trumpetts will greatly disturbe and hinder both the ministers and parishioners in tyme of devine service."[1] Apparently the special effects of the theaters were sufficiently realistic to inspire an early instance of a "not-in-my-backyard" sentiment in the community. Twenty or so years earlier, the city fathers had even claimed that the queen's subjects risked "slaughters and mayhemynges . . . by engynes, weapons, and powder used in plays."[2]

As we have seen, many details of staging are inscribed in elaborated entries and dumb-show directions that specify props, blocking, costumes, action sequences, and spectacle. On the other hand, as a scene unfolds much that is implied in the dialogue may never be confirmed in explicit stage directions, and cues for sound and other special effects have been described as "extremely haphazard."[3] For example, some royal entrances are accompanied by a flourish, while others are not, and a modern editor must decide if the omission is deliberate or inadvertent. Nonetheless, midscene directions for action and special effects are fairly common, especially in the first half of the period. Chapter 3 has already examined their place in the visual design of early modern playtexts; an examination of their grammatical form will complete our investigation of the voice of Elizabethan stage directions.

Like chapter 3, this chapter focuses on freestanding midscene directions: that is, directions for action and special effects that are not part of an elaborated entry, dumb-show, or exit direction. In general, I have judged a direction to be freestanding if it is not on the same line as another direction or grammatically part of it, or if it is visually distinct in some way, such as set off by rules or brackets. In addition to calls for special effects that obviously stand alone, I have included those that precede, in a separate grammatical period, an elaborated entry or exit. While these cues are clearly meant to accompany an entrance or exit, they are grammatically independent, and so can be considered separately. Thus, for example, the formula *"Sound trumpets. Enter . . ."* I consider as a sound cue followed by an entry. The formula *"Enter . . . with drum and colors"* may imply that the drums are heard, but the sound cue is expressed as part of an elaborated entry, and thus is governed by the conventional grammar discussed in chapter 5.

Finally, though their freestanding status might be questioned, participles and adverbs that appear as extensions of speech prefixes have also been included in the tallies below. *Aside* and *within* appear in this position fairly frequently, and to ignore them would misrepresent the frequency of adverbial modifiers. Participial extensions of speech prefixes are rare but are interesting for that very reason; therefore, I have taken them into account when tallying the use of freestanding participial directions. The deciding factor in including these cases was my desire to note the incidence and contribution of directions *not* governed by a finite verb.

For convenience, midscene directions can be discussed under two headings: directions for action, gesture, and vocal delivery aimed at one or more players on the stage; and directions, usually aimed at a backstage audience, calling for stage properties (*"A bed brought out"* or *"low stools"*), sound (music, ceremonial flourishes, military signals, and so on), or other special effects (such as thunder and lightning). Midscene directions addressed to these different audiences seem to have followed their own trajectories with regard to grammatical form.

Some types of midscene directions can appear under both of these headings: cues for unison dialogue and offstage sound are sometimes cast as instructions to actors and sometimes as impersonal calls addressed to backstage personnel. When expressed as an instruction to a specific actor or actors (*"All cry,"* or *"York knocks"*), they are counted below as directions for action; when expressed impersonally (*"Loud shouts,"* *"Chambers discharg'd"*), they are counted as calls for special effects. Similarly, the adverb *within* appearing alone in the margin opposite a speech or as an extension of a speech prefix I have treated as an instruction to an actor (where he should be standing to speak the line); noun phrases such as *"shouts within,"* however, I treated as calls for special effects (to be provided by whoever can be mustered offstage to create the desired effect). As we shall see, one of the trends in plays for the London theaters is for such cues increasingly to appear as impersonal backstage calls, rather than as directions addressed to actors.

As in chapter 3, my attempt to describe Elizabethan and Jacobean practice with respect to mid-scene directions is based on a sample of plays composed between 1530 and 1642, though some were published as late as 1661. The sample is larger than that relied on in chapter three, though many of the same plays are included. Since I assume that the grammatical form of a stage direction owes more to authorial and scribal hands than to the printing house, I have grouped plays by probable date of composition not date of publication.[4] The groupings thus differ from those in chapter three, in which plays were grouped by date of publication.

The sample includes a total of sixty-one plays divided into four chronological periods: seven Tudor interludes (to provide a baseline of early practice, particularly with regard to verb mood); twenty-three plays written for the London theaters to 1599 (an arbitrary cutoff for early plays); ten plays from 1600 to 1613 (the burning of the Globe being a convenient event to demark a middle period); and eight plays composed between 1613 and 1642 (though some were not published in quarto until 1661). In addition, eleven plays published in the three folio collections (Jonson's, Shakespeare's, and Beaumont and Fletcher's) will be examined to suggest the extent to which mid-scene directions in folios adhere to or depart from the grammatical conventions of plays in manuscript or quarto. As in the discussion of page design in chapter 3, I have made no effort to exclude "bad" quartos, since a description of communal practice is the goal.

Unlike the visual conventions discussed in chapter three, the grammatical conventions for midscene directions do not differ significantly in manuscripts and printed plays. Consequently, in this chapter I consider manuscripts and printed plays together. Although the number and distribution of the *kind* of directions may vary between an extant manuscript and its printed edition, the grammatical *form* is largely consistent among plays that are contemporaries, whether manuscript or printed. (For example, the manuscript of Beaumont and Fletcher's *Bonduca* has only five directions for sound effects and the printed [folio] edition has thirty-three, but in both manuscript and printed text nearly all of them are expressed as noun phrases.) History plays form a large portion of the sample, and they are useful because they tend to have many midscene directions (for battle sequences, court scenes, and the like). However, the romances, tragedies, and city comedies in the sample, though often less fully annotated, observe the same grammatical conventions. Even Jonson's folio plays, which differ so radically in their visual design, fall well within the norms of his fellow dramatists' practice with respect to the grammar of midscene directions.

The plays, by short title and approximate date, are as follows (the editions used are listed in the bibliography):

Tudor Interludes, Humanist plays:

King Johan, MS, c. 1530–60
Cambises, c. 1561, Q 1570
King Darius, Q 1565
Horestes, Q 1567
Like Will to Like, Q 1568
Richardus Tertius, MS, c. 1580

London plays to 1599:

The Spanish Tragedy, c. 1582–88, Q 1594
Famous Victories, c. 1583–88, Q 1598
John a Kent, MS, c. 1587–90
George a Greene, c. 1587–91, Q 1599
Edmond Ironside, MS, c. 1590
Mucedorus, c. 1588–98, Q 1598
1 Contention, c. 1590, Q 1600[5]
Edward I, c. 1590–93 Q 1593
Richard III, c. 1592, Q 1597
Edward II, c. 1592, Q 1594
Woodstock, MS, c. 1592

Sir Thomas More, MS, c. 1592
1,2 Edward IV, c. 1592–99, Q 1600
Richard II, c. 1595, Q 1597
The Blind Beggar of Alexandria, c. 1596, Q 1598
Captain Thomas Stukeley, c. 1596, Q 1605
1 Henry IV, c. 1596–97, Q 1598
2 Henry IV, c. 1598, Q 1600
Every Man Out of His Humour, c. 1599, Q 1600
Sir John Oldcastle, c. 1599, Q 1600
Old Fortunatus, c. 1599, Q 1600
Henry V, c. 1599, Q 1600

London plays 1600–1613:

Thomas Lord Cromwell, c. 1600, Q 1602
Bussy d'Ambois, c. 1600–1604, Q 1607
Sir Thomas Wyatt, c. 1602–7, Q 1607
If You Know Not Me, c. 1604–5, Q 1605
When You See Me, You Know Me, c. 1604–5, Q 1605
King Lear, c. 1605, Q 1608
The Miseries of Enforced Marriage, c. 1606, Q 1607
The Roaring Girl, c. 1604–11, Q 1611
Pericles, Prince of Tyre, c. 1607–8, Q 1609
A King and No King, c. 1611, Q 1619
Bonduca, MS, c. 1611–14

London plays 1614–61:

Sir John Van Olden Barnavelt, MS, c. 1619
Hengist, King of Kent, MS, c. 1616–20, Q 1661[6]
The Changeling, c. 1622, Q 1653
Duchess of Suffolk, c. 1623, Q 1631
King John and Matilda, c. 1628, Q 1655
Perkin Warbeck, c. 1628–30, Q 1634
Alphonsus, Emperor of Germany, Q 1654

Folio editions:

2 Henry VI, c. 1590, F 1623
3 Henry VI, c. 1590, F 1623
Richard III, c. 1592, F 1623
King John, c. 1592–93, F 1623
Richard II, c. 1595, F 1623

Every Man In His Humour, c. 1598, F 1616
2 Henry IV, c. 1598, F 1623
Henry V, c. 1599, F 1623
Henry VIII, c. 1612–13, F 1623
Bonduca, c. 1611–14, F 1647

Examples may be cited from other plays, but these were the basis of my effort to tally the grammatical conventions of midscene directions.

In the plays listed above, directions for action and special effects tend to fall into one of three general grammatical categories, which may in turn be usefully subdivided. The first category is finite verbs that specify what the actor(s) or other personnel should *do*. Within this category there are interesting shifts in verb mood (indicative or imperative), address (second- or third-person), and syntactical completeness (full sentences or elliptical phrases). The second category is modifying phrases that specify *how* something is to be done or a line is to be spoken. The most common forms are present participles, prepositional phrases, and adverbs (such as *aside* or *within*). The third category is nouns or noun phrases that specify *what* is to be done. Nouns may stand alone or be modified by adjectives, participles, or prepositional phrases. In the sections that follow, I will discuss each of these grammatical categories in turn as they are exemplified by directions for action and for sound and other special effects.

FINITE VERBS

In all the plays of my sample, directions for onstage action most often take the form of a finite verb—that is, a verb specific in tense, mood, and person that appears as the predicate of a full sentence or of an elliptical sentence with an implied subject (see table 6.1).

Table 6.1. Directions for Action

Plays	Finite verb	Modifying phrase	Noun phrase
Interludes	230	12	17
to 1599	541	101	50
1600–13	128	7	4
1614–61	133	12	11
Folio eds.	142	9	12

On average, when calling for onstage action, these plays prefer a finite verb 87 percent of the time.

Directions for sound and special effects exhibit a different pattern. (The interludes are omitted below since they contain no identifiable free-standing cues for sound or special effects.) London plays to 1613 express only half of their cues for special effects as finite verbs; the other half appear as nouns and noun phrases, and after 1613 the proportion of nouns increases sharply (table 6.2).

Table 6.2. Directions for Special Effects

Plays	Finite verb		Modifying phrase		Noun phrase	
to 1599	75	(53%)	2	(3%)	66	(46%)
1600–13	24	(50%)	0		24	(50%)
1614–61	8	(9%)	1	(1%)	84	(90%)
Folio eds.	21	(14%)	0		128	(86%)

If some directions I have tallied as "for action" had been classified as "for sound," the number of directions containing verbs would be somewhat larger. For example, the following direction clearly results in an offstage sound, though it is cast as an instruction to an individual actor (and was so tallied above):

Count knocke within.

(*Blind Beggar of Alexandria*, TLN 1020)

Even if one takes these additional directions into account, however, beginning with the earliest plays in my sample, many special effects are "objectified," imagined not as actions to be performed but as effects to be supplied, and this trend increases over the period surveyed.

VERB MOOD: IMPERATIVE, SUBJUNCTIVE, INDICATIVE

The preference for finite verbs in mid-scene directions for action is clear, but ambiguities do arise with respect to verb mood. The presence of ambiguous instances can be understood in part as a legacy from the earlier drama, in which stage directions move freely among imperative, subjunctive, and indicative verbs, and thus among second- and third-person address, even within a single direction. Sometimes the effect is that of carelessness or incoherence, as in an example quoted earlier:

> Go afore her and let her fall down upon thee *and al[l] to beate* him.
> (*Horestes*, TLN 755–61; emphasis added)[7]

But often, what seems like linguistic incompetence is the result of ellipsis. The direction below does shift between second- and third-person address, but it is consistent in mood if the third clause be understood as elliptical:

> Up with thy staff, and be ready to smite, but [let] *Hodge smit first, and let the vice twacke them both and run out.*
> (*Horestes*, TLN 175–85; emphasis added)

The seemingly ungrammatical *"Hodge smit"* makes sense if it is understood to be an abbreviated instance of the jussive subjunctive or third-person imperative that was the norm for stage directions in the medieval Latin and vernacular religious drama.

When a direction takes the form of several independent clauses, as in the example above, a judgment about verb mood can reasonably draw on the mood of other verbs in the sentence. The problem is greater, however, when the direction has only one verb, and even greater if that verb stands alone without an explicit subject. Third-person *singular* indicative phrases pose no problem, having their distinctive "-s" or "-es" ending (*"Kneels," "Dies"*). But since English, unlike Latin, is not a fully inflected language, it is not always possible to distinguish definitively between an elliptical third-person plural indicative phrase and a second-person imperative. For example, forms such as *"Fight," "Dance,"* or *"Sit down"* clearly addressed to more than one character, could be construed grammatically no less than three ways. They might be viewed as second-person imperatives (*"[You] fight," "[You] dance," "[You] sit down"*). Alternatively, they could be viewed as an elliptical indicative phrase (*"[They] fight"* or *"[They] dance"*). A third possibility is to construe them as third-person imperatives (*"[Let them] fight"* or *"[Let them] dance"*). To complicate matters even further, the first two examples, *"Fight," "Dance,"* might even be construed as nouns (*"[A] fight," "[A] dance"*).

Sometimes a pronoun makes it clear which person and mood of the verb is meant. In directions such as *"Make thy battle long"* the second-person address is explicit. Alternatively, given the third person pronouns in the examples below, an elliptical third-person imperative *("Let him/ them . . .")* can safely be inferred:

> *Draw* their *swords.*
> *Run* his *way out while she is down.*
> > (*Cambises*, TLN 202, 838; emphasis added)

> *winde* his *horn,*
> *look in* his *glasse*
> > (*John a Kent*, TLN 469, 736; emphasis added)

By this principle, the following series of directions from *The Spanish Tragedy* (the first for Hieronimo, the last two for Bel-Imperia) also seem to be elliptical subjunctives. They read:

> *Stab him.*
> *Stab him.*
> *Stab herself.*
> > (IV.iii. 85, S.D.-100, S.D.)

Given their proximity in the text, and the third-person pronoun "*herself,*" it seems likely that the writer of these directions thought in terms of a series of third-person subjunctive phrases:

> *[Let him] Stab him* [i.e., Lorenzo].
> *[Let her] Stab him* [i.e., Balthazar].
> *[Let her] Stab herself.*

Telltale pronouns are rare, however, so ambiguous instances remain.

In attempting to tally evolving practices, my solution has been to treat these elliptical instances conservatively. Prior commentators (notably Greg)[8] have noted the ambiguity but construed them as "imperatives," and I shall do likewise. If they are meant as third-person jussive subjunctives *("[Let them] Dance"* or *"[Let them] sit down"*), they are rightly grouped with their second-person counterparts. However, I will note the number of ambiguous instances in parentheses in order to show that in later plays a relatively large proportion of the total imperative instances might be construed as plural indicative phrases.

As noted in chapter 4, in plays from the London theaters directions with imperative and subjunctive verbs soon give way to directions in the third-person indicative. The break with the imperative and subjunctive mood

preferred by Tudor interludes occurs by the 1590s and is sustained throughout the period, as table 6.3 shows (ambiguous instances counted as imperatives are indicated by ±):

Table 6.3. Directions for Action

Play group	3d pers. Subj/ 2d pers. Imper	Indicative
Interludes	158 ±6 (68%)	73 (32%)
to 1599	36 ±8 (6%)	505 (94%)
1600–1613	14 ±10 (11%)	114 (89%)
1614–61	12 ±9 (9%)	121 (92%)
Folio eds.	14 ±9 (10%)	127 (90%)

Tudor interludes prefer third- or second-person commands (100 and 58
instances, respectively) more than two to one. Plays for the professional
theaters more than reverse the preference, opting for the indicative sentence or finite verb phrase about 90 percent of the time. The overall significance of this change from imperative to indicative verbs has already been
discussed at length in chapter 4: it contributes to the self-effacing quality
of Elizabethan directions, in contrast to the self-conscious voice of the
medieval production narrative. While the unique form of entry and exit
directions may, as Greg argued, "be felt as an imperative," the minute-by-
minute business of a scene is conducted in the present indicative. Indicative mid-scene directions permit the action to unfold objectively (that is, in
the third person) in the here and now of the fictive world.

The preference for the indicative in midscene directions is so complete
that, in plays written after 1600 or published in late quartos or folios, the
number of ambiguous instances nearly equals the number of imperatives
and subjunctives. In the ten plays composed between 1600 and 1613, ten
of the fourteen imperatives could be indicative phrases; in the plays from
1614 to 1661, nine of the twelve might be indicative; and in the folio plays,
nine of the fourteen. More and more, stage directions impart instructions to
the actors indirectly and impersonally, without the relative fanfare of the
imperative or subjunctive moods.

In addition to maintaining the unobtrusive, third-person point of view,
most midscene directions are brief and simple, almost atomistic, noting
events singly as they are performed and as they might (*pace* gestalt psy-
chology) register on the consciousness of a member of the audience:[9]

he sees their handes.
he offers to depart
he pulles his beard
Sydanen and h[e] conferre.

(John a Kent, TLN 244, 254, 299, 412)

He strikes him on the eare.
He carries the letters.
She receives and peruseth them.
They discourse privately.
They are all in a muse.

(James IV, TLN 327, 765, 767, 896, 941)

Mucedorus killeth him.
The clowne sings.
she sits her downe.
Shee kneeles.

(Mucedorus, B4ᵛ, C4, D2, D2ᵛ)

In contrast to elaborated entries, which employ compact, Latinate constructions in order to pack maximum information into a single grammatical period, most midscene directions are studiedly brief and simple. After the entry direction establishes the gestalt or the context of the scene, playwrights and playhouse annotators let the action unfold with minimum intrusion from the voice of stage directions.

There are of course exceptions. In early history plays battle sequences are conveyed in more elaborate directions; though many of these are entries, some are for characters already on stage and thus qualify as midscene directions. Thomas Heywood sometimes uses detailed midscene directions, not only for battle sequences but for ordinary business. Thus in *1 and 2 Edward IV*, along with brief directions, such as *"She weeps"* and *"He is led forth,"* one finds:

> *The Lord Maior brings a bowle of wine, & humbly on his knees offers it to the king*
>
> <div align="right">(<i>Part 1</i>, D4ᵛ)</div>

> *As Jane kneels on one side the King, so the Queen steps and kneels on the other.*
>
> <div align="right">(<i>Part 2</i>, Q2ᵛ)</div>

The second example, particularly, with its adverbial clause *("As Jane kneels"),* is a departure from the norm. Similar directions can also be found in the anonymous *Alphonsus, Emperor of Germany* (Q 1654):

He reads a note which he finds among his books.

(B1ᵛ)

As Bohem. is a drinking, e're he hath drunk it all out, Alphonsus pulls the Beaker from his mouth.

(F1ᵛ)

Here the late date of the quarto may have occasioned these highly descriptive directions, but the example of Heywood shows that earlier playwrights might also opt for fuller midscene directions. These exceptions aside, however, the great majority of midscene directions are exceedingly brief.

Like directions for action, directions for special effects that contain a finite verb prefer the indicative to the imperative or subjunctive mood. But in these directions, the preference is not as overwhelming (table 6.4).

Table 6.4. Directions for Special Effects

Play group	3d pers. Subj/ 2nd pers. Imper		Indicative	
to 1599	21	(28%)	54	(72%)
1600–1613	11	(46%)	13	(54%)
1614–61	2	(22%)	7	(78%)
Folio eds.	7	(33%)	14	(67%)

Indicative cues for sound and special effects include the ubiquitous *"The trumpet sounds,"* and directions such as:

The cocke crowes.
. . . a peece goes off.

(*Hamlet,* Q 1604–5, B3 and N4ᵛ)

The Drumme soundeth a-farre off.

(*The Valiant Welshman,* B2 and B2ᵛ)

On the other hand, the imperative form, such as *"Sound an alarum,"* persists as a significant minority longer than in directions for action. In plays between 1600 and 1613, imperative directions for onstage action account for only 10 percent of the finite verbs, whereas 46 percent of the sound cues are still in the imperative mood. If one were to include cues tallied above as "action" that do produce a sound effect (such as *"York knocks"*), this percentage would decline slightly (since directions for action

strongly prefer the indicative), but even so the longer tenure of the imperative in cues for special effects is clear.

VERB PHRASES

The desire for brevity in midscene directions is even more evident when a
stage direction takes the form of an elliptical verb rather than a full sentence (*"Weeps"* or *"Sits"* rather than *"He weeps"* or *"She sits"*). In my
sample, the number directions for action expressed as elliptical verb phrases
steadily grows (table 6.5).

Table 6.5. Directions for Action

Play group	Subjunctive/ Imperative	Indicative sentence	Indicative phrase
Interludes	158 ±6 (68%)	72 (31%)	1 (0.4%)
to 1599	36 ±8 (6%)	448 (83%)	57 (11.0%)
1600–1613	14 ±10 (11%)	91 (71%)	23 (18.0%)
1614–61	12 ±9 (9%)	67 (50%)	54 (41.0%)
Folio eds.	14 ±9 (10%)	72 (51%)	55 (39.0%)

Whereas elliptical indicative phrases are virtually nonexistent in the interludes surveyed, they account for 11 percent of the finite verbs in the plays
to 1599, 18 percent of those in plays 1600–1613, and 41 percent of those in
plays composed after 1613. These late plays provide nearly half their directions for action in an abbreviated, shorthand form. In Middleton's *Hengist*
one finds, for example:

Stabs him.

(I2)

Throws meal in his face,
takes his purse,
and exit.

(I2ᵛ)

And in Thomas Drue's *The Duchess of Suffolk*:

Goeth up the ladder and works.

(C3ᵛ)

Sits downe.

(G4ᵛ)

Strikes him.

(H1)

Climbs up the tree.

(H1)

If all the ambiguous verbs were judged to be elliptical plural verbs (*"[They] Fight"*) rather than imperative or subjunctive commands, the practice after 1613 would be evenly split between full sentences and elliptical phrases. It is true that thirty-six of the fifty-four instances in the latest group are concentrated in two late plays, *The Duchess of Suffolk* (c. 1623) and *King John and Matilda* (c. 1628). However, the proportion in the folio plays is nearly as high, and here conscious revision seems to be responsible for the increase. In the folio texts of plays previously published in quarto, some full-sentence directions are shortened to phrases, and the reverse almost never happens. Consider these examples from the Shakespeare Folio:

Quarto:	Folio:
She spitteth at him.	*Spits at him.*
	(Richard III, TLN 334)
He pluckes it out of his bosom and reades it.	*Snatches it.*
	(Richard II, TLN 2442)
He throws the bottle at him.	*Throws it at him.*
	(1 Henry IV, TLN 2949)
He takes up Hotspur on his back.	*Takes Hotspur on his back.*
	(1 Henry IV, TLN 3093)
He strikes him.	*Strikes him.*
	(Henry V, TLN 2723)

While the second of these examples is squeezed flush right of a line of dialogue, others are indented on their own line of text, so shortage of space in setting the type cannot account for the Folio revisions.

Unlike directions for action, directions for special effects that contain a finite verb hardly ever take the form of an indicative verb phrase (table 6.6).

Table 6.6. Directions for Special Effʻcts

Play group	3rd pers. Subj/ 2d pers. Imper		Indicative sentence		Indicative phrase	
to 1599	21	(28%)	54	(72%)	0	
1600–1613	11	(46%)	13	(54%)	0	
1614–61	2	(22%)	6	(67%)	1	(11%)
Folio eds.	7	(33%)	14	(67%)	0	

The total number of verbs in directions for special effects is low, since, as noted above, between 50 and 90 percent of them are expressed without benefit of a verb. Compared to the growing frequency of indicative verb phrases in directions for action (increasing from 11 percent to 39 percent over the course of my sample), the use of indicative verb phrases in cues for special effects is virtually nil. The road to brevity and economy for these directions took the form of nouns and noun phrases that simply name the effect desired.

MODIFIERS AND NOUN PHRASES

Although directions with finite verbs are the norm, midscene directions for action sometimes appear as grammatical fragments, including modifying phrases and noun phrases. Directions expressed as modifiers may take the form of participles, prepositional phrases, and adverbs. Nouns may stand alone or be modified by adjectives or by prepositional or participial phrases (in which case they constitute ablative absolutes). Since participles, adverbs, prepositional phrases, and ablative absolutes are the main constituents of elaborated entries, their presence in other kinds of directions is not hard to understand. It is as if the descriptive components of an entry had been deconstructed and redistributed to various points in the scene.

Modifiers and nouns constitute a small but fairly consistent minority of directions for midscene action. In my sample, their frequency is as shown in table 6.7.

Certain italicized phrases, such as *"The Song," "The letter,"* and *"His oration to his Souldiers"* (*Richard III*, TLN 3702), I have construed as textual titles rather than stage directions per se, and I have excluded them from my tallies. If they were included they would raise the frequency of noun phrases a percentage point or two, but they would not alter the minority status of phrasal directions.

Table 6.7. Directions for Action

Plays	Total Action SDs	Modifiers	Noun Phrases
Interludes	259	12 (5%)	17 (7%)
to 1599	692	101 (15%)	50 (8%)
1600–1613	139	7 (5%)	4 (3%)
1614–61	156	12 (8%)	11 (7%)
Folio plays	129	9 (6%)	12 (7%)

Indeed, the largest percentage above (15 percent for plays to 1599) may somewhat overstate the frequency of fully freestanding phrases. In these plays, some directions in a series seek economy by omitting the verb that governs the series after the first direction. In *3 Henry VI* (F 1623), for example, a messenger addresses himself to several people in a single speech, and three directions highlight the changes in his orientation:

Speaks to Warwick. . . .
To Lewis. . . .
To Margaret.

(TLN 1906-9)

A similar series occurs *1 Henry IV*, although only one element of the series omits the verb:

Glendower speakes to her in Welsh. . . .
The Lady speakes in Welsh.
The Lady again in Welsh.
The Lady speakes again in Welsh.

(F 1623, TLN 1732–51)

A final example can be cited from Munday's holograph of *John a Kent*, showing that ellipsis may result from the author's hand as well as a scribe's or bookkeeper's:

The chime plays, and Gosselin with the Countesse goes turning out. . . .
The chime again, and they turn out in like manner.
The chime again, and so they.

(TLN 1158–64)

Here, both an action cue *("and so they")* and a sound cue *("The chime again")* are expressed as noun phrases. The elliptical elements of these series are visually independent (and I have tallied them as freestanding), but grammatically they are still governed by the initial verb.[10]

The degree to which a phrase is freestanding may also be restricted if it occurs as an extension of a speech prefix. In this case, such a phrase is clearly detached from a governing verb, but it is combined with another direction. In *Sir John Oldcastle*, for example, *"imbracing her"* follows a speech prefix at TLN 686, and a pair of directions cue the carrier humorously named "Club." The first is clearly a freestanding noun plus participial phrase; the second appears as part of an extended speech prefix:

> *The carrier calling*
> *Club calling*. Hoste, why ostler, zwookes. . . .
>
> (TLN 2247–48)

Such forms are not new with Elizabethan directions. In *Le Martire S. Estiène*, a saint's play c. 1450, speech prefixes plus participial phrases constitute much of the production narrative:

> *Annas, en gregnant les dens et en estoupant ses oreilles*
> [Annas, grinding his teeth and stopping his ears.]
>
> *Le Premier, en ferant du poing*
> [The First {false witness} striking {Estiène} with his fist]
>
> *Le Second, en frapant comme l'autre, die en ferant.*
> [The Second {witness} striking like the other, says while doing so.][11]

Prepositional phrases and adverbs may also extend a speech prefix to indicate how or to whom a speech is addressed. In the Anglo-Norman *Adam*, for example, prepositional phrases occasionally appear as extensions of speech prefixes: *"Figura ad Evam"* [The Figure {of God} to Eve]. *Sir John Oldcastle* contains several similar forms:

> *Doll to the Priest.*
>
> (TLN 709)
>
> *King in great hast.*
>
> (TLN 1329)
>
> *Roch[ester] within.*
>
> (TLN 2057)

Examples can be found in other plays as well:

Gloster and Jone hand in hand.

(*Edward I*, TLN 1659)[12]

Gh[ost] to Ri[chard]. . . .
Ghost to Richm[ond].

(*Richard III*, F 1623, TLN 3563–66)

Boy within.

(*Sir John Van Olden Barnavelt*, MS, TLN 1671)

If the phrases that extend speech prefixes were not included in my tallies above, the percentage of freestanding phrasal directions would be even smaller. However, since they are often felt as parenthetical additions and represented as such in modern editions, I have included them so as not to understate the role of grammatical fragments in midscene directions.

The most common adverbial modifiers are *aside* and *within*, appearing after a speech prefix (in prose passages) or to the right of the dialogue (in verse). In *Sir John Oldcastle*, for example, four out of five asides in the prose passages are marked by an extended speech prefix, while one stands alone in the "margin" (i.e., flush right). Both that occur in verse speeches appear to the right, independently.[13]

Thus, though a definite minority, midscene directions for action may appear as freestanding phrases, including adverbial constructions:

Roundly off.
Hastilie.

(*Captain Thomas Stukeley*, TLN 9, 2805)

Round in his eare.

(*John a Kent*, TLN 551)

participles:

Shrugging gladly.
flinging up cappes.

(*Sir Thomas More*, TLN 240, 710)

Pointing to old Kno'well.

(*Every Man In His Humour*, F 1616, IV.x.41, S.D.)

prepositional phrases:

> *to him-*
> *self*
>
> (*King Leir*, TLN 404–5, 414–15)

> *To the King.*
>
> (*King John and Matilda*, H1ᵛ)

> *At the Fether shop now.*
> *At the Sempsters shop now.*
>
> (*The Roaring Girl*, C4ᵛ, D1)

and even nouns:

> *action* [i.e., Lifter picks a purse]
> *kinde salutations.*
>
> (*Sir Thomas More*, TLN 237, +1532)

> *The Fethershop againe.*
>
> (*The Roaring Girl*, D1ᵛ)

Even if what I construe to be textual titles, such as *"The Song"* and *"The letter"* were included in the tally, nouns are the rarest form for a direction for action. By far the most common is the familiar term *Excursions* that cues episodes in a battle sequence. *"Skirmish,"* an alternative to *"Excursions,"* also appears once as a noun:

> *Here another Skirmish.*
>
> (*1 Henry VI*, TLN 629)

It also appears in a prepositional element of an entry direction and as a verb:

> *Enter in skirmish with bloody Pates.*
>
> (*1 Henry VI*, TLN 1298)

> *Here they skirmish againe.*
>
> (*1 Henry VI*, TLN 441)

Fifteen of the fifty nouns tallied in the plays to 1599 occur in one scene of Jonson's *Every Man Out of his Humour*. In a series of prose speeches, an abbreviated direction in parenthesis "(*Tab.*)" repeatedly cues a character when to take a puff on his pipe of tobacco. In a sly metadramatic or metatextual comment on this unusual direction, a character observes "I never knew Tabacco taken as a *parenthesis* before" (Q 1600, TLN 2528).[14]

It also should be noted that in my sample midscene directions for action expressed as phrases are concentrated in the plays of Anthony Munday. His autograph manuscripts of *John a Kent* and *Sir Thomas More*, and the quarto of *Sir John Oldcastle*, a play on which he collaborated, account for 52 of the 152 modifiers and nouns in the twenty-three plays to 1599 (they contribute 17, 17, and 18 instances, respectively). So, there is some basis for seeing these forms as a "Munday signature." Heywood's two parts of *Edward IV* are also heavy contributors to the total of phrasal directions before 1600; the two plays account for 22 instances, many of them simple notations for asides. The habits of these two authors might thus account for the relatively higher percentage of such directions up to 1599. But their contributions notwithstanding, it is clear that a small minority of action directions were expressed as phrases throughout the period.

Unlike directions for action, directions for sound and other special effects are routinely expressed as grammatical fragments, chiefly nouns and noun phrases, as shown in table 6.8.

Table 6.8. Directions for Special Effects

Plays	Finite verb	Modifying phrase	Noun phrase
to 1599	75 (53%)	2 (0.3%)	66 (46%)
1600–1613	24 (50%)	0	24 (50%)
1614–61	8 (9%)	1 (1.0%)	84 (90%)
Folio eds.	21 (14%)	0	128 (86%)

In relying on noun phrases as much or more than on finite verbs, directions for special effects resemble the bookkeeper's annotations regarding sound and props that appear in some playhouse manuscripts. In the theatrical "plots" that have survived,[15] one finds lists of props and stage furnishings, such as these lurid reminders of objects needed for *The Battle of Alcazar*:

> raw
> flesh
> Dead

mens heads
& bones
banquett
blood[16]

Notes added to the *Woodstock* manuscript also typically take the form of nouns or noun phrases: *"flourish"* (TLN 628), *"Book"* (TLN 664), *"Petitions/ [deletion]: Mace"* (TLN 789–90), *"Blanks"* (i.e., blank charters, TLN 1136), *"George"* (presumably the name of the actor playing the Servant who enters a few lines later, TLN 1405), and *"A bed / for woodstock"* (TLN 2377–78).

Two examples in *John a Kent*, however, clearly show that directions written in the main hand of the manuscript, in this case Munday's, might also appear as noun phrases. Munday's directions are on the right, the bookkeeper's additions on the left:

Musique	*Musique*
	whi<le?. . .
	(TLN 777)

Musique. Chime	*A daynt<y fit>*
	of musi<que
	(TLN 1140–41)

Two exit directions in Munday's hand also contain sound cues expressed as noun phrases:

The chime again, and they turn out in like manner. . . .
The chime again, and so they.

(TLN 1161–64)

Similarly, in the portions of *Sir Thomas More* ascribed to Munday, one finds a prop notation as a freestanding direction in his hand: *"low stools"* (TLN +1413). Although the manuscript evidence is rather weighted toward one author, in this case his practice does not seem to be idiosyncratic, as the increasing frequency of noun phrases in all plays in my sample suggests. Indeed, the highest percentages occur in the folio plays, in which Munday presumably had no hand. Overall, whereas directions for action remained chiefly in the form of full sentences with finite verbs, sound and special effects became objectified, conceived as effects to be named, rather than as actions to be performed.

AUTHORITY AND AUDIENCE IN MIDSCENE DIRECTIONS

Directions for special effects

Like initial entries and many midscene directions for action, directions for special effects evolved in the direction of economy, unobtrusiveness, and a kind of terse, matter-of-fact authority. They move from full-sentence descriptions to brief but syntactically complete sentences, significantly terser than most dialogue, to noun phrases or even single words. Syntactically, they come to resemble bookkeeper's notations, which characteristically also take the form of lists of nouns or noun phrases.

These simple nouns and noun phrases are still, I think, felt as imperatives, as "calls" for certain effects, as I have often termed them here. In their extreme abbreviation, however, they are less formal and more confident in tone than ordinary imperatives: there is no need for discussion and no room to question such a simple signal. Like their modern equivalents "Lights, camera, action!," they seem more a means of coordinating agreed-upon group activity than a formal command. Their terseness implies not coercion but communal action.

Indeed, this commonality can been seen in the frequency with which the bookkeeper reiterates in his own hand directions already present in the hand of the author or the main scribe of a theatrical manuscript. The bookkeeper, in effect, re-authorizes or internalizes the stage directions written by others. The audience for most bookkeeper's notes is not the individual actor or the general reader but the bookkeeper himself. Thus their extreme simplicity is understandable; writer and audience are one. What is interesting, as we have seen, is that directions for special effects written by the author or other intermediary also adopt the simple, concise form of nouns and noun phrases.

In general, I speculate, directions for special effects wield great authority both with the bookkeeper and the players for whom they were initially designed. Together with the bookkeeper's annotations (if any survive), they are records of how a particular group (or groups) realized the play's spectacle. At the same time, the backstage directions that survive in printed texts, while prized by theater historians, often have less authority with later interpreters, who are working with different players, different resources, and different theaters. Not all modern productions of the history plays resound with flourishes, drums, and trumpets, just as not all productions of *Macbeth* actually treat their audiences to visions of the "armed head" or the "bloody child."

Directions for Action

As we have seen, although the use of elliptical verb phrases increases after 1613, directions for action most often appear as finite verbs, in the indicative mood, and usually in full (though brief) sentences. This preference may seem entirely predictable; what better way to indicate action than with a verb? In the most basic way, the preference for finite verbs suggests the degree to which stage directions primarily encode physical actions, as opposed to the internal reactions or emotional states that are inscribed in many modern stage directions. As David Bevington and others have shown,[17] on the Elizabethan stage "Action is eloquence"; the physical body and actions of the player are primary signifiers of emotional, social, and moral meaning. The term "actor" is in flux during the early modern period, referring first to the characters of the play and later to the players that impersonate or "act" them. Thus, for example, the dramatis personae, or the list of what we would term the "characters," that concludes the Folio text of *2 Henry IV* is entitled "The Actors Names." At the same time, in the front matter of the 1623 Folio, a list of the members of the King's Men is similarly entitled "The Names of the Principall Actors." Like the predominance of active verbs in the stage directions of the period, the use of "actor" attests to action as the essence of playing: both character and player were actors, not merely speakers *(interloquitores)* of their lines.

The preference for finite verbs and full sentences, however, is harder to explain. Given all the other trends in the evolution of Elizabethan stage directions (i.e., the movement towards economy, unobtrusiveness, and a distinctive voice to distinguish them from the dialogue), one might expect that elliptical verbs would have become the norm. First, a verb phrase provides greater economy. As we saw in chapter 3, after 1600 more than half of all midscene directions for action and special effects appeared flush right of the dialogue, in a "marginal" position. Consequently, brevity and economy of syntax would, one supposes, be especially desirable. Second, a verb phrase arguably makes the directions for action even less obtrusive and more easily absorbed into the text. At the same time, it preserves a distinctive, shorthand style and laconic tone that would help distinguish the voice of the directions from the voices of the dialogue. In the light of all these factors, it is rather surprising that elliptical verb phrases did not become more common or eventually become the norm.

By the same token, participial phrases might have served as well as or better than finite verbs. Participles are economical and clear without being overly precise. Indeed, the indefiniteness of a participial phrase suggests ongoingness, a sustained period of dialogue-plus-action, and thus might be viewed as even more dynamic and well suited to coordinating word and action on the stage than a finite verb. Many modern plays use participial phrases as often as (or more often than) finite verbs.[18] Why did participles not become more common, even become the norm for Elizabethan directions for action? What accounts for the persistence of full sentences and finite verbs?

Sometimes full sentences are preferable because clarity requires including a specific subject for the relevant verb. If two or more characters are involved, or if the action is to be performed by a nonspeaking character, the subject of the verb needs to be explicit. For example, a series of directions in the folio edition of *Richard III* illustrates the utility of full sentences during the melodramatic business of the wooing scene:

She looks scornfully at him.

(TLN 362)

He lays his breast open: she offers at [it] with his sword.

(TLN 371)

She falls the sword.

(TLN 376)

Full sentences are helpful here because all these actions occur during Richard's long speech of seduction; without the pronouns, who's doing what would not be as clear.

It is also possible that finite verb phrases themselves were not viewed as syntactically incomplete by the Elizabethans. Like their Latin counterparts, elliptical English verb phrases may have been seen as syntactically complete. *Exit, Exeunt, Manet,* and *Manent* stand alone, and they are usually translated as full sentences, the subject being implied in the inflected verb. This might also have been true of the third-person singular in English, where ambiguity is reduced by the inflected ending ("-s" or "-es"). A direction from *Hengist*, quoted earlier, seems to imply just such an equivalence of the English and Latin forms:

> *Throws meal in his face,*
> *takes his purse,*
> *and exit.*

(I2ᵛ)

In this case, two English indicative phrases seem to be offered as directly parallel to the Latin *"exit"* [he exits]. If this is how such verb phrases were viewed, it might explain why they came to be used roughly as often as brief full sentences: the two forms were felt to be equivalent, economical but syntactically complete.

The need for clarity aside, however, it seems to me that the degree of formality conferred by syntactical completeness was itself desired. A brief full sentence maintains a degree of authority and formality that a shorthand phrase relinquishes. Phrases and simple lists sufficed for backstage directions, but the character/actor continued to be addressed more formally. Just as an old-fashioned courtesy once governed backstage forms of address ("Five minutes, Miss Fontaine!"), early modern directions address the actors in full sentences.

Conclusion

It is beyond the scope of this book to trace the later development of English stage directions comprehensively or in detail, but I would like to conclude by looking very selectively at the stage directions in some eighteenth-century "acting" editions of Shakespeare and in some well-known plays of the nineteenth and twentieth centuries. Just as examining medieval directions highlights key aspects of the Elizabethan code, so glancing at the directions of later editions and dramatists suggests how elements of that code were adapted to the needs and visions of later theatrical communities. Overall, aspects of Elizabethan page design have proved remarkably durable, aided, as one might guess, by the ascendancy of Shakespeare as the preeminent English dramatist. The diction and syntax of English stage directions, on the other hand, have varied widely, but particularly in the late twentieth century the impersonal and objective tone of Elizabethan directions seems influential in the works of important contemporary playwrights.

EIGHTEENTH-CENTURY EDITIONS OF SHAKESPEARE

The text of Shakespeare's plays underwent sometimes radical alteration and "improvement" during the eighteenth century, but visual aspects of the Elizabethan code for stage directions were transmitted largely intact, not only in the scholarly editions of Theobald, Johnson, and Malone, but also in the so-called acting editions of Garrick, Bell, and Mrs. Inchbald.[1] While eighteenth-century acting editions of Shakespeare were usually based on the Folio texts, rather than the quartos emphasized in this study, many aspects of the design of the page were carried over unchanged:

1. Directions appear in italics in contrast to the dialogue in roman.
2. Speech prefixes appear on the left-hand side of the text column, slightly indented, one speech prefix to a line.

3. Initial entries are prominent on the page, centered within the text column or written across the entire column.

4. Midscene entries are also usually centered, highlighting the arrival of a new character upon the scene.

5. Midscene directions (other than entries) are usually set on their own line, indented to the right as far as convenient.

6. Exits generally appear to the right, even flush right, either on a separate line or flush right at the end of a line of dialogue.

During the eighteenth century, some Elizabethan conventions, such as italicized directions and centered entries, seem to have been standard for dramatic texts of all kinds. Others, though not universal, seem retained in these editions in deference to Shakespeare. For example, the left-hand, indented speech prefix is retained by Garrick, even though in his own plays and his non-Shakespearean adaptations he preferred a centered speech prefix, which separated each speech by vertical white space.[2]

One innovation in the apparatus of many eighteenth-century editions of Shakespeare is the locale provided at the beginning of each scene along with act and scene headings. The location of the action is sometimes noted in Folio plays at the *end* of the text, along with the dramatis personae. (This is the case, for example, in *The Tempest* and *Measure for Measure*.) But stage directions indicating the location of the action in each scene do not regularly appear in Elizabethan plays. In Dryden's 1752 version of *Henry VIII*, for example, an indication of locale introduces the first scene of each act:

S C E N E, *an Anti-chamber in the Palace.*

(I.i.0)

And for subsequent scenes in each act, the formula is:

S C E N E *changes to the* Council chamber.

(I.ii.0)

S C E N E *changes to* York-house.

(I.iv.0)

This edition thus alternates between a noun phrase, such as those used for special effects in Elizabethan texts (*"Cornets, Hoboyes"*) and a direction in which the scene is active, like a character ("S C E N E *changes*"). A similar duality can be found in Elizabethan plays with respect to introducing prologues: one could use a textual heading, usually in roman type ("The

Prologue") or an italic entry direction, which treated the prologue as a character *("Enter Prologue")*.

Two other acting editions of *Henry VIII*, Garrick's[3] and Bell's, do not add scene-by-scene locations, but Dean's edition inserts a general statement at the end of the dramatis personae *("The* SCENE *lies mostly in London and Westminster; once at Kimbolton")* and indicates the location of each scene with either a noun phrase ("*The Council-Chamber*," I.ii.0), or a combination of a scene heading and "scene change direction" (as in the Dryden edition):

> *SCENE IV.*
> *Changes to York-place. . . .*
>
> (I.iv.0)

With Kemble's edition of 1804, however, the pattern of scene heading plus a brief location seems to become the norm:

> *SCENE II.*
> *The Council-chamber. . . .*
>
> (I.ii.0)

This pattern is reproduced in Mrs. Inchbald's 1808 edition and retained in Kemble's edition of 1815.

One innovation embraced by Garrick (and also found to a greater extent in Pope) is not continued in the later editions. Instead of the Elizabethan convention that a cleared stage signals the end of one scene and the beginning of another, Garrick observes the neoclassical or French convention in which a new scene begins when a new character or group of characters enters.[4] This convention, however, was not retained in later editions, where, as in the Folio, a cleared stage defines a scene.

As we saw in chapter 5, entries with their codified, Latinate grammar are among the most authoritative and distinctive of Elizabethan directions. To a great extent their conventions still obtain in eighteenth-century acting editions of Shakespeare. Here is an entry from the first scene of *Henry VIII*, followed by its counterparts in later editions:

> *Enter Cardinall Wolsey, the Purse borne before him, certaine*
> *of the Guard, and two Secretaries with Papers: The*
> *Cardinall in his passage, fixeth his eye on Buck-*
> *[ing]ham, and Buckingham on him,*
> *both full of disdaine.*
>
> (F 1623, TLN 175–79)

Enter Cardinal Wolsey attended, Secretary with papers, the
Cardinal in his passage fixeth his eye on Buckingham
and Buckingham on him, both full of disdain.

(1752, Dryden)

Enter Cardinal Wolsey, and Cromwell, the purse borne,
before him, certain of the guard, and two secretaries
with papers; the Cardinal in his passage fixeth his
eye on Buckingham, and Buckingham on him, both
full of disdain.

(1762, Garrick)

Enter Cardinal Wolsey, and Cromwell, the purse borne,
before him, certain of the guard, and two secretaries
with papers; the Cardinal in his passage fixeth his
eye on Buckingham, and Buckingham on him, both
full of disdain.

(1774, Bell)

Enter footmen—Guards—Gentlemen—one Gentleman bearing the
broad seal,—another the Cardinal's hat,—two Gentlemen
with silver pillars,—two Priests with silver crosses,-
-Serjeant at Arms with mace,—two Gentleman-ushers
bareheaded with wands,—Cardinal Wolsey,—two Pages
bearing his train,—Cromwell with dispatches,—two
Secretaries with bags of papers,—Chaplains,—
Gentlemen,—Footmen,—Guards.

Wolsey in his passage fixes his eye on Buckingham, and Buckingham
on him, both full of disdain.

(1804, Kemble; roman type in original)

Up to Kemble, the form and content (with minor excisions and substitu-
tions) remain remarkably similar. The number of characters varies and the
anonymous "secretary" is early on conflated with a named character (Cromwell), perhaps to enlarge an actor's part or save doubling. Kemble's version reflects his particular staging, with additions of props, supers, etc.[5]
Nonetheless, despite the additions, the form of an entry direction remains:
the initial uninflected *"Enter,"* elaborated with the characteristic syntax,
chiefly ablative absolutes.

The survival of these conventions seems to be another indication of the
increasing deference to Shakespeare's text. George Coleman's edition of
Fletcher's *Bonduca* for *Bell's British Theatre*, for example, regularly changes

the grammar of all the entries. The unique, unvarying verb is naturalized and inflected depending on the number of characters entering: *"Junius and Petillus enter"* (I.i.0), but *"Curius enters"* (II.i.0). Similarly, Charles Johnson's *Love in a Forest*, an 1723 adaptation of scenes from *As You Like It*, employs neoclassical entries and invents a new form: *"Orlando and Adam entering"* (I.i.0). But when representing Shakespeare's own texts, editors adhere to the conventions of the originals.

Occasionally in these editions, one finds entries in the neoclassical form or so-called massed entries: the characters in the scene are simply listed at the beginning without use of the word *"enter."* None occur in the Folio text of *Henry VIII*, but several occur in Garrick's edition and in Bell's.[6] Further, in keeping with the different resources and practices of the eighteenth-century theater, some "entries" become "discoveries." The eighteenth-century stage had a proscenium arch, from which a "house curtain" might be hung, and wings on grooves that could be opened to reveal a fully dressed stage. Discoveries occur in the folios and quartos, too, of course, but usually not on this scale:

> *Discover'd at the trial. Captain, six guards behind the*
> *throne. King on the throne. Norfolk and Suffolk*
> *on each side. Lord Chamberlain and Surry on a*
> *step. Sands and Lovel on another. Two Lords.*
> *Two Cardinals, on two stools, facing the audience.*
> *Cromwell at a table, in the middle, a mace on it. . . .*
>
> (Garrick, II.iv.0)

> *A state for the Cardinal, and a Table for the Guests. Anne Bullen, Lady*
> *Denny, and other Ladies and gentlemen, as guests, Wolsey's Servants*
> *attending them, discovered.*
>
> (Kemble, II.iv.0)

The diction of the details is non-Elizabethan: the references to a *"step"* on the stage and, more striking, to *"facing the audience"* by way of indicating the blocking. Nonetheless, the syntax remains close to that of Elizabethan directions for special effects: compact noun phrases, including one ablative absolute *("a mace on it")*.[7]

NINETEENTH- AND TWENTIETH-CENTURY DIRECTIONS

The scope of nineteenth-century and early-twentieth-century stage directions differs in many ways from that of Elizabethan directions. Influential playwrights in the realist movement provided detailed descriptions of sets and often lengthy descriptions of a character's appearance and personality attached to the dramatic personae or to his or her first entrance.[8] For example, consider the opening directions in an English translation of Ibsen's *A Doll's House*:

> *A comfortably and tastefully, but not expensively furnished room. Backstage right a door leads out to the hall; backstage left, another door to Helmer's study. . . . Engravings on the wall. A what-not with china and other bric-a-brac. . . . A winter day. . . .Nora enters the room.*
>
> *. . . Nora closes the door. She continues to laugh happily to herself as she removes her coat, etc. She takes from her pocket a bag containing macaroons and eats a couple. Then she tiptoes across and listens at her husband's door.*
>
> *Nora*: Yes, he's here. *(Starts humming again as she goes over to the table, right.)*
>
> *Helmer (from his room):* Is that my skylark twittering out there?
>
> *Nora (opening some of the parcels):* It is! . . . *(Pops the bag of macaroons in her pocket and wipes her mouth)* Come out here, Torvald, and see what I've bought.
>
> *Helmer:* You mustn't disturb me! *(Short pause, then he opens the door and looks in, his pen in his hand.)* Bought did you say? All that?[9]

The set is described in detail; much action is provided for Nora that is not implied in the dialogue. In addition to changes in scope and content, the diction and syntax of these directions also differ from Elizabethan norms: the verb in the entry direction is inflected: *"Nora enters the room."* Offstage spaces are not alluded to in terms of theater architecture, as they tended to be in Elizabethan plays; rather they are imagined in terms of the fictive space of the realistic set: Helmer speaks *"from his room,"* not *"within."* Similarly, when characters leave the stage they no longer simply *"exit"*; they go *"out into the hall"* or *"the study."* Fictive terms for theatrical space are dominant, not occasional as they were in Elizabethan times.

In addition, directions for stage business are far more frequent, often in the form of elliptical verbs and participles: Nora *"Starts humming again"* and speaks while *"opening some of the parcels."* The characters' actions are far more densely scripted than in Elizabethan times. In *Death of a Sales-*

man, the following are only some of the participial directions for business that accompany the two brothers' reminiscences in act 1:

> *getting out of bed,*
> *sitting down on his bed,*
> *holding out a pack of cigarettes,*
> *taking a cigarette.*[10]

Despite these differences, a few formal features are familiar in both Ibsen and Miller: participles and elliptical verb phrases to indicate action; ablative absolutes to establish hand-props involved in an entry (*"his pen in his hand"*); noun phrases to indicate stage furnishings (*"engravings on the wall"*), and so on. In their impersonal tone, too, these directions have some things in common with Elizabethan practice.[11]

Some twentieth-century stage directions differ more radically in tone and function from Elizabethan practice than Ibsen's and Miller's. Free-standing participles and other phrases indicating the character's emotional state are common in many modern plays. I encountered only a handful of such directions in sixty Elizabethan plays, chiefly these in *Sir Thomas More*:

> *shrugging gladly*
>
> (TLN 240)
>
> *pondering to himself*
>
> (TLN +1575)
>
> *kind salutations*
>
> (TLN +1532)
>
> *in great reverenc<e*
>
> (TLN +1237)

By contrast, in one half-page of dialogue in Fugard's *"Master Harold"* . . . *and the Boys*, several phrases convey Hally's inner state:

> *sharply,*
> *Seething with irritation and frustration,*
> *Trying to hide his feelings,*
> *Before he can stop himself.*[12]

Such emotional pointers serve as both descriptions for the readers and instructions for the actors, but they tend to reduce the objectivity of the dramatic script. They assume that the reader/actor is not responsible for inferring the emotional coloration of the speech from the lines themselves or the context, or providing one of his own. Further, they may seem to close down options for other moods or modes of delivering a line that might be possible.

Although modern authors often provide such stage directions, contemporary theater professionals, as noted in the introduction, often pay them little mind. Jerry Turner, director and translator of Ibsen, concludes that although Ibsen worked as a director and stage manager, he wrote "superfluous" stage directions (such as *"amazed"* or *"swooning")* because he didn't "trust the actors."[13] In Turner's view, I infer, such directions are "superfluous" because they either state the obvious or reduce the emotional richness of eloquent concrete actions, such as Nora's tarantella or the intimacy of her gesture in lighting Dr. Rank's cigar.

Even more distant from the impersonal, objective tone of Elizabethan stage directions is the tone of writers like G. B. Shaw or Tennessee Williams. Shaw's directions sometimes engage in highly self-conscious parody of traditional stage effects, as in this direction from the opening scene of *Pygmalion:*

> *He opens the umbrella and dashes off Strandwards, but comes into collision with a flower girl, who is hurrying in for shelter, knocking her basket out of her hands. A blinding flash of lightning, followed instantly by a rattling peal of thunder, orchestrates the incident.*[14]

In *Cat on a Hot Tin Roof,* Williams's directions sometimes take the form and tone of personal reverie on his characters, addressed to the reader/actor as if to an intimate friend:

> *Her [Maggie's] voice has range, and music; sometimes it drops low as a boy's and you have a sudden image of her playing boy's games as a child.*[15]

Marsha Norman, in *'night, Mother,* provides a literary-critical comment within a stage direction:

> *As Jessie and Mama replace the slipcover on the sofa and the afghan on the chair, the physical struggle somehow mirrors the emotional one in the conversation.*[16]

In contrast to Ibsen, the voices of these directions step entirely outside the fictive world of the play to address the reader/actor in a self-conscious and literary way.

Some more recent playwrights, however, have returned to a more objective voice, close to that of Shakespeare and the Elizabethans. Beckett and Pinter reject the overt psychologizing and personal tone of novelistic directions. With the simple direction *"Pause,"* they manipulate the rhythm of the dialogue, focusing on silence and enigmatic timing, rather than on the explicit emotional coloring of a speech. Further, the atomistic simplicity of their directions for onstage action recalls the brevity and unobtrusiveness of most Elizabethan directions. However, in Beckett's case the sheer number of these directions makes them anything but unobtrusive; to read them or to witness the repetitive actions they prescribe powerfully communicates Beckett's mechanistic, oppressive universe, as in this passage from *Endgame:*

> *Clov*: What did I do with that steps?
>   (*He looks around for ladder.*)
>   You didn't see that steps?
>   (*He sees it.*)
>   Ah, about time.
>   (*He goes toward window left.*)
>   Sometimes I wonder if I'm in my right mind. Then it
>   passes over and I'm as lucid as before.
>   (*He gets up ladder, looks out of window.*)
>   Christ, she's under water!
>   (*He looks.*)
>   How can that be? . . . Ah what a fool I am! I'm on the wrong
>   side!
>   (*He gets down, takes a few steps towards window right.*)
>   Under water!
>   (*He goes back for ladder.*)
>   What a fool I am!
>   (*He carries ladder toward window right.*)[17]

Sam Shepard's directions similarly tend to focus on pauses and specific physical actions; they assume the reader/actor can, in the context of the dialogue, interpret their emotional significance. In *Fool for Love*, for example:

> [*May*] *crosses fast to bathroom, steps over Eddie, goes into bathroom, slams door, door booms. Pause as Martin stares at bathroom door. Eddie stays on floor, grins at Martin.*

> *Martin*: She's not mad or anything is she?
> *Eddie*: You got me, buddy.

Martin: I didn't mean to make her mad.
(*Pause*.)[18]

Also Elizabethan in feeling is Shepherd's shorthand syntax, the avoidance of connectives and articles (*"goes into bathroom, slams door, door booms"*). When he does include a direction for specific emotion, Shepard tends to phrase it as an action: *"grins, gets embarrassed, looks at bathroom door"*;[19] this also contributes to the objective tone.

The Elizabethan form for stage directions is as integral to Elizabethan dramatic discourse as Shaw's and Beckett's are to their plays. Yet in many ways the Elizabethans provided the basic code on which later dramatists depended as they modulated the voice and content of the stage directions to suit their own ends and theatrical circumstances. Director Jonathan Miller once lamented that dramatists, and especially Shakespeare, present the performers with texts "which are almost bereft of collateral instructions telling one what the characters are and what they mean by what they say."[20] Despite the apparent tone of despair, I suspect that this is precisely as many performers (and readers) of drama like it. In such "bare" scripts readers and actors alike must ponder the text, collaborate with the author, and construct their own meaning. Although we may now consider that readers construct the meaning of all texts, the pleasure of doing so is especially characteristic of drama as a genre. To judge from their practices, Elizabethan playwrights and theater people accommodated and nurtured this pleasure by creating a code for stage directions that provides the essentials of speech, action, props, and costume authoritatively, objectively, and unobtrusively, and yet leaves much room for interpretation. Elements of their code survive not only in contemporary drama, but also with some modification in such unlikely venues as the Saturday morning cartoons, when the Pink Panther prefaces his escape from his pursuers by the catchphrase, "Exit, stage right."

Notes

PREFACE

1. Alfred Harbage, *Shakespeare and the Rival Traditions* (New York: Macmillan, 1952).

2. Peter Arnott, *Greek Scenic Conventions in the Fifth Century b.c.* (Oxford: Clarendon Press, 1962), quoted in Gary Chancellor, "Stage Directions in Western Drama: Form and Function" (Ph.D. diss., University of Wisconsin, 1980), p. 14. Chancellor argues that the horizontally rolled scrolls on which Greek plays were written left no room for explicit stage directions, but it seems to me room would have been made for them if there were any. Chancellor's main interests are the influence of a reading public on the balance between the two "forms" of stage direction (implicit and explicit) and the aesthetic effects achieved by the density and frequency of explicit stage directions in dramatists such as Lessing, Hauptmann, and Ionesco.

3. Chancellor, "Stage Directions in Western Drama," p. 71.

4. David Bevington, *Action is Eloquence: Shakespeare's Language of Gesture* (Cambridge: Harvard University Press, 1984).

INTRODUCTION

1. That is, in the usual sense of explicit written directions in a playscript, rather than the many performance cues in the dialogue. The definition offered in the *Oxford Companion to the Theatre*, ed. Phyllis Hartnoll, 3d ed. (London: Oxford University Press, 1967) reads: "notes added to the script of a play to convey information about its performance not already explicit in the dialogue itself" (p. 912). For the purposes of this discussion, I will consider (as is customary in Shakespeare studies) all stage directions, even those that confirm action already clear in the dialogue.

2. See Marga Munkelt, "Stage Directions as Part of the Text," *Shakespeare Studies* 19 (1991): 253–71.

3. Michael Issacharoff, "Inscribed Performance," *Rivista di Letterature moderne e comparate* (Pisa) 39, no. 2 (April–June 1986): 101.

4. David Bradley, *From Text to Performance in the Elizabethan Theatre: Preparing the Play for the Stage* (Cambridge: Cambridge University Press, 1992), pp. 4–5, 25.

5. Patricia A. Suchy, "When Words Collide: The Stage Direction as Utterance," *Journal of Dramatic Theory and Criticism* 6, no. 1 (fall 1991): 74.

6. Janusz Głowacki, interview on *Fresh Air,* National Public Radio, July 1991.

7. Joel Engel, ed., *Screenwriters on Screenwriting* (New York: Hyperion, 1995), p. 140, cited in Louis Phillips, "The Pleasure of His Company," *Shakespeare Bulletin* 13, no. 4 (fall 1995): 13.

8. See Michael Issacharoff, "Texte théâtral et didascalecture," *Modern Language Notes* 96, no. 4 (1981): 809–23, esp. 813–20. His taxonomy is also summarized in a later essay, "Stage Codes," in *Performing Texts*, ed. Michael Issacharoff and Robin F. Jones (Philadelphia: University of Pennsylvania Press, 1988), p. 63. Marvin Carlson provides a very similar list of categories in "The Status of Stage Directions," *Studies in the Literary Imagination* 24 (fall 1991): 37–38.

9. Issacharoff, "Inscribed Performance," p. 94.

10. Suchy, "When Words Collide," p. 71.

11. The incident is discussed in ibid., p. 70. The production, which I saw, was subversive to Beckett's intention, but powerful all the same.

12. Silvia Drake, "Few Fears in This 'Virginia Woolf,'" Los Angeles *Times*, 1 October 1989.

13. Cited in E. A. G. Honigmann, *The Stability of Shakespeare's Text* (London: Edward Arnold, 1965), p. 12.

14. From the company's complaint against Brome, 12 February 1639/40, quoted in G. E. Bentley, *The Profession of Dramatist in Shakespeare's Time, 1590 to 1642* (Princeton: Princeton University Press, 1971), p. 143.

15. Carlson, "The Status of Stage Directions," p. 26.

16. Suchy, "When Words Collide," p. 74.

17. See for example, Bernard Beckerman, *Shakespeare at the Globe, 1599–1609* (New York: Macmillan, 1962); Bentley, *Profession of Dramatist;* T. J. King, *Shakespearean Staging, 1599–1642* (Cambridge: Harvard University Press, 1971); Andrew Gurr, *Playgoing in Shakespeare's London* (London and New York: Cambridge University Press, 1987); S. P. Cerasano, "Editing the Theatre, Translating the Stage," *Analytical and Enumerative Bibliography*, n.s., 4 (1990): 21–34; and John H. Astington, "Descent Machinery in the Playhouses," *Medieval and Renaissance Drama in England* 2 (1985): 119–33; and idem, "The London Stage in the 1580s," in *The Elizabethan Theatre XI*, ed. Augusta Lynne Magnusson and C. E. McGee (Port Credit, Ont.: Meany, 1990), pp. 1–18.

18. William B. Long, "'A bed / for woodstock': A Warning for the Unwary," *Medieval and Renaissance Drama in England* 2 (1985): 91–118, esp. 92. See also Cerasano, "Editing the Theatre," who likewise stresses the irregularity of the stages and staging practices.

19. See, for example, Alan Dessen, *Elizabethan Stage Conventions and Modern Interpreters* (Cambridge: Cambridge University Press, 1984) and idem, *Recovering Shakespeare's Theatrical Vocabulary* (Cambridge: Cambridge University Press, 1995).

20. Issacharoff, "Inscribed Performance," pp. 95–96. Patrice Pavis, speaking of the stage directions in classical French drama, hears the voice of "un observateur extérieur, un narrateur qui nous dit ce qui se passe" ("Remarques sur le discours théâtral," *Degrés* 13 [1978]: h2). Neither of these formulations quite describes the voice of Elizabethan stage directions, but I am indebted to Issacharoff and Pavis for raising the issue.

21. Suchy borrows these terms from Barbara Herrnstein Smith. Suchy goes on to argue that in some modern plays, directions are multiple-voiced and have elements of both

fictive and natural discourse (see "When Words Collide," p. 71). As noted previously, however, she views directions in pre-eighteenth-century drama as largely unproblematic examples of "natural discourse."

22. See the preface for a brief discussion of the absence of explicit directions in classical drama and Chancellor, "Stage Directions in Western Drama," for a more extended analysis.

23. From the opening direction of *The Bald Soprano* in *Four Plays*, trans. Donald M. Allen (New York: Grove Press, 1988), p. 8.

24. Walter J. Ong, *Orality and Literacy: The Technologizing of the Word* (London and New York: Methuen, 1982), p. 7.

25. Wilhemina Frijlinck, ed., *1 Richard II or Thomas of Woodstock* (Oxford: Oxford University Press, 1929), pp. xi–xv.

26. T. H. Howard-Hill, *Ralph Crane and Some Shakespeare First Folio Comedies* (Charlottesville: University Press of Virginia, 1972), p. 24.

27. William B. Long, "Stage-Directions: A Misinterpreted Factor in Determining Textual Provenance," *TEXT* 2 (1985): 125.

28. William B. Long, "Deciphering a Layered Manuscript: *John of Bordeaux* and the Playhouse." A paper delivered at the First International Conference of the Malone Society, 29 June–1 July 1990, Stratford-upon-Avon, p. 11.

29. Antony Hammond, "Encounters of the Third Kind in Stage Directions in Elizabethan and Jacobean Drama," *Studies in Philology* 89, no. 1 (winter 1992): 71–99, esp. 78–81.

30. Bradley, *From Text to Performance*, p. 24.

31. I cite Donald C. Baker, J. L. Murphy, and Louis B. Hall, eds., *The Late Medieval Religious Plays of Digby 133 and e Museo 160*, Early English Text Society (Oxford: Oxford University Press, 1982). The manuscript also preserves a number of stage directions in a narrative form suitable for public recitation or private reading. For example, "said Joseph" appears as part of a line of dialogue rather than giving Joseph's name in the margin as a speech attribution. A later hand has carefully crossed out these narrative-style directions and added speech attributions and directions for action in the margins.

32. See David Bevington's appendix in *From "Mankind" to Marlowe: Growth of Structure in the Popular Drama of Tudor England* (Cambridge: Harvard University Press, 1962), p. 268.

33. In discussing ironic or "autonomous" directions in contemporary plays, Suchy makes the same point ("When Words Collide," p. 76).

34. See Susan Basnett-McGuire's discussion of the differences between "literary" and "theatrical" reading in "An Introduction to Theatre Semiotics," *Theatre Quarterly* 38 (summer 1980): 47–53.

35. Based on Alleyn's surviving side for *Orlando Furioso*, as partly reproduced by W. W. Greg, *Dramatic Documents from the Elizabethan Playhouses* (Oxford: Clarendon Press, 1931), pp. 180–81, I infer that an actor's side was annotated on different principles and more sparsely than a promptbook. Alleyn's part contains exits and midscene directions for action (some in Latin), but few entry directions and no speech prefixes (all the lines are Orlando's, of course, except the cues).

36. Bentley, *Profession of Dramatist*, p. 76. For an insightful discussion of the history and meaning of this theatrical practice from the Renaissance to modern times, see Peter Holland, "Reading to the Company," in *Reading Plays: Interpretation and Reception*, ed. Hanna Scolnicov and Peter Holland (Cambridge: Cambridge University Press, 1991), pp.

8–29. Based on the evidence of Henslowe's diary, Holland, like Bentley, concludes that an authorial reading of the script was a "normal stage, between the acceptance of proposals for a new play from one of the many regular writers used by the company and the beginnings of rehearsals" (p. 12).

37. Bentley, *Profession of Dramatist*, pp. 76–77.

38. See ibid., p. 79, regarding Daborne's apparent submission of some manuscript pages to Henslowe.

39. Ibid., p. 77.

40. Ibid.

41. Ibid., p. 79.

42. Ivan Illich, *In the Vineyard of the Text: A Commentary on Hugh's Didascalion* (Chicago: University of Chicago Press, 1993), p. 69.

43. In our own day, however, some Shakespearean actors approach their roles, in part, via highly literary reading practices. Actors like Michael Pennington, Patrick Stewart, and Sinead Cusack, read and reread, noting images and stylistic features, as well as (or even more than) cues for action and gesture. See the discussions provided by the first three named in Philip Brockbank, *Players of Shakespeare* (New York and Cambridge: Cambridge University Press, 1985), esp. pp. 11–28, 123–24. Patrick Stewart mentions profiting as he prepared to play Shylock from an article by Alan Dessen on the Elizabethan stage Jew (p. 23).

44. Marvin Carlson notes the partial exception of the information about time and place usually included in modern playbills ("Status of Stage Directions," p. 38).

45. R. B. McKerrow, "The Elizabethan Printer and Dramatic Manuscripts," *Library*, 4th ser., 12 (1931): 274.

46. From the company's complaint against Brome, 12 February 1639/40, quoted in Bentley, *Profession of Dramatist*, p. 143.

47. Frederick Kiefer, *Writing on the Renaissance Stage: Written Words, Printed Pages, Metaphoric Books* (Newark: University of Delaware Press; London: Associated University Presses, 1996), pp. 66–67; emphasis added.

48. Quoted in ibid., p. 67.

49. The printer asserts he has omitted some "Gestures . . . unmeet" to be "mixtured in print with . . . so honorable and statelie a history," "though (happly) they have bene of some vaine conceited fondlings greatly gaped at, at what times they wer shewed upon the stage" ("To the Gentleman Readers: and others who take pleasure in reading Histories," Q 1590). John D. Jump, editor of the Regents Renaissance Drama edition (Lincoln: University of Nebraska Press, 1967) notes this claim, but asserts that no one would suspect anything was missing without it. He speculates that whatever was cut (if anything) might have been a later addition. See note p. 3, note to lines 8–9.

50. See the preface of the stationer, Humphrey Moseley, in the folio of 1647.

51. See Greg, *Dramatic Documents*; J. Dover Wilson and Arthur T. Quiller-Couch, eds., *The New Shakespeare* (Cambridge University Press, 1921–67); and A. W. Pollard, *Shakespeare's Fight with the Pirates* ([London?], 1920). See also McKerrow, "The Elizabethan Printer."

52. Ironically, authorial directions were supposed to be less authoritative about some things. For example, they might contain errors and inconsistencies in entrances, exits, or speech prefixes that would be noticed and corrected in rehearsal. McKerrow argued, for example, that what he viewed as the high rate of error in printed dramatic texts might be ascribed to their routinely being set from (messy) foul papers rather than from (clear, cor-

rect, and legible) prompter's copy ("The Elizabethan Printer," p. 275). Assumptions about the relative neatness of the bookholder's or prompter's copy have recently been challenged by William B. Long; see "'A bed / for woodstock,'" p. 108.

53. Dessen cites Greg's and Richard Hosley's judicious initial discussions of these terms. See *Elizabethan Stage Conventions and Modern Interpreters* (Cambridge: Cambridge University Press, 1984), pp. 27–28.

54. See for example, R. C. Bald on the differences between the ms. and folio versions of plays in the Beaumont and Fletcher canon in *Bibliographical Studies in the Beaumont and Fletcher Folio of 1647* (Oxford: Oxford University Press for the Bibliographical Society, 1938), pp. 74–79.

55. R. B. McKerrow, while challenging the reliability of the distinction as an indication of provenance, nonetheless contributed this last, influential set of criteria for the directions in prompt-copy. See "The Elizabethan Printer," pp. 270–72.

56. I am indebted to Alan Dessen for calling my attention to Greg's and McKerrow's caveats; he supports their view that theater-wise authors and other theater professionals would be equally likely to write directions from a technical/theatrical or a fictive/literary point of view; see *Elizabethan Stage Conventions*, pp. 26–27, 34–35.

57. McKerrow, "The Elizabethan Printer," p. 274.

58. For the provenance of the ms. and alterations in the directions of the quarto, see R. C. Bald's edition for the Folger Shakespeare Library, *Hengist, King of Kent, or the Mayor of Quinburough* (New York: Charles Scribner's Sons, 1938), p. xxxix.

59. Those who came after Greg and McKerrow nonetheless continued to stress the difference between "literary" directions for readers and "theatrical" directions ostensibly originating in the playhouse. Bald contrasts the theatrical directions of the *Hengist* ms. with those in the quarto of 1661, which are "more literary in type, and seem to be there to help a reader who has not actually seen the play on the stage." The ms. has more "backstage" directions (it has twenty-four cues for sound effects, the quarto only four), but the quarto directions for stage action are more descriptive and more complete than those in the extant transcript. Bald offers a list of fifteen instances in which the quarto supplies a detailed direction where the ms. has a minimal one or none at all (*Hengist, King of Kent*, pp. xxx–xxxi). Bald speculates that the directions in the quarto may have originated with the author or may have been added later in the transmission of the text (p. xxxi n. 1).

60. F 1616, pp. 387, 388. Jonson's neoclassical practice with respect to stage directions and his revisions of the directions in the folio of 1616 are discussed in chapter 5.

61. T. H. Howard-Hill, "The Evolution of the Form of Plays in English during the Renaissance," *Renaissance Quarterly* 43, no. 1 (spring 1990): 112–45. I am indebted to Bernice Kliman for calling this article to my attention.

62. Ibid., p. 113.

63. Howard-Hill examines all plays in English up to the 1590s, whereas I include early medieval plays in Latin and Anglo-French and follow the conventions to the closing of the theaters in 1642, with a glance beyond that. In addition, Howard-Hill does not discuss the form of playhouse manuscripts, which I see as an important step in the evolution of the code for stage directions.

64. Howard-Hill, "Evolution," p. 140. While I don't entirely disagree with this view, I see classical apparatus as symptomatic of a more fundamental difference between the physically concrete native theatrical tradition and the more literary and logocentric classical tradition.

65. Ibid., p. 112.

CHAPTER 1. DISTINGUISHING DIRECTIONS FROM THE DIALOGUE

1. *A Midsummer Night's Dream* III.i.100.

2. This taxonomy based on theatrical function seems to me more useful for the discussion of Elizabethan directions than that of Michael Issacharoff, which is based on the relationship of the direction to the dialogue and on its content (what it tells us). For a summary of Issacharoff's categories, see pp. 16–17 in the introduction. Antony Hammond ("Encounters," 78–81) lists six kinds of Elizabethan directions, which correspond more or less with the ones I list here. The chief difference is that he creates a separate category for directions for properties, which leads him to think of elaborated entry directions—i.e., those that specify props, costume, and manner of entry *("running")*—as "hybrid" forms. For my discussion of these entries, see chapter 5.

3. Robert S. Knapp, *Shakespeare—The Theatre and the Book* (Princeton: Princeton University Press, 1989), p. 151.

4. Marion Trousdale, "Critical Bibliography and the Acting of Plays," *Shakespeare Quarterly* 41 (1990): 90.

5. See, for example, William B. Long's discussion of the irregularities and inconsistencies in extant Elizabethan playbooks: "Play manuscripts originate in an oral, not a written tradition. . . . Only printing and a print culture demand regularity, consistency, and other such modern expectations . . ." ("Stage-Directions: A Misinterpreted Factor," pp. 122–23).

6. See also plate 4 in Ian Lancashire, *Dramatic Texts and Records of Britain: A Chronological Topography to 1558* (Toronto and Buffalo: University of Toronto Press, 1984).

7. Walter J. Ong, *Ramus, Method, and the Decay of Dialogue: From the Art of Discourse to the Art of Reason* (Cambridge: Harvard University Press, 1958), p. 311.

8. Ong, *Orality and Literacy*, pp. 119–25.

9. This text is regarded as an "extra-liturgical ceremony," related to but no longer embedded in the church liturgy. See David Bevington, *Medieval Drama* (Boston: Houghton Mifflin, 1975), p. 75. The play is also known by its Latin title, *Ordo Repraesentationis Adae*, and as the *Jeu d'Adam*. The dialogue is in Anglo-Norman, the directions are in Latin. As Bevington points out (p. 78), Anglo-Norman was the official language of the English court, so this *Adam* and other Anglo-Norman plays may have been known in England.

10. A photo-reproduction of the complete Tours manuscript can be found in Leif Sletsjöe, ed., *Le Mystère d'Adam: Edition diplomatique* (Paris: Librairie C. Klincksieck, 1968), p. 4. From this photographic facsimile, I would guess that the stage directions on the opening page are in a lighter ink, possibly red as in some of the later manuscripts discussed below. I have not found any mention of red ink in modern editions of the play, however, and, in any case, on later pages the stage directions and speakers' initials appear to be in the same color ink as the dialogue.

11. For help in deciphering the script of this and other plays in the Macro manuscript, I relied on David Bevington, *The Macro Plays: The Castle of Perseverance, Wisdom, Mankind: A Facsimile Edition with Facing Transcripts* (New York: Johnson Reprint Corporation; Washington, D.C.: The Folger Shakespeare Library, 1972). I also consulted Mark Eccles, ed., *The Macro Plays* (London: Oxford University Press, 1969).

12. Bevington, *Medieval Drama*, p. 901.

13. Most cues for action, entrance, and exit are found in the dialogue itself, as in the case of the otherwise unmarked entrance of Nowadays and Nought, "Mak rom, sers, for we have be longe!" *Mankind*, in Bevington, ed., *Macro Plays*, line 330.

14. See the photo-reproduction of fol. 129 in Bevington, ed., *Macro Plays*.

15. This is especially true in the latter half of the manuscript. For examples, see lines 477, 482, 486, 549, 565, and 725 in ibid.

16. Ibid., p. xx.

17. Donald C. Baker, John L. Murphy, and Louis B. Hall, eds., *The Late Medieval Religious Plays of Bodleian MSS Digby 133 and e Museo 160*, Early English Text Society (Oxford: Oxford University Press, 1982), p. lxxxi.

18. See the photo-reproduction of fol. 155v in ibid., facing p. 112.

19. Bevington makes no mention of the use of red or contrasting ink in *Mankind*.

20. Bevington, ed., *Macro Plays*, pp. xviii–xix.

21. Norman Davis, ed., *Non-cycle Plays and the Winchester Dialogues: Facsimiles of Plays and Fragments . . .* (Leeds: University of Leeds School of English, 1979), p. 34.

22. Ibid., p. 50.

23. E.g., *"Tunc intrat Mak, in clamide se super togam vestitus"* (*Secunda Pastorem*, 189, S.D.) and *"Here knele all the thre kingys downe"* (*Magi*, 510, S.D.).

24. See the photo-reproduction of fol. 51^v in A. C. Cawley and Martin Stevens, eds., *The Towneley Cycle: A Facsimile of Huntington MS HM 1* (San Marino, Calif.: The Huntington Library, 1976).

25. Ibid., p. vii.

26. This may be because the manuscript was not intended as a practical script for performance, but scholars are not agreed about its character. According to Martin Stevens, it is likely that the Towneley ms. is "something like a presentation copy" rather than a "register" or a script used by the players. See *Four Medieval Mystery Cycles: Textual, Contextual, and Critical Interpretations* (Princeton: Princeton University Press, 1987), p. 94.

27. See the photo-reproduction of Digby fol. 158 in Donald C. Baker and J. L. Murphy, eds., *The Digby Plays: Facsimiles of the Plays in Bodley MSS Digby 133 and e Museo 160* (Leeds: University of Leeds School of English, 1976). I was alerted to the use of colored inks in medieval dramatic manuscripts by the beautiful color plates that serve as frontispieces to this edition. The scribe who wrote the Digby *Wisdom* also wrote *The Killing of the Children*, which is written in brown ink throughout (see pp. xiii–xiv).

28. Baker et al., eds., *Late Medieval Religious Plays*, p. lxxx.

29. Davis, ed., *Non-cycle Plays*, p. 93.

30. For help in deciphering this much annotated manuscript, I relied on the Malone Society type-facsimile edited by Wilhelmina P. Frijlinck (1929; reprint, Oxford: Oxford University Press, 1961).

31. Greg, ed., *Dramatic Documents*, 1:207.

32. Like the use of contrasting ink in medieval texts, the use of italics in Elizabethan texts is not wholly devoted to theatrical elements. Foreign words, proper names, sententiae, and other textual elements may also appear in italics.

33. *John a Kent and John a Cumber* (Oxford: Oxford University Press, 1923), p. ix.

34. Sometimes they seem more indented to the right as a block than "centered," but in either case white space on one or both sides visually interrupts the text column and distinguishes them from the dialogue. Hereafter, in using the term "centered" I refer to directions that break the text in a way that medieval directions placed in the central column did not.

35. The *Ironside* manuscript also centers extended directions for fight sequences; see the Malone Society type-facsimile. The *Hengist* manuscript emphasizes initial entries with double rules above and below; see R. C. Bald's type-facsimile (New York and London: C. Scribner's Sons, 1938).

36. Two appear in the 1608 quarto of *King Lear*. Other exceptional cases are discussed in chapter 3.

37. This practice was revived by Ben Jonson (or his printer) in the layout of the 1616 folio of his works; the quartos of Jonson's plays for the professional theaters, however, follow the more standard form.

38. See John S. Farmer, gen. ed., *Cambises, King of Persia*, The Tudor Facsimile Texts ([Edinburgh?]: T. C. and E. C. Jack, 1910).

39. See Martin Elsky, *Authorizing Words: Speech, Writing, and Print in the English Renaissance* (Ithaca: Cornell University Press, 1989), p. 125.

40. For other accounts of the significance of different typefaces, see Charles C. Mish, "Black Letter as a Social Discriminant in the Seventeenth Century," *PMLA* 68 (1953): 627–30, and Rudolf Hirsch, "Classics in the Vulgar Tongues Printed During the Initial Fifty Years," *Papers of the Bibliographical Society of America* 81 (1987): 249–337, both cited in Howard-Hill, "Evolution," p. 136 n. 75.

41. Howard-Hill, "Evolution," pp. 129–31.

42. Ibid., p. 138. For a fuller account of "the synthesis" of native and classical styles, see pp. 138–44.

43. Ibid., p. 138.

44. Ong, *Orality and Literacy*, p. 132.

Chapter 2. Speech Attributions

1. Quoted by Jerome Taylor in the introduction to his and Alan Nelson's anthology, *Medieval English Drama: Essays Critical and Contextual* (Chicago: University of Chicago Press, 1972), p. 14. Marius Sepet is discussed by E. Catherine Dunn in her contribution to the volume.

2. For plays in the Digby and e Museo manuscripts that are not included in Bevington's anthology, I have relied on Baker and Murphy, eds., *Digby Plays*. Where I was uncertain of the script, I relied on Baker et al., eds., *Late Medieval Religious Plays*.

3. My text is *King Johan* edited by Barry Adams (San Marino, Calif.: The Huntington Library, 1969).

4. According to Howard-Hill, in manuscripts of English plays written before the advent of printing, speeches "shared by a number of characters ('omnes') are always controlled by stage directions rather than by speech prefixes ("Evolution," pp. 118–19).

5. The presence of these speech prefixes in an early religious drama would seem to challenge Howard-Hill's view that the strict economy of single initials as speech prefixes originated in imitation of classical practice. See ibid., pp. 133, 135.

6. Davis, ed., *Non-cycle Plays*, p. 94.

7. Baker et al., eds., *Digby Plays*, p. x.

8. See William Gribbons, "Visual Literacy in Corporate Communication: Some Implications for Information Design," *IEEE Transactions on Professional Communication* 34, no. 1 (March 1991): 48.

9. See Greg, ed., *Dramatic Documents*, 1:207 n. 2.

10. Long, "Deciphering a Layered Manuscript."

11. Ong, *Orality and Literacy*, p. 119.

12. On the *Sir Thomas More* manuscript, see Greg's note to lines 21–35 in the Malone Society edition (Oxford: Oxford University Press, 1961), p. 91. On the *Thomas of Woodstock*

manuscript, see Frijlinck's introduction (p. x) and the note to line 6 in the Malone Society edition (1929), p. 3. Medieval scribes also are said to have added stage directions after the dialogue was completed; see Richard Beadle and Peter Meredith, *The York Play: A Facsimile of British Library MS Additional 35290* . . . (Leeds: University of Leeds School of English, 1983), p. xxx.

13. Derrida discusses logocentric drama in *L'Écriture et différence*; see the postscript in Issacharoff and Jones, eds., *Performing Texts,* pp. 138–43: "The stage, Derrida argues, is theological as long as it is dominated by the Word, a primary logos, alien to the theatrical space that it governs from a distance" (p. 140).

14. See the textual note in the edition of A. C. Cawley (Manchester: Manchester University Press, 1961), p. xxxvii. Like most modern editors of early plays, Cawley places all speech prefixes on the left in accordance with modern expectations, regardless of their placement in the early text. Howard-Hill notes that a placement of speech prefixes in the opposite margins of facing pages is attempted in one of the extant manuscripts of *Gismond of Salerne* (MS Lansdowne 786, c. 1566), but the scribe "became confused" ("Evolution," p. 137).

15. William H. Bond, "Casting Off Copy by Elizabethan Printers: A Theory," *Papers of the Bibliographical Society of America* 42 (1948): 281–91.

16. One special case might be noted. In *Old Fortunatus* (Q 1600), in the opening scene (gathering A) two embedded prefixes occur in the inner forme and eleven in the outer. All occur in an extended prose scene. This case, however, is unusual, since the second "speaker" is a presumably offstage "Echo," which repeats the last words of Fortunatus's lines of dialogue. Thus the running together of the two speakers in one line seems a logical exception to the usual convention. It might even represent another instance of mimetic textual design. See the discussion of mimesis below.

17. I cite the facsimile published by Theatrum Orbis Terrarum (Amsterdam, 1972). The line occurs at II.iii.85 in the edition of Donald K. Anderson Jr. (Lincoln: University of Nebraska Press, 1965). Anderson, like nearly all modern editors, alters his copytext to conform to the more common Elizabethan layout that we have been describing here.

18. Classical and neoclassical apparatus, with its scene and act headings, sparse staging information, and so-called massed entries tends to highlight conceptual and poetic rather than theatrical aspects of a dramatic text. For a discussion of neoclassical conventions (such as massed entries) versus the conventions of the professional London theaters, see chapter 5.

19. Ong, *Orality and Literacy*, p. 100.

20. See the New Mermaids edition, ed. Elizabeth Cook (London: A. and C. Black; New York: W. W. Norton, 1991), p. xxxi.

21. Howard-Hill, "Evolution," p. 139 n. 10.

22. No speech prefix for the Officer follows, though modern editors may provide one (as the Riverside editor does, see I.iii.74). It is possible, perhaps, that the Mayor proclaims the text himself, not giving the Officer a chance to do his part, or that the Officer repeats the text after him in a declamatory style, either line by line or as a whole.

23. The F1 compositor may be responsible for this design or he may be faithfully reproducing his copytext (Q5); see the textual notes in the Riverside edition.

Chapter 3. Midscene Directions

1. Bookkeepers' notations may also emphasize the information contained in initial entries. These redundant notations were passed over in chapter 1 for the sake of simplicity,

and since, from a design point of view, they merely intensify the prominent position of an initial entry, which was the theme of that chapter.

2. I follow the Malone Society editor who represents Munday's inconsistent Italian hand sometimes as italics and sometimes as roman.

3. See Howard-Hill, *Ralph Crane*, p. 54 n.

4. See Long, "A bed / for woodstock," p. 108.

5. I rely on Scott McMillan's dating of the original version of the play in *The Elizabethan Theatre and "The Book of Sir Thomas More"* (Ithaca: Cornell University Press, 1987), chap. 3, esp. p. 72. He dates the revised version c. 1603 (chap. 4, esp. pp. 90–91), but Vittorio Gabrieli and Giorgio Melchiori, the editors of the Revels edition (Manchester: Manchester University Press, 1990) place them in 1593/4. In the light of this disagreement, I have only tallied Hand S, Munday's portion of the manuscript.

6. Howard-Hill, *Ralph Crane*, p. 31.

7. See the edition in Bald, *Bibliographical Studies*, p. xxix.

8. The sixth play, *The Two Noble Ladies* (c. 1622) is linked with the Red Bull Theatre. Writing in 1930, Malone Society editor Rebecca Rhoads identifies it with "the Revels Company," and notes that the Children of the Revels were performing at the Red Bull from 1619 to 1623. More recently, however, Andrew Gurr identifies the play with "the Red Bull Company," one of the professional men's troupes (see *The Shakespearean Stage, 1574–1642*, 2d ed. [Cambridge: Cambridge University Press, 1980], p. 228).

9. These are the scribe's own words; see Greg's introduction to the Malone Society print facsimile, p. xi.

10. See the Malone Society facsimile edited by Charles J. Sisson, pp. xii, xxi, and xxxiii.

11. Middleton's autograph copy of *A Game at Chess* (the Trinity manuscript, c. 1624, one of several manuscripts of this play apparently prepared for private use) has also been reviewed. Its design seems an imitation of a printed quarto, which it resembles in size (18.7 x 14.6 cm in contrast to the folio-sized playhouse manuscripts and transcripts listed above). For example, speech prefixes are located not in the left margin but as the first word (unindented) of the text line. Because its size and layout are different from the other manuscripts, it was not included in my baseline sample. For a description of the manuscript, see the introduction to the Malone Society facsimile edited by T. H. Howard-Hill, John Creaser, and H. R. Woudhuysen, pp. x–xii.

12. I say "within" rather than "centered" because this manuscript represents both initial entries and other directions as blocks of text indented well to the right, rather than as centered with an equal amount of white space on each side.

13. The stage directions in this manuscript are sometimes in an Italian hand and sometimes not. I have followed the Malone Society editor in representing them here.

14. Many of the centered midscene entries in *Ironside* participate in battle sequences; this is one of the shorter ones.

15. Robert J. Lordi's list of the stage directions in all nine extant manuscripts shows that all but four of the thirty-two directions are run in the margins alongside the passages to which they are relevant. See *Thomas Legge's Richardus Tertius: A Critical Edition with a Translation* (New York: Garland, 1979), appendix C.

16. I am indebted to G. Blakemore Evans for this formulation.

17. I follow the Malone Society editor in representing the scribe's intermittently Italian hand for the directions in this manuscript.

18. I borrow this phrase from William B. Long.

19. They seem rather to have been intended "to centre the text on the page and to align

recto and verso." See the introduction to his Malone Society edition of *Sir John Van Olden Barnavelt*, p. xi.

20. In some playhouse manuscripts, bookkeepers' additions tend to appear on the left. In the *Woodstock* manuscript, sixteen bookkeepers' notations are on the left and only two on the right. All five notations in *Edmond Ironside* appear on the left. But in *Sir John Van Olden Barnavelt*, as we have seen, the bookkeeper's notes appear in both margins.

21. Many exits are merely implied by the dialogue and not marked by an italicized direction.

22. My authority for printers whose names do not appear on the title pages is W. W. Greg, *A Bibliography of the English Printed Drama to the Restoration*, 4 vols. (Oxford: Oxford University Press, 1939–59). See the list of plays and editions for full bibliographic information on each title.

23. Jaggard is given as the "probable" printer in Glenn Blaney's introduction to the Malone Society edition (1963), p. v.

24. See Ong, *Ramus, Method, and the Decay of Dialogue*.

25. Although this play was revised and performed, apparently without permission, by the King's Men, it was originally written for the Children of the Queen's Revels; like many other boys' plays it differs from most plays for the men's companies in several other respects as well. For example, in addition to containing directions as genuine marginalia, it observes scenes based on the neoclassical or "French" principle (as opposed to the cleared stage) and other conventions that distinguished the learned from the popular drama. I refer to the third 1604 edition, containing Webster's induction and other revisions for the King's Men. See the note to the Scolar Press facsimile (1970) for an account of the three 1604 editions and the surreptitious procurement of the play by the King's Men. The unusual circumstances of the play's production are the subject of Webster's humorous induction added for the occasion.

26. See Peter M. Wright, "Jonson's Revision of the Stage Directions for the 1616 Folio *Workes*," *Medieval and Renaissance Drama in England* 5 (1990): 257–85, for a full account of the differences between the quarto and folio editions in Jonson's plays.

27. This might suggest that in 1598 the printer of *The Famous Victories* was working from a (now lost) earlier printed edition, which like *Edward I* or *1 Contention*, tended to center midscene directions more often than later editions did.

28. In Q 1594, printed by Thomas Creede, the speech prefixes are italicized, but the stage directions are not except for proper names. In Q 1600, printed by Valentine Simmes, normal italicized directions are provided.

29. Several directions are not italicized in this quarto.

30. See Bond's discussion of quartos in "Casting Off Copy" and the brief summary of his analysis in chapter 2.

31. The preferred locations for different sorts of midscene directions will be discussed below.

32. Contrary to what one might expect, the closing of the theaters did not entail the disappearance of quartos of previously unpublished plays from booksellers' shops. Judging from Greg's *Bibliography of the English Printed Drama*, although new titles numbered only 8 from 1642 to 1646, previously unpublished plays from the repertory of the professional theaters appeared in print during the Commonwealth at about two-thirds the rate that characterized the previous twenty-five years: 288 new titles appeared between 1616 and 1642; 198 appeared between 1643 and 1660. These estimates do not take reprints into account in either period. The publication of the Beaumont and Fletcher folio in 1647 accounts for 43

of the titles that appeared during the Commonwealth, but apparently it was profitable to provide new plays for the reading public even after the theaters had been closed.

33. An early humanist use of extended speech prefixes is illustrated in Bale's *King Johan* (c. 1530–60). Usurped Power and Private Wealth are instructed to enter *"singing one after another"* (763, S.D.), and their Latin (sung) lines are introduced by *"Us.P (sing this)"* and *"Pr.W (sing this),"* respectively. What is interesting here, I think, is not the extension of the speech prefix per se, but the directorial redundancy (one might even say overkill) that characterizes this and other early interludes, and the emphasis on vocal effects (singing) rather than bodily action.

34. "Self-consciousness" as an aspect of the voice of stage directions is the topic of chapter 4.

35. E. A. G. Honigmann, "Re-enter the Stage Direction: Shakespeare and Some Contemporaries," *Shakespeare Survey* 29 (1976): 117–25, esp. 118.

36. *William Shakespeare: The Complete Works* (Oxford: Clarendon Press, 1986). The editors discuss their rather free approach to remedying the "deficiencies" of the original stage directions in their introduction to this modern spelling edition, pp. xxxv–vi, and refer readers to their original spelling edition (also 1986) for the stage directions as they appear in their copytexts.

37. Evelyn Tribble, *Margins and Marginality: The Printed Page in the Early Modern Period* (Charlottesville: University Press of Virginia, 1993), pp. 129, 103.

38. Ibid., p. 103.

39. Ibid., p. 131. The decision of some recent editions of Shakespeare's plays to put notes and commentary on the verso pages, rather than in foot- or endnotes, seems a revival of the early modern spirit of marginal commentary.

40. Unitary texts and unitary meanings are currently out of fashion. See, for example, Michael Warren, *Parallel King Lear* and Randall McCloud, "UN Editing Shak-speare," *SUBSTANCE* 33/34 (1981/82): 26–55. Both Warren and McCloud, for different reasons, call into question the modern tradition of edited texts, which, it might be argued, begins when the printing houses of the early modern period produced relatively readable texts from the often confusing and hard-to-read manuscripts of the professional theaters, or altered the design of a playscript in ways that created a more linear text.

CHAPTER 4. SELF-CONSCIOUS AND SELF-EFFACING DIRECTIONS

1. Once again, my text for medieval plays cited by line number, unless otherwise noted, is Bevington's *Medieval Drama.*

2. I cite the Regents Renaissance Drama edition of R. Mark Benbow (Lincoln: University of Nebraska Press, 1967).

3. On the biblical echoes of the Latin subjunctive, see the comments of Robin F. Jones quoted in chapter 5.

4. I cite Arthur H. Nethercot et al., eds., *Elizabethan Plays*, rev. ed. (New York: Holt, Rinehart, and Winston, 1971); I have also consulted the quarto.

5. These numbers may also reflect a difference in custom between the professional and occasional playwrights.

6. See, for example, the abbreviated indicative plural *"[They] Sit to the banquet"* (*The Spanish Tragedy* I.iv.12, S.D.). For a more detailed discussion of ambiguous verb mood, see chapter 6.

7. See Long, "'A bed / for woodstock,'" p. 111.

8. In a 1978 promptbook of *Richard III* in Ashland, Oregon, for example, the major characters are identified as "R" (Richard) or "Buck" (Buckingham), but smaller parts and extras are identified by their own names, "Berman, Smith, Denison, Olson" (see notes to the opening of IV.ii). A similar practice is common at the Royal Shakespeare Company. I am indebted to Lisa Brandt and other librarians of the RSC archives at the Shakespeare Centre in Stratford-upon-Avon and to Kathleen Leary, archivist of the Oregon Shakespeare Festival, for their kind assistance in my study of these materials.

9. These are found in *The Slaughter of the Innocents* from the Fleury collection of plays. See Bevington, ed., *Medieval Drama,* pp. 67–72.

10. For example: *"Dunt s'en alerent dous des serganz, / Lances od sei en main portanz. / Si unt dit a Longin le ciu, / Que unt trove seant en un liu"* [Then the sergeants went away, carrying their lances in their hands. Thus they said to blind Longinus, whom they found sitting in a place] (lines 91–92). See *La Seinte Resurrection* in ibid. Similarly rhymed, narrative "stage directions" occur in *Christ's Burial*; see the notes to Baker et al., eds., *Late Medieval Religious Plays.*

11. Ong, *Orality and Literacy,* p. 119.

12. Ibid., pp. 122–25.

13. Ibid., p. 133.

14. See for example the Wakefield *Noah,* in Bevington, ed., *Medieval Drama,* pp. 291, 307.

15. M. Eduoard Fournier, *Le Théâtre français avant la renaissance, 1450–1550* (1873; reprint, New York: Burt Franklin, 1965), pp. 2, 6; my translation.

16. It is possible some medieval nonliterate performers learned their lines indirectly by having them read to them. It is hard to say much about what the individual professional player actually had to hand when he learned his lines. If we judge by the few "sides" or acting parts that have survived, the text in the possession of any given actor was fragmentary. It contained his own lines with brief cue lines from other speakers in the scene and directions for midscene business. See the facsimiles in Greg, ed., *Dramatic Documents,* and the discussion of Alleyn's part for Greene's *Orlando Furioso* in Hammond, "Encounters," pp. 83–85. Both players and other playhouse personnel presumably would consult the version of the stage directions posted on the "plot" as a reminder during performance. The importance and function of the "plot" is the focus of Bradley, *From Text to Performance.*

17. For a list of the extant plays in this category with transcriptions of their title pages, see Bevington, *From "Mankind" to Marlowe,* pp. 265–73.

18. In Nethercot et al., eds., *Elizabethan Plays.*

19. Ibid.

20. Actor as well as playwright, Heywood (like Munday and unlike Shakespeare) exhibits unusual freedom in the form and content of his midscene directions (see chapter 6).

21. See also, *"Here Gloucester's men beat out the Cardinal's men ..."* (I.iii.56, S.D.), *"Here they shoot, and Salisbury falls down ..."* (I.iv. 69, S.D.), and *"Here Salisbury lifteth himself up and groans* (I.iv.103). The instances, for some reason, are concentrated in act 1.

22. See also *1 Henry IV,* II.ii.92, S.D., and III.i.244, S.D.; *King John,* II.i.299, S.D.; and *Richard II,* V.v.107, S.D.

23. I am indebted to Peter M. Wright for sharing this data with me.

24. See Evans's textual notes in the Riverside edition.

25. A detailed discussion of the differences between page design in the manuscript tradition and in printed plays for the London theaters can be found in chapter 2.

26. Quoted in Bevington, ed., *Medieval Drama*, pp. 48–49.

27. Both dialogue and directions are in the same black-letter typeface in the original. I italicize the directions here since they appear in Latin.

28. Though the manuscript as it stands lacks competent doubling instructions, there is an apparent report of a performance of the play in 1539 for Cranmer. See Barry Adams's edition, pp. 6, 20.

29. See Alan Dessen, "Much Virtue in *As:* Elizabethan Stage Locales and Modern Interpretation," in *Shakespeare and the Sense of Performance*, ed. Marvin and Ruth Thompson (Newark: University of Delaware Press, 1989), pp. 132–38, and idem, *Elizabethan Stage Conventions*, pp. 27, 30–34.

30. See Dessen's expansion of his 1989 essay, also entitled "Much Virtue in *As*," in *Recovering Shakespeare's Theatrical Vocabulary*, pp. 127–49.

31. Long, "A Misinterpreted Factor," p. 127.

32. I cite the edition of John Quincy Adams in *Chief Pre-Shakespearean Dramas* (Boston: Houghton Mifflin, 1924), pp. 117–24.

33. I cite Adams's edition in ibid., pp. 225–42.

34. This direction is in Latin in the original (which mixes Latin and English directions): *"Difidendo dicat ista verba."* I cite the Revels Plays edition of Paula Neuss (Manchester: Manchester University Press; Baltimore: Johns Hopkins University Press, 1980).

35. This edition is a quarto in eights, hence the unusual siglia.

36. I cite the edition of A. H. Bullen, *The Works of Robert Davenport*, Old English Plays, n.s., vol. 3 (London: Hansard Publishing Union, 1890), pp. 83–84.

CHAPTER 5. ENTRIES AND EXITS

1. Bradley, *From Text to Performance*, p. 29. Bradley argues that Elizabethan scenes, the "natural" divisions of the action, are unmarked by anything more than *exeunt* followed by an initial entry, whereas act divisions introduced in imitation of classical drama require textual headings such as *Actus Primi* or *Finis Actus Primi*, "because they are *un*natural divisions" (p. 29).

2. Marvin Spevack, *Concordances to Stage Directions and Speech Prefixes, A Complete and Systematic Concordance to the Works of Shakespeare*, vol. 7 (Hildesheim and New York: Georg Olms Verlag, 1975).

3. See Howard-Hill, "Evolution," p. 135.

4. Robin F. Jones, "A Medieval Prescription for Performance: *Le Jeu d'Adam*," in Issacharoff and Jones, eds., *Performing Texts*, pp. 102–3.

5. Hartnoll, ed., *The Oxford Companion to the Theatre*, p. 912. Southern traces *manet/manent* "as far back . . . as 1698," but it is common a century before that in Elizabethan and Jacobean drama.

6. To begin a scene in this play, Marlowe observes the neoclassical convention regarding entries; that is, he lists the names of the speakers without using the word "enter." Only entries later in the scene are marked by the verb. See the discussion of this rival tradition later in this chapter.

7. See McMillin, *Elizabethan Theatre*, pp. 154–59.

8. According to Warren D. Smith, although exit directions per se are often omitted, nearly every exit is cued somehow, by the dialogue or a rhyme tag. See "Shakespeare's Exit Cues," *JEGP* 61 (1962): 884–96.

9. "Ruffian" appears to be shorthand term for a rough fellow, poorly dressed, perhaps a discharged soldier, once associated with Vice characters of the past; Huf, Snuf, and Ruf, cohorts of Ambidexter in *Cambises*, are introduced as "three ruffians" (1ine 159, S.D.).

10. I quote here from the quarto of 1661 to show a late instance of the form. For the comparable direction in the Folger manuscript of this Middleton play, c. 1616–20, see below.

11. Ablative absolutes are compact constructions, common in Latin, as their grammatical name suggests. They are usually composed of a participle plus a noun, adjective, or prepositional phrase. They are rather loosely connected to the rest of the sentence, adding new information or ideas rather than modifying a word present in another clause. Ablative absolutes common in English include "God willing" and (not surprisingly) legalistic expressions such as "Evidence to the contrary notwithstanding." A classic Latin example is *"The road completed*, Caesar advanced." The extreme economy of ablative absolutes made them useful to composers of telegrams or cables, but in normal English prose they are usually rendered as dependent clauses that articulate their implied connection to the rest of the sentence: *"Once the road was completed*, Caesar advanced." The important point regarding stage directions is that the compressed Latinate form is preserved, rather than "Englished."

12. Comparison of quarto and Folio directions in Shakespeare indicates the trend towards increased economy. In *1 Henry IV*, for example, where the (good) quarto reads *"Enter the travellers"* and *"Enter the thieves again,"* the Folio reads *"Enter Travellers"* and *"Enter Thieves again"* (see II.ii.77 and 97, S.D.). A further change in these directions suggests an increased tendency to identify walk-on roles with proper nouns rather than common nouns, somewhat analogous to changing "the prologue," a generic textual title, to "Prologue," a character's name. I am indebted to Peter Wright for the loan of the database he has prepared to facilitate comparison of Folio and quarto directions in Shakespeare.

13. The repetition of the entry direction in normal syntax is obviously unusual. It appears that the accumulation of details in this particular direction necessitated a fresh start.

14. I have only come across one elaborated *manet* direction, a noncanonical one in English: *"Exeunt. Lafew and Parolles stay behind commenting of this wedding"* (*All's Well That Ends Well* II.iii.183, S.D.).

15. This direction seems to require the character to enter a discovery space rather than to exit the stage entirely; otherwise his action of locking the door would not be visible.

16. These directions are also unusual for their self-conscious reference to each other (*"in like manner,"* *"so"*). Only the *"exeunt"* is reproduced in italic type in the Malone Society facsimile and in Pennell's edition. See Arthur E. Pennell, ed., *An Edition of Anthony Munday's "John a Kent and John a Cumber"* (New York: Garland, 1980), p. 10.

17. On translating Latin into idiomatic English, see Fredric M. Wheelock, *Latin: An Introductory Course* (New York: Barnes and Noble, 1963), p. 111, and Frederick F. Bruce, *The English Bible: A History of Translations*, rev. ed. (New York: Oxford University Press, 1970), p. 16.

18. See Dessen, who quotes W. W. Greg on this subject, *Elizabethan Stage Conventions*, p. 27.

19. Alarums, excursions, and battle sequences might have been treated here, since they tacitly involve entries and exits. See the discussion of battle sequences in chapter 6.

20. The various texts of the play-within-the-play in *Hamlet* illustrate three different formulae for introducing a dumb show:

> *Enter in Dumb shew, the King and the Queene, he*
> *sits downe in an Arbor, she leaves him. . . .*

(Q1 [1603])

> *The trumpets sounds* [sic]. *Dumb show followes.*
> *Enter a King and a Queene, the Queene embracing him, and he*
> *her . . .*

(Q2 [1604])

> *Hoboyes play. The Dumb shew enters.*
> *Enter a King and Queene, very lovingly; the Queene embracing him.*

(F1 [1623])

21. Visually, this direction is distinguished by larger roman typeface rather than the usual italics.

22. The single use of *"then"* in the direction occurs within the basic entry, indicating the order of persons entering.

23. *The Misfortunes of Arthur: A Critical Old-Spelling Edition*, ed. Brian Jay Corrigan (New York: Garland, 1992), pp. 1–2.

24. The edition is based on the manuscript in the Folger Shakespeare Library (New York and London: Charles Scribner's Sons, 1938).

25. This list includes the entries and exits from Bald's comparison of manuscript and quarto directions on pp. xxx–xxxi and other parallel pairs of directions. Line numbers refer to Bald's edition of the manuscript; quarto directions not cited on pp. xxx–xxxi are recorded in his notes.

26. Stanley Wells and Gary Taylor, general introduction to *The Complete Oxford Shakespeare* (Oxford: Oxford University Press, 1986), pp. xxxiii–xxxiv. Wells and Taylor further consider the so-called bad quartos to be the texts most closely linked to the circumstances of actual production.

27. For a discussion of Jonson's practice see Wright, "Jonson's Revision," pp. 257–85.

28. I am indebted to Alan Nelson and the materials he provided at the U.C. Shakespeare Conference, February 1990, for calling the printed editions of university plays to my attention.

29. The term *interloquitores* appears beneath the act 2, scene 4 heading in *Misogonus*, before the list of characters involved in the scene. See Ernest B. Lester's edition, Ph.D. dissertation, University of Arizona, 1967.

30. See John D. Jump's edition for The Regents Renaissance Drama Series (Lincoln: University of Nebraska Press, 1967), pp. xxv–xxvi.

31. The direction that begins each scene sometimes merely lists the initial speakers: *"D'Ambois with two Pages with tapers"* (V.iii.0, S.D.). But on other occasions the usual formula is used: *"Enter Monsieur and Guise"* (V.i.0, S.D.).

32. Wright, "Jonson's Revision," p. 262.

33. Ibid. Wright also notes that Jonson's plays of "language and debate" for the boys' companies, such as *Cynthia's Revels* and *Poetaster*, were published with massed entries. Wright appears to use the term "massed entries" to refer to the timing issue only; he cites as "massed entries" instances from the quarto editions of *Cynthia's Revels* that do contain the word *"Enter."*

34. Ibid., p. 278.

CHAPTER 6. ACTION AND SPECIAL EFFECTS

1. Quoted in Gurr, *Shakespearean Stage*, p. 144.

2. Quoted in ibid., pp. 7–8.

3. See, for example, A. R. Braunmuller's discussion of cues for flourishes to accompany royal entrances in "Editing the Staging/Staging the Editing," in Thompson and Thompson, eds., *Shakespeare and the Sense of Performance*, pp. 141–42.

4. My authority for probable dates of composition is appendix C, "Annals, 1552–1616" in the Riverside Shakespeare, pp. 1853–93, and Gurr's appendix, "Select List of Plays," in *Shakespearean Stage,* pp. 216–28.

5. My analysis is based on the quarto of 1600, which differs slightly from the earlier edition of 1594.

6. Both the manuscript and printed versions have been analyzed for this study. There are some variations in the form of stage directions common to these two texts, but the chief differences are the presence of many sound cues in the manuscript that are lacking in the quarto and the presence of seven additional directions for action in the quarto that are lacking in the manuscripts.

7. The direction (and others quoted from this play) runs in the outer margin opposite the lines cited in the Malone Society reprint. Since verbal, not visual, matters are now our focus, I have not preserved the line breaks within these marginal directions.

8. Greg construes the mood of many stage directions as imperative: *"enter* is an imperative, and though *exit* and *manet* are grammatically indicatives, the frequency of their use where several characters are concerned suggests that they were rather felt as imperatives." But he does note many ambiguous instances: "'kiss' may be an imperative, or it may merely be a shortened form of 'they kiss.'" See *Dramatic Documents from the Elizabethan Playhouses*, vol. 1 (Oxford: Clarendon Press, 1931), p. 209.

9. I am indebted to Marie Plasse for this point.

10. Yet another series from *John a Kent* shows an initial freestanding participial direction further abbreviated to two noun phrases:

> Suddenly starting to him, after the other hath do<n>e . . .
> he sudden<ly> t< . . .
> he suddenly too.
>
> (TLN 1257–71)

11. Fournier, *Le Théâtre français*, p. 5, my translation.

12. This direction is centered, but it serves as the speech prefix for the following line, "We humbly thank your majesty."

13. Presumably they were placed flush right in verse passages so as not to disrupt the pentameter line.

14. Later in the same scene, Jonson uses a repeated parenthetical direction *"(hum, hum)"* to cue a character's sawing away on a viol while he unsuccessfully tries to woo his lady (TLN 2541–45). These are the only onomatopoeic sound cues I have encountered, other than those in the dialogue, such as "hem" for a cough.

15. That is, the summaries of a play, scene by scene, prepared as an aid to theatrical production. They often consist chiefly of the initial entry direction for each scene, plus marginal annotations, presumably by the bookkeeper. See Greg, ed., *Dramatic Documents*, vol. 2 for examples.

16. Reproduced in Greg, ed., *Dramatic Documents*, vol. 2, n.p.

17. See Bevington, *Action Is Eloquence;* and, among others, Michael Goldman, *Shakespeare and the Energies of Drama* (Princeton: Princeton University Press, 1972); Manfred Pfister, "Reading the Body: The Corporeality of Shakespeare's Text," in Scolnicov and Holland, eds., *Reading Plays;* and Gail Kern Paster, *The Body Embarrassed: Drama and the Disciplines of Shame in Early Modern England* (Ithaca: Cornell University Press, 1993).

18. Some examples from *Death of a Salesman* and *"Master Harold"* . . . *and the Boys* are discussed in the concluding chapter.

CONCLUSION

1. My remarks are based on a study of six eighteenth-century acting editions of Shakespeare's *Henry VIII*: Dryden's, Garrick's, Bell's, Dean's, Inchbald's, and Kemble's. For full bibliographic references, see the list of plays and editions at the end of this book.

2. See, for example, the printed edition of *Bon Ton: or High Life above Stairs* (1775) or the photographic facsimile of his manuscript for *The Meeting of the Company*, both in Gerald Berkowitz, ed., *The Plays of David Garrick*, vol. 2 (New York: Garland Publishing, 1981).

3. Garrick's version of *Macbeth*, as it appears in Bell's series, does have locations for each scene on the model of the Dryden edition (*"Scene, an open Place"* [I.i], *"Scene changes to a Palace . . ."* [I.ii]). Unlike the 1762 *Henry VIII*, this 1774 text of *Macbeth* is rather fully annotated by Francis Gentleman, who may have added the scene indications.

4. For example, I.i of the Folio text becomes three different scenes: scene 1, the opening with Buckingham and Norfolk; scene 2, when Wolsey enters with his train; and scene 3, when Brandon enters to arrest Buckingham. This change might matter little to a spectator, but a reader would lack the appropriate signals for the scenes that were the fundamental unit of Shakespeare's dramaturgy.

5. Comparison with his 1806 promptbook suggests that this expanded direction may still not include all the details actually realized on stage.

6. For example:

> *A small table under a state for the Cardinal, a longer table*
> *for the Guests. Anne Bullen, and divers other Ladies*
> *and gentlemen, as guests. Enter Sir Henry Guilford.*

(I.iv.0, S.D.)

> *The Queen and her Women, as at work.*

(III.i.0, S.D.)

7. One other point regarding entries might be mentioned. Dean's edition and Bell's 1786 edition, both based on Johnson-Steevens, employ the term *"re-enter"* when the character exits and returns to the stage.

> *Cardinal goes out and re-enters with Gardiner.*

(II.ii)

Re-enter Griffith, with Capucius.

(IV.ii)

Re-enter Denny and Cranmer.

(V.i)

"Re-enter" is (as far as I know) not found in Elizabethan directions, which typically operate within the immediate moment, rather than stepping outside it.

8. Brief character sketches can be found in some of Jonson's plays.

9. In Carl H. Klaus et al., eds., *Stages of Drama*, 3d ed. (New York: St. Martin's, 1995), p. 558.

10. Ibid., pp. 865–67.

11. Whether or not these directions have this form in the original Norwegian text, they are presented to English readers in a grammar largely familiar since Elizabethan times.

12. Athol Fugard, *"Master Harold"* . . . *and the Boys*, in Klaus et al., eds., *Stages of Drama*, p. 1138.

13. Interview at the Oregon Shakespeare Festival, 13 July 1990.

14. In Klaus et al., eds., *Stages of Drama*, p. 651.

15. In ibid., p. 909.

16. In ibid., p. 1224.

17. In ibid., p. 1001.

18. In ibid., p. 1198.

19. In ibid., p. 1199.

20. Quoted in Ralph Berry, *On Directing Shakespeare* (London: Croom Helm; New York: Barnes and Noble, 1977), p. 29.

Bibliography

PLAYS AND EDITIONS CITED

Plays or collections are listed alphabetically by title. In the case of Tudor and Stuart plays, the short title is followed by the name of the author(s) or probable author(s) and the date of the quarto or folio text cited. Manuscripts cited are identified by " MS" and an approximate date.

Medieval Plays

Chief Pre-Shakespearean Dramas. Edited by John Quincy Adams. Boston: Houghton Mifflin, 1924.

The Digby Plays: Facsimiles of the Plays in Bodley MSS Digby 133 and e Museo 160. Edited by Donald C. Baker, John L. Murphy, and Louis B. Hall. Leeds: The University of Leeds School of English, 1976.

Everyman and Medieval Miracle Plays. Edited by A. C. Cawley. London: J. M. Dent, 1993.

The Late Medieval Religious Plays of Bodleian MSS Digby 133 and e Museo 160. Edited by Donald C. Baker, John L. Murphy, and Louis B. Hall. Early English Text Society. Oxford: Oxford University Press, 1982.

The Macro Plays. Edited by Mark Eccles. London: Oxford University Press, 1969.

The Macro Plays: The Castle of Perseverance, Wisdom, Mankind: A Facsimile Edition with Facing Transcripts. Edited by David Bevington. New York: Johnson Reprint Corporation; Washington, D.C.: The Folger Shakespeare Library, 1972.

Medieval Drama. Edited by David Bevington. Boston: Houghton Mifflin, 1975.

Le Mystère d'Adam: Édition diplomatique. Edited by Leif Sletsjöe. Paris: Librairie C. Klincksieck, 1968.

Non-cycle Plays and the Winchester Dialogues: Facsimiles of Plays and Fragments in Various Manuscripts. . . . Edited by Norman Davis. Leeds: University of Leeds School of English, 1979.

Le Théâtre français avant la renaissance, 1450–1550. Edited by M. Eduoard Fournier. 1873. Reprint. New York: Burt Franklin, 1965.

The Towneley Cycle: A Facsimile of Huntington MS HM 1. Edited by A. C. Cawley and Martin Stevens. San Marino, Calif.: The Huntington Library, 1976.

The York Play: A Facsimile of British Library MS Additional 35290. . . . Edited by Richard Beadle and Peter Meredith. Leeds: University of Leeds School of English, 1983.

Tudor and Stuart Plays

The Alchemist. By Ben Jonson. Edited by Elizabeth Cook. The New Mermaids. London: A. and C. Black, 1991.

Alphonsus, Emperor of Germany. Q 1654. Facsimile reprint. New York and London: G. P. Putnam's Sons, 1913.

Antonio and Mellida and *Antonio's Revenge.* By John Marston. Q 1602. Edited by W.W. Greg. Malone Society Reprints. Oxford: Oxford University Press, 1921.

Believe as you List. By Philip Massinger. MS c. 1631. Edited by Charles J. Sisson. Malone Society Reprints. Oxford: Oxford University Press, 1928.

The Blind Beggar of Alexandria. By George Chapman[?]. Q 1598. Edited by W.W. Greg. Malone Society Reprints. Oxford: Oxford University Press, 1928.

Bonduca. By John Fletcher. MS c. 1609–14. Edited by W. W. Greg. Malone Society Reprints. Oxford: Oxford University Press, 1951.

Bussy d'Ambois. By George Chapman. Q 1607. In *Elizabethan Plays,* edited by Arthur H. Nethercot et al. Rev. ed. New York: Holt, Rinehart, and Winston, 1971.

Cambises, King of Persia. By Thomas Preston. Q 1584. Edited by John S. Farmer. Tudor Facsimile Texts. [Edinburgh?]: T. C. and E. C. Jack, 1910.

Captain Thomas Stukeley. Q 1605. Edited by Judith C. Levinson. Malone Society Reprints. Oxford: Oxford University Press, 1975.

The Changeling. By Thomas Middleton and William Rowley. Q 1653. In *Stuart Plays,* edited by Arthur H. Nethercot et al. Rev. ed. New York: Holt, Rinehart, and Winston, 1971.

*1 Contention [The First Part of the Contention betwixt the Two Famous Houses of Yorke and Lancaste*r]. Q 1594. Malone Society Reprints. Oxford: Oxford University Press, 1985.

*1 Contention [The First Part of the Contention betwixt the Two Famous Houses of Yorke and Lancaste*r]. Q 1600. Private photostatic copy.

Cynthia's Revels. By Ben Jonson. F 1616. Copy in the Houghton Library, Harvard University.

Cynthia's Revels. By Ben Jonson. F 1616. In vol. 4 of *Ben Jonson,* edited by C. H. Herford and Percy Simpson. Oxford: Oxford University Press, 1932.

The Death of Robert, Earl of Huntingdon. By Anthony Munday [and Henry Chettle?]. Q 1601. Edited by John C. Meagher. Malone Society Reprints. Oxford: Oxford University Press, 1967.

The Duchess of Suffolk. By Thomas Drue. Q1631. Copy in the Houghton Library, Harvard University.

Edmond Ironside. MS c. 1590. Edited by Eleanore Boswell. Malone Society Reprints. Oxford: Oxford University Press, 1927.

Edward I. By George Peele. Q 1593. Edited by W. W. Greg. Malone Society Reprints. Oxford: Oxford University Press, 1911.

Edward II. By Christopher Marlowe. Q 1594. Edited by W. W. Greg. Malone Society Reprints. Oxford: Oxford University Press, 1926.

1, 2 Edward IV. By Thomas Heywood. Q 1600. A facsimile reprint. Philadelphia and New York: Rosenback Co., 1922.

Enough is as Good as a Feast. By William Wager. Edited by R. Mark Benbow. Regents Renaissance Drama Series. Lincoln: University of Nebraska Press, 1967.

Everyman. Edited by A. C. Cawley. Manchester: Manchester University Press, 1961.

Every Man out of his Humour. By Ben Jonson. Q 1600. Edited by F. P. Wilson. Malone Society Reprints. Oxford: Oxford University Press, 1921.

The Famous Victories of Henry V. Q 1598. Edited by John S. Farmer. Tudor Facsimile Texts. [Edinburgh?]: T. C. and E. C. Jack, 1913.

Friar Bacon and Friar Bungay. By Robert Greene. Q 1594. Edited by W. W. Greg. Malone Society Reprints. Oxford: Oxford University Press, 1926.

George a Greene. Q 1599. Edited by F. W. Clarke. Malone Society Reprints. Oxford: Oxford University Press, 1911.

Hamlet. By William Shakespeare. Q 1604–5. The Shakespeare Association. The Shakespeare Quartos in Collotype Facsimile, no. 4. London: Sidgwick and Jackson, 1940.

Hengist, King of Kent, or the Mayor of Quinburough. By Thomas Middleton. MS c. 1616–20. A print fascimile of the Lambarde manuscript. Edited by R. C. Bald. New York and London: Charles Scribner's Sons for the Trustees of Amherst College, 1938.

[Hengist, King of Kent, or] The Maior of Quinburough. By Thomas Middleton. Q 1661. Ann Arbor: University Microfilms International.

1 Henry IV. By William Shakespeare. Q 1598. In *The Riverside Shakespeare*, edited by G. Blakemore Evans et al. Boston: Houghton Mifflin, 1974.

1 Henry IV. By William Shakespeare. F 1623. In *The First Folio of Shakespeare: The Norton Facsimile*, prepared by Charlton Hinman. New York: W. W. Norton, 1968.

2 Henry IV. By William Shakespeare. Q 1600. Edited by Thomas L. Berger and G. R. Proudfoot. Malone Society Reprints. Oxford: Oxford University Press, 1990.

2 Henry IV. By William Shakespeare. F 1623. In *The First Folio of Shakespeare: The Norton Facsimile*, prepared by Charlton Hinman. New York: W. W. Norton, 1968.

Henry V. By William Shakespeare. F 1623. In *The First Folio of Shakespeare: The Norton Facsimile*, prepared by Charlton Hinman. New York: W. W. Norton, 1968.

Henry VIII. By William Shakespeare. F 1623. In *The First Folio of Shakespeare: The Norton Facsimile*, prepared by Charlton Hinman. New York: W. W. Norton, 1968

Horestes. The Interlude of Vice (Horestes) Q 1567. By John Pikeryng. Edited by Daniel Seltzer. Malone Society Reprints. Oxford: Oxford University Press, 1962.

If You Know Not Me, You Know Nobody. By Thomas Heywood. Q 1605. Edited by Madeleine Doran. Malone Society Reprints. Oxford: Oxford University Press, 1934.

James IV. By Robert Greene. Q 1598. Edited by A. E. H. Swaen and W. W. Greg. Malone Society Reprints. Oxford: Oxford University Press, 1921.

John a Kent and John a Cumber. By Anthony Munday. MS c. 1589. Edited by Muriel St. Clare Byrne. Malone Society Reprints. Oxford: Oxford University Press, 1923.

John a Kent and John a Cumber. By Anthony Munday. MS c. 1589. Edited by Arthur E. Pennell. In *Renaissance Drama: A Collection of Critical Editions,* edited by Stephen Orgel. New York: Garland, 1980.

A King and No King. By Francis Beaumont and John Fletcher. Q 1619. Copy in the Houghton Library, Harvard University.

A King and No King. By Francis Beaumont and John Fletcher. Q 1619. Edited by Robert K. Turner. Regents Renaissance Drama Series. Lincoln: University of Nebraska Press, 1963.

King Darius. Q 1565. Edited by John S. Farmer. Tudor Facsimile Texts. [Edinburgh?]: T. C. and E. C. Jack, 1909.

King Darius. Q 1577. Edited by John S. Farmer. Tudor Facsimile Texts. [Edinburgh?]: T. C. and E. C. Jack, 1907.

King Johan. By John Bale. MS c. 1530-60. Edited by Barry Adams. San Marino, Calif.: The Huntington Library, 1969.

King John. By William Shakespeare. F 1623. In *The First Folio of Shakespeare: The Norton Facsimile*, prepared by Charlton Hinman. New York: W. W. Norton, 1968.

King John. By William Shakespeare. In *The Riverside Shakespeare*, edited by G. Blakemore Evans et al. Boston: Houghton Mifflin, 1974.

King John and Matilda. By Robert Davenport. Q 1655. Copy in The Huntington Library, San Marino, Calfornia.

King John and Matila. By Robert Davenport. Ann Arbor: University Microfilms International.

King John and Matilda. By Robert Davenport. Q 1655. Edited by A. H. Bullen. *The Works of Robert Davenport*. In *Old English Plays,* n.s., vol. 3. London: Hansard Publishing Union, 1890.

King Lear. By William Shakespeare. Q 1608. Photographic facsimile. Shakespeare Quarto Facsimiles, no. 33. London: Praetorius, 1885.

King Lear. By William Shakespeare. Q 1608 and F 1623. In *The Parallel King Lear: 1608–1623,* prepared by Michael Warren. Berkeley: University of California Press, 1989.

King Leir. Q 1605. Edited by W. W. Greg. Malone Society Reprints. Oxford: Oxford University Press, 1908.

Like Will to Like. By Ulpian Fulwell. Q 1568. In *Two Moral Interludes*, edited by Peter Hoppé. Malone Society Reprints. Oxford: Oxford University Press, 1991.

Love's Labour's Lost. By William Shakespeare. Q 1598. Edited by W. W. Greg. Shakespeare Quarto Facsimiles, no. 10. Oxford: The Clarendon Press, 1957.

Magnificence. By John Skelton. Edited by Paula Neuss. Manchester: Manchester University Press; Baltimore: The Johns Hopkins University Press, 1980.

The Malcontent. By John Marston. Q 1604. Photographic facsimile of the copy in the British Museum. Menston, U.K.: Scolar, 1970.

The Marriage Between Wit and Wisdom. By Francis Merbury. MS c. 1579. Edited by Trevor N. S. Lennam. Malone Society Reprints. Oxford: Oxford University Press, 1971.

The Miseries of Enforced Marriage. By George Wilkins [and Thomas Heywood?]. Q 1607. Edited by Glenn H. Blayney. Malone Society Reprints. Oxford: Oxford University Press, 1964.

Misogonus. MS c. 1577. Edited by Lester Ernest Barber. Ph.D. diss., University of Arizona, 1967.

Mucedorus. Q 1598. Edited by John S. Farmer. Tudor Facsimile Texts. [Edinburgh?]: T. C. and E. C. Jack, 1910.

Old Fortunatus. By Thomas Dekker. Q 1600. Photographic facsimile. Menston, U.K.: Scolar Press, 1971.

Pericles, Prince of Tyre. By William Shakespeare. Q 1609. In *The Riverside Shakespeare*, edited by G. Blakemore Evans et al. Boston: Houghton Mifflin, 1974.

Perkin Warbeck. By John Ford. Q 1634. Theatrum Orbis Terrarum. Amsterdam: Da Capo Press, 1972. Photographic facsimile.

Perkin Warbeck. By John Ford. Q 1634. Edited by Donald K. Anderson Jr. Regents Renaissance Drama Series. Lincoln: University of Nebraska Press, 1965.

Richard II. By William Shakespeare. Q 1597. Shakespeare Quarto Facsimiles, no. 13. Oxford: The Clarendon Press, 1966.

Richard III. By William Shakespeare. F 1623. In *The First Folio of Shakespeare: The Norton Facsimile*, prepared by Charlton Hinman. New York: W. W. Norton, 1968.

Richard III. By William Shakespeare. In *The Riverside Shakespeare*, edited by G. Blakemore Evans et al. Boston: Houghton Mifflin, 1974.

Richardus Tertius. By Thomas Legge. MS c. 1580. Edited with a translation by Robert J. Lordi. *In Renaissance Drama: A Collection of Critical Editions,* edited by Stephen Orgel. New York: Garland, 1979.

Richardus Tertius. By Thomas Legge. MS c. 1580. Edited with a translation by Dana F. Sutton. American University Studies, series 13. New York: Peter Lang, 1993.

The Rival Friends. By Peter Hausted. Q 1632. Copy in the Huntington Library.

The Rival Friends. By Peter Hausted. Q 1632. Facsimile reprint. In *The English Experience,* no. 601. Amsterdam and New York: Da Capo Press, 1973.

The Roaring Girl. By Thomas Middleton and Thomas Dekker. Q 1611. Edited by John S. Farmer. Tudor Facsimile Texts. [Edinburgh?]: T. C. and E. C. Jack, 1911.

Sir John Oldcastle. By Anthony Munday, Michael Drayton, Robert Wilson, and Thomas Hathway. Q 1600. Edited by Percy Simpson and W. W. Greg. Malone Society Reprints. Oxford: Oxford University Press, 1908.

Sir John Van Olden Barnavelt. By John Fletcher and Philip Massinger. MS c. 1619. Edited by T. H. Howard-Hill. Malone Society Reprints. Oxford: Oxford University Press, 1980.

Sir Thomas More. By Anthony Munday et al. MS c. 1592–1600[?]. Edited by W. W. Greg. Malone Society Reprints. Oxford: Oxford University Press, 1911.

Sir Thomas More. By Anthony Munday et al. MS c. 1592–1600[?]. Edited by Vittorio Gabrieli and Giorgio Melchiori. The Revels Plays. Manchester: Manchester University Press; Baltimore: The Johns Hopkins University Press, 1990.

Sir Thomas Wyatt. By Thomas Dekker and John Webster. Q 1607. Edited by John S. Farmer. Amersham: Issued for subscribers by the editor of the Tudor Fasimile Texts, 1914.

The Spanish Tragedy. By Thomas Kyd. Undated quarto. In *Elizabethan Plays*, edited by Arthur H. Nethercot et al. Rev. ed. New York: Holt, Rinehart, and Winston, 1971.

1, 2 Tamburlaine. By Christopher Marlowe. Q 1590. Edited by John D. Jump. Regents Renaissance Drama Series. Lincoln: University of Nebraska Press, 1967.

Thomas Lord Cromwell. Q 1602. Edited by John S. Farmer. Tudor Facsimile Texts. [Edinburgh?]: T. C. and E. C. Jack, 1911.

Thomas of Woodstock [or I Richard II]. MS c. 1592. Edited by Wilhelmina P. Frijlinck. Malone Society Reprints. Oxford: Oxford University Press, 1929.

Tom a Lincoln. MS c. 1607–16. Edited by G. R. Proudfoot and H. R. Woodhuysen. Malone Society Reprints. Oxford: Oxford University Press, 1992.

The Two Noble Ladies. MS c. 1622–23. Edited by Rebecca G. Rhoads. Malone Society Reprints. Oxford: Oxford University Press, 1930.

The Valiant Welshman. By "A.R." Q 1615. Edited by John S. Farmer. Tudor Facsimile Texts. [Edinburgh?]: T. C. and E. C. Jack, 1913.

Wealth and Health. Q undated [1565?]. Edited by W. W. Greg. Malone Society Reprints. Oxford: Oxford University Press, 1907.

When You See Me, You Know Me. By Samuel Rowley. Q 1605. Edited by F. P. Wilson. Malone Society Reprints. Oxford: Oxford University Press, 1952.

Post-Renaissance Plays

Bonduca : A Tragedy. Altered from Beaumont and Fletcher, and adapted to the stage by George Coleman. In vol. 26, no. 2 of *Bell's British Theatre*. London: George Cawthorn, 1796.

King Henry VIII by Shakespeare. As Performed at the Theatre-Royal, Covent Garden: Regulated from the Prompt-Book. With Permission of the Managers, by Mr. Younger, Prompter. An Introduction and Notes Critical and Illustrative are added by the Authors of the Dramatic Censor. 2d ed. London: Printed for John Bell, 1774.

King Henry VIII: A Historical play in five acts . . . as performed at the Theatre Royal, Covent Garden . . . with remarks by Mrs. Inchbald. London: Longman, Hurst, Rees, and Orme, 1808.

King Henry VIII: A Tragedy . . . Adapted for Theatrical Representation, as performed at the Theatres-Royal, London. In vol. 21 of *Dean's Edition of the British Theatre*. Manchester, 1801.

King Henry VIII: A Tragedy. . . . with alterations by Dryden, as it is now acted in the Theatres Royal of London and Dublin. Dublin: James Dalton, 1752.

King Henry VIII With the Coronation of Anne Bullen . . . With Alterations, As it is Performed at the Theatre-Royal in Drury-Lane. London: C. Hitch and L. Hawes et al., 1762. (Garrick's version).

The Plays of David Garrick. Edited by Gerald Berkowitz. 2 vols. New York: Garland, 1981.

Shakespeare's King Henry the Eighth. A Historical Play. Revised by J. P. Kemble. And Now first published as it is acted at the Theatre Royal in Covent Garden. London: Longman, 1804.

Stages of Drama: Classical to Contemporary Theater. Edited by Carl H. Klaus, Miriam Gilbert, and Bradford S. Fields Jr. 3d ed. New York: St. Martin's Press, 1995. For plays of Ibsen, Miller, Beckett, Norman, Williams, Fugard, Pinter, and Shepard.

REFERENCES

Astington, John H. "Descent Machinery in the Playhouses." *Medieval and Renaissance Drama in England* 2 (1985): 119–33.

———. "The London Stage in the 1580s." In *The Elizabethan Theatre XI*, edited by Augusta Lynne Magnusson and C. E. McGee, pp. 1–18. Port Credit, Ont.: Meany, 1990.

Bald, R. C. *Bibliographical Studies in the Beaumont and Fletcher Folio of 1647*. Oxford: Oxford University Press, 1938.

Basnett-McGuire, Susan. "An Introduction to Theatre Semiotics." *Theatre Quarterly* 38 (summer 1980): 47–53.

Beckerman, Bernard. *Shakespeare at the Globe, 1599–1609*. New York: Macmillan, 1962.

Bentley, G. E. *The Profession of Dramatist in Shakespeare's Time, 1590 to 1642*. Princeton: Princeton University Press, 1971.

Berry, Ralph. *On Directing Shakespeare*. London: Croom Helm; New York: Barnes and Noble, 1977.

Bevington, David. *Action Is Eloquence: Shakespeare's Language of Gesture*. Cambridge: Harvard University Press, 1984.

———. *From "Mankind" to Marlowe: Growth of Structure in the Popular Drama of Tudor England*. Cambridge: Harvard University Press, 1962.

Bond, William H. "Casting Off Copy by Elizabethan Printers: A Theory." *Papers of the Bibliographical Society of America* 42 (1948): 281–91.

Booth, Wayne C. *The Rhetoric of Fiction*. Chicago: The University of Chicago Press, 1961.

Bradley, David. *From Text to Performance in the Elizabethan Theatre: Preparing the Play for the Stage*. Cambridge: Cambridge University Press, 1992.

Brockbank, Philip. *Players of Shakespeare*. New York and Cambridge: Cambridge University Press, 1985.

Carlson, Marvin. "The Status of Stage Directions." *Studies in the Literary Imagination* 24 (fall 1991): 37–48.

Cerasano, S. P. "Editing the Theatre, Translating the Stage." *Analytical and Enumerative Bibliography*, n.s. 4 (1990): 21–34.

Chancellor, Gary. "Stage Directions in Western Drama: Form and Function." Ph.D. diss., University of Wisconsin, 1980.

Craik, T. W. *The Tudor Interlude*. London: Leicester University Press, 1958.

Dessen, Alan C. *Elizabethan Stage Conventions and Modern Interpreters*. Cambridge: Cambridge University Press, 1984.

———. *Recovering Shakespeare's Theatrical Vocabulary*. Cambridge: Cambridge University Press, 1995.

Drake, Silvia. "Few Fears in This 'Virginia Woolf.'" *Los Angeles Times*, 1 October 1989, pp. 4, 6.

Elsky, Martin. *Authorizing Words: Speech, Writing, and Print in the English Renaissance*. Ithaca: Cornell University Press, 1989.

Greg, W. W. *A Bibliography of the English Printed Drama to the Restoration*. 4 vols. Oxford: Oxford University Press, 1939–59.

———. *Dramatic Documents from the Elizabethan Playhouses*. 2 vols. Oxford: Clarendon Press, 1931.

Gribbons, William. "Visual Literacy in Corporate Communication: Some Implications for Information Design." *IEEE Transactions on Professional Communication* 34, no. 1 (March 1991): 42–50.

Gurr, Andrew. *Playgoing in Shakespeare's London*. London and New York: Cambridge University Press, 1987.

———. *The Shakespearean Stage, 1574–1642.* 2d ed. Cambridge: Cambridge University Press, 1980.

Hammond, Antony. "Encounters of the Third Kind in Stage Directions in Elizabethan and Jacobean Drama." *Studies in Philology* 89, no. 1 (winter 1992): 71–99.

Harbage, Alfred. *Shakespeare and the Rival Traditions.* New York: Macmillan, 1952.

Hartnoll, Phyllis, ed. *The Oxford Companion to the Theatre.* 3d ed. London: Oxford University Press, 1967.

Hirsch, Rudolf. "Classics in the Vulgar Tongues Printed during the Initial Fifty Years." *Papers of the Bibliographical Society of America* 81 (1987): 249–337.

Holland, Peter. "Reading to the Company." In *Reading Plays: Interpretation and Reception,* edited by Hanna Scolnicov and Peter Holland, pp. 8–29. Cambridge: Cambridge University Press, 1991.

Honigmann, E. A. G. "Re-enter the Stage Direction: Shakespeare and Some Contemporaries." *Shakespeare Survey* 29 (1976): 117–25.

———. *The Stability of Shakespeare's Text.* London: Edward Arnold, 1965.

Howard-Hill, T. H. "The Evolution of the Form of Plays in English during the Renaissance." *Renaissance Quarterly* 43, no. 1 (spring 1990): 112–45.

———. *Ralph Crane and Some Shakespeare First Folio Comedies.* Charlottesville: University Press of Virginia, 1972.

Illich, Ivan. *In the Vineyard of the Text: A Commentary on Hugh's "Didascalion".* Chicago: University of Chicago Press, 1993.

Ionesco, Eugène. *The Bald Soprano.* In *Four Plays,* translated by Donald M. Allen. New York: Grove Press, 1988.

Issacharoff, Michael. "Inscribed Performance." *Rivista di Letterature moderne e comparate* (Pisa) 39, no. 2 (April–June 1986): 93–105.

———. "Stage Codes." In *Performing Texts,* edited by Michael Issacharoff and Robin F. Jones, pp. 59–73. Philadelphia: University of Pennsylvania Press, 1988.

———. "Texte théâtral et didascalecture." *Modern Language Notes* 96, no. 4 (1981): 809–23.

Jones, Robin F. "A Medieval Prescription for Performance: *Le Jeu d'Adam.*" In *Performing Texts,* edited by Michael Issacharoff and Robin F. Jones, pp. 101–15. Philadelphia: University of Pennsylvania Press, 1988.

Kiefer, Frederick. *Writing on the Renaissance Stage: Written Words, Printed Pages, and Metaphoric Books.* Newark: University of Delaware Press; London: Associated University Presses, 1996.

King, T. J. *Shakespearean Staging, 1599–1642.* Cambridge: Harvard University Press, 1971.

Knapp, Robert S. *Shakespeare—The Theatre and the Book.* Princeton: Princeton University Press, 1989.

Lancashire, Ian. *Dramatic Texts and Records of Britain: A Chronological Topography to 1558.* Toronto and Buffalo: University of Toronto Press, 1984.

Long, William B. "'A bed / for woodstock': A Warning for the Unwary." *Medieval and Renaissance Drama in England* 2 (1985): 91–118.

———. "Deciphering a Layered Manuscript: *John of Bordeaux* and the Playhouse." A paper delivered at the First International Conference of the Malone Society, 29 June–1 July 1990, Stratford-upon-Avon.

———. "Stage-Directions: A Misinterpreted Factor in Determining Textual Provenance." *TEXT* 2 (1985): 121–37.

McCloud, Randall. "UN Editing Shak-speare." *SUBSTANCE* 33/34 (1981/82): 26–55.

McKerrow, R. B. "The Elizabethan Printer and Dramatic Manuscripts." *The Library*, 4th ser., 12 (1931): 253–75.

McMillan, Scott. *The Elizabethan Theatre and "The Book of Sir Thomas More."* Ithaca: Cornell University Press, 1987.

Mish, Charles C. "Black Letter as a Social Discriminant in the Seventeenth Century." *PMLA* 68 (1953): 627–30.

Munkelt, Marga. "Stage Directions as Part of the Text." *Shakespeare Studies* 19 (1991): 253–71.

Ong, Walter J. *Orality and Literacy: The Technologizing of the Word*. London and New York: Methuen, 1982.

———. *Ramus, Method, and the Decay of Dialogue: From the Art of Discourse to the Art of Reason*. Cambridge: Harvard University Press, 1958.

Pavis, Patrice. "Remarques sur le discours théâtral." *Degrés* 13 (1978): h–h10.

Pollard, A. W. *Shakespeare's Fight with the Pirates*. London [?], 1920.

Spevack, Marvin. *A Complete and Systematic Concordance to the Works of Shakespeare*. 7 vols. Hildesheim and New York: Georg Olms Verlag, 1975.

Stevens, Martin. *Four Medieval Mystery Cycles: Textual, Contextual, and Critical Interpretations*. Princeton: Princeton University Press, 1987.

Suchy, Patricia A. "When Words Collide: The Stage Direction as Utterance." *Journal of Dramatic Theory and Criticism* 6, no. 1 (fall 1991): 69–82.

Taylor, Jerome, and Alan Nelson, eds. *Medieval English Drama: Essays Critical and Contextual*. Chicago: University of Chicago Press, 1972.

Thompson, Marvin, and Ruth Thompson, eds. *Shakespeare and the Sense of Performance*. Newark: University of Delaware Press, 1989.

Tribble, Evelyn. *Margins and Marginality: The Printed Page in Early Modern England*. Charlottesville: University Press of Virginia, 1993.

Trousdale, Marion. "Critical Bibliography and the Acting of Plays." *Shakespeare Quarterly* 41 (1990): 87–96.

Warren, Michael, prep. *The Parallel King Lear: 1608–1623*. Berkeley: University of California Press, 1989.

Weitz, Shoshana. "Reading for the Stage: The Role of the Reader-Director." *Assaph: Studies in the Theatre* (Tel Aviv), sec. C, no. 2 (1985): 124–41.

Wells, Stanley, and Gary Taylor, gen. eds. *William Shakespeare: The Complete Works*. Oxford: The Clarendon Press; New York: Oxford University Press, 1986. Modern spelling edition.

Wilson, J. Dover, and Arthur T. Quiller-Couch, eds. *The New Shakespeare*. Cambridge: Cambridge University Press, 1921–67.

Wright, Peter M. "Jonson's Revision of the Stage Directions for the 1616 Folio *Workes*." *Medieval and Renaissance Drama in England* 5 (1990): 257–85.

Name Index

231

Subject Index

Ablative absolutes: 149; defined, 217n.11; in elaborated entries, 148; translation of, 217n.11

Abraham and Isaac (Brome), 41, 135

Abraham and Isaac (Northampton), 40

Act and scene divisions: significance of, 207n. 64; as unnatural, 216n. 1. *See also* Neoclassical conventions

Acting editions of Shakespeare, eighteenth-century, 193–97;

Action, directions for: authority and audience of, 190–91; brevity of, 177–79; direct address in, 176; in elaborated entries, 169; and finite verbs, 173–74; freestanding, 169–70; and full sentences, 190–92; in manuscripts and printed plays, 171; and participles, 184–85; and prepositional phrases, 184–86; and verb mood, 174–77; verb phrases in, 180–81. *See also* Midscene directions

Actor: address of, as character, 116–17, 133–34; ambiguity of term, 190; and direct address, 115, 117, 192; as *interloquitor,* 9, 190; as reader, 22, 206n. 43

Adjectives, in elaborated entries, 148

Adverbs, 169, 185; in elaborated entries, 148. *See also* Asides

Alarums, 140. *See also* Noun phrases; Special Effects

Alchemist, The (Jonson): Gothic typeface in, 70

Alphonsus, Emperor of Germany: midscene directions in, 178–79; theatrical self-consciousness in, 133

American Repertory Theatre, 18

Appositives, 148

Arden of Feversham, 121

Aristippus, 92

"As," directions beginning with, 124, 128–29

Asides, 104, 185; marginal, 71

Asterisks, 104–5

Attributive directions, 16

Audiences, of stage directions, 21–26

Authority: 17–18, 19; of authorial directions, 206n. 52; of directions for action, 190–91; and entries, 152, 165–66; and calls for special effects, 189

Autonomous directions, 16

Battle of Alcazar, The (Peele), 187–88

Believe as You List (Massinger), 81, 84, 85, 88

Bell's British Theatre, edition of *Henry VIII,* 193, 195, 196

Bible: and red ink, 141; and medieval directions, 58

Blind Beggar of Alexandria, The (Chapman?), 98, 174

Bonduca (Fletcher): 81, 83, 88; eighteenth-century edition of, 196

Bookkeepers' notations, 88; and midscene directions, 75–76; in modern promptbooks, 215n. 8; placement of, 213n. 20; ready directions, 76

233